SUMMER NIGHTS

A SINGLE FATHER NOVEL

WESTON PARKER

STAR KEY PRESS

Summer Nights
A Single Father Novel

First Edition.

Editor: Eric Martinez
Cover Designer: Ryn Katryn Digital Art

FIND WESTON PARKER

www.westonparkerbooks.com

1

LANDON

I struggled to hold in my laughter as I stood by, watching my son kick an eighty-six-year-old's ass in a game of chess. Colten was ten, but the expression of intense concentration on Chester's face made it seem as if he considered the boy a master.

"Kids these days have a leg up from practicing on computers," Chester grumbled and stuck his unlit pipe between his teeth. "Back in my day, the only practice we got was when our butts were in a rickety wooden chair and we had a friend willing to play with us."

The game had attracted a bit of attention in the rec room of the elderly care home, and several of the other residents guffawed at Chester's griping while smiling proudly at Colten. We came to Green Acres Senior Living Facility at least once a week and many of these people saw Colten as a grandson of sorts, spending more time with him than with their own grandkids. They appeared to be delighted that he was beating the resident Grouch today.

I bit my tongue in an attempt not to chuckle at their expressions of glee and Chester's of absolute disgust. He resigned by flicking his king over before he slowly pushed to his feet. "Good game, kid. I'll teach you a thing or two next time."

Colten stood and offered the old man his hand, but Chester was already shuffling away from the table to brood in the corner of the rec room. Finally losing my battle, I chuckled under my breath and Colten playfully looked around the room, grinning at all the white-haired folks.

He even arched a cocky little eyebrow at them. "Is anyone interested in challenging me, the victor?"

I laughed in earnest, pushing off the wall I'd been leaning against and sliding my arm around his shoulders before I ruffled his hair. "Alright, buddy. Knock it off with the bravado. No one likes a bragger."

Colten sighed heavily, humor in his kind green eyes as he glanced up at me. "I wasn't bragging. I was simply stating a fact. I *am* the victor."

"Yeah, yeah." I hid my amused smile as I turned toward the table. "Let's pack this up. Grandpa should be done with his physio appointment soon."

"Maybe he'll play me," Colten said hopefully, but I shook my head.

"Let's pack it up. I'm sure he'd love to try his luck against you later, but we should probably ply him with some coffee and treats outside first. Just to make sure he still loves us when we leave. Unlike Chester, who I'm sure is going to be avoiding us from now on."

Colten shrugged. "He won't avoid me. He's too proud for that."

"Fair enough. When did you get so good?" I asked.

"Since Mr. Lafferty put me in the chess club at school."

I grimaced. My work really had been keeping me way too busy. Too busy, it seemed, to keep tabs on my own son's extracurricular activities. "How long have you been in the chess club?"

"Since January," he said, picking up the game when we were done and stowing it back on the shelf behind him.

Meanwhile, I was reeling a little bit. *Since January? That's six months. How could I have missed it for that long?*

As we packed up the chess board, I watched him stow each piece meticulously and I wondered what had happened to the kid who used to just stuff things back into his toy bag on the rare occasion I could convince him to actually help clean up before he was ready.

"I'm super proud of how well you're treating this board right now."

"Thanks," he said. "Mr. Lafferty says we have to respect the pieces as part of the game itself."

"That's great. It's also very true. It's important to learn how to take care of your things." It was also important that your parents knew what you were being taught, which I was apparently failing at dismally.

Before I could beat myself up too much about it though, my step-father emerged from the hallway, clearly finished with his physio appointment for the day. Walter lived here at Green Acres, which was the best place my money could buy.

If I didn't work so much, I would have had Walt live with us, but I would never be able to give him the care he needed to be healthy. Seventy-eight and unsteady on his feet, he still broke into a wide smile when he saw us, as enthusiastic as ever. He pulled Colten into a hug.

"My boys!" He beamed at me in turn, reaching out to shake my hand as he let go of my son. "How are you two doing?"

"We're good. Happy Father's Day, Walt." I gave his hand a firm shake before pulling him in for a quick hug.

"Oh. Happy Father's Day, Grandpa. Guess what?"

"What?" he asked eagerly as he released me. "Happy Father's Day to you too, Landon. You're a wonderful dad. Never doubt it."

My heart swelled. Coming from a man who'd been the best father he could be to a boy who wasn't even biologically his, that meant a lot. Walter and Colten turned to head outside, and Colt looked up at him with his chest puffing out a little.

"I just beat Chester at chess," he said happily.

"Is that so?" Walter laughed, clapping him on the back as they walked. "That's great, Colt. He's a sour old grouch who deserves to lose every now and then. He keeps telling us he was named after that game. Makes him insufferable. We're never going to let him live this down."

"You're getting mean in your old age," I joked as I stepped up beside him, joining them for a stroll down the wide corridor that led to the gardens and patio outside. "I've never known you as one to gloat."

"My ten-year-old grandson kicked his butt. Of course, I'm going to gloat."

I chuckled. "Yeah, fair enough."

With my head shaking, I fell silent as Colten caught him up on every move of the game, and to my surprise, Walter seemed to have known about chess club. "That Mr. Lafferty is teaching you well. Is he still challenging you to matches during lunch?"

"He is," Colt said, practically bouncing on the balls of his feet. "He says it's to hone my skills. I didn't know what *hone* meant, but I looked it up and it's a good thing."

"Indeed," Walter said as we stepped outside.

Since it was Father's Day, the facility was expecting more visitors than usual and they'd laid out a nice spread of snacks for the visitors and residents alike. Long tables lined the walls on the patio, urns filled with coffee and iced tea beside them.

"We should go find a spot in the shade before they're all taken," Walter said as we strode toward the coffee. He looked around the activity on the lawns today, sighing when he realized his favorite bench was already taken. "I suppose we're going to have to find a different spot for our visit."

I grinned at him. "Change is as good as a holiday, Walt. Cheer up. We'll find an even better spot."

Grumbling softly, he waited as I fixed our coffee and Colten helped himself to juice from a jug on the table. Then we meandered away from the building in search of a suitable place to sit. Some of the younger residents were lawn-bowling a little ways down, and Marge spotted Colten, immediately smiling and waving him over.

"Colty! Come join us. Let Aunty Marge show you how it's done."

He glanced at me and I nodded, taking his juice. He hurried away to join them. Walter sighed. "The only thing she's going to teach him is how to cheat."

"Don't be a sore loser." I smirked as we sat down at a small table under a canopy of branches overhead. "She didn't cheat last week. We beat you guys fair and square."

"Keep telling yourself that."

I set our drinks down, offering him a hand to help him sit, but he swatted it away, managing just fine on his own.

As I took a seat across from him, I cast a glance at Colten to make sure he was okay before I looked back at my stepfather. He was really getting on in age now, with most of his previously blond hair gone and only a few strands of wispy white left on top of his balding head. His goofy smile, glasses, and kind brown eyes had remained the same though, which was comforting.

"How are they treating you here?" I asked, starting each visit with the same question as the last. "You're looking well, so I'm assuming you like this new chef they hired."

"He's fine." Walter waved me off. "We don't need to keep having the same old boring conversation, my boy. I'm fine. I like it here. They've always treated me well. I'm more interested in hearing about you. Has that job sucked out your soul yet?"

"Not since last week," I joked.

Walter was the closest thing I had to a parent. My mom had passed shortly after they'd gotten married and he'd raised me ever since. He considered me his son by every definition possible and I felt the same way about him. We were family. If I couldn't be honest with him, then I wouldn't be able to admit this to anyone.

I sighed when he cocked his head at me, waiting patiently for the truth to come out. "My last case was a doozie."

Being a criminal defense attorney wasn't an easy or an enviable job. I knew that, and yet, I was one of the most in-demand ones in all of Los Angeles. A fact I was no longer sure I was proud of.

Walter nodded slowly. "What happened?"

"I, uh, I got some threatening letters in the mail again. My car got vandalized. It's getting harder to explain it all to Colten." I paused for a beat. "I'm just not sure if it's worth it anymore."

"That child is too clever for his own good." Walt pushed his glasses firmly into place on the bridge of his nose. "If it's not worth it anymore, why keep doing it? You've got your inheritance now. With all that money, you could retire and live comfortably for the rest of your days without ever working again, so why are you still putting yourself through it?"

"I don't know." I shrugged. "I wish I had a good answer for you, but I don't. It's just a part of who I am, I guess. I'm a defense attorney. That's what I do."

"You're right," he said dryly. "That's not a good answer. Try harder."

When I didn't immediately respond, he sighed and rubbed the shiny skin on top of his head. "I realize this isn't the first time you've received threats for doing your job, but your car has never been vandalized before. That's an escalation, son. It's going to keep happening too, with you becoming more well known and getting higher profile cases."

"I know, but what I do is part of my identity," I explained, digging deep to try and put words to the way I felt. "I genuinely believe in the legal system. I know it's not perfect, but every now and then, I defend someone who's legitimately innocent, and in those cases, my commitment and representation have saved someone from serving time for a crime they didn't commit."

I drew in a deep breath, trying to imagine quitting and never getting to help someone like that again. The thought was inconceivable to me. "Those cases are why I do it and those moments make it all worth it." I shot him a look and arched an eyebrow. "Should I keep trying, or was that better?"

"Marginally," Walter said, chuckling at something happening at the lawn bowling.

I turned to see Colten taunting Chester to come join them, and the old man actually shuffled his way toward the green. As I watched Colten hand over some bowls, I smiled. "I'm missing out with him. I think that's what's been bothering me the most. It's not that I don't love my job. I'm only wondering if it's worth representing the clients who are assholes when I could be spending that time with him."

"You *are* missing out," he agreed emphatically. "For no good reason. You have nearly one billion dollars sitting in an account somewhere. You've had access to it all year, and yet, here you are. Have you even touched it?"

I shook my head, watching Chester show Colten some tricks while Marge collected her bowls to get ready for the next game. "It's a life-changing amount of money, Walt. I can't touch it until I know I'll be using it to change our lives for the better."

I could feel Walt's eyes on me and knew he was thinking. Considering. Finally, he spoke, and I could tell his words were chosen carefully. "The best years of my life were those I spent with you when you were a boy," he said quietly. "Don't let this precious time slip through your fingers. You'll regret it, and not even all that money can buy you back so much as a minute of that time. When it's too late, it's too late."

"What should I do?" I asked, genuinely needing his advice about this.

Walter shrugged. "Rent a house on a lake somewhere for the summer and show your son a good old-fashioned time. No screens. No video games. No distractions. Just fun, sunshine, water, and making memories. You'll have a bit of a different perspective on things by the time you get back."

I had no doubt that he was right. I just didn't know if I'd be able to swing a trip to a lake this summer. But as I watched Colten laugh while Marge chased him around the green, I decided to try. I couldn't remember the last time he and I had had fun together, and Walt was right. I'd let too much time slip through my fingers already.

2

JEWEL

Elbow deep in a porcelain throne, I was sweating profusely and strands of hair that had fallen out of my ponytail were sticking to my neck. I sighed, annoyed with my hair, but there was nothing I could do about it right then. Thick, plastic cleaning gloves covered my hands up to my elbows and there was no way I was taking them off until I was done here.

The scent of bleach wafted up my nostrils, and even though it was probably going to singe my nose hairs soon, it was still a lot better than how it had smelled when Brittany and I showed up to start working.

A shudder raced down my spine at the mere thought of the scent that used to hang in the air in here. But that was one of the things I loved most about my job. Not the scent, *obviously*, but the fact that the stench could be strong enough to make someone's eyes water, and a couple hours later, an entire house would be sparkly clean and lemon scented.

Brittany and I both had a knack for cleaning, and over the years, we'd devised a pretty efficient system. We owned a residential cleaning business together and I wondered if I could ask *her* to remove the hairs stuck to my neck. Glancing away from the toilet, I saw her on her hands and knees in the shower—also wearing thick plastic gloves.

That's a no, then.

Resigned to waiting until I was done, I scrubbed the tiles around the throne when I finished with the inside. Then I finally got to my feet and carefully pulled off the gross gloves. "Is it just me, or is it like a sauna in here?"

Brittany widened her eyes at me and nodded enthusiastically. "I know the Rogers family isn't fond of wind, but I think we should open the windows to let in a bit of fresh air. I'll text them about it."

As I opened the faucet and washed my hands, I looked around the little bathroom, spotting one tiny window right above where I'd been working before. "I'm on it."

I wiped my hands on a clean rag we'd brought along, fixed my ponytail, and pushed up on my toes to open that window. Then I strode out into the master bedroom to open a few more. The Rogers were an elderly couple who'd just moved to June Lake and they had a terrific view of the mountains and the shimmering water in the distance.

We still had some work left to do in their condo, but I paused at the window for a moment to admire the view. I'd lived in this town, or village rather, my entire life and I *still* hadn't grown tired of that view.

The heavily wooded forest between the lake and the condo was completely green, the majestic pines at their happiest in the summertime like now. Crystal clear, blue water stretched from the edge of the forest to the mountains, the very tops of them still wearing little white caps of snow.

I sighed dreamily, leaning against the windowsill and then suddenly realizing that I hadn't cleaned it yet. My fingers came away dusty and I groaned, sad to leave the view but knowing that I had to get a move on.

Brittany and I had started *Tidy Touch* almost four years ago and we had a list of loyal clients in June Lake, but we wouldn't keep them if I sullied our spotless—pun intended—reputation by getting starry eyed over the views instead of actually cleaning. Most of our clients were older folks who needed help maintaining their homes and young working professionals who just couldn't get around to everything by themselves. We also had a couple of younger families, but a cleaning service just wasn't necessarily in their budget around here.

Either way, we always did our very best and the Rogers deserved that too. Especially since we were hoping to sign them on for our weekly service.

When I walked back into the bathroom, Brittany had just gotten done in the shower. Her short, curly hair clung to her neck as well and she pushed some of it off with her forearm as she removed her gloves. "We're almost done, right?"

"Yep. I just want to dust the windowsills in the bedrooms, but we should be out of here in about ten minutes."

"Good," she said. "I'm boiling. I'll double-check the kitchen and the living areas if you take care of the bedrooms?"

"Deal," I replied easily, grabbing a soft cloth and a spray bottle out of my caddy before heading back into the bedroom.

After dusting the remainder of the surfaces, I gave the room a last onceover, ensuring that the bedding was fitted perfectly and the floors were immaculate. Satisfied that we'd done a good job, I headed to the small guest bedroom and did the same thing there. When that was finished, I smiled at the cloudless blue sky outside and checked the time.

11:37 a.m. Awesome.

Brittany was wrapping up when I skipped down the stairs, packing all our supplies and equipment into her trunk. She perked up when she saw me, her light brown eyes sparkling in the summer sunshine. "All good?"

"All good." I locked up behind me and left the keys in the spot the Rogers had designated. Then I stripped off my disgusting cleaning clothes to reveal my bathing suit underneath.

Brittany did the same thing, bagging up our clothes before tossing them in the back and wrestling the top of her ancient car down once more. "Are you ready?"

"So ready." I hopped into her car and grabbed my sunglasses off the dashboard. I slid them on as she slid in behind the wheel.

We raced away from the Rogers' place, smiling. The wind whipped through our hair and the hard work of the morning melted out of our tired muscles. Zipping along the winding mountain road, I relaxed into my seat, proud of another job well done.

A few minutes later, Brittany pulled over on the side of the street in our usual spot, grabbing a bottle of sunscreen from her glove compartment and slathering it on before she grinned at me. "Let's go."

I chose to forego the sunscreen, but my skin wasn't nearly as fair as hers. Sun-kissed already, I didn't burn as easily and I wanted to get a bit more color now that summer had officially arrived. She and I ran to our rock next to the road, not pausing for even a beat before we jumped off, happily leaping into the crystalline waters of the alpine lake below.

It was clean, fresh, and pristine, and as soon as I hit the cool surface, I felt refreshed, going under and lazing around underwater for as long as my lungs would allow before I kicked my way back up. Giggling as I surfaced, I looked around for Brittany, finding her flopping onto her back just a few feet away.

"God, I love summer," she whooped happily, her eyes closing as she spread her arms to her sides. "We don't have any meetings this afternoon, right?"

"Not as far as I know," I replied, slicing silently through the water and splashing her as soon as I was close enough.

She sputtered before she squealed with laughter, splashing me back when I spun to race away. We goofed off in the water for a little while before we swam to the shore, stretching out on our favorite rocks to lounge in the sun as we dried off.

Across the lake, sunlight reflected off the windows of *The Manor*. It had been one of the first homes that had been built in town as far back as 1920. The original owners had lived there until they'd passed away, leaving it to their grandson who now used it as an AirBnB. He accommodated ultra-wealthy guests coming to vacation in our simple small town during the summer and the winter, to enjoy either a sun-washed holiday or the snowy ski hills.

Beside me, Brittany was admiring it as well, sighing and murmuring aloud as she settled down on her rock. "Just once, I'd love to see the inside of that house."

"I know," I agreed. "Maybe we should offer to go spruce it up for free before his next guests arrive?"

She let out an unladylike snort and shook her head. "I don't want to see it *that* badly. Have you seen the size of the place? It'd take us a whole day and we won't even be getting paid for it. No, thank you."

I remained propped up on my elbows, momentarily unable to stop staring. There was something about that house that was just so compelling that it always drew me in. It was old, sure, but classic and timeless with sprawling grounds meticulously cared for by a groundskeeper who lived just down the road.

I'd considered offering him a free cleaning or two to let me into the house, but I'd never been able to bring myself to follow through. It seemed too dishonest. Instead, I drooled over the place from a distance, constantly trying to devise a plan to get me in the doors that didn't involve spending all the money I made in a few months just to stay there for a single night.

"It'd be worth it, though," I said, my voice hushed for even just admiring the splendor from afar. "How dirty would it really be? I'm sure they have it cleaned after guests have stayed there. All we'd have to do is give it a bit of spit and polish, and we'd get to look around to our hearts' content."

"It's just a house, Jewel," Brittany said, never understanding my utter fascination of it. "We'll get to take a peek inside sooner or later. You just have to be patient."

I wrinkled my nose. "It's been twenty-six years. I've been patient. It's time to become proactive instead."

She chuckled, rolling her eyes at me before she closed them and tipped her face to the sun. "I'm curious too. You know that, but we've seen the listing and it's still just a house. Even if it is an old, beautiful one."

"It's not just a house, though," I protested as I kept staring at the striking structure across the lake. "Mrs. Styles waited for her husband to come back from the war in that house. They raised their children there. Decades of lives were lived there and it just looks like this perfect time capsule, don't you think?"

One day, I'd see the guts of that old house and I was sure it would be everything I imagined and more.

Brittany shoved me playfully. "We're going to have to find a way to get richer clients if you ever want to afford to stay in that house for a night."

"I've already thought of that, and I think offering to clean it before new guests arrive is a more realistic option. There are only so many people in this town, and even if we clean every day for all of them, we still wouldn't be able to afford staying there."

"You just have to be patient," she repeated before stretching her arms above her head and yawning. "We probably need to start heading back to town for lunch. I have to do some invoices this afternoon and you need to do inventory."

I groaned, casting another longing look at Styles Manor before I got up and followed her to her car. I loved this town, but if there was one thing I knew for sure it was that living here meant never getting rich enough to see the inside of that house by paying for it. It also meant never getting rich enough to buy a new car or to own a house myself, but I was at peace with that.

We lived a simple life here and I was okay with it, but just once before I died, I wanted to go into Styles Manor. If I could just do that, I would truly die happy.

3

LANDON

Standing in a grassy quad outside of Colten's classroom, I waited to pick him up from his last day of school before the summer break. A guy around my own age emerged from a small crowd of parents chatting nearby, looking around until he zeroed in on me. Wearing a bow tie with a tweed jacket and thick glasses, he smiled, but he also suddenly seemed nervous for some reason.

James Lafferty was Colt's teacher and, as I'd recently learned, was responsible for encouraging him to play chess. He and I had had a few talks since Colt had joined his class, but he'd never pulled me aside like he did now.

"Mr. Payne, may I speak to you for a moment?"

I nodded. "Of course. What's up?"

"Colten is a brilliant young student," he started hesitantly. "He's got a great head on his shoulders, his reading comprehension is staggering, and his mathematics are getting sharper every day. He's a natural problem solver, which is wonderful for his age."

Having said all that, he stopped speaking and I frowned. My head lowered slowly to one side as I looked at the man. "All of those sound like good things to me, so what's the catch?"

"Well, I'm afraid his social skills aren't developing quite as well." Fidgeting with his hands, he averted his gaze and sighed before he looked back at me. "He doesn't socialize well with the other kids, Mr. Payne. He doesn't fit in and he doesn't seem to care."

My heart thudded against my ribs. "As far as I know, he's been playing chess with you during lunch to hone his skills. Could it be that he's simply more interested in chess than the other children at this stage?"

He shook his head. "I've been trying to encourage him to go out with his classmates to play during their lunch hour, but he always chooses to stay in the classroom with me instead. He just doesn't seem interested in going anywhere."

Sucking in a deep breath, he swiped his tongue across his lips and then reached up to straighten his already straight glasses. "I don't want to cause any trouble by making unfounded allegations, but while I haven't seen any proof of this, I'm worried he's being bullied. I wanted to bring it to your attention."

"Thank you," I said, overwhelmed and uncertain how to handle this but grateful for a teacher like Mr. Lafferty watching out for my son. "We're spending all summer together in lake country. I'll talk to Colt. If anything comes out that involves the school, I'll be sure to let you know. Thanks again, James."

He inclined his chin at me, grasping my hand warmly before he left. "I'm happy to help, Landon. You have a truly wonderful son and I'm sure he's going to have a blast this summer. It's marvelous you're going to be spending the whole break together. He's a lucky boy to have a father who's willing to do that."

Surprised by the compliment, I watched him turn and hurry back into his classroom. A minute later, kids started running out of it and the quad was suddenly filled with noise, laughter, and chatter.

Colten was one of the last kids to leave the room and he paused in the door, searching before he made a beeline for me. "Straight to the airport?"

"Straight to the airport," I said, grinning at him as he hiked his backpack higher on his shoulder.

We strode out of the building together and I was curious to see if he'd run into a single friend, but we made it all the way to the car without him even acknowledging anyone else.

Worry started gnawing at my insides. I'd missed that he'd joined a chess club, but I would've noticed if he was being bullied.

Right?

While I wasn't in the habit of doubting myself as a counselor, being a single parent was tough sometimes. I had no one to use as a sounding board and no one to share these observations with. It'd never bothered me, but finding out one's own son might've been in peril at school without you ever having considered it a possibility had a way of getting in one's head.

Wondering if I should give Walter a call to find out if he knew anything, I drove us to the airport, parking close to the private plane I'd chartered. After we boarded, Colten immediately picked a seat, opening his iPad to start playing chess, and I decided I'd speak to Walter later.

Right now, it seemed to me that the person I had to speak to the most was right here. I sat down next to him and plucked the computer out of his hands. "This summer is about disconnecting, Colt. I'm not even going to look at any work and you're not going to bury your face in a screen either."

He groaned, protesting throughout our preparation for takeoff and until we'd reached cruising altitude. "That's not fair. We're on a plane. What else am I supposed to do?"

"Take in the view," I suggested. "Talk to your old man. Play *I Spy*. Just be bored for a change. Take your pick."

"I want to play chess," he said, turning to face me and sticking out his lower lip. "That's not the same as normal screen time. That melts your brain. Chess strengthens it. It's all about strategy and stuff. It's good for me."

"It sure is," I agreed. "So is being bored and all those other things I mentioned. You're a kid, Colt. Act like one."

"I am. Can't you see? I'm pouting." He stuck his lower lip out further and widened his eyes.

I chuckled. "I can see, but it's not going to work."

He tried a few more arguments, but I held my ground. Between what Walter had said and what James Lafferty had told me earlier, it was more important than ever that I got caught up with my son.

"Are you going to miss your friends while we're gone?" I asked, trying to change the subject.

Colten crossed his arms and looked out the window. "Not really."

I exhaled slowly through my nostrils, wondering if he even had any friends at all. He'd never invited anyone over, but I hadn't thought much of it before.

How could he when his father was never home?

Most kids their age wouldn't get left alone without a parent in the house for a play date and I usually only got home long after he'd gone to bed. If I went home at all. Oftentimes, I simply crashed in my office for a few hours before I got back to work.

A driver picked Colt up from school every day, bringing him back to our estate where he worked on his homework with his tutor. He had dinner made for him by our chef and then he wound down for the night by himself, but under the watchful eyes of Mrs. Neil, our housekeeper.

I squeezed my eyes shut for a moment, my mind racing as I thought back over the last few years. Colt and I had been close when he was younger. We'd spent a lot more time together than we did now, but as he'd gotten busier at school, I'd taken on more work.

Quickly rising from obscurity, I'd made something of a name for myself and I was doing pretty darn well. It was a point of great pride for me that I'd done it all without my late parents' money. Walter had never been rich and he'd been frugal with the allowance he'd received from the trust to cover my expenses.

As a result, I'd grown up respecting the value of money and the effort put into earning every dollar. I'd never become obsessed with making as much as I could, but in retrospect, I had been prioritizing work above Colten in recent years.

Exhaling slowly, I opened my eyes and tried to recalibrate my brain. "Do you want to see the house we're going to be staying at?"

Suddenly even more eager to reconnect with my baby, I hoped this would be the kind of summer Walter thought it would. Colten arched an eyebrow at me though, not nearly as enthusiastic now that I'd taken away the iPad. "I thought I wasn't supposed to look at screens?"

Smart ass, I thought, but I chuckled and shrugged my shoulders as I leaned back in my seat. "Fair point. It would spoil the surprise anyway."

A little while later, we landed at a tiny airport surrounded by rocky mountains and tall pines. The sky was an azure blue and there wasn't so much as a wisp of cloud in sight. Colten leaned forward to study the landscape through the window, skepticism in his eyes as he glanced at me.

"What are we doing here again?"

"Taking a real break," I replied firmly, unbuckling when the plane came to a full stop. "Some fresh air and bright sunshine never hurt anybody."

"But we live in *LA*," he said as he followed me to the door. "There's plenty of sunshine at home. Fresh air nearby too."

"That may be true, but there's also a lot of distractions there. We won't have that here. It's just going to be me, you, and the lake."

When we stepped off the plane, the sun beat down on our shoulders, but we were only uncomfortable for a minute. Piling into a large SUV with the AC blasting, we waited while our bags were loaded in the trunk and then we set off on a winding drive that eventually led us through the tiny town that was June Lake.

Colten blinked hard as he stared out the window. Then he gave me a completely incredulous look. "We have to spend a whole summer *here*? When you said it was just going to be you, me, and the lake, I thought you were being metaphorical."

"Look at your vocabulary coming along," I said lightly, ignoring his question because as I looked through my own window, I was starting to have doubts too.

On the internet, the town had looked pleasant and quaint, but now, it only looked simple. *Maybe a little too simple for my liking.*

"Just give it time," I told Colten, but I was speaking to myself as well. "It will grow on you."

It didn't take more than a minute before we'd driven through the entire town and started traveling down a lakeside road that soon began offering the most incredible views. Even Colten relaxed a little bit as he appreciated them, gluing his nose to the window and looking out at the glittering lake below.

I did the same thing, not at all ashamed of acting like a ten-year-old. It was stunning out here, and as much as I was hopeful that I would get to reconnect with my son this summer, I was also keen to have some time to reconnect with myself.

It had been a long time since I hadn't had work looming over me, and at this point, I didn't even know who I was without a case to work. After my conversation with Walter on Father's Day though, I'd realized it was time to figure it out.

Just as I was really starting to lean into the idea of this vacation despite the simplicity of the town, the SUV came to a complete stop. Right in the middle of the road.

There was no house nearby and no driveways leading off this road either, which meant we certainly hadn't reached our destination. Sighing as I leaned forward, I looked at the driver. "Why have we stopped?"

"There's a car blocking our way, sir," he responded. "Just a minute. I'll sort it out."

I frowned. *What is this all about? And why, oh why, did it have to happen right the hell now?*

"No," I said firmly. "I will. Who the hell parks right in the middle of a goddamn road? On a mountain, no less. I'll get them to move. Don't worry. Just be ready to get us to the house as soon as they're out of the way."

4

JEWEL

After another grueling day at work, Brittany and I were cooling off in the lake after cleaning a mansion that had been occupied by teenagers for the week. They'd left their host's house in a terrible state and both of us had been eager to get into the water once we were done.

As we floated and tried to cleanse our souls from the sights and smells we'd had to endure earlier, voices filtered down from the road above. I shielded my eyes against the sun as I glanced up. Then I cursed under my breath.

"Shit," I muttered. "I told you we should have pulled over all the way."

"Way ahead of you, girl," Brittany replied. She and I took off, swimming hurriedly to the shore. We waded out of the shallow water and she cupped her hand around her mouth to call out to whoever was up there. "We'll be up in a minute! So sorry about this!"

Hightailing it up the slope to the road, we tried to cover the twenty-foot rise in elevation from the shore to where we'd parked as fast as we could. Almost slipping a few times with our wet feet on the rocks, we made it without serious incident, but I was out of breath and probably red faced by the time we reached the road.

As luck would have it, that was when I first locked eyes with the most handsome man I'd ever seen. I stopped in my tracks, breathing hard and struggling to coax air into my lungs. He just stood there, perfectly put together in a pair of navy slacks, a crisp white button-down, and leather loafers on his feet.

Our gazes clashed and his regal brow furrowed, but I didn't care that he was scowling at me. I was too busy trying to wrap my head around the fact that there was a guy who looked like *him* only a few feet away from me. *They sure don't build 'em like that in this town.*

With short brown hair touched with a warm gold, perfectly trimmed facial hair, and intensely green eyes, he looked like a celebrity. He was tall too, freakishly so, and built, but not absolutely jacked.

As my gaze swept across his features, that scowl chilled me to the bone despite the summer heat. It had sharpened while I'd been staring at him like a stalker, and right then, it felt like he might slice me in half with a single look.

Clearly, the man had perfected the art of silent intimidation. With a slight lift of his chin, his eyes moved from mine to Brittany's and back again.

"Your car is in my path," he informed me, his voice crisp and clear, but also authoritative in a way I definitely wasn't used to. It was the kind of voice that could command armies and rally enemies into a united force at a simple instruction.

Brittany wasn't used to being spoken to like that either. She squeaked in response and rushed to the driver's door of her car.

Meanwhile, I tried to play it off. We had been in the wrong, but the transgression hardly warranted this kind of treatment.

"Nobody ever uses this road. Sorry about that. We were being thoughtless," I said, taking an even closer look at him. "Are you going to be staying at Styles Manor?"

A sleek, black SUV stood beside Captain Intimidation, the engine still running and the outline of a man visible behind the steering wheel. I couldn't see him clearly since the windows were tinted, but I had a suspicion he was a hired driver.

There weren't that many houses out on this road—which was why we'd thought it was safe to just stop—and a guy like him wouldn't be staying at any old holiday rental. The math hadn't been that hard to do, but the slight cant of his head told me he was surprised.

He still nodded though, only slightly, but it had definitely been a nod. No acknowledgment at all of my apology, however. *Okay then.*

His standoffish body language suddenly made me acutely aware of the fact that I was half naked in a bikini in front of him. My boobs were very much on display in the plunging top, and the bottoms that tied on the hips didn't cover much either.

It was meant for tanning, not running up to the road to move a car and talk to a grumpy stranger. Inappropriate clothing aside, however, this man was going to be staying in a home I'd been enthralled by my entire life.

He might've been born to melt panties and conquer enemies with nothing more than a look, but I had been born to charm unsuspecting tourists into possibly letting me have a peek inside that house. With that thought in mind, I smiled at him.

"It's the nicest house in June Lake." Not that I knew from personal experience, of course. I'd scrolled through the handful of pictures on the internet a few times, though. The Styles' grandson hadn't put nearly as much effort into the property listing that I would've, which was disappointing considering it meant that I still didn't really know what to expect from the inside.

Brittany's engine sputtered a few times and I winced, trying desperately to engage him while she tried to start the old car. "I'm sure you're going to have a wonderful time there. How long are you staying?"

He remained silent, eyeing me suspiciously, but I kept smiling. *Right. So he doesn't talk much. That's okay.*

"There's a country market in town every morning from eight a.m. until one p.m. all summer long," I said lightly. "It's the best place to buy fresh goods. Talya's Butchery is also pretty good. You can call her in the morning to put in your order for the day."

The engine finally roared to life behind me and relief trickled down my spine. As soon as Brittany started creeping onto the shoulder, Captain Intimidation offered me a dismissive nod. "Thanks."

Climbing back into his fancy SUV, he left without another word, and Brittany and I shared a look as they raced away.

She scoffed, her head shaking as she brought her gaze back to mine. "What an ass."

"Seriously," I said. "And those shoulders? Yowza."

"Well, I meant he was an asshole, but now that you mention it, he was pretty easy on the eyes."

"Right." I shook my head. "Too bad he's a jerk."

He was perhaps the rudest person I'd ever not met and yet, there was definitely something intriguing about the man. No one I knew could stare at another person that intently. It made me curious about him, how he had gotten to be that way and if he was like that all the way through or if there was more to him. I sighed as Brittany and I headed to her car. "What do you think a guy like that is doing in a place like June Lake?"

She shrugged. "Writing a murder mystery novel?"

I laughed, but she shared a few more ideas as we climbed in. "Planning a murder? Running from the law? Witness protection?"

"Stop it." I shook my head, but I couldn't stop myself from twisting in my seat to glance at the SUV again before it disappeared around the bend.

Honestly, I had no idea what a guy like him was doing in a place like this, but I couldn't deny that he'd commanded my attention. It was unlikely that I'd see him again, though. The tourists who stayed at Styles Manor tended to have people who did things like grocery shopping for them, preferring to spend their days on or next to the lake.

I couldn't blame them. I wouldn't have moved from there either, but I was weirdly disappointed about encountering a person like Captain Intimidation without the opportunity to scratch a bit at the surface. Find out what might be hiding beneath.

Sighing as Brittany turned the car around and started driving back toward town, I tried my best to focus on the afternoon ahead. I was already borderline obsessed with the house he would be staying in for the summer. The last thing I needed was to project that obsession onto the house's temporary resident.

Ultimately, it was just a house and he was just a guy. Neither had any real bearing on my life. It was a nice fantasy, though, imagining what life in that place could be like and even nicer to imagine spending it there with a guy who looked like him—minus the spiky personality.

What could I say? I was a romantic to the core and the history of that house played into my idle fantasy, knowing that such an epic love story had been lived out there once before. That was all it would ever be, though. An idle fantasy that played out in my head on the short drive back to my town.

To my real life. In which neither houses like Styles Manor nor men like Captain Intimidation would ever play any real role.

Sad as it was, there wouldn't be an epic love story in my future. Unless my love for *Tidy Touch* counted, in which case, I was already living it—and that was perfectly fine by me.

My empty bed didn't bother me—most nights.

5

LANDON

To end our journey, we traveled down a long driveway lined with perfectly manicured lawns, beautifully trimmed hedges, and towering pines surrounding the edge of the expansive property. Up ahead, the manor awaited our arrival, along with an old lady that was reminiscent of something out of a movie.

Colten inched forward on his seat, scooting all the way to the edge as he ducked his head, gaping as he stared at the place through the windshield. He was clearly in awe and I had to admit, he wasn't the only one.

It was difficult to imagine a place like this existing just outside of the tiny town we'd passed through to get here. Almost just as difficult as it was to imagine a woman like that one I'd seen earlier just appearing like a siren from the water below.

We hadn't even climbed out of the SUV yet, and already, June Lake was surprising me. I grinned as Colten unbuckled his seatbelt without moving his stare away from the house. His mouth dropped open as he got out and studied the exterior.

Proud that I'd managed to shock him into silence, I followed him out of the vehicle and chuckled. "Cat got your tongue?"

He finally managed to tear his gaze away from the house to gape at me instead. "We're staying here all summer?"

"Yep."

"No. Way." Suddenly, he let out an enthusiastic yell before taking off, running around the loop in the driveway and up the front steps to the door.

Barely stopping to open it, he burst inside and I heard another shriek of excitement before he disappeared from view. The driver chuckled as he unloaded our bags.

"The Manor has that effect on people," he said. "It's got a rich history too. I know some of it, if you're interested."

I dipped my chin in a curt nod, taking a look around while he emptied the trunk. The property was sprawling. Massive, really. The listing for the rental had said that the house was set on seven acres, but I hadn't really believed it until now.

Right on the lake, it was a brick mansion and one of the most magnificent buildings I'd ever seen. I was in awe of the architecture, almost castle-like with modern updates.

"A wealthy couple from England started building it in 1915," the driver said as he shouldered all the bags he could carry at once. I picked up the others, following him as he told the story. "The husband, Mr. Styles, survived World War I and the manor became their family estate until they grew old and gray together."

"That's impressive," I said, finding it hard to comprehend the events that must have happened here. "Does it still belong to the family?"

"Yes, sir," he said immediately. "Their oldest grandson inherited it and he's the one you'd have rented it from. He's had it listed for a few years now as a vacation rental, though I'm not sure I'd have wanted to share a home like this with anyone else."

I chuckled, nodding my agreement as he walked inside. Dropping the bags with dull thuds, I pulled off my sunglasses and let out a low whistle. "Yeah, there's no way I'd have rented it either."

Finding myself in an expansive entry hall, I took a minute to take it all in, my gaze wandering from the large, polished tiles beneath my feet, to the high ceilings, the elaborate chandeliers, and the curving staircase that led to the upper level.

The driver carried our bags to the base of the staircase. "Would you like me to take these up for you? I'm sure you know this from the ad, but there are five bedrooms. All upstairs, I'm afraid."

"That is no problem," I said, my voice hushed with the awe that was rolling over me until I cleared my throat. "We'll take care of it. Thanks for everything."

"You're very welcome, sir. Is there anything else I can do for you before I leave?"

"No, thank you," I replied, my gaze leaving his again as I took a few steps forward. "I doubt we'll be going anywhere else today."

"Very well, sir." He tipped his hat at me and left, and I blinked hard, wondering where Colten had gone off to.

Deciding to take our bags upstairs later, I set off in search of my son, walking through a formal living room featuring windows on three sides and a marble fireplace, but Colt wasn't there. Nor did it appear that the doors leading outside had been opened, which meant that he hadn't run to the swimming pool, the lake, or the patio.

As I left the living room, I entered a large, double-island, gourmet kitchen that opened to a breakfast area as well as a space for larger gatherings. In the corner was a pantry the size of my childhood bedroom and I peeked inside, relieved at the foresight I'd had to ask for the basics to be stocked.

Still not having found any trace of my son, I kept going, striding into a large dining room next. I found a paneled den with an ornate fireplace and a built-in bar. *Jeez, this place just keeps getting better and better.*

Eventually, I found Colten in a lavish room at the end of the house. Billiard tables and dart boards dominated the space, making me think that it was definitely a game room, and lo and behold, it even had a chess table with hand-carved pieces right in front of a picture window facing the lake.

Naturally, that was where I found Colten. He'd already taken a seat and was marveling at the board when I walked in. It took him a moment to realize I was there, but when he looked at me, he immediately pressed his palms together in a praying motion.

"Can we play, Dad? Please?"

I glanced at the grounds beyond the window and the sparkling lake, then shook my head when I looked back at him. "How about we hold off on the chess for now and go exploring?"

He frowned but was quickly distracted when I arched an eyebrow at him. "How about this? Whoever finds the best room first gets to claim it for themselves for the summer. No arguments. You just get the one you want as long as you were in it before me."

Colten's green eyes lit up, and before I could say another word, he was on his feet and racing to the door. I laughed, taking off after him but he'd already disappeared up the stairs when I reached them. Grabbing some of the bags, I carried them up with me, smiling at the squeals of laughter emanating from the room he was in.

Later that night, I sat on the edge of his bed, knowing it wasn't strictly necessary to tuck him in anymore but also relishing the opportunity. I grinned as I took another look at the room he'd won.

"You definitely got the best one in the house, you little brat."

He smirked at me, shrugging his shoulders as he leaned back against his pillows. "You said whoever found it first got to claim it. I found it first."

"Does it matter that I stopped to bring up your things?" I asked, but I wasn't about to welch on our deal.

He shook his head, grinning like a cat who had gotten the cream. "Nope. That wasn't part of the terms of our agreement."

"The terms of our agreement?" I chuckled, surprised, but it was the most adorable thing he'd ever said to me. "Is that right?"

"Yep." His grin widened. "I've heard you on the phone enough to know that anything that isn't on paper isn't part of the agreement. You didn't say we had to stop to bring up bags, so the room is mine."

"Fair enough, little man." I reached out to ruffle his hair, pride surging through me as I looked into those eyes he'd inherited from me. "You really are too clever for your own good."

"Nah, but I am going to be a lawyer one day."

"Nope," I said firmly, my head shaking as I chuckled. "Over my dead body. You certainly have the brains for it, though, kiddo."

His eyebrows tugged together as he frowned at me. "Why not? You love your job."

"Sometimes, yeah, but I'm tied to my office and courthouses. I'm sure there's something better out there for you."

Something that doesn't involve threats and danger to your family.

Colten sighed. "Something better like what?"

I shrugged. "I don't know. Thankfully, we still have a lot of time to figure it out. Plus, the world is changing so fast these days that what you're going to end up doing for a living may not even be a career yet."

"I think I like the sound of that," he said, smiling as he took another look around. "I love this house. Did you see my tub?"

I laughed, following his gaze as it moved to the bathroom. "Oh, you mean your private pool? I saw it."

The soaker tub could fit at least eight people, but then again, he hadn't only won the best room in the house. He also had the best adjoining bathroom.

"Maybe not being tied to an office or a courthouse would be good," he mused a few seconds later. "Do you think I could find a job I could do from here?"

"I'm sure you could, buddy, but you're getting way ahead of yourself." I studied his serious expression, the furrow on his brow making him look older than his years.

It wasn't like I never saw the kid when we were home. We visited Walter together every Sunday. Saturday nights, we watched movies together. Yet somehow, looking at him now, I felt like I'd missed a huge chunk of his life.

Since when was he thinking of becoming a lawyer? Why was he thinking about it when he was only ten? At that age, I wanted to be an astronaut. Or an elephant trainer. Or maybe that had been my F1 driver year.

I couldn't remember which, but *lawyer* definitely hadn't been on my radar. *How long has he been taking himself this seriously?*

I sighed, smiling at him as he picked up a book on strategy in chess. “Don’t stay up too late, okay?”

“We didn’t play today,” he said, his features falling as he let out a disappointed breath. “Is it too late now?”

“We’re going to play a ton of chess while we’re here,” I promised, leaning over to press a kiss to his forehead. “I could use the lessons.”

He finally returned my smile. “I’m going to whoop you.”

I laughed, ruffling his hair before I stood up. “Tomorrow is the first day of the best summer ever. Get some sleep, okay?

Nodding, he lowered his gaze to his book as he opened it to a page that had been earmarked. I strode to the door, looking back at him for just a moment. The four-poster bed was so big that he looked ridiculously small in it, yet I knew he wasn’t so small anymore.

At the rate he was growing, he would be a teenager before I knew it. Then he’d be going off to college, and if I was lucky, I’d see him for the holidays. I ran my fingers through my hair as I left his bedroom, leaving the door ajar just in case.

Grappling with the realization that I had maybe eight years left of being with him full-time, I headed downstairs to that built-in bar I’d seen earlier and poured myself a stiff drink. It was downright scary to think how time had flown, and I had a feeling it would only speed up from here.

Yep. It’s a good thing I’ve taken this time off. I have a lot to think about.

6

JEWEL

Brittany and her little sister climbed out of my brother's truck when we arrived at the boat launch at the lake. I got out too, moaning as the sun washed over my skin.

"What kind of person do you have to be to torture other people like that?" I complained, stripping off my shirt to let the sun warm me as much and as fast as possible.

Scott, my only family and the driver of the Arctic Express today, winked at me. "A person who knows how to enjoy the few luxuries he's got in life. It's a million degrees out today. You should've appreciated the AC while you had it."

I shivered again just thinking about the drive from town and slammed the door in his face. All the way here, he'd refused to adjust the temperature setting in his truck to one designed for human survival. "Lizard man."

Brittany laughed. She and Tiffany pulled off their shirts as well. At twenty-one, Tiff was five years younger than us, but she was Brittany's double. With the same short, curly hair, the same soft, light brown eyes, and the same petite build, she could've been her twin.

While Scott backed his boat into the water, the girls and I stood beside the launch, trying to defrost. At least, *I* was trying to defrost.

Brittany and Tiff were staring at Scott's truck like it held the secret to eternally youthful skin.

"What?" I asked eventually, still unable to feel my fingers and toes. "Are there icicles sticking to the backseat or something?"

"No, it's not that," Brittany said, her voice oddly breathy. "There's just something so hot about watching a man in a big truck."

I shouldered my friend, my features scrunching up as I shuddered. "Ew. That's my brother you're talking about."

Tiff giggled, her gaze as glued to the truck as her sister's was. "Yeah, but he's not *our* brother."

"Really, you too?"

"Me too." She shrugged, pumping her eyebrows at me as she let out an almost dreamy sigh. "You can't be that surprised. Your brother is hot and you're the only woman in town related to him. To the rest of us, he's the prize."

"The prize?" I scoffed back a laugh. "You guys are ridiculous. He's an idiot. With an internal temperature regulation issue."

"Well, that last part may be true," Brittany said. "If I had him to keep me warm though, I wouldn't mind it so much."

I groaned playfully, scrubbing my palms over my face as I shook my head. "You'd mind it once you got pneumonia and ended up losing a lung."

She laughed, then shrugged at me. "I don't know. Losing a lung might be worth it."

"Maybe you're the idiot," I joked.

The truth was that I adored my brother. We had an amazing relationship and we were closer than any other siblings I knew. Our parents were gone and they had been for a long time. Although Scott was only three years older than me, he was my rock, my go-to for advice, and my one true hero.

Besides, I knew all the women in town were gaga over him. Six feet tall, he kept in great shape and he was always showing it off by wearing solely board shorts, sandals, and loose tanks. He kept his blond hair in a short buzz cut and his strong jaw clean shaven. To top it all off, he had eyes the color of freshly bottled honey, with a personality sweet enough to match.

Eventually, one of the women chasing him was going to catch him. I just hoped that whoever she was, she was good enough for my fiercely loyal, even-keeled brother.

"Okay, ladies!" he shouted from the water, jerking me out of my reverie. "Let's go. We're burning daylight here."

Brittany and Tiff started toward the boat immediately and I rolled my eyes but followed them, hopping on and grabbing a coveted spot at the front where I could relax. Unsurprisingly, both my friends stayed close to the helm—and my brother behind the wheel.

After we'd piled in, Scott drove smoothly away from the shore and I watched as the young families who had congregated there for the day grew smaller and smaller. He opened it up when we were far enough away, heading to the far end of the lake where we'd be able to float in peace.

I closed my eyes, relishing the wind in my hair and the warm sun on my skin. *This is the life.*

Nobody said much until he slowed again, and my eyes opened to see that he'd driven us almost all the way to Styles Manor. Up ahead on the shore, she sat in all her glory.

Once again, I ogled her for a moment. "She's especially beautiful today, don't you think? I love that garden in the summertime when it's all green and lush."

"It's just a house," Scott said, rolling his eyes.

Brittany nodded her agreement. "I keep telling her that."

"There are a lot of words to describe the manor, but 'house' and 'just' have no place among them," I said. "It's the most incredible structure in town. Maybe even in the whole world."

In my opinion, it was definitely the most incredible structure in the world, but to be fair, I hadn't seen more of it than June Lake and its surrounds. I was also probably just biased, being so well read on the history of the house.

I'd fallen in love with the romance behind it years ago and it was a love that lasted to this day. After years of uncertainty of whether he would survive the war, Mr. and Mrs. Styles had settled here to live out the rest of their days in peace.

They'd built the place to their exact specifications over the course of several years. She'd given birth to her three children right here in town, and they'd lived a beautiful life here after that.

While I was daydreaming about the house, Scott spun the wheel to bounce over some waves he'd created, and since I hadn't been paying attention, the sudden jolt made me land on my ass. I scowled at him, fixing my sunglasses that had fallen off my nose.

"Jerk," I said.

He laughed, his eyes almost closing with glee. "Welcome back to earth, sis. Did you have a nice imaginary trip to the past?"

"I really did," I said as I stood up and resumed my seat, keeping an eye on him this time. "You didn't have to be mean about it. You could've just said my name."

"I did. A few times." He jerked his head at the Manor. "You were too busy over there."

I exhaled through my nostrils. "So what? It's a nice place and I appreciate the history."

He chuckled. "Uh huh. You do know that you won't get that same kind of romance just by admiring the house, right?"

My cheeks flushed and I flipped him off. "So sue me for being a romantic. At least I have a sense of romance. Unlike you, you caveman."

"What, you mean taking a girl fishing and expecting her to gut her own catch isn't romantic?" He batted his eyes innocently at me.

Brittany's nose wrinkled. "There's nothing wrong with some good old-fashioned guts and gore."

I snorted, trying to hold back my laughter. "Sure, as long as the girl he's trying to woo is a psychopath, which you're not. We've long established that being capable of gutting your own fish doesn't mean you should be forced to do it when you're on a date." I shook my head. "The men in this town."

"What can I say?" Scott asked, smirking as he connected his phone to the sound system on the boat. "We're old-school romantics."

"Yeah, like, dawn of time old school," I muttered. Then the music started and I opened our cooler, passing out some snacks and drinks.

We chatted while we ate, waiting until we were all hot and sweaty before we leaped into the lake. Brittany ogled Scott when he pulled off his tank and I had to resist the urge to throw up over the side. Eventually, I chose to plunge into the cool water instead, swimming under it and feeling my hair making a cloud around my head.

When I finally broke the surface, Tiff was scrolling through her phone, filming videos for her social media page. She had the most followers in town—by a landslide.

"Smile, Jewel," she called as she aimed her camera in my direction. I gave her a cheeky wave before ducking under again, kicking my way back to the boat.

When I broke the surface, her phone was still pointed in my direction and she smiled, winking at me. I sighed but returned her smile. Social media wasn't really my thing and I didn't quite understand why she was always so busy uploading things, but I appreciated that it was important to her, so I rolled with it.

When I climbed back onto the boat, Scott tossed me a bottle of water and moved us closer to the shore. Then he tossed an inner tube into the water. "Anyone for tubing?"

"Me!" I volunteered immediately, leaning over to the side to grab the tube before it drifted away. "I don't mind waiting, though."

"I'll go too," Brittany said.

She and Scott bantered for a minute, but I wasn't paying much attention to them. Eyes peeled, I glanced at Styles Manor, unable to resist now that we were so much closer. To my surprise, I spotted movement on the property.

"Check it out," I said, pointing at the lawn. "That's him."

Scott raised a hand to shield his eyes from the sun. "The asshole from the road?"

I nodded. *Asshole? Check. Sexiest man I've ever laid eyes on? Also check.*

"I wonder how long they're staying," I mused aloud.

"Don't get any ideas," Scott warned me, then shoved Brittany overboard. "You're going first, babe. Grab the tube, will ya?"

She sputtered as she came up, but she flashed him a cheeky smile. "Do your worst, Pendleton."

He arched an eyebrow, his gaze locking on hers as a smirk tugged at the corners of his lips. "Oh, I will. You're going down, Brit."

I chuckled at the exchange, putting my money on Scott on this occasion. He loved taking us out on the lake. It was his slice of paradise and he spent a lot of time messing around out here. Brittany and I worked hard, but we played hard too when we had the chance.

Just not as hard as Scott. In any challenge involving the water, my money would always be on my brother.

As they got themselves ready, Tiff held up her phone again, panning it from Scott, to Brittany, to the shore. I cast another glance that way myself, acutely aware of Captain Intimidation's presence not so far away.

I knew I shouldn't be indulging this curiosity about him. Nothing could come of it and it was so silly, but he'd been wandering around in the back of my mind since we'd had our run-in with him.

Scott pushed forward on the throttle, making me lurch as he opened up. I turned my back on the shore, grinning as I held on to my sunglasses and put my focus back where it belonged.

Not on some tourist who was only passing through but on my friends and family. The people who would still be here long after he left.

7

LANDON

I frowned at the nearly empty fridge in the main kitchen. There were three in total—completely unnecessary in my opinion—but all of them were about as well stocked as this one right now.

Colten sat at the expansive kitchen island, impatiently waiting for me to come up with something for us to eat. "I'm starving. What's for breakfast?"

"That's a good question," I said, scratching the side of my neck as I considered our options.

We'd eaten through the loaf of bread and the ready-made meals I'd had delivered before we'd arrived. Of the grocery items that had been stocked before our arrival, we had some basics left, like butter, milk, and coffee, but nothing we could eat as a meal.

The eggs were gone and so was the pasta. I'd seen rice in the pantry, but I had no idea what to do with it. As I stared into that fridge after having spent equally long staring at empty containers on the shelves in the pantry, I realized I was ill equipped to prepare meals.

I'd spent so much time working that I'd never really learned how to cook—beyond ramen and eggs. Walter had done the bulk of the cooking when I'd been growing up. Then I'd gone to college. Hence the ramen and the eggs, and then I'd lived on takeout and restaurants for a while before I'd hired my chef.

Guilt gnawed at my insides when I realized I hadn't cooked a proper meal for my son *ever*. As a baby, I'd fed him but it'd never been food I'd made myself. In the morning, we had cereal for breakfast, but that came out of a box. At all other times, I either got us takeout or we relied on our chef to come up with something.

My automated systems at home allowed him to add items to a grocery list on a tablet in the kitchen. The tablet was linked to an online shopping app and the groceries were delivered to our home once he ordered them. When it arrived, the staff packed it away and the cycle started all over again.

All of that and I never had to do a thing other than pay our monthly bill. I raked a hand through my hair as I thought it over.

"It looks like we're going to have to take a drive into town and check the place out," I said as I closed the fridge. "There must be a decent place to grab waffles."

At the word *waffles*, he perked up but then sighed. "Do we need to call the driver and wait? How long will that take?"

I shook my head. "There's a truck in the garage for guests to use."

A grin spread on his lips. "I love waffles."

He got up and followed me to the door leading to the garage. I unlocked it, flipping the switch for the lights and finding a solitary truck in the center of a space meant for at least four vehicles. The air was stale in here, but the gleaming blue truck was clean and relatively new.

Looking around, I found the keys hanging on a hook on the wall and I grabbed them before inclining my head at Colt to follow me. I'd been a touch worried that the battery would be dead despite the seemingly good condition of the truck, but it roared to life when I turned the key and I grinned.

"Decent waffles, coming right up," I said as I hit the button for the garage door and waited for it to slide open.

While we waited, I opened the windows. Colt switched on the

radio and fiddled with it for a moment before he settled on a catchy pop song, turning up the volume as I backed out of the garage.

The sun was high in the sky as we drove along the winding roads to the tiny little town. It glinted off the surface of the lake, its waters the same incredible blue as the sky itself. Colt grinned and peered down to the slope to the shore, watching the activity for a minute before he looked at me.

"There's tons of people down there. The water is packed. We should go."

"One of these days, we will." I wasn't too keen on sand, sunscreen, and congested beaches full of strangers, but that was one of the reasons we'd come out here.

At some point, I'd have to suck it up and go join the summer *fun*. These last couple days, Colt and I had been settling in, playing chess, and lounging around the swimming pool. That had been great. We'd been able to see the lake without having to deal with any of those other things.

I knew it wouldn't last all summer, though. Eventually, we'd go to the lake. I was even considering chartering a boat to take us out, but that wasn't happening today.

As we drove into town, I was struck again by how underwhelming it was. The tallest building was no more than two stories, and while the streets were flanked on either side by parked cars, it wasn't exactly a bustling metropolis.

I parked in a spot along one of the side roads, pulling up the emergency brake and sliding my sunglasses over my eyes. "We're going to have to walk it. Explore a little until we find someplace that looks good."

He nodded, opened his door, and climbed out. I followed him, aware of how everyone we passed was looking at us as we walked down the sidewalk and popped into the only cafe we could find. A little bell above the door jingled when I pushed it open, and the only server around smiled brightly when she looked at us.

"Inside or outside, boys?"

"Outside," I decided immediately, figuring that we might as well get a feel for the town by being able to see it while we ate.

She finished pouring the coffee she'd been busy with, then chatted to the people at the table she'd been serving for a moment before she nodded and turned back to us. Motioning that we should follow her, she plucked two menus out of a stand on our way out and led us to the streetside seating.

Bordering the sidewalk, it was separated by only a low metal trellis that appeared to have seen better days, but the umbrellas covering the tables and the faux plants hanging from the wall and trellis gave it a cozy feel.

As we sat down, she dropped the menu on the table and slid a notepad out of the pocket of her apron. "What can I get you to drink?"

"Coffee," I said immediately.

Colten chuckled. "Orange juice, please."

"You got it, baby boy," she said before she smiled again and took off.

In her fifties and wearing neon pink lipstick with an apron to match, it turned out that our server's name was Verna and she fancied herself as the town's welcome committee. As she brought our drinks, she peppered us with questions.

"Where are you folks staying?" she asked conversationally. "Have you been here long? If you need anything, you should just ask. Anyone from around here would be happy to answer any questions you might have or to show you around."

"Thank you," I said politely. "We're staying at the Styles Manor and we're doing okay so far. We'll be sure to keep that in mind, though."

"The Styles Manor?" Her purple eyeshadowed eyes widened. "Is that so? It's the nicest house in town."

"So I've heard," I murmured. "Do you sell waffles?"

She grinned. "Only the best in town. Two?"

"Yes, please," Colten said. "For me. I don't know what Dad wants."

She giggled, but I flashed her a tight smile. "He's serious. He'll have two and I'll have one as well."

"Perfect." She grinned at him in that grandmotherly way that made me wonder if she was going to pinch his cheek next. "I forget sometimes that boys have such healthy appetites. My own are fully grown and they flew the coop ages ago. I'll bring your food in a few."

She took off and I picked up my coffee, taking a small sip and expecting the worst, but by some miracle, it was actually pretty good. Colten lifted his juice to his lips, also seeming tentative until he'd had the first sip.

We watched as people strolled by, many greeting one another on the street and having quick chats before they separated. The pace of the town was mesmerizing to me, so slow and lazy that even the people who appeared to be in a hurry were practically moving in slow motion.

I couldn't understand how anyone got anything done. It was a weekday morning, and sure, it was summer, but no one seemed too stressed out about work.

I envy them that, I realized as I watched them. I would never be able to live like this myself, but it had to be nice.

Verna came back with our waffles, also not seeming to be in a rush to get back to her other tables. "You guys should come to the Friday Night Market tonight. It's at the bandstand, which is a landmark in town so you'll see the signs for it."

"A night market?" I asked.

She nodded and offered me a wide smile. "There will be live music, great food, face painting, and plenty of kids' activities."

Turning to Colt next, her smile softened. "There are lots of boys your age who will be there. Maybe you'll meet some friends for the summer? It's no good for a child to rattle around that big old house all by himself."

I was about to protest that he wasn't all by himself when she winked at me. "You know what I mean. Kids need kids, or they get bored unless you entertain them."

Colten shrank in on himself and I wondered why the idea of

making some friends seemed to have suddenly shut him down. Resolving to ask in a minute, I glanced up at Verna. “Thank you for the invitation. We might see you there.”

She nodded as she spun away and Colten picked up his cutlery, but he poked at his waffles instead of devouring them like I’d thought he might. While we ate, I glanced at him from across the table, taking in his slumped shoulders and the forlorn expression on his face.

“What do you think about going tonight?” I asked. “It could be fun.”

He shrugged and responded without looking up at me. “It’ll be fine, I guess.”

I sighed but let it go, thinking back to what Mr. Lafferty had said about suspecting that Colten was being bullied at school. I’d tried to broach the subject a few times, but he kept dodging it, finding a way to avoid the question before he changed the topic.

Maybe this is just what he needs. Some small-town kids who know how to have good old-fashioned fun and aren’t obsessed with their social media following or designer shoes.

While I paid the bill, he went to wait outside by the truck, and when I caught up to him, I saw him talking to some local kids. *Well, look at that.*

Hanging back for a moment, I watched him, noticing how awkward and unsure he was, his hands in his pockets and his gaze averted. The kids ended up leaving, but one of them turned back to holler at Colt over his shoulder as they rode off on their bikes. “You should come tonight!”

Once they’d turned the corner, I smiled as I approached him. “Who was that?”

“Just some locals,” he murmured, turning toward the truck and reaching for the door. “It was no big deal.”

“Yeah, of course. They seemed nice, though.”

“I guess.” He shrugged. “Can we go now?”

“Sure.”

We climbed into the truck and drove around the block back to the main street, and I glanced at him. "Are those kids going to the market tonight?"

"Yes."

I grinned. "We should definitely go, then. I can get you a bike to use while we're here, if you'd like. It looked like you might need one."

"No, I'm fine."

I frowned. "Are you sure? I used to love my bicycle when I was your age. Our neighbors and I—"

"It doesn't matter, Dad," he grumbled. "They're not my friends and I don't know them. I don't need a bike to ride with kids who don't even know my name."

"That's why they invited you to the market," I reasoned. "To get to know you. Who knows? They might just become your friends."

"They won't," he said confidently.

My frown deepened and I considered pulling over to talk to him but decided to keep it casual at the last minute. "Why not? The kids in towns like this are usually different to—"

"No."

Frustration started bubbling in my veins and my grip on the steering wheel tightened. "If you opened up to them, they might become your friends, but that means you have to try."

"I don't want to."

I blew out a heavy breath, shaking my head at him. "Just give them a chance, Colt."

"Can we just stay home tonight?" he asked, completely ignoring what I'd said. He sounded so defeated that I didn't push it, though.

Clearly, there was more to this than him just wanting to spend his lunch hour honing his skills with his teacher. Intent on finding out what it was, I debated my next move internally. Getting in an argument with him about this wouldn't help, but I also didn't know just what the hell would.

Damn it. Why don't kids come with manuals? That sure would've been helpful right around now.

8

JEWEL

On Friday morning, I hurried around town, trying to get to the hardware store. They were the only supplier around here for the cleaning products Brittany and I liked to use, and I hadn't noticed that we'd run out of floor cleaner—until I'd started looking for it halfway through our first house of the morning.

Having to bail in the middle of a job wasn't pleasant, and if I didn't haul ass, Brittany was going to wind up doing the lion's share of the work by herself. *Darn it. I should've done inventory yesterday instead of spending the afternoon on the lake.*

On the other hand, we'd had a blast tubing with Scott and it'd been worth a tiny touch of stress this morning. Hurrying across the sidewalk, I yelped when a huge blue pick-up truck barreled out of nowhere and nearly ran me over.

Leaping back, I glared hotly up at them, cursing under my breath. "Freaking tourists never paying attention to the crosswalk!"

My heart was racing and my cheeks were flushed. My hand flew to my chest and my lips parted. *Wow. That was a close call!*

A scowl tightened my features. My eyes adjusted to the glint of sunlight off the windshield and I finally managed to get a good look at my would-be murderer. When our eyes locked, recognition rippled through me and I groaned. My heart skipped before it started thudding against my ribs at the sight of those intense green eyes burning into mine.

"Seriously?" I muttered. *How do I keep running into this guy, and why is it always on such bad terms?*

Captain Intimidation scowled right back at me, another cutting glare coming my way as he opened his window and stuck his head out. "Watch where you're going!"

I scoffed. My eyes widened and my fingers curled into fists at my side. *The nerve of this guy.*

"It's a crosswalk, dude!" I yelled right back at him, not afraid to get loud when I had to. "I don't know where you're from, but you're the one who should've been watching out. You could've turned me into roadkill."

I planted my hands on my hips and narrowed my eyes as I lifted my chin. The man was impossible. First, he'd refused to accept my apology graciously the other day, and now, it seemed he was allergic to offering one of his own.

Most people would've just said they were sorry and gone on their merry ways, but not this guy. As if he hadn't even *heard* the part where I'd told him it was a crosswalk, those strong features of his remained impassive and he didn't say anything at all.

I rolled my eyes, so over his silent, haughty arrogance. I didn't even care that this was only our second encounter. He was already getting to me, him and his superior attitude and that cutting glare that said he thought he was better than me.

To be honest, he probably *was* better than me—financially, anyway—but I definitely won in the humanity and politeness category.

This time, he'd been in the wrong, and yet, there wasn't even a hint of remorse on his handsome face. Being hotter than the surface of the sun didn't give him the right to ignore the rules of the road. If I had been someone else, perhaps even a child, this could've ended in disaster.

Bet he wouldn't have been so fucking arrogant about it then.

Standing my ground, I met those gorgeous green eyes and stared into them intently. "I'm not moving until you apologize."

In my periphery, I suddenly noticed that there was a passenger in the truck and I almost did a double-take when I realized it was a kid. A kid who inched forward and rolled his eyes at Captain Intimidation. He muttered something, but I obviously couldn't hear what it was.

The man shook his head, then broke eye contact with me for a moment as he unbuckled himself and opened his door. The kid sighed, the rising and falling of his chest a dead giveaway. I stole a closer look at him, noticing the similarities between the two and coming to the conclusion that the kid had to be his son.

They had the same dark hair. The same attractive, downturned eye shape. The same straight-as-an-arrow nose and high cheekbones. Add a bit of scruff to the kid's jaw and a few years to his face, and I'd have thought they were twins.

If they weren't father and son, then they had to be related some other way but they clearly came from a family who had been blessed by the gene fairy. The kid was going to be a stunner when he got older, but right now, he looked exactly like what he was—a disgruntled, irritated child who wished he could be anywhere else in the world.

Meanwhile, his father had climbed out of the truck and was coming around the hood of it. The man moved in a smooth, almost graceful way, one stride flowing seamlessly into the next. He didn't look at the ground once. Didn't seem worried that he'd trip or step in a hole. Like he expected the universe to literally pave the way ahead of him, making it as smooth as glass without a single obstacle in his way.

I nearly snorted out loud at the thought. *At least that means he's not only an arrogant ass to me. He even expects the damn stars to align for him in his everyday life.*

"Move," he said, his voice once again a quiet command that made the hairs on my arms threaten to rise.

I didn't know if it was because of attraction or annoyance, though.

It didn't matter. I wasn't moving. I didn't obey the orders of men—no matter how hot they were.

By now, the incident—and the truck currently blocking a lane of Main Street—had attracted a bit of an audience. Most of them, I recognized as locals and they were chuckling, knowing me for these kinds of antics.

They knew I wouldn't back down. I was quick to apologize if I was in the wrong and I expected the same from other people.

Even big-city bastards who thought they owned the whole world and everyone in it.

It also didn't matter that I was so intrigued by this guy and where he was staying. Right was right and wrong was wrong.

Slowly crossing my arms over my chest, I shrugged and met his gaze without wavering. "I'm not moving until you say those two little words. *I'm. Sorry*."

He ran his fingers through his thick dark hair, exasperation flaring to life behind those eyes as he scoffed at me. I frowned, cocking my head as I studied him and realized that *he* wasn't about to back down either.

"Why is it so hard to just say it?" I asked. "You're the one who messed up. Not me. It's easy. Quick. We could've been done here already, so just say it and then we can both move on with our days."

His teeth were clenched, the column of his elegant throat moving as he swallowed something. *Probably a string of curse words.*

"Maybe you could just forgive me and take the stick out of your ass," he suggested, those eyes never leaving mine. "You did run into a road, after all. Crosswalk or not, it's advisable to look left and right before you cross, no?"

I laughed with my head tipped back and my hands on my hips. "Fat chance, buddy. I didn't do anything wrong, yet you chose to yell at me. Apologize and I'll move. Simple as that."

As he held my gaze, he paused for a beat, his eyes moving from one of mine to the other before a smirk ghosted across his lips. "Shouldn't we just call it even? You were in my way the other day and now you're in my way again."

I didn't budge.

Our stare-off continued, drawing even more of an audience, but I didn't care about any of that. Standing up for what was right was important to me. It always had been, and there were far too many people in this world who thought the rules didn't apply to them.

While I wasn't some kind of keyboard warrior or self-righteous serial killer in the making, I did make a point of taking a stand when it was necessary. Like now. It could be a kid next time, and then what?

Finally, his son stuck his head out of his own window. "Just say you're sorry already, Dad!"

Glancing at the boy, I smiled. "Thank you." I looked back at Captain Intimidation. "Why does your kid have better manners than you do?"

His nostrils flared and he sucked in a deep breath, but he kept his cool. Sliding his sunglasses back over his eyes from the top of his head, he ground out, "I'm sorry."

Giving me a curt nod, he stomped back to the truck and got in, slamming the door behind him. I stepped aside, giving a little curtsy. He accelerated through the crosswalk and flew down the road. The onlookers laughed, giving me a round of applause. Some of them even whooped.

I smiled, allowing myself a moment to indulge them and be goofy before I hurried to go grab that floor cleaner. Brittany was going to be furious that it had taken me so long, but I knew she would understand once I told her what had happened.

I shopped, raced to the cash register, and paid before hightailing it back across town. The whole time, I thought over the encounter and shook my head. Scott had been right about that guy. He really was an asshole. As much as he had intrigued me after our first meeting, perhaps it was better that I took my brother's advice.

Don't go getting any ideas. I nodded to myself as I walked back into the house we were cleaning. I wouldn't get any ideas. He was just a tourist, passing through like all the others. From now on, I wasn't even going to think about him anymore.

9

LANDON

"That was so embarrassing," Colten grumbled as we drove away from the crosswalk and the scene it had turned into. "Now I *definitely* don't want to go tonight."

"We're going." I inhaled deeply in an attempt to keep my temper under control. "No more negotiations. We're going to be in this town for almost two full months. We might as well put ourselves out there and get to know people. They can't all be as bad as the bimbo."

Fuck. I shouldn't have said that.

Colt frowned. "What's a bimbo?"

I winced. *I really have to start remembering to be more careful about what I say.*

"I'm sorry, Colt. My mouth ran away with me there. It's not a very nice word and I didn't mean it. That woman just gets under my skin. She's always in the wrong place at the wrong time, and she's... willful."

Stubborn, more like, but I didn't say that. I'd already called her a bimbo in front of him. The least I could do now was to rein in my frustration and not say any other words with less than pleasant connotations.

"I think she's cool," he said, and I nearly rolled the goddamn truck as shock ricocheted through me.

"What? Why?" I didn't look at him, intent on keeping my full attention on the road now that I'd learned the people around here just stormed into it whenever they saw fit.

Spotting a grocery store next to the road, I pulled into the parking lot. Breakfast hadn't been the only thing we needed to get while we were in town. Colt shrugged when I finally looked at him after I'd parked.

"She stood up for herself," he muttered. "She was right and you were wrong, and she made you apologize for it even if you didn't want to. That's cool. Not a lot of people have the guts to do that. Especially when there are so many others watching."

What the hell? I shook my head, but I didn't respond immediately. I knew how to bite my tongue when I needed to—and how to consider whether there was something I might learn from the person I was speaking to.

It was a skill I'd acquired over the years in my job, not running my mouth while people often left all sorts of clues if you let them run theirs instead. I had already let it get away from me just a few minutes ago. I wasn't about to let it happen again.

As I considered what he'd said, I realized that he had a point. So had I, but I might've overreacted back there. That woman—the Bimbo Siren—had been standing up for herself, which she'd had every right to do.

She hadn't had to make such a scene about it, but in retrospect, I could see why Colten might think she was cool. He was right about something else too. There weren't a lot of people who had the guts to do what she had.

Sighing, I climbed out of the car and waited for Colten. We headed toward the grocery store together. A bulletin board was up on the wall outside it, full of community events, jobs, items for sale, and that kind of thing.

All sorts of advertisements stared back at me, both seekers and providers taking the opportunity to get their needs out there. It was cute. Wholesome.

We'd had these in LA too when I'd been growing up, but I hadn't been to a grocery store in so long that I had no idea if it was still a thing. Either way, as I paused in front of the board, I wondered if I could take advantage of this.

Colten and I needed someone to cook at least dinners for us. Between cereal, eggs, and toast, we had breakfast covered, and making sandwiches for lunch was easy enough, but dinners were going to get the better of me.

A brilliant idea popped into my head and I grinned. Colten frowned up at me. "Why did we stop? If you're looking for a bicycle, I told you, I—"

"It's not that," I assured him. "I still think it'd be nice for you to have one here, but I can wait until you realize it too."

Scanning the board, I found what I was looking for posted right at the bottom. A flyer so old that the paper was yellow and wavy. Everyone who lived in town had probably seen it a million times, but I was still careful when I tore some paper off the bottom of it.

The information on the flyer remained undamaged, and I was satisfied that I hadn't been a pompous ass by destroying someone else's ad. Turning the scrap over in my hand, I slid my pen out of the pocket of my shirt and scrawled my number on it, adding that I was at the Manor at the end of the lake and looking for a chef for the summer.

With that done, I borrowed a pin from another ad and stuck it to the board, proud of my handiwork and my own initiative. Colt shook his head at me, a pained expression on his face as his gaze met mine.

"Is that really necessary?" he asked. "You can grill, right? We'll just have hamburgers every night."

"I can grill more than just a hamburger," I said, feigning insult. "I'd just rather not have to do it every night while I'm on vacation. Besides, this helps the local economy."

Just as I was about to turn away from the board, a flyer for a residential cleaning service caught my eye. Acting on impulse, I tore off one of the phone numbers at the bottom and tucked it into my pocket.

The Manor could've come with house staff, but I hadn't been interested in having a bunch of people around us at all times. I was having second thoughts about that now though, since I also didn't want to spend our entire vacation cleaning up.

This summer was supposed to be about my son and me, but having someone pop in every now and then to clean and having a cook just for dinners sounded like the perfect balance to me. Otherwise, I might end up giving us both food poisoning and I doubted that was the kind of memory Walter had been encouraging me to make with my son.

Reaching out, I ruffled his hair and looked into those unhappy green eyes. So far, I wasn't doing a very good job of making the right kind of memories. I smiled through my disappointment, my mind whirring for ways to make it up to him. "How about we do our shopping and then we head back to the Manor for a swim in the lake?"

"For real?"

I nodded. "For real. It'll be fun."

A wide grin split his face as he nodded enthusiastically. "That sounds good. Do you think they've got any inflatables at the house we can borrow?"

"Like what?" I asked. "I know you can swim."

"Yeah, but like, maybe a boat we can float on or even just one of those fun, ride-on sharks or something. An inner tube at least."

I chuckled. "I didn't see it mentioned in the listing, but maybe we can get something while we're here."

Finally leaving the bulletin board behind, we grabbed a cart on our way into the store and Colt glanced at me. "Even if you don't want to cook burgers every night, do you think we can maybe just do it once?"

"Of course," I said immediately. "We can even do it a few times. It's just that having a cook around will mean that I can focus on you without having to worry about what we're eating as well."

He rocked his head from side to side as he considered it, then nodded. "Yeah, I suppose that's fine."

Satisfied that I had explained my reasoning properly this time, we turned left as we entered the store and took the aisles one by one. The place wasn't great or huge. We certainly wouldn't find any upper-end, gourmet products here, but we managed to load up our cart with snacks and basic foodstuffs. I even got some pancake mix, intent on giving it a try at least once.

Colten and I could do it together, and barring any kitchen disasters, it would be worth the memory no matter how bad they turned out. Once we'd made our way through all the aisles containing food, we walked to the other end of the shop, finding them surprisingly well stocked with summery things.

There were camping chairs and swim towels, portable grills only meant to be used once, beach toys for children, and fortunately an entire wall dedicated to all sorts of inflatables to play around with in the water.

Colten bounced on the balls of his feet when he saw the selection, his eyes lighting up with glee. I stepped up beside him, checking them out myself. He reached for a box that supposedly contained a boat.

"I wonder if we need oars to go with this," he said, then spotted a bucket with a few oars in it a couple yards away. "I think we do."

Leaving him to do his thing, I went in search of a device to inflate these for us. I definitely wasn't doing it all with breath out of my lungs. I'd never survive.

After finding an electric compressor that promised to do what I needed it to, I strode back to Colten and our cart, finding that he'd added a ride-on creature that might or might not have been a dragon. After grabbing a floating mat for myself as well as a miniature, inflatable volleyball net and a ball, I nodded at him.

"I think that's enough, don't you?"

He shrugged, eyeing our haul before he grabbed two pairs of goggles and dropped them in too. "Now it's enough."

I chuckled, but considered myself lucky that he was so excited about this. At least it meant that I wasn't too late. He wasn't a slave to a screen—or a chessboard—just yet.

As we made our way to the exit, I spotted a few cheap fishing rods and wondered if we should get some of those too, but I had a feeling I might be able to find some at the Manor. Deciding to check there first, we continued to check out and then loaded an impressive amount of shopping bags onto the back of the truck.

A fresh breeze had started up while we'd been inside, and I found myself smiling as I stood in the sunshine with the wind in my hair. Behind the grocery store was a line of towering green pines, the lake glinting in the distance.

Despite the encounter with the Siren this morning, I was taking more and more of a liking to this picturesque town. At first glance, it was a little simple and a lot small, but there was something enchanting about it that was definitely getting to me.

Colt and I had our windows down on the way back to the Manor, both lost in thought but smiling as I drove us home. It'd been a long time since I'd felt so at peace. So relaxed.

I could see Colt felt the same. This summer was going to be good for us. I could feel it in my bones. If I had known then how it was going to turn out, I probably would have tucked tail and run for the hills, but I had no clue what was coming for us.

So I drove back to the Manor, blissfully ignorant of the changes about to happen, and spent the afternoon in the water with my son. Sunscreen and sand be damned. We were here to have a good time, and from the look of his smile and the sound of his laughter, that was exactly what Colten had.

10

JEWEL

Early on Friday evening, Scott and I arrived at the bandstand for the night market. It was outside of town hall, in Heritage Park, and it was shaping up to be a beautiful night for being outdoors. Twinkle lights had been strung in the trees and a popular local band was playing *Brown-Eyed Girl*.

The sun had started to set in the distance, painting the sky in pinks and oranges while a nice breeze drifted off the lake to break the heat of the day. Surrounded by laughter and chatter, Scott glanced at me and motioned toward a stand selling cold lemonade.

"You want one?"

"You bet," I said, grabbing his arm and pulling him toward the stand. It was manned by a kid I knew from our neighborhood and I'd promised her I'd stop by. Peeling off a couple bills, I handed them over and smiled at her. "How are you doing tonight, Lacey? We'll take two please."

"You came!" she said excitedly as she added our money to her box and grabbed two plastic cups. "It's not going so well yet, but it will. People are only really starting to get here now."

I nodded, waiting patiently as she poured our drinks. "It's nice and warm tonight. I'm sure you're going to make a killing, but even if you don't, it's still fun, right?"

She smiled. "Sure is! Would you mind spreading the word that it's the best lemonade you've ever tasted?"

"Consider it done, kiddo," Scott said, grinning. He took his first sip. I watched him closely, nearly laughing at his attempt to fight a grimace. Thankfully, he succeeded and gave her a wide grin instead. "Yum, that's great. Did you add the sugar to this yourself?"

"I tweaked my mother's recipe," she said, beaming at him.

Understanding flashed in his eyes as he gave her another smile. Then I took my cup from her as well and thanked her before we took off. I glanced at him. "It can't be that bad."

"It's ninety-nine percent sugar," he said, giving my drink a pointed look. "Taste it. You'll see."

"Doesn't matter. We're going back to get another one after this, and you promised we'd spread the word."

He sighed. "Sure. I'll do it, but we might need to warn people."

I chuckled. "Lacey's lemonade has always been sweet. It'll be fine."

"Not this sweet." He held his nose as he drank the rest of his in one gulp, then tossed the cup in the nearest recycle bin and winced once he was done. "I need a beer. You see any yet?"

"I think Britt mentioned there's a beer tent outside of Gaston's," I said. "Which makes sense, considering it's a pub."

"Let's go," he said and we wandered through the crowd, greeting people we knew—which was almost everyone.

We hardly ever missed a Friday night market in the summer, and besides, there wasn't much to do in a town like ours, so almost everyone always showed up for this. It was a favorite event for every local, and as a result, most tourists in the area got invited too.

At the thought, Captain Intimidation's face flickered through my mind and I groaned softly, reminding myself that I'd resolved not think about him anymore. I focused on chatting to nice people instead of wasting my brain power on the rudest one I'd ever met.

As the sun set and the band kept playing golden oldies that

everyone knew, kids chased each other through the crowd and adults congregated in front of the band to dance. Parents filmed their kids or dragged them over to dance with them. Older siblings on babysitting duty pouted and the scent of barbecue and onions wafted in the air.

When we finally reached Gaston's, a pub bordering the park, Brittany and Tiff were already there and I downed my sickly sweet lemonade before gratefully accepting a glass of beer from Tiff's pitcher. We sat down with them at a small table, catching up before we went in search of food.

"Oh, Susie's here," Tiff said happily, sending us an apologetic smile. "I'll see you guys later, okay?"

"See you later," Brittany called when her sister took off to join her friends. Then she groaned as she glanced at me. "Why is it that whenever her friends show up, we're not good enough anymore?"

"Because we're old and boring," Scott joked. "I'd rather spend time with her friends myself, to be honest."

I rolled my eyes at him. "So go then. Go be old and boring among the youngsters. We'll see how long it takes them to send you back to us."

"Probably won't be long," he admitted, laughing as he guided us toward the section of the park containing the food trucks. "What are you guys in the mood for?"

"Retirement," Brittany lamented. "My body is so sore from all the cleaning today. We need to find a spot to sit. I can't walk much more tonight."

"Oh, wow. You really *are* old," I teased. "I'm feeling fine. Sprightly, even."

"Sprightly?" Scott chuckled as he arched an eyebrow at me. "Weren't you *just* complaining about your back before we got here?"

I waved him off. "It was just a joke. No backache here. I'm too *sprightly* for that."

As he laughed, Brittany's gaze suddenly left us and zeroed in on something behind my back. "Isn't that the fancy city boy and his son?"

She inclined her head at the duo, and I spun around. My eyes narrowed when I realized he was probably going to ruin it for me. *Crap.*

I knew it was better to turn around and walk away, but I stayed rooted to my spot like a deer in the headlights, just waiting to be hit. In my defense though, all three of us watched them as they started strolling through the market.

Locals sold hand-crafted products and baked goods here, as well as home-brewed wine and beers. There was no shortage of talent in our town, and to my surprise, Captain Intimidation actually stopped to look at a few things.

Wow. I'd have thought anything here was beneath him. But nope. He even purchased a leather belt and some kind of game for his son before they'd even been there two minutes.

"Verna told me they're in town all summer," Brittany murmured. "I went to grab a coffee earlier and she mentioned there were people living in the Styles Manor. I asked how she knew and she said they came in this morning."

"That must've been where they were coming from when they nearly ran me over," I mused out loud, huffing out a heavy breath. "That's great, though. That they're going to be hanging around for the whole damn summer. Think we can cancel the season and try again next year?"

Scott shrugged. "I mean, we could try, but it probably wouldn't be a great idea. If we cancel it, he might leave but so will all the other tourists, which wouldn't be good for anyone."

I sighed and sent him a disappointed pout. "Stop with your crazy logic."

He chuckled. "Just stay out of his way, Jewel. Literally."

Just as the ass took a sip of the lemonade he'd purchased, he glanced my way and our eyes locked. Despite the distance between us, it was intense.

I felt a sudden rush of vulnerability, like he was looking right into my soul, and I quickly averted my gaze, turning toward Brittany. "Is he still staring?"

"Yep," she responded.

"He's also walking this way," Scott added. "Probably wants to give you a piece of his mind after your little showdown this morning. Run, Brit. Or else we're going to need popcorn for this."

My traitorous friend giggled like Scott had said the funniest thing ever. Then she jerked her head toward Elvis, who was legitimately walking around with a tray of popcorn he was selling. "Would you look at that? I don't even need to run. Elvis is bringing the popcorn to us."

Searching wildly for an escape, I came up empty. I glanced over my shoulder, seeing that he was moving too fast. The only way of getting out of this would've been to flee, and I definitely wasn't giving him that kind of satisfaction.

Before I even knew it, I felt a tap on my shoulder. My breath caught and I turned around, bracing myself for his bad attitude and piercing glare. But instead, I wasn't greeted by any of that.

A smile that shocked me with how kind it looked graced his face, and his green eyes were warm as they hooked on mine. *Jeez. If he keeps this up, I'm going to need to come up with a new nickname for him.*

"Hi," he said in a voice as warm as sunshine and as sweet as honey. "I'm sorry for interrupting you. I just wanted to apologize for earlier."

My eyes widened as shock cascaded through me. When he glanced at his son, I looked too, leaning past him just in time to see him giving his dad an enthusiastic thumbs-up. The man chuckled, the sound rich and surprisingly easy.

I wouldn't have thought he knew how to laugh. Let alone how to do it while making it look natural. He succeeded spectacularly, though.

Moving those eyes back to mine, he even managed to seem genuine. "My son gave me a lesson in manners today. I haven't been very kind or even very polite to you at all, and I'm sorry."

Shocked speechless, I just stood there staring at him like an idiot while he rubbed the back of his neck and disarmed me with another smile. "Really. I've been a jerk. I was taking some pent-up stress out on you and that's not right."

When I still didn't say anything, Brittany jabbed me in the ribs and I blinked hard, clearing my throat as I held out my hand. "It's okay. I'm Jewel. It's, uh, it's interesting to finally meet you."

He chuckled again, sliding his palm into mine and making tingles race up my arm at the touch. "Landon. It's interesting to finally meet you too." Doing a half-turn, he motioned for his son to come closer. "This is Colten. The ten-year-old I got schooled by today."

I grinned at the boy, extracting my hand from his father's to offer it to him instead. "Hi, Colten. I'm Jewel. Thanks for teaching your dad a lesson."

"No problem," he said as he returned my grin. "He had it coming."

"He sure did." I chuckled, then swept a hand toward my friend and my brother. "This is Brittany and Scott."

Landon shook with them, his gaze lingering on Scott's before he turned back to me. "Okay, so thanks for hearing me out."

"Not so fast," I said. "You owe me a lemonade at least."

He glanced at Scott again but then agreed with a curt nod and a sweep of his arm toward Lacey's stand. "That seems fair. Shall we?"

"We shall." I took a step away from my little group and turned to wink at them as I walked away with Landon and Colten.

Brittany shot me a thumbs-up and Scott rolled his eyes, but neither of them tried to stop me. As we joined the line for some more lemonade, I smiled at my new companions. "Since I probably owe you too, how about I take you guys on a tour of the market? I know where all the best stuff is, and since you're going to be here all summer, you're probably going to come to the market every weekend. It'll help to get to know the vendors."

Landon glanced back in the direction we'd come from. "Wouldn't your boyfriend mind?"

"Boyfriend?" My face scrunched up and I burst out laughing when I figured out who he was referring to. "Oh, no. I'm sorry. Scott isn't my boyfriend. He's my brother."

Landon blinked a few times in surprise, then smiled and rubbed his eyes with his thumb and index finger. "Wow. That's embarrassing for me, but in that case, we'd love to take you up on the tour."

We got our too sweet lemonades, then strolled through the market. I pointed out my favorite places to stop every Friday night. Colten and Landon seemed happy to listen, and I was genuinely surprised by how pleasant he was being.

"How did you know we were going to be here all summer?" he asked.

I chuckled. "Verna. From the cafe? You should be careful about what you tell people around here unless you want everyone to know about it. We're a pretty tight knit community."

"I'm starting to realize that," he said good-naturedly. "Thank you for the tour, though. And the warning. There's a surprising amount of booths here."

Instead of admitting that it was because most people in town made and sold things to supplement their income, I finally blurted out the question I'd been wanting to ask him since that day on the road. "I hope this isn't too intrusive, but why on earth did you pick June Lake for your vacation? No offense, I mean, I love this town and everything, but you're not the typical tourists we get around here."

A faint frown creased his brow. He gave his head a quick shake and chuckled. "Yeah, why is that? What exactly is it that makes us so different?"

11

LANDON

The June Lake Friday night market was small but larger than I'd expected. A quick look around had told me that the local vendors were about quality and not quantity, and that was something I could get behind.

Best of all was our tour guide, though. I'd been incredibly surprised when she'd accepted my apology so readily and even more surprised when she'd offered to show us around. On the other hand, people here seemed to be ridiculously friendly.

Jewel introduced us to vendors and other shoppers alike, and not only did they all go out of their way to suggest things we could do, but they all knew who we were. "The guy from the city with the kid staying in the Manor."

That was what I heard all around. So when she finally blurted out the question about what we were doing here, I wasn't as surprised by her bluntness as I would've been before I'd realized that the towns-people seemed to be direct and honest.

I chuckled. "We're here for a good time in a small town, and you know how it is with kids and water. A small town by a lake sounded like a good combination, but we didn't want somewhere overly crowded."

She arched a sassy eyebrow at me. "For those of us who are from around here, this *is* overly crowded."

Colten frowned at her. "Really? You think *this* is crowded?"

He took a look around the park like he was waiting for more people to jump out and surprise him. Jewel gave him a friendly smile when he looked back at her. "I don't know where you guys are from, but to us, this is a lot of people."

"It's pretty here," he said kindly. "Maybe that's why so many people come. The lake is great."

Nice save, buddy, I thought as I reached out to ruffle his hair. "That's another reason we're here. I spent a lot of time around lakes and rivers growing up, but Colt has never spent a summer or even a week in a place like this. We figured we'd come have good, old-fashioned fun."

That explanation seemed a lot simpler than admitting I was here to make memories, to make sure I didn't have any regrets, and to disconnect from work so I could reconnect with my son. *Oh, and also to take advice from the man I respected more than anyone in the world.*

Fun summed it up nicely.

"Well, you've come to the right place for good, old-fashioned fun," she said easily. "June Lake might not be fast paced, but it's top notch. And you can't beat the scenery."

She winked, her entire face animated as she spoke of her town. *Speaking of scenery, damn, she's cute.*

As I looked at her, illuminated by the string lights in the trees, I noticed things about her that I hadn't before. Her eyes were a honey gold, her skin was kissed by days in the sun, and a smattering of freckles covered her shoulders and cheeks.

When I'd first seen her in that scrap of fabric pretending to be a bikini, I'd noticed her amazing figure. It had been impossible to hide her curves when she hadn't been wearing much. That was why I'd been thinking of her as a Siren from the deep, coming to land to lure poor, horny assholes to their deaths, but now?

All these new little things about her struck me as nothing less than beautiful. I glanced down at my lemonade. *Is there vodka in this?*

I'd thought of women as many things after Colt's mom, but beautiful hadn't often been one of them. As I stared deeply into the lemonade and wondered if the girl who had sold it to us had added a little something other than sugar, I realized I'd missed what she'd said.

She gave me an amused look. "Were you listening?"

"Uh, no," I admitted honestly. "Sorry. I missed that."

To my surprise, she shared a look with my son, who shrugged at her before he turned to me. "Jewel was telling us about some of the stuff happening around town this summer."

"Oh, right," I said, clearing my throat as I focused on the information she was giving us. "You mean there's more to this place than markets?"

Laughter shimmered in her eyes as she nodded. "There's a fair in two weeks, and next weekend, we have our Lake Warrior contest." A twinkle joined the shimmer in her eyes. "You should sign up. It's a blast."

Lake Warrior contest? What the hell is that?

Before I could ask, she shifted her attention back to Colten. Nodding toward a bright blue tent with a gladiator on it, she urged him on. "You can sign up right over there, or at least grab a brochure. You guys will enjoy it."

"How do you know?" I asked lightly. To my utter dismay, I sounded like I was flirting—and flirting poorly at that.

Jewel didn't seem to realize it, though. Or if she did, she didn't show it. She flashed me a bright, happy smile. "Everyone loves the Lake Warrior contest. I mean, come on. What's not to love?"

Since she seemed more focused on Colten than on me, I decided to encourage him. If it was a kid thing, he should definitely participate. "Go on, bud. Jewel is right. We should at least grab a brochure while we're here. The tent is right there. It'd be silly to leave without getting some information."

Colt sighed but finally slid his hands into his pockets and cocked his head as he started toward the tent. "Wait for me here."

I grinned at him. "You got it."

As I watched him approach the tent with far too much caution and suspicion for my liking, I glanced at her. "Thanks for that. The kid definitely needs to let his hair down and make some friends this summer."

She grinned. "You definitely came to the right place for that too. We know how to have good, old-fashioned fun, but we're also pretty friendly. Bring him to the beach tomorrow. We'll take him out on my brother's boat and show him how we play here in June Lake."

"That's very hospitable of you," I responded, glad that the dismal flirting had been momentary. "We might just take you up on the invitation, but I'm afraid Colten may not warm up to the way you play here in June Lake in just one day."

I had no issue flirting with her. It was the realization that it had been *awful* flirting that had gotten to me. Once upon a time, I'd had game. And sure, it'd been a long time ago, but surely, it still had to be in here somewhere.

Jewel watched as Colten chatted to the man under the tent. "You've been here a few days. To be honest, I'm surprised he hasn't made any friends yet. The kids here usually try to recruit any new arrival to their ranks, but he'll warm up to us. I guarantee it."

I chuckled. "It's not on the kids. Some of them tried to *recruit* him earlier, but we haven't spent much time outside of the house until today and he wasn't exactly enthusiastic about spending time with them."

"He'll get there." She smiled. "I wouldn't have wanted to spend any time in town either if I could've been spending it there instead. It's the nicest house in town."

"So I've heard," I said, then smirked at her. "From you, among others."

Her cheeks flushed a gorgeous, rosy pink. "Right. I forgot. How has your stay been so far? Living up to the hype, I hope."

"It's an amazing house," I replied, holding her gaze for a moment. "I think it's the perfect place to unwind for a couple months. So your brother has a boat, huh? Are you sure he won't mind if we join you tomorrow?"

"The more, the merrier," she said with yet another smile on her lips. "A day on the water is just what any child needs to ease into our way of living."

"Does your way of living include parking in the middle of the road to go for a swim often, or was that a one-off thing?"

"Oh, no. It definitely wasn't a one-off thing." Her eyes widened as they darted in the direction of the lake. "Tell me you could live on a lake like this and not take a dip every day the weather allows? It's irresistible."

"Yeah, it is," I agreed, taking in those freckles and her golden skin. It wasn't just the lake that was irresistible to me.

June Lake was already starting to rub off on me, thanks in no small part to the girl I was looking at right then. The level of attraction I felt toward her was unfamiliar and not in the comfortable way.

She was a beautiful, small-town, girl-next-door type and not only did I not know anyone else like that, but I also had no idea why I was suddenly noticing things like the way she tucked her hair behind her ears whenever it came loose and how she constantly seemed to be rubbing the pads of her index fingers over her thumbnails as we spoke.

There has to be vodka in the lemonade. It's the only explanation.

After going years without ever even really looking at a woman, there was not a chance in hell that this one had gotten to me so fast. It just wasn't possible.

Besides, I certainly couldn't act on the attraction. Flirting was one thing, but it couldn't go any further than that.

"Do you think Colten would like tubing?" she asked, blissfully unaware of the direction my thoughts had taken.

When I blinked myself out of my head and refocused on her, I saw her looking at him where he was still talking to the Lake Warrior guy. Once again noticing something I shouldn't have, I studied the fond softness on her expression and wondered if it was for Colt or the contest representative.

"I think he'd love it if he gave it a try." I responded to her question instead of letting my mind run away with me again.

I'd already assumed her brother was her boyfriend. I couldn't exactly ask her about this guy too without coming off as an intensely creepy stalker who was jealous of any potential romantic entanglements she might have.

Jewel glanced away from Colten to look back at me, sliding her fingers into the back pockets of her denim shorts as her eyes sparkled with humor. "Don't worry about that. We can be very persuasive when it comes to tubing. All you need to do is show up and we'll encourage him to live a little."

Suddenly, I had no doubt that they would. Their definition of living a little was very different to what I'd become used to, but I liked it. It seemed to me that the people around here were not only friendly but carefree.

They adored their town and the water it had been settled here for, and they knew how to live life outside of the rat race. It made me more convinced than ever that I'd chosen the right spot for our vacation, but looking at Jewel now, I wondered if our time here would hold any more surprises.

Somehow, I was sure it would, and strangely, I didn't mind the thought so much. I wasn't generally a guy for surprises, but with her being the thing that had surprised me most so far, I couldn't say I was opposed to finding out more.

To being surprised. To unwinding in ways I hadn't done since I'd become an adult. *Yeah, we made the right decision coming here.*

Now I just had to find a way to keep my hands to myself and then I'd really be able to enjoy the time I suddenly suspected we'd be spending together for the months I'd be here. But until I figured out how to keep my attraction contained, I mirrored her move and slid my fingers into my pockets to keep from doing something stupid.

And that was where they stayed for the rest of the night. *See? It's not that hard. I just have to hope I packed enough pants with pockets—or that I can work out how to use the washer back at the Manor without burning everyone's favorite house to the ground.*

12

JEWEL

While Scott backed his boat into the lake, I slapped on some sparkly lip gloss and smiled. I hadn't expected Landon to take me up on my offer to join us today, but he'd surprised me when we'd said goodbye last night, asking which beach to meet us at this morning.

"Why are you all dolled up?" Scott asked as he joined me after putting the boat in the water. His eyes drifted across my face and obviously noticed that I'd applied some light makeup this morning. "Are you really that eager to impress Mr. Big City Ass?"

"He's new," I said flippantly. "I'm just a little curious. Sue me."

Scott grunted and shook his head before he headed back to his truck to load the cooler onto the boat. I couldn't blame him for not understanding why I'd made something of an effort for Landon. Our first impressions of the man certainly hadn't been good, but the fact of the matter was that not much happened in June Lake that wasn't mundane or repetitive.

I loved my life here, but there was something about Landon that made me kind of excited. After how different he'd been last night, I was more curious about him than I had been before and I was looking forward to seeing what else he was hiding under that prickly exterior.

As Scott hoisted the cooler off the back of his truck, he glanced at me. "Anyone can be charming for a day. Even a week, or a month, or however long he's going to be in town for. That doesn't mean he's a good guy. So what if he apologized? Have you forgotten what he put you through just because he suddenly smiled at you?"

"No." I scoffed softly, arching an eyebrow at my brother as he passed. "I simply happen to believe in second chances. He was rude a couple times, but that's it. He didn't '*put me through*' anything."

I made air quotes around the words and Scott rolled his eyes. "Being rude to you for no reason is putting you through something, sis. First impressions count for a reason, and you should trust his raw reactions when he's under pressure if you're looking to find out who he is."

"He apologized," I said simply. "Besides, it's not like I caught him in the act of murdering someone before. He was grumpy and he made a point of saying he was sorry for it. End of story. He didn't commit some unforgivable sin."

"He treated you like you were an inconvenience to him."

"Don't be such a pessimist," I said. "He was rude. That's it. Kind of like you're being right now. Since when are you such a caveman anyway? I thought you and I were more evolved than that. You've never had a problem with me liking a guy before."

"Those guys weren't him," he shot back without hesitation. Then he dragged his hands through his hair and pulled in a deep breath. "All I'm saying is to remember that he's not from around here. He's not like us, which is fine. I'm sure that's part of what makes him so appealing. I won't stop you from having your fun. I'm just asking you to be caref—"

He cut himself off when Brittany climbed out of her car after parking next to his. As I watched, my brother seemed to forget that I was even here. His eyes widened, his jaw clenched, and his throat started working, but he didn't appear to be upset or angry.

This was something completely different and I didn't care to put a name to it. Even in my head.

To be fair to him, Brit had really brought it today, showing up looking like a ten out of ten in a red bikini with a matching, opaque cover-up. Large sunglasses covered her eyes and her light brown curls were damp and bouncy.

Damn, girl.

I nudged my brother with my elbow. "Keep your eyes in your head."

He grunted, either not bothering with a response or not capable of forming one just yet. I was pretty sure it was the latter.

For at least the last four years, my brother and my best friend had had a very flirty dynamic but nothing had come of it just yet. Even so, I was confident that one day, Brit was going to be my sister-in-law—even if it did give me a bit of the ick to think about them together.

If I really dug deep though, I could admit that they were probably the only people in town I thought were good enough for the other. But whatever happened, as long as they were happy, I would be too.

That didn't mean I was going to make it easy on them. I gave Brit a knowing grin as she strode up to us. "Now that's a bikini. Since when do we buy something new for a day on the boat?"

"I didn't buy it," she said. "I went to one of those exchange thingies. You know, the ones where you take a few of your old clothing items, and as long as they're in good condition, you get to choose from the stuff other people brought in?"

"Oh, right." I smiled. "That was a great choice."

Meanwhile, my brother had managed to roll his tongue back into his mouth and he'd finally gone to put the cooler in the boat. He climbed on after, extending his hand to help Brittany on at the same time that Landon's blue truck pulled up.

They parked a ways away from us and I squared my shoulders as I gave my brother a look that should've told him I meant business. "I'm going to go flag them down. Be nice. Please?"

"I'm always nice."

My eyes rolled, but since I wanted to be welcoming, I couldn't get into it with Scott right then. Hurrying across the crowded parking lot, I waved them over and smiled. "Hey, guys. How are you today?"

"We're good," Landon said from behind a pair of aviators, looking like a model in his turquoise board shorts and black vest. "You're still sure it's okay if we join you, right?"

"Absolutely. Follow me and we'll get you sorted." I turned and started back to the boat, not wanting to look like I'd been waiting for them as eagerly as I had been.

Scott and Brittany muttered greetings as we piled onto the boat with them. Then Scott reached for a life jacket he'd had waiting for Colten. "You're going to have to put this on, buddy."

The boy's face fell and he looked utterly demoralized. "I know how to swim."

"Yeah, but you don't have a choice, kiddo," Landon explained. "It's for safety. Knowing how to swim won't help you much if you fall off and get disoriented as you hit the water. It's as hard as concrete if you're going fast enough."

Colten sighed and accepted the life jacket, but he looked so broody that I threw Landon a bone and intervened, grinning at his son as Scott got us underway. "Have you ever been on a boat like this?"

"I've been on a yacht," he said.

I blinked hard and glanced at his father, who gave me a sheepish smile and shrug in return. *Wow, they really must be loaded.*

Inhaling deeply, I tried to hide my surprise and grinned at him again. "Okay, well, this isn't much like a yacht at all. Far from it, in fact, but the best spot to sit is the very front."

I guided him over to the seats in front of the windshield that got the most air over waves, and Scott left the shore, slow and steady like always. Once we were clear and we were all seated, he called out, "Okay, people. Hold on."

Colten's fingers tightened around a handle, but his eyes still went wide as Scott opened up, pressing down on the throttle and letting out a delighted whoop. In turn, Colten grinned from ear to ear, shrieking with laughter, and he gripped the line around the front of boat for dear life. I threw my arm over my head like I was on a roller coaster and beamed into the wind.

So far, this seems to be going pretty well.

I glanced over my shoulder at the others, wondering if Scott was keeping his promise to be nice to Landon, but he was too busy flirting with Brittany to be noticing the other man at all. And Landon? Well, he was grinning too, but he was looking right at me.

That megawatt smile stole the control I had over my body, making a tingle rush down my spine and goosebumps rise on my skin. My nipples hardened and my lips parted.

Undeniable lust raced through me and he swiped his tongue across his lips, making me wonder if he felt it too. Something zapped through the air between us, but then Scott suddenly pulled up short, waiting until the boat had almost stopped gliding through the water on its momentum alone before he shoved Brittany right off.

She landed with a splash and came up sputtering and laughing. Then she started splashing water at him. Goofing off was part of our way of life and we always made sure to do it safely, but Colten and Landon seemed a bit shocked at first.

At least it broke the spell between us when he snapped his head toward my brother and my friend, staring at them with confusion on his features until he realized what was going on. Immediately joining in the fun, he got up, strode over to us, picked Colten up, and leaped over the side with him in his arms.

Colten shrieked and clung to Landon, taking a deep breath just as they hit the water. I chuckled, diving in after them since I wasn't about to wait for someone to toss me in against my will. Just as I came up, Scott sent a massive spray of water right at my face and I yelped. Then I went under and launched an offensive of my own.

I grabbed his ankle and yanked him down, only to realize it hadn't been his ankle, but Landon's that I'd tugged. I squealed with surprise when I realized it.

He smirked and came at me. "You've gone and done it now."

I laughed at his playful threat, flipping over onto my front to slice through the water with powerful strokes. It turned out they weren't powerful enough, though. He reached me quite easily, dunking me before his son jumped on his back and dunked him in turn.

After that, a full-fledged water war broke out and we messed around until we were all too tired to keep at it, so we got back on the boat and Scott drove us to a secluded beach on the far shore. As he unpacked our cooler of waters and food, I smiled at Landon and Colten, finding us a spot in the shade to sit in.

"This is called Soulmate Beach," I said. "Coincidentally, it's where Mr. and Mrs. Styles had their first date after they moved here and it's also where he proposed to her."

Scott heard what I was telling them as he and Brittany came over to join us, and he rolled his eyes at me. "Not this nonsense again. They've been dead nearly two decades! Leave them to rest in peace, would you?"

I sighed dreamily. "That's true, but there's something about them that has always captivated me. You know that. Besides, it's not like I'm disturbing their graves. I'm keeping their love story alive. I'm sure they're resting more peacefully than ever knowing that their romance lives on."

Colten's nose wrinkled, but then he shrugged. "I don't know about their romance, but their house is huge!"

"It's almost too big," Landon said. "When I booked the place, I said I didn't want the staff that should've come with it, but I've had to call a cleaning company to come help us stay on top of things. It's that big. Their story is pretty awesome too, though. Just not as awesome as their house."

My eyebrows crept up, my heart beating just a little bit faster. "Is the cleaning service you contacted called *Tidy Touch*?"

Surprise flashed in his eyes before he nodded. "How did you know? Are they any good?"

I smiled. "There's only one residential cleaning company in June Lake, and it just so happens that Brittany and I own it."

13

LANDON

She's a maid?

I barely managed to keep my jaw from dropping as I stared back at Jewel. Sitting there in that bikini that had nearly made my eyes fall out of my head that first time I'd seen her, it was hard to imagine her on her hands and knees, scrubbing someone else's toilets and floors.

I wasn't sure I would've been able to handle that. I understood that people had to do what they had to do to make ends meet, but shit. Being a house cleaner seemed like a rough way to do it.

Wishing for the first time in a long time that I hadn't said anything, I wondered if I would really be able to have this beautiful woman cleaning up after us. Honestly, I didn't think so.

"You're in the best hands with our company," she gushed, seeming downright giddy. "Brittany and I are excellent at what we do. You can check out our reviews on social media. You won't be sorry you hired us. I promise."

Scott handed a water to me and clapped me on the shoulder. "Just watch out. My little sister has had the girl version of a hard-on for the house since she was a kid."

"What does that mean?" Colten asked curiously as he glanced between her brother and me.

Scott turned neon pink and shot me an apologetic look. "I'm sorry. I'm not around kids much. I wasn't thinking. She just really likes the Manor."

I chuckled, but thankfully, Jewel saved me from having to have that extremely uncomfortable conversation with my son in front of an audience by defending herself. Her golden-brown eyes flashed with indignation as she cocked her head at her brother.

"This has nothing to do with how much I appreciate that beautiful old house. It's business and Brittany and I are the best."

"You're also the only people in your business," he replied with a teasing smirk. "That means you may be the best, but you're also the worst."

"We've never had one bad review," she scolded him, her cheeks flushed as she glanced at me. "Really. You can look it up. Every last one of our clients love us. We're thorough, efficient, and respectful. We're also reliable and affordable."

"I never said you weren't," he retorted, his voice thick with barely restrained laughter. "I was just being nice. They should know that if they hire you, you're going to spend the first day or so just gaping and *then* you'll get to work. I'm sure you'll be plenty thorough and efficient once you get started. It's just that you won't be getting started immediately."

She scoffed at him. "That's not true. I can marvel and work at the same time."

Her brother guffawed, but she ignored him, turning back to me instead with a pleading look in those bright eyes. "Don't listen to him. I'm a professional. What do you say, are you going to hire us?"

I was uncomfortable letting her—of all people—come in to clean our house, but I couldn't say no when she was looking at me like that, so I nodded. "Of course. Yes. Sure."

Tossing her arms up in the air, she did a little jig and stuck her tongue out at her brother, but my gaze had dropped to her chest. It was only for a second, but I hadn't been able to help myself when she'd done her victory dance.

Her cleavage was so pronounced in that bikini top, the curves of her breasts so round and voluptuous, that I kind of wanted to bury my head between them. I groaned internally, silently begging her to put her damn arms down and stop moving before my problem became too obvious.

Mercifully, Scott had walked back to the boat and he came back with a football from a storage area under one of the seats. He tossed it to Colten, who fumbled it terribly, picked it up, and handed it to me instead of throwing it back at Scott.

"I'm not really a sports person," he explained quietly. "Chess is more my thing."

To my surprise, Scott grinned at him. "Well, that's okay. I'll teach you how to throw a football, kid. By the time I'm done with you, the NFL is going to be knocking at your door."

As he motioned for Colten to get up and join him, a flare of annoyance shot through me. If anyone was going to teach my son how to play ball, it should've been me. *Yeah, but you've had years to teach him and you've never done it. Why?*

Exhaling slowly, I realized that the guy wasn't stepping on my toes. He was doing me a favor by getting Colten on his feet and out of his head.

Watching them on the beach, with Scott patiently taking the time to explain to him what to do and how to hold the ball, I felt guilty as hell. This man, with his faded cut-off T-shirt and his board shorts that had seen better days, had met my son last night and he was already getting more involved with him than I was.

Jewel chuckled at my side, poking me in the ribs with her thumb. "You should go join them. I might even join them myself. Brit and I are pretty good, though. Maybe it'll be better for Scott's ego if we pretend to let him be doing the teaching before we kick his ass."

Scott must've heard her because he laughed and cocked an eyebrow at her. "Oh, we've got a big mouth today, have we? Come on over here and prove how much better you are."

"Fine," she agreed immediately, getting up without wasting any time. "The teacher is about to become the student, though. Watch me, Colt. You might just learn something you wouldn't have from this old man."

As she dusted some sand off her butt, she suddenly broke into a run, laser-focused on her brother. He pulled his arm back, letting the ball fly toward her without appearing to be pulling any punches. I nearly fell over when she caught it perfectly and dodged him when he launched himself at her. She threw a perfect pass to Brittany, who I hadn't even noticed standing up.

Clearly, these three did this often, but when the ball came back to Jewel, she called a heads-up to Colten, who let out an *oooof* when he caught it, but then he shot a proud grin at me and held it up above his head.

"Look, Dad! I did it! I got it."

"Yeah, you did," I said, trying to be encouraging. "It's just, uh, you're supposed to pass it back to Scott."

"That's okay," he said, clapping his hands as he grinned at Colt. "You're a fast learner, bud. How about you toss it back to me and we'll do it again?"

He seemed determined to teach Colten how to play, and I realized I was the only one whose ass was still on the sand. *Way to go, Dad of the Year.*

I almost rolled my eyes at myself, but I wasn't one to sit around and mope. I didn't know why I hadn't thought of it before, but I got up when they started again, joining in the fun instead of just watching.

Working with Scott instead of being a dick about it, I managed to teach Colten with him, and by the end of the day, my boy was catching almost every pass. Scott ruffled his hair when he took the ball back from him for the last time.

"It's getting late. We should probably start getting back."

I glanced at my watch, blinking a few times when I realized how many hours had gone by. Jewel looked up at the sky instead of at a watch. “Crap. It *is* late. What do you think, about an hour until sunset?”

Scott dipped his chin in a nod. “Maybe an hour and fifteen, but no more than that.”

Brittany reached up to rub her own shoulders. “Thank God. Don’t get me wrong, that was fun, but my arms are killing me.”

As she started toward the boat, Scott murmured something to her I couldn’t hear, but it brought a deep flush to her cheeks. I glanced at Jewel, wondering if she’d seen it too, and she rolled her eyes, the ever-present smile on her lips as she strode over to the spot we’d been sitting and started gathering her things.

Climbing back on the boat, we were all sleepy and blissed out from a day in the sun. Colten seemed happy, though. With a faint smile on his lips, he gripped the line and held on as Scott drove away from the shore.

For the first time in a long time, he actually looked his age, relaxed and little smug too. I smiled and Jewel winked as she sent a pointed look at my son. I nodded at her, a silent thank you for having included us in the day.

After we arrived back at the beach, we were loading our things back into the truck when Colten caught my gaze. “I had fun today. I’d really like to do it again.”

“So would I, buddy,” I said honestly. “Let me talk to Jewel and see about making plans for it, okay?”

I’d been wanting to charter a boat while we were here, but now that we’d been out with them, I doubted Colt would have as much fun with only me. These people knew the lake and what to do on or around it. We hadn’t gotten around to tubing today, but she’d mentioned how much they enjoyed it.

I glanced at where she was helping her brother secure the boat and wondered if I could impose. Then I remembered that she was going to be cleaning our house soon. *Shit.*

While I looked forward to seeing her regularly while we were in town, I was seriously doubting hiring her as a cleaner. It was bound to be uncomfortable, but I had already said yes.

"How about this?" I said to Colten, deciding against inviting ourselves on another outing with them until *after* she'd spent her first day on the job. "If Jewel ever wants to spend time with us again after she's seen the mess we've made back at the house, I'll talk to her about it."

Colt blanched. "Yeah. Maybe we should straighten up a bit ourselves tonight?"

I dipped my chin in a nod as I shut the tailgate. "Sounds like a plan, kiddo, but we're going to have to straighten up more than just a little bit if we want to get invited back out on the lake with them."

Just like that, I was going to be paying someone to do the cleaning while also being a lot neater about things myself. But if that was the cost of giving Colten another day like today while getting to see more of Jewel at the same time, I would happily fork over the cash.

Fuck. Maybe the vodka wasn't just in the lemonade. It's got to be in the air around here or something. I'd never had those kinds of thoughts before, but it seemed June Lake was scrambling my brains.

The worst part of it was that I honestly couldn't say I minded.

14

JEWEL

I'm on the property! I'm on the property!*

For twenty-six years, I'd done nothing but admire the place from afar—until today. Today, I was finally on the property and I was going to be spending the day *inside* the house.

I'd never been as ecstatic for a job, and while I'd given Scott some hell for warning Landon about it, I knew my brother had probably been right. For at least this first day that I was going to be cleaning here, I was not going to be as efficient as usual.

Already, I had slowed down. From the moment I'd pulled up at the address, I'd felt this intense desire to soak in every minute of this day. Deliberately driving at a snail's pace, my head was on a swivel as I crept from the ornate metal gates, down the winding drive, to the front of door of Styles Manor.

I hadn't even stopped yet, and the place was already exceeding my expectations from this close up. The grass was even greener now that I was here, the hedges the most immaculately kept I'd ever seen. Right at the top of the drive was a loop around a little garden containing a gorgeous water feature and I couldn't wait to get a closer look at that too.

Beyond the massive structure, the front garden led all the way to a tiny stretch of private beach with the glittering waters of the lake beyond. Excitement bubbled within in me, little sparks of joy shooting through my veins.

It had taken me all of my twenty-six years to get through those gates, but here I was. My car was loaded up with cleaning supplies, and since this was a new gig, I was on my own while Brittany flew solo on our regular Monday cleans.

My friend was a bit sour about it, but she hadn't fought me to be the first to come. She knew this was the opportunity I'd been waiting a lifetime for, seeing the inside of the Manor. Besides, she also trusted me to do a good job, in which case, she'd get her turn to see it for herself sooner or later.

I kind of wished she was with me, though. It would've been nice to have someone to share this moment with, but instead, I took about a zillion mental pictures and thanked my lucky stars that my dreams were finally coming true.

I stopped under the porte cochere, the elaborate covered entrance meant for dropping off people. I pulled off my sunglasses and blinked up at the wide, double front doors, taking in the traditional brick and plaster of the exterior before I remembered I was here to do a job. Forcing myself to focus, I turned back to my beat-up old Mazda-rati—which was my fun nickname for it—and grabbed all my supplies.

The equipment weighed me down. The mop, bucket, vacuum, and caddy with liquids were a lot to handle by myself, but not even that bugged me today. I was in seventh heaven and it was like I could carry the whole world into that house without flinching.

As I made my way up the few stairs, the door suddenly opened and Landon appeared, his hair wet and slicked back and the scent of a masculine shower gel wafting to my nostrils. He grinned, and my heart nearly gave out.

"Can I help you with that?"

I shook my head, hoping he couldn't hear how dry my mouth had gone. "No, thanks. I'm okay. This is part of my job. I've got it handled."

"Right. Of course." He nodded a few times slowly, then smiled and stepped aside. "Welcome to Styles Manor, Jewel. I hope it lives up to the hype."

I chuckled when I recognized my own words coming out of his mouth and he winked at me. I stepped inside and the last bit of moisture that had remained in my mouth evaporated. The place was so much more spacious than I ever would've been able to imagine, and so graceful and elegant that it almost made me weep.

High ceilings and gorgeous chandeliers, polished, patterned tiles, and original wooden fixtures. Finally getting to see it for myself brought actual tears to my eyes, but I fought them back, swallowing hard as I took in the magnificence of the main room and the view beyond.

There weren't that many photos online, only a few of the exterior, the gardens when they'd been used for special events, and the main sitting room. The rest of it was unlike anything I'd ever seen, and it was definitely making me far more emotional than I'd expected.

Clearing my throat, I made myself focus and turned back to Landon. Those eyes of his burned into mine like twin balls of green fire, his sharp features seeming nervous for some reason or another.

"Would you mind showing me to the primary suite?" I asked, doing my best not to sound all husky because of the way he was looking at me. "I always start there. It gives you someplace to retire to while I finish up the rest."

He blinked. "My bedroom?"

"Yep." I shouldered the mop bucket and nearly dropped everything, but then I grinned. "I hope you're not hiding anything in there."

"Nothing to hide," he said, but faint red streaks appeared at the tops of his cheeks. "Follow me. Colten and I are each in a master suite, but if you ask me, he got the better one. I let him choose first."

"In this house, I think they're all the better one." I couldn't stop staring at every little thing as I traipsed after him, enthralled by the crown molding along the ceiling, the large windows, and the wide corridors.

"I bet the Styles' kids had fun here," I murmured once we got upstairs, feeling like I could practically still hear the echoes of their laughter in the air. "Imagine the races you could have and the games you could play right here when the weather is too bad outside."

"That's a good point," he said. "I hadn't thought of it before, but these are big enough to play baseball in."

"Provided Mrs. Styles had insurance on all her windows." I marveled every step of the way and then suddenly fell silent when we stopped in a large bedroom at the end of the hall.

"This is it," Landon said, his voice slightly hushed. "I'll, uh, I'll leave you to it."

He took off quickly, and I realized he might've been embarrassed that I would be cleaning the room he was staying in. Truth be told, I was glad he had gone. It was something of a double whammy for me, knowing I was standing in what might've been Mr. and Mrs. Styles' bedroom—and that Landon was now sleeping in it.

Deciding to focus on the former instead of the latter, I tried to imagine her here, Mrs. Styles as she watched her kids play outside or she lay on the giant bed reading a book. It worked to take my mind off imagining Landon in that enormous bed—perhaps even rolling around with me.

The room was quite possibly the largest bedroom I'd ever been in, with a massive picture window complete with a built-in daybed overlooking the gardens and the lake below. Two walk-in closets about twice the size of my bedroom flanked the door to the adjoining bathroom, with an antique dresser spanning one entire wall.

The four-poster bed with its nightstands dominated the center of the room, positioned to face the view, and I moaned softly when I envisioned waking up in it. But as I took it all in, I also got to work, cleaning the space as meticulously as I'd ever cleaned anything before.

In fact, I might've even cleaned it lovingly, polishing the surfaces, dusting the antiques, and scrubbing everything that needed scrubbing. When I got to the bathroom, I realized Landon's hair must've been wet from a shower because that same scent I'd gotten from him earlier permeated the air in here as well and some droplets of water still clung to the glass walls.

I inhaled deeply, allowing myself precisely five seconds to consider the fact that I was standing in a room that he'd been naked in not so long ago. Then I kept going. Time flew by and I stopped to eat the lunch I'd brought along on a flowery patio overlooking the water.

The door behind me opened and Colten stepped out, his cheeks reddish and a sheepish grin tugging at his lips. "Was my bedroom okay? I tried tidying it up for you."

"You're the neatest boy I've ever met," I said easily, waving for him to join me if he wanted to. "Don't worry about tidying up, though. You're on vacation. You should relax."

He took a seat and I offered him half of my sandwich. "It's turkey and lettuce."

"Are you sure?" he asked.

I nodded and set it down in front of him. "Go for it."

"Thank you," he said softly. "I could just go make my own. I think we've got turkey and lettuce downstairs."

"Sure, but this saves you the trip." I smiled. "Did you have fun yesterday?"

"So much," he gushed, a smile lighting up his entire face as he nodded. "It was, like, the best day ever. Your brother and your friend are so cool. Hey, do you play chess?"

A bit taken aback by the very sudden change in subject, I nodded. "I used to play more often when my gran was still alive, but it's been a while."

Excitement splashed over his features as he jumped up. "Will you play me? Just one game. Hang on. Let me grab my board."

He ran into the house before I could stop him and we played a match. When it was over, I chuckled and offered him my hand. "Well done, Colten. I guess I'll have to get some more practice if I don't want to be beaten by a ten-year-old again, but you're very good. I didn't mind losing to you."

"I barely beat you, though," he said, his voice soft and almost awed as he glanced up at me from the board. "You're an excellent player."

I smiled. "Thank you, but you're better. I should get back to work, Colten. That was a great game, though. It was fun. Thank you for suggesting it."

As I walked to the door, I gave him a final smile, but he surprised me by getting up and following after me. "Can I help you?"

I laughed. "Why would a kid your age, on vacation no less, offer to help me clean the kitchen?"

He shrugged. "My dad is making some calls for work and I have nothing else to do."

"Oh, uh, sure." I agreed, handing over a rag and a spray bottle when we reached the kitchen. "Would you mind wiping the surfaces for me and then giving them a spray with that? I'll come clean them after I'd done with the floors in the scullery and the pantry."

He nodded, doing what I'd said with an easy, almost practiced way about him. It made me wonder how often he offered to help the people who worked for them, but even though we had a chat while we cleaned, he didn't offer much information about himself.

While he seemed generally optimistic, he was rather reserved, kind but not very easy to talk to, so I took the lead, sharing random things about myself in the hopes that he'd open up too. "I was born and raised right here in June Lake."

"How was that?" he asked curiously. "It's a very small town."

I chuckled. "It is, but in the summer, we get to spend our days on the lake, and in the winter, we do the same on the mountains. I couldn't have asked for much better than that. Everyone comes here to ski and snowboard once it's too cold for swimming, and until we've got enough snow on the slopes, we have some amazing hikes. It's the best of all worlds, really."

"I've never skied or snowboarded," he revealed shyly.

My mouth dropped open. "Okay, that's it. You guys have to come back here in the winter!"

I said it completely without thinking, but as Colten started nodding slowly, I realized I might just see them again after this summer—and I hated the hope that flared to life inside me when I pictured a future in which they might just become a regular fixture.

15

LANDON

Colten and I stood shoulder to shoulder, peering into the fridge while Jewel packed up her cleaning supplies. I was trying my best not to seem as uncomfortable as I was about the fact that she'd spent an entire day cleaning up the mess we'd made, and then I realized it was about to get worse.

"I'm hungry, but there's nothing in here."

"What are you talking about?" I scoffed playfully. "The entire fridge is packed. We've got enough food. It's just a matter of deciding what we want to eat."

I sensed movement in my periphery, but before I could turn to look at Jewel, she suddenly poked her head in next to mine, her body so close that I felt her chest against the back of my arm whenever she inhaled. A sweet, citrusy scent had come with her and I breathed it in, finding it clean and feminine.

"You've got everything you need to make a good casserole," she suggested helpfully, clearly unaware that her presence in my personal space was causing my muscles to tense with restraint. I wanted this woman something fierce, and I couldn't have her, which naturally only made me want her more. "You can never go wrong with a good casserole."

I glanced at Colten, sharing a look with him that told me he didn't know how to make a good casserole either. Jewel planted a hand on her hip as she looked between us. "Don't tell me you're so rich that you've never had casserole before?"

"It's been a while," I admitted, thinking back to my youth and the meals Walt used to prepare for me as a child.

Well, *prepare* was a strong word. Walter had always been better at picking out frozen meals at the grocery store than he'd been at cooking. Somehow, he even managed to botch those sixty percent of the time. But my memories of that period in my life were happy ones, even if my tongue had suffered for them.

Amused exasperation danced across her pretty face. Her eyes were alight with humor but her lips were slightly pursed as she tilted her head to the left. "Let me stay and make you dinner. Consider it a June Lake welcome party."

"I should say no, but I'm not going to." I gave her my best attempt at puppy eyes. "Instead, I'm just going to say yes, please, and be grateful."

She smiled, nodding as she deftly stepped in front of me and opened the fridge that I'd just closed. "You two go wash up and I'll get the ingredients out, but get ready to work. You're going to help me."

Colten seemed happy to help. Smiling, he raced to the sink and poured a generous amount of soap into his palms. I followed him, relieved that she was staying to help us. Even if it was just for one night, at least it was one night I wouldn't have to worry about cooking.

"Chopping board?" she asked as I lathered my hands with soap.

I glanced at her over my shoulder and grimaced. "We, uh, haven't tracked those down yet."

More amusement flashed in those golden eyes, but then she nodded and started rummaging through the cabinets. When she'd finally found everything she needed, Colten and I sat at the kitchen island, him grating some cheese and me slicing the onions while we watched her cook.

"Would you like some wine?" I asked once the potatoes were in a pot and the meat was still defrosting. "This doesn't have to be a marathon and you're definitely staying for dinner."

She lifted both eyebrows at me. 'Are you sure? I was just going to wait until it all goes into the oven before I leave."

"No, stay." I got up and pulled a bottle out of the wine fridge in the corner. "Red or white?"

"White," she decided out loud, then wagged her index finger at me. "Only one glass, though. I'm driving."

"Of course." I reached for two glasses then, filled them up, and added some ice before I poured a glass of soda for Colten.

Picking it all up, I handed theirs over and settled down with my own glass in front of me. "So, how do you know how to cook?"

Sliding the onions into a pan, she shrugged and shot me a small smile. "Both of my parents passed away a long time ago. Scott and I were older when it happened, so we had a handful of recipes from our Mom and some dishes she taught us how to cook, but we had to perfect them ourselves."

I nodded slowly. "I get that. My mom passed when I was a child and my stepdad tried to teach me how to cook on top of everything else, but we never had time to get much further than boiling eggs and chopping stuff."

She chuckled as she turned the heat on the onions a little bit higher. "I get that. How about you, Colt? Have you learned how to cook yet?"

"Nope," he said with a one-shouldered shrug, glancing at me. "I'm trying to hang around the kitchen at home more, but no one wants me holding the knives or setting the house on fire."

She laughed, nodding her agreement. Then she took her first sip of wine and her eyes flew wide open. "Wow. That is amazing. It's the best wine I've ever had. Where's it from?"

"New York," I said vaguely, not telling her how much it cost or that it had come from a private reserve. I'd developed some pretty particular tastes in wine, and I'd had a few crates delivered before we'd arrived. "What is it about the scent of frying onions that makes you feel like you've walked into your home for Sunday dinner with everyone you've ever cared about?"

Jewel took another sip of her wine and smiled. "I don't know, but that's so true. It's one of my favorite scents in the world."

"Same," Colten said, giving her a happy smile. "Thank you for staying to cook for us."

"You're very welcome." She added the chicken to the onions and focused on the stovetop for a while.

Soon, the kitchen was filled with delicious aromas. Once the dish was in the oven and the scent of melted cheese joined the fray, my mouth was watering. Trying to stave off my hunger, I sipped my wine and peered at her curiously. "You grew up here, right?"

She nodded. "I sure did. How about you? I've just realized I don't even know where you're from."

"Los Angeles," I said. "Born and raised."

Spinning to face me, her eyes were wide and suddenly shining with excitement. "Really? That's so cool. I don't think I've ever spoken to anyone who grew up there. Aren't most people transplants?"

I shrugged. "Some. Those who go there for Hollywood, anyway. There are also plenty of people who have no interest in joining the entertainment industry, though. A lot of those are locals."

"Ah." She smiled. "I guess that's true, but I never thought about it as just another city. It's all about fame there, right?"

"Nah. Not for everybody."

Colten laughed suddenly. "Only for most people."

She shot a finger gun at him. "That's kind of what I thought. How is it going to school there?"

While he answered her question, we drank some more of our wine, and by the time she put dinner on the table, I was positively ravenous—and then I took my first bite.

I nearly gagged. It was horrific. So salty that I could barely swallow it. The potatoes were still hard, the chicken reminiscent of rubber, and the vegetables like a soggy soup under a layer of slightly burnt cheese.

She made Walt look like a five-star chef.

Colten chugged all of his soda and half his glass of water after just his first bite, looking like he'd seen a ghost when he came up for air. He glanced at me desperately to save him from this night, but I fixed him with a glare.

Jewel had spent all day cleaning our house and then she'd stayed to cook for us. The least we could do was to be polite.

She flashed us a proud smile as she joined us, mixing everything around in her bowl. It made squelching sounds and I hid a grimace by fixating on my own food while Colten gripped his stomach, looking woozy all of a sudden.

I nudged his shin under the table, waiting until she wasn't looking before I mouthed, "force it down and puke later."

He winced, but then he glanced at her and sighed. We suffered through the meal, choking on each bite, but Jewel was none the wiser. She chatted throughout, asking us more about LA and apparently not noticing that neither of us were sitting at the table while we ate.

Colt and I both kept getting up, pretending to eat while we got something else to drink and dropping little bits of our food into the trash once we were out of sight. About halfway through, I considered getting a dog to feed in case she ever offered to cook for us again, but I didn't think it would be fair to the dog.

One day, I knew we'd be laughing about our attempts to empty our bowls without offending her, but that day wasn't today. By the time I gingerly scraped my teeth across my fork on my very last bite, I felt ill, but I still smiled at her.

"Thank you, Jewel. Would you like some more wine?"

16

JEWEL

After saying goodnight to Colten, Landon came outside to meet me on the patio. I was curled up on a lounger with a mug of green tea, a blanket tucked around my legs as I stared out at the lake glittering in the moonlight.

I heard the soft padding of his footsteps as he approached and I glanced at him, watching as he lowered himself into the chair beside mine. He had turned out so differently from how I'd summed him up after our first meeting.

Right then, his features were relaxed, his feet bare, and his long fingers wrapped around a cup of coffee. There was no trace of that scowl I'd thought was a permanent feature on his face. His teeth weren't grinding or tense and I no longer thought he had a carrot up his butt.

Knowing that he was preoccupied with sitting down and getting comfortable, I let myself really look at him for just a moment, admiring the strong line of his jaw, the way his eyes managed to sparkle in the evening light even though the sun had long since gone down, and the rise of his chest as he stretched out and inhaled deeply.

He turned to face me, catching me staring, and smiled instead of calling me out on it. His lips curved slowly upward as he held my gaze. He opened his mouth to speak, but I interrupted, needing to change the subject before he asked why I'd been looking at him like that.

"You have a good kid," I said softly. "He and I spent some time together today. We even played some chess when I took my lunch break. He's an amazing player."

"That he is," Landon agreed, taking in a deep breath. He released it slowly before the corners of his lips pinched. "He can be a handful, though. The preteen is strong in that one."

"Really?" I chuckled as I tried to imagine it. "He's still more kid than preteen though, right? When does he officially become a preteen?"

"I'm not sure when it's supposed to happen, but with him, it started last year." A thoughtful gleam entered his eyes before he blinked it away. "He's developing that teenager's attitude fast and it's really giving me a run for my money as a father, but I'm proud of him every day."

"Teenager's attitude," I repeated slowly, trying to remember what Scott and I had been like back then. So much had changed for us since, with our parents' passing and starting to work and all that, but I had so many memories of us digging in our heels when we were told to do things. "You mean the stubbornness?"

"Yep." He raked the fingers of his free hand through his hair as he shook his head and chuckled. "The stubbornness, the impulsivity, the emotional outbursts."

"Ooooh, I remember all that," I said with a soft giggle. "My mom always used to tell me that it was like our brains were on fire with emotion at that age. Technically, I think it's the hormones, but I suppose that's what causes the emotion."

"Absolutely, but he's not even a teenager yet. I thought I had more time before it all kicked in, you know?"

"I think that's one of the cornerstones of the human condition," I mused. "We always think we have more time."

He glanced at me. "That's very true. I'm just not sure I'm ready for it. Don't get me wrong. I love that kid more than life itself and I really am proud of him, but I'm worried about him too. And there's enough going on that it would be nice not to worry about everything that's going to come when he does become a teenager on top of everything else."

I cocked my head at him. "How so? He doesn't look like a kid you need to be worried about."

Landon shrugged, glancing back out at the lake before he finally seemed to decide to share with me. "It's, uh, it's nothing huge, I guess. I don't even really know if it's anything at all, but it seems like he's not having the best time at school. He doesn't 'fit in.' Whatever that means."

"What makes you think that?" I asked. "Did something happen?"

"Well, his teacher spoke to me on the last day of school. Apparently, he's more interested in chess than going out during their lunch break. He doesn't want to play football at all. All the friends he used to have seem to have *outgrown* him, if that makes sense."

"It does." I sensed the genuine hurt in Landon's voice and I saw that he wanted better for his son. It endeared him to me even more and I smiled softly. "Kids can be mean. Thoughtlessly so sometimes. But at the same time, not all friendships were built to last. Maybe it's better that he's not trying to fit in with kids whose interests aren't aligned to his own anymore."

He paused for a moment as he thought it over, then nodded his agreement. "I hadn't looked at it like that, but I guess you're right."

"To me, it was all about finding my own rhythm and where I fit in. Maybe he just hasn't found his place yet, you know? It's a tough lesson to learn at such a young age, realizing that people you thought you'd go the distance with just aren't like you anymore, but I think the sooner you can make peace with something like that, the happier you'll be later on."

Gaze lingering on mine for a moment, he suddenly chuckled and dragged both palms over his cheeks. "Go figure you'd also be some kind of kid guru. I honestly hadn't even thought about it as part of the process of growing up, and I definitely didn't see that silver lining, but

I think you're right. Better to realize you don't fit in with the kids you used to like than to spend years trying, only to realize later that it's okay to have your own interests and not to share it with them."

"I'm from a small town, remember? Everything is amplified here. There's no space to get away from whatever issues you're facing, which makes them more intense while you're facing them but it also forces you to actually face them. That kind of makes things simpler."

"Maybe we should move here," he joked. "It sure seems like you guys have got life figured out. I mean, where else do you go to work and then go tubing or sunbathing right next to the road?"

I groaned. "You're never going to let me live that down, are you?"

"Nope, but not in a bad way. It was just my first taste of what your lives here are like, and I guess I didn't handle it very well because I didn't understand it at all."

"How about this?" I suggested. "I know some local kids I can connect Colten with. Like everywhere, there is a mean kid or two in June Lake, but for the most part, everyone here is well rounded and they're just eager to enjoy the summer. Maybe that would help Colten, if he's around kids who are growing up with taking a dip in the lake after work and whose parents don't really care where they park while they're doing it cause there's just not much traffic?"

"That would be good for him, I think." He stared deep into my eyes for a beat before he smiled. "Thanks, Jewel. Are you sure you wouldn't mind?"

"Not at all. Scott has an ex with a son who's about Colt's age. I'll call her and set it up. He's a good kid too, so maybe they'll hit it off?"

"I would appreciate that greatly," he said. "I know it's probably silly to be so focused on him making friends just for the summer, but it just feels like it would help if he knew there are kids out there who are more like him. I feel like it might encourage him to connect with other kids even after we get home."

"If nothing else, at least it will help him not to be lonely while you're here. Kids always want friends around, right? Even if they don't have any, they'd still *like* to have them."

"That's what I think too, but I'm not him. I don't think it could hurt, though. To try, I mean." He leaned back on his chair and turned toward the lake, kicking his legs up on the lounger and glancing at me. "For now though, I'd like to know more about you. Why a cleaning service? Is that your passion? Are you one of those clean freaks who gets off on a job well done?"

I laughed. "Not really. I do enjoy the instant-gratification aspect of it, but I just saw a need in our town and we filled it."

"Are you really the only cleaning service around?"

I nodded. "Most of our clients are elderly and they need some help keeping up with their houses. That's all. Before we started *Tidy Touch*, there used to be a group of people from the church who helped out when they could, but it just wasn't enough. Brit and I joined them a few times, saw that they needed more, and decided to provide the service."

"What's your real dream then?" he asked. "No offense, but everyone who's simply filling a need has something that they'd rather do. What's your something?"

"It's silly," I admitted after hesitating for a beat. "There's a reason I never have and never will pursue it full time."

"It doesn't matter if it's silly," he said. "Lay it on me. What is it you'd like to do that would make you happier than the instant gratification you get from your current job?"

I groaned, covering my face with my hands and peeking out at him from between my fingers. "It really is silly."

"Not if it's your dream."

I sighed, closing my eyes as I pulled my hands back to my sides. "I make suncatchers. They're these odd, quirky little things that I used to try to sell at the Friday night market, but no one really wanted them, so I stopped bothering. It's more like a fun hobby now."

He blinked a few times. "Would you make one for Colten? I think it would be a nice memento for him to bring home after our summer here and I don't think that's silly at all. I used to love suncatchers. Especially after my mom died. I don't really know why, but I always thought the rainbows in my room when the crystals caught sunlight was her way of smiling at me from above."

Surprised by the depth of his admission, I couldn't deny that it made me feel all warm and tingly inside. "That's funny. That's what my mom used to say too. Of course, I'll make him one. I'd love to."

Landon grinned before he turned to the lake once more. "I might need one myself to remember this place by. When we first got here, I won't lie. There were moments when I asked myself what the hell I was thinking, bringing us to a town so small for a whole summer, but I'm glad we came."

"So am I," I said softly, not really knowing why it was so easy for us to be so honest with one another. Generally, I was a very honest, open person, but with him, I felt safe being that. Safe enough that the vulnerability that came with a personality like mine didn't feel like a risk at all, which was odd, considering all that conflict between us when we'd first met. "In fact, I've already told Colten that I think you guys should come back here in the winter."

Landon chuckled, his gaze remaining on the water as he nodded. "That might not be the worst idea I've ever heard, Jewel, but maybe we should just try to get through the summer first."

17

LANDON

Late that night, Jewel groaned when she checked her watch. "I should get going. I have no idea how I lost track of so much time, but we're both going to be dead on our feet tomorrow."

Discreetly checking my wrist, I couldn't understand how the evening had flown by so quickly. It had been three hours since Colten had gone to bed and we were still talking.

Stretching her arms out above her head, she yawned and then slowly got up as she relaxed out of the stretch. "Thank you for a wonderful evening, Landon. I'm sorry I kept you up so late."

"It's no problem," I said as I stood up as well, sweeping a hand out to let her precede me to the back door. "I'm as much to blame as you are, and at least I'm already home. Would you like me to drive you? I can collect you in the morning so you can come get your car."

"No, that's okay," she said sweetly. "I'll be fine."

"Are you sure?" I asked, worry nagging at me when I thought about the long, winding mountain road back into town. "I wouldn't mind at all. It sure is dark around here at night."

"Nah, it's perfect," she said, chuckling as she turned to me when she walked back into the house. "Don't worry. I'm used to it, and I prefer total darkness to pretend darkness with so much ambient light that you can see everything anyway."

I nodded sharply, still not quite comfortable with the idea, but she had a point. She'd grown up here. She was obviously used to it.

Walking her out to her car, I said goodbye and watched as she climbed in, but the engine didn't turn over when she turned her key. I frowned, but she just sighed, shaking her head before sending me a reassuring grin.

"Don't worry about this either," she said after manually winding down her window. "It happens all the time. Sasha just needs some love to start when she's feeling neglected."

"Sasha?" I asked, inclining my head toward the vehicle. "Why Sasha?"

She chuckled. "It was the name of the old lady I bought her from. It seemed a nice way to remember her. She gave her to me for a really good deal."

Turning back to the ignition, she tried the key again, but it wouldn't work. I drew in a breath, striding to the hood and praying my limited knowledge would be enough to help her with the problem. "Why don't you open this for me? I can't guarantee anything, but I can try to help you get it going."

Her cheeks turned that rosy hue of pink again and she nodded. The hood popped open with a mighty creak. Wincing, I lifted it and found that the arm to keep it open had rusted off. After taking a cursory look, I discovered a loose connection on her battery and jiggled it a bit, hoping it was the issue.

"Try it again."

She did and I waited with bated breath to see what would happen. Mercifully, the engine turned over this time but the noise coming out of it wasn't normal. I gave it a wary look, wondering if this thing was even going to get her home, but I knew I couldn't insist that she stay.

I could, however, try to convince her. Walking to her window after shutting the hood, I looked into her eyes and hoped she'd take me up on the offer.

"The magic I just worked isn't going to last long, so drive straight home, okay?" I said, taking a brief pause before I added, "Or you could just stay over for the night?"

She shook her head, a soft smile on her lips. "That's very kind of you, but I'll be okay. Sasha's just temperamental, is all."

Shit. "Once you turn it off, it might not start again, so it might be best to get to wherever you're going to be sleeping and then call a mechanic first thing in the morning."

She arched an eyebrow at me, humor once again flaring to life behind her tired eyes. "I'll be sleeping at home, so I'll take your initial advice and drive straight there. Scott can get Sasha up and running for me again in the morning, and he's free labor, so he's better than a mechanic."

Laughing as she said it, she gave me a little wave and eased her foot down on the gas, creeping out from underneath the porte cochere before rumbling down the drive. I watched her go, knowing that if Colten hadn't been asleep inside, I would have jumped into the truck and followed her home just to make sure she got there okay.

I really didn't like the thought of her on these pitch dark, narrow roads all by herself in that hunk of junk. While I was by no means an expert on anything automotive, I did know that it was only a matter of time until that thing conked out for good—I just hoped it didn't happen on her way back to town tonight.

Worry sat like a rock in the pit of my stomach. I checked in on Colten and leaned against his door for a moment as I watched the rhythmic rise and fall of his chest in his sleep. It calmed me, but it also allowed me to feel something that had been tugging at my insides for the last couple days.

I'd been trying to shut it out, but right then, it was so persistent and loud that I couldn't ignore it any longer. *This is where we're supposed to be.*

It just felt so damn right that somehow I knew that we'd been meant to land here for the summer. I wasn't really one for fate and stuff, but this sure as shit felt like exactly that. I had this one summer to make the most of things.

That was why we'd come here—existentially as well as literally. Soon, my son wouldn't be a boy anymore and I needed to squeeze every last drop of bonding I could out of the next couple months.

I owed it to Walt and to myself, but most of all, I owed it to Colten. This place would be good for his soul if he let it. He could learn a lot here and it could change his perspective before he went into his next school year.

Nodding to myself as I pushed off the door, I had to admit that I felt better for having acknowledged the tugging in my gut. Heading back downstairs, I pulled my phone out of my pocket and called the senior living facility to check on my stepfather.

This had been the first week in a very long time that we hadn't gone to visit, and I was kicking myself for not bringing him with us. It was late and he would be asleep now, but at least I would be able to make sure that he was okay.

"Walter?" Gabi, one of the nurses, said after I'd asked. "Oh, he's fine, sir. He's been in good spirits and he spent most of the afternoon bragging about his grandson's chess skills, much to Chester's irritation."

I chuckled. "Sounds about right. Alright, thank you, Gabi. Will you tell him I called?"

"Of course. Have a good night, sir."

"You too." I hung up as I walked outside to collect Jewel's tea cup and my mug.

Carrying both back to the kitchen, I set them down in the sink and rinsed them before adding them to the load in the dishwasher. Inhaling deeply, I smiled. The scent of Jewel's cleaning products was still in the air—along with that of her God-awful cooking.

Standing alone in the kitchen now, I laughed out loud when I glanced at the stove. How she had eaten that casserole without even flinching, I didn't know. Her taste buds must be dead.

Still chuckling, I switched on the dishwasher and turned off the lights. Then I went upstairs, winding down for the night in my bedroom after a quick shower. For the first time in years, I was truly looking forward to tomorrow.

There would be no guilty criminals to defend. No strategies to formulate. No court appearances. No judges to contend with or juries to convince.

Just sunshine, simple living, quality time with my son, and a beautiful girl to get to know better.

At that last part of my thought, I exhaled sharply in the dark of my bedroom. Having her in the house today hadn't been easy. Not because she'd been in the way or anything, but because all I'd wanted to do was spend time with her.

Eventually, I'd broken the promise I'd made to myself and had logged into my work emails on my phone just so I'd have a distraction. As I looked around the room now, even in only the silver moonlight filtering in from outside, I imagined her in here earlier.

In fact, the last person to have touched this bedding had been her. My cock stirred and I scrubbed my palms over my jaw. Groaning, I squeezed my eyes shut.

Ever since that very first time I'd seen her, she'd plagued my thoughts at night. At first, it had frustrated me to no end that I saw her endless curves every time I closed my eyes, but now, with the sound of her easy laughter in my ears and more memories of her in a swimsuit, it was even worse.

But it didn't annoy me anymore. It was a whole different kind of frustrating now. The kind that made me want to reach down and take matters into my own hands.

I cut off that line of thinking. Breathing in and out deeply, I tried to focus on the fun I'd had playing football with them yesterday and on some of the work I'd gotten done today. Jewel was still hovering in the back of my mind though, and as soon as I fell asleep, my subconscious went to the place my conscious mind wouldn't let me go while I'd been awake.

Since Jewel and I were outside in the pool for this dream and I wasn't worried about Colten coming home, I knew it wasn't real, but it felt like it was. A gentle breeze cooled my skin as I sat on the step with her on my lap, her body hot against mine from a day spent in the sun.

She smiled, her eyes sparkling as she brushed her fingers through my hair. Ducking her head, she slanted her lips over mine, moaning as my tongue dove between them. I was hard as a rock, aching to get inside her. She kissed me, grinding against me in a way that was going to make me lose it any second.

Her breathy moans got louder as I ran my hands up and down her sides, then finally tugged at the knot keeping her bikini top tied around her neck. The straps fell free immediately and I ran the flat of my hand along her spine until it brushed the knot there as well. I reached for the ends, freeing them and letting the bikini top float away.

Bringing my hands back to her ribs, I let them rest there for a moment, so turned on at the sensation of her pebbled nipples against my chest that I couldn't bear to touch them. I was breathing hard, fighting for control as our kisses grew harder and more purposeful.

Jewel rolled her hips against mine. "Landon, I want you."

Her voice was a husky whisper, the words spoken into my mouth. I swallowed them hungrily, reaching for the front panel of her bikini bottoms, and just as I was about to pull them away, my eyes opened and I sat bolt upright in bed.

Alone and panting, I groaned, my cock straining against my boxers for attention. Dropping back down on the mattress, I had no idea what had woken me up, but I was taking it as a sign that I shouldn't be having sex dreams about a girl who loved her simple life here in June Lake.

A girl who probably wouldn't be interested in a summer fling—and I wasn't interested in that either. As attracted as I was to her, Jewel and I weren't going to happen.

Now I only had to find a way to convince my cock to stop trying to make it happen.

18

JEWEL

My ruby-colored crystals glowed a deep, rich red in the sunlight shining in through my open window. They were spread out on my coffee table along with other supplies I needed to make my suncatchers, and I smiled as I looked at them and remembered the conversation I'd had with Landon last night.

That big-city man is just one surprise after another, I thought as I picked up one of the crystals, adding it to the intricate design I was working on for Colten. Soft country music played on my TV, my only company as I pored over the suncatcher meant to remind Colten of this summer.

I moved onto the azure blue crystals next, hoping that he'd understand the story I was trying to tell with it once I explained it to him. Happiness filled my soul as I imagined handing it over once it was done. Making these was my one true love and I was grateful for the motivation and the opportunity to spend the day doing it.

Scott was working on my car at his house, so until he was finished this afternoon, I was stuck here. Brittany and I had pushed our Tuesday cleans to Thursday because of our transportation issues—

her car was in the shop too—but I was okay with it even if it meant that Thursday was going to be crazy.

I hardly ever got to spend my time with my suncatchers anymore. Too busy with work and life, I always put it off until later and it was great that *later* had finally come.

As I sat in my mother's old rocking chair in my living room, I kept my body moving gently back and forth as I threaded the crystals and tied off the ends of each different layer of my design. Faint sounds of cars and people filtered into my loft apartment from the street below, and I wondered idly if I could really just spend the whole day indulging in my hobby.

Life was happening outside right now and here I was, missing out on a sunny summer's day, holed up in my little place above some of the businesses on the main drag in town. I chewed on my lower lip, then decided that for just one day, life outside could go on without me.

It was after ten a.m. and I was still happily sipping coffee, having showered earlier and changed into clean pajamas to be comfortable while I worked. I *never* took days off like this, but the fact that my car and Brittany's broke down at the same time told me karma herself wanted us to do nothing for a change.

Either that, or the mechanic in town who had repaired both of our cars the last time they'd been in had used crappy parts. It was likely that this was the real explanation, but I was going with karma or fate.

The suncatchers against my ceiling cast reflections all around my apartment, at least a dozen of them scattered around the room. Whenever I was sad, I made one of these. Excited? Same thing. The list went on, but while I gifted most of them, I'd kept all those that meant the most to me.

As I looked at them now, tears filled my eyes when I thought back to the times I'd made them. One for each of my parents. One for the day we'd decided to start *Tidy Touch* and another for the first time I'd paid my rent with the money we'd made from it.

Landon was right to have asked me to make one of these for Colten to remember the summer by. If the boy had even an ounce of the appreciation I did for these things, it would be a reminder he'd keep forever.

Lazy but focused, at peace and humming along to the song on my radio, I felt happier than I had in a while as I worked on his suncatcher. Until I heard the roar of a loud engine outside.

I groaned loudly, getting up and poking my head out the window to see a flashy, cherry red sports car parking on the street below. My stomach sank and disgust rolled through me.

Dallas Styles, Jr.

I freaking loathed the guy. If there was one unromantic thing about the Manor and its history, it was the eldest grandson who currently owned the place. He was a reckless idiot with an entitlement complex who didn't appreciate what he had at all.

Down below, Dallas climbed out of his car, his blond hair slicked back and his dull brown eyes covered by a pair of fancy sunglasses. He always stopped in on me when he was in town, and he lowered them as he spotted me, pulling them down to the end of his nose and staring at me over the frames.

"Hey, baby," he called up to me with a cocky grin on his lips. "Looking good!"

My nose wrinkled and I pretended to gag, reaching for my window to close it. I had no idea why he always came to see me, but whenever I heard the roar of that engine it was like my soul got encased in concrete.

Dallas was toxic, a poison to town and everyone in it, and he was the only person I'd ever met who truly made my skin crawl. He was average looking at best, but his ego made him believe he was God's gift to women.

He saw me pretending to gag and he threw his head back, laughing like he thought I was the funniest person he'd ever met. "Don't play so hard to get, Jewel. You know you want this."

Gesturing at himself in a designer suit that had no place in a town like June Lake, he didn't seem to care that everyone on the sidewalk could hear him. Such was the extent of his hubris that it never mattered what I did. He simply believed I was joking.

There was no way a girl like me wouldn't want him. I nearly rolled my eyes at the thought, but I was interrupted by his next display of dangerous overconfidence.

"*Everybody* wants this, baby!"

"Only in your fantasies, buddy." I murmured to myself as I shook my head at him.

Even from up on my second level unit, I could see the sweat glistening on his forehead and I felt my stomach roll. Instead of engaging him, I reached for my window and closed it before I went back to work.

Dallas needed to get over himself, but since hearing it from me hadn't worked so far, I figured it wasn't worth wasting my breath to tell him again. Besides, what I was busy with was far more important than trying to get it through his thick skull that I did not, nor would I ever, want him.

I poured my heart into the suncatcher I was making for Colten, meticulously choosing each and every bead, crystal, and feather I used on it. Thankfully, Dallas never tried to come up, nor did he hang around outside trying to get my attention.

He simply came by, made sure I knew he was here, and then he took off again. Which suited me just fine. Of course, I would have preferred if he never came at all, but in the absence of that, at least he never wasted too much of my time.

While I was working, my phone rang and my heart skipped when I saw it was Samantha returning my call. At least Scott's ex and I were on good terms. This was a small town. Their breakup hadn't meant that she and I, or even her and Scott, weren't civil to one another anymore.

Sam and I weren't friends, exactly, but since there was no avoiding one another around here, we still saw each other and spoke quite often. I slid my thumb up from the green circle on my screen, smiling as I pressed the device to my ear.

"Hey, Sam," I said. "Thanks for calling me back."

"Of course," she replied easily. "Sorry I missed you. Brody took off with Cole and some of the other kids and I had to track him down for a doctor's appointment."

"Is he okay?" I asked, genuinely concerned.

In June Lake, everybody looked out for everybody. We were a real close-knit community that way. Samantha chuckled. "He's fine if you don't count the fact that he skinned his knee when he tried to run away from me. He just had to go for a checkup for an ear infection he had last week."

I sighed. "Summer equals swimming equals ear infections. I remember those days."

She laughed. "I'm living them all over again, so what's up?"

"Oh, uh, I was wondering if Brody could show a new kid around town this week?" I asked. "Colten's here for the summer with his dad and he's ten. I thought it might be nice if some of the kids could involve him a little bit?"

"Ten, huh? Well, Brody only turned eleven a couple weeks ago, so it shouldn't be a problem. I'll talk to him, but why are you playing matchmaker for a tourist kid?"

That's a darn good question. "Landon, the dad, hired *Tidy Touch* to help them out while they're here. I spoke to the kid a little bit when I was there yesterday and he seems pretty lonely. All he wants to do is play chess and Landon is worried about him, just wanting to sit inside when he could be out enjoying the sunshine with other kids."

"Wait," she said slowly, dragging out the word. "Are you talking about the single father and his son who are living at Styles Manor for the summer?"

"You've heard about them?"

She let out a bark of gleeful laughter. "Everybody has heard about them. I also heard that the dad, Landon then, is hot as hell."

"That he is," I agreed. "So damn hot, but he's also a really good dad who's worried about his kid. I haven't made any promises, but I said I'd reach out to you and find out if maybe Brody and his friends could hang out with Colten once or twice. Just see if they hit it off?"

"It must be terrible for a boy that age to be stuck inside that big old house with only his dad," she said sympathetically. "Not that *I'd* mind being stuck in that house with his dad, but kids need other kids who can keep up with their energy and get into mischief together."

"My thoughts exactly," I said. "Will you talk to them?"

"Sure," she replied. "I can't guarantee anything, but I'm sure they wouldn't mind a bit of extra company. He's gone back to the park with Cole for now. As soon as he comes home later, I'll talk to him and let you know?"

"Thanks, Sam," I said, relieved and excited on Colten's behalf. "I'll talk to you later."

We said our goodbyes and I went back to the suncatcher, eager to hear from Sam but knowing that it wouldn't happen for a few hours. Once kids like Brody and Cole hit that park on their bicycles, they'd only go home once the streetlights came on.

I smiled as I envisioned Colten with them, carefree and grinning like he had on that beach with us while we'd been tossing the football around. From the sounds of things, the kid just needed a break and I was so happy I might just be able to give him one.

19

LANDON

After that day on the beach with Scott, Colten was slightly more open to tossing a football around than he had been before. I'd packed one on the off chance that we got around to using it, but I'd been surprised when Colt had left the chess board earlier to ask me if I'd come play outside with him for a while.

Wrapping my fingers around the ball, I let it fly. Colt dashed across the expansive lawn behind the house, his arms outstretched to catch it. I shielded my face from the sun with my hand as I looked up, following the ball as Colten leaped to grab it out of the air. It landed with a *thwack* in his arms, and pride surged through me.

"I got it," he yelled.

My arms shot into the air and I rushed at him, grinning like a madman as I ran. "You did it! Great catch, bud. Wow!"

I didn't stop when I reached him, wrapping my hands around his hips instead and hoisting him onto one of my shoulders. "Hold on tight!"

Colten squealed with laughter as I raced around the lawn with him, and with the sun sitting high in the sky and warmth washing over us, I wished there had been someone around to photograph this moment. It was a big one, considering that nothing like it had ever happened before.

When I finally reached the place I'd been standing, I set him back down on his feet and motioned at the tree line near the fence. "Do you want to try running that way and catching it while you're on the move?"

He grinned. "Sure. This is pretty fun, huh? That's why everyone's always talking about football?"

I chuckled. "That's one of the reasons. Okay, so go—"

A red Ferrari tore through the gates then, burning rubber and coming in hot. Colten yelped, ducking in behind me, and I felt a rush of protectiveness over him, stepping in front of him as the car came to a stop.

What the fuck is this?

The gates had opened, so the well-dressed man climbing out of the car had to have legitimate access to the Manor, but whoever he was, I didn't approve of his sudden, unannounced arrival, nor the way in which he'd come in here.

His front tires were on the lawn right where I'd been running a minute ago, and he held his hands up as he climbed out, grinning as he invited me to toss him the ball. I didn't.

The man's grin faded some and he slid his hands into his pockets. He nodded and took a few steps forward. "Hi there, folks. I'm Dallas Styles. The owner of this place. I hope you don't mind me popping in. I just have to pick up some things inside."

For the daily rate I was paying for the place, I hadn't expected impromptu visits from the owner. In fact, I'd been guaranteed complete privacy, but the longer I took to let him get whatever he needed, the longer he would be here, interrupting what could be a pretty special day for Colten and me.

"Go ahead," I said, my tone sharper than usual but not nearly as sharp as it could've been. "We'd sure appreciate a heads-up if you need to drop in again."

The man chuckled, shrugging his shoulders. His slicked-back

blond hair shimmered in the sunshine. *Jesus, how much product does this guy use?*

"Sure thing, Lando. I'll just a be a few minutes. How are you enjoying your stay so far?"

"We were enjoying it just fine," I said. "And it's Landon."

I emphasized the 'n' and turned back to Colten. "Maybe we wait a few before we try running, huh? Why don't you just back up a bit and we'll keep just tossing it around until he leaves?"

Colt nodded and Dallas must've caught the hint because he shrugged again and strode toward the front door. Pushing it open without breaking stride, he went inside and left it open behind him. More irritation rippled through me.

Were you raised in a barn?

It was hard to believe a slick dick like him could be related to the people who had built this house. Since we'd arrived, I'd heard quite a lot about the Styles family and I definitely didn't expect one of them to be a forty-something wannabe cool guy with zero regard for his tenants.

Letting out a deep sigh, I scratched the back of my neck and convinced myself to let it go. The younger generation of families like his were never as classy or gracious as their predecessors. It was unfortunate, but generational money didn't always breed generational refinement.

I was a prime example of that myself, going into criminal defense when my parents, grandparents, and all those who had come before me had built their empire in high-end real estate. Shaking my head, I waited until Colten had backed up enough. Then I passed the ball to him. He tossed it back and I caught it once more.

Dallas took much longer than the few minutes he'd promised, and by the time he emerged, I realized it was because he seemed to be carrying half the house away. He came out with what looked like an old wooden jewelry box and a few other knickknacks. He opened his trunk and set them inside before he headed back in.

I frowned, curiosity trickling through me. *What are you up to, Dallas Styles?*

Colten and I continued tossing the ball, but he fumbled it more often than he caught it, his own eyes darting from the man adding more things to his trunk and the trunk itself. Eventually, I waved him over. "Let's take a break."

"What is all of that?" he asked, peering past me with confusion furrowing his brow. "He's not taking anything of ours, right?"

"I doubt it, but I don't know what it is," I said. "Maybe we should ask."

When he came back outside again, I strode up to him, getting in his way between him and his car. "What is all of that?"

I glanced at the box of leather-bound journals he had in his hands. He gave me a cocky grin, stepping around me to deposit it in his trunk as well. Once he'd set it down inside, he dusted off his hands and turned back to me.

"It's my grandmother's old jewelry collection and her journals. She wrote in them almost every day of her life. Apparently, that means something to certain people."

A trickle of discomfort slid down my spine. I imagined it would mean a lot to many people, but since he looked and acted the way he did and had phrased it the way he had, I assumed he wasn't one of those people. "What do you mean?"

"An antique collector is interested in these items. He wants to buy 'em off me. Can you believe that?"

What I couldn't believe was that he'd rented out the house with his grandmother's jewelry in it, and that he'd want to sell any of it at all. I lifted my chin. "How much has he offered you?"

"Half a million," Dallas said, even cockier now than he had been before. A smirk appeared on his lips as he stared me down. "They're not worth anything to her now, are they? I might as well get something out of it."

I hadn't suggested that he shouldn't sell his grandmother's things, yet he was defending himself for doing it as if I had said something. Assuming it meant he was feeling a little insecure about it despite the smirk, I decided to take my chances.

"How about I buy them off you here and now? Save you the trip to the collector. I'm willing to offer you six hundred thousand."

Dallas's muddy brown eyes widened and he sputtered. Then he stuck his hand out. "Let's make the deal, Lando."

I gritted my teeth but didn't bother correcting him again. Instead, I slid my palm into his and made the damn deal. "Wait here. I'll go write you a check." Turning to my son, I nodded at the trunk. "Do you mind helping me take all this stuff back inside?"

He blinked a few times but then came over and lifted the jewelry box out first. As he carried it back in, I brought up the rear with the journals and another box of haphazardly packed stuff on top of it.

"Your check better be good," Dallas called after me, trying to sound good-natured but he wasn't fooling anyone—least of all me.

"It's good. Don't worry. Besides, you know where to find me if it's not."

He chuckled. "Good point!"

Instead of responding again, I kicked the front door shut behind me, not wanting him to follow us inside. Colt was ahead of me and he shot me a questioning look over his shoulder. "Where do you want it?"

"Kitchen," I said since it was the first place that came to mind.

When we walked in, he set the jewelry box down carefully on the center island and immediately lifted the lid, peering inside and starting to pull things out. I was about to tell him to be careful when I realized he already was, running the items gently through his fingers as he examined them.

I wrote the check on the same island, distracted by the beauty of the jewelry I was about to own. I had absolutely nothing in mind for it and no one in my life to give it to, but I could appreciate it all the same.

Colten removed an oval-shaped locket engraved with what appeared to be initials, an ornate bracelet, and a ring that resembled the one that used to belong to the Princess of Wales. Glancing up at me, he frowned as he put it all back into the box and closed the lid.

"These are pretty, but why did you buy them?"

I shrugged. "It was a spur of the moment decision."

After writing the check, I cracked open one of the journals, deciding on a whim that I probably needed to make sure at least that I wasn't paying over half a million dollars for empty notebooks. Immediately, my gaze fell upon page after page filled with an elegant, feminine handwriting and I shut the journal again, feeling like I was intruding.

When I looked up, I found Colten eyeing me skeptically. "You made a spur of the moment decision to spend half a million on this junk, but you won't buy me Nike sneakers?"

"It's not junk." I chuckled. "It's history. The Styles family meant a lot to the people in this town and all this stuff used to belong to them, which makes it part of their history too, not just the family's."

His nose wrinkled as he shrugged. "It's a lot of money for some jewelry and a few notebooks. You said the sneakers were too expensive."

"I'll buy you the sneakers for back to school in the fall," I conceded. "I said they were too expensive for just another pair because you already had three pairs of sneakers, but by the time you go back to school, I'm sure those will be too tight anyway."

He cocked his head at me. "The town already has history too. Why did we need this stuff?"

"Because it's special," I said emphatically.

"To who?"

I held up the journal in my hand and swiped the check into the other. "To Jewel. Let's go give that man his money so we can get back to football and stop pouting. You're getting the sneakers when we get home."

20

JEWEL

On Wednesday evening, Brittany and I sat around the little metal table in Scott's backyard. She had driven me over to collect my car, which had taken longer to repair than expected, and my brother had invited us to stay for dinner.

While he was at the grill barbecuing some burgers, we lounged around, getting caught up and sipping soda water with lime and mint. I inhaled deeply, almost moaning at the scent of the grilling meat as the sun started setting on the horizon.

Scott's house was small and set a ways out of town on a hill not overlooking the lake, but he still had a pretty decent view. Even if it was obscured by his neighbors and towering pines.

"Tomorrow is going to be so tough," Brittany complained good-naturedly. "I can't believe we did this to ourselves. Making up for the cleans we missed and doing our usual jobs? What were we thinking? We should've just walked it."

"With all our supplies in tow?" I lifted my eyebrows at her. "I doubt we'd have gotten much done walking from house to house with our mops and buckets, babe. Besides, we'll pull it off. We always do."

She sighed, toying with her light brown hair as she glanced at Scott before looking back at me. "Yeah, you're right. We'll get stuff done. All we need to do is power through."

"Exactly." I ignored the obvious longing in her eyes when she'd glanced at Scott, knowing she was also referring to him when she said she needed to power through.

While they'd been flirting for ages and ages, he'd never made a move and I was starting to wonder if he was just toying with her, but I was staying out of it. Besides, my brother wasn't a player. He'd dated a lot, but I couldn't imagine he'd be stringing her along.

Whatever his reason for not going after her, I knew it would be good. As much as I would have liked to know it, I didn't want to pry or get involved, so I stayed in my own lane, changing the topic when he glanced at her as he took another sip of his beer.

"Why have neither of you asked me what it was like to have finally set foot inside the Manor?" I asked teasingly. "It's only a dream come true, so you know. No biggie."

Brittany laughed and Scott rolled his eyes at me, but at least he obliged. "What was it like setting foot inside Styles Manor after all this time, and did you steal a key so you can go back whenever you want?"

I scoffed. "No. I'm not a burglar or a trespasser."

He chuckled. "When that place is in the mix, I wouldn't put it past you, but go on then. I know you're dying to tell us."

"Bursting at the seams," I said excitedly as I thought back to the first moment I'd walked inside. "It was amazing. Everything I ever dreamed it would be and more. On top of that, I also had a really nice evening with Landon and Colten, so it was a definite red-letter day for me."

Scott groaned. "Let's stick to details about the house. I don't really want to hear about Mr. Big City."

"Disagree," Brittany said incredulously. "The house has been there for about a hundred years. It can wait. Tell us about your date with the hottest single dad in town."

I smiled, giggling when Scott threw his hands up in defeat and focused on the grill again instead of listening to this part of the story. "It wasn't a date. They asked me to stay for dinner, is all. Afterward, he put Colten to bed and I had some tea before I went home."

"Uh huh. How much tea?" she asked with a glint of laughter in her eyes. "I bet it wasn't just one cup."

"It was two," I admitted. "Drunk over about three and a half hours."

"You spent three and a half hours with him after the kid went to bed?" Her eyes widened and a knowing grin spread her lips. "Pray tell, Jewel. What on earth were you doing with him that it took you so long to drink two cups of tea?"

I laughed. "Talking. That's it. I promise."

"Do you mean you were communicating with your bodies, or actually talking with your mouths?" she asked.

Scott scrunched up his face and spun around, grumbling under his breath. "I'm going to need another beer if we're really going to be talking about this."

"You don't have to listen if you don't want to," Brittany called after him in a sing-song voice before turning back to me with a grin that was borderline evil on her lips. "Who knows? Maybe if he hears that even his sister is getting some, it'll make him realize that I need to get some too. From him."

I wrinkled my nose and shook my head. "Nope. I'm not touching that and I also didn't touch Landon. We just talked. With our mouths. I promise."

She let out a disappointed sigh and tracked my brother's movements as he came back out with a fresh beer in his hands. "Fine. I believe you. How did you just talk to a guy that looks like him for so long? I would've at least tried for something more."

"Nah. It was a really good conversation. Surprisingly good, actually." I gave my brother a pointed look. "He's more than just Mr. Big City. There's real depth there, and he's an excellent father."

"I saw that," Brittany said with a fond smile, all the humor and teasing now gone from her features "That day on the boat, he was so sweet with Colten. It's obvious he really cares about him."

'He does, but I think there's also a lot of guilt there." Brittany and Scott were my people. I shared everything with them and they always helped me gain perspective. "I'm not entirely sure why, but I suspect he's not as involved when they're home as he is here."

"Well, to be fair, no parent is," Brittany said. "That's what vacations are for, right? Getting away as a family and having your parents' undivided attention? At home, there's always other stuff to do and to worry about, and that's not even mentioning work."

"Sure," Scott said, playing devil's advocate. "Yet there are many working parents who still manage to make time to spend with their kids. It doesn't matter what you do for a living. Prioritizing is a real thing. A lot of folks will tell you that they just can't make time, but it's just not true. Maybe there will be periods that you're busier than others, but in general, it's a matter of deciding what's more important to you."

"Nuh uh," Brittany countered instantly. "If you can afford to prioritize, then sure. What about people who work specific shifts or whose jobs depend on the amount of hours they can put in? Most people can't afford to say no to their bosses just so they get home in time to tuck their kids in."

Scott shrugged. "Maybe most people can't, but people who can afford to stay in Styles Manor for two months sure can."

She held his gaze for a beat. "Okay, I hear you and I'm not saying you're completely wrong, but the money has to come from somewhere. Staying in Styles Manor for a summer costs a bundle. We all know that, which means they can't exactly be hurting, but at the same time, we don't know how much work he has to do in a normal month to be able to stay on top of providing that kind of lifestyle."

I put my hands up and shook my head at both of them, chuckling as I intervened. "I think you're both right. He probably could prioritize his son a little more, but I think that's why they're here. That being said, Scott, you should know that I got in touch with Samantha.

I called her up to ask if Brody would mind spending some time with Colten this summer."

"That was a good idea," he said without even needing to think about it. "Brody is a good kid and Colten definitely needs to get out a little more. What kind of ten-year-old boy doesn't like tossing a ball around?"

I pursed my lips at him. "The kind who prefers to play chess. Not every kid needs to be a football player."

"Sure, but even if you don't want to play, it's nice to just spend some time in the sunshine, running around with the ball. You never played football and yet, you've always enjoyed it."

"Fair enough," I said. "I also had you as a brother, though. Tossing a ball around wasn't optional for me."

He chuckled. "When are you seeing them again?"

"On Monday," I said, excitement creeping back into the center of my being and making my heart flutter like little butterfly wings being tried out for the very first time. "I'd have liked to see them again sooner, but I guess I'll just have to wait until I go clean again."

Brittany suddenly scowled. "You're abandoning me again?"

"This is going to be an all-summer thing, Britt," I warned, frowning at her when I realized this had come as a surprise. "Did you not see the contract he signed?"

"I did, but I guess I didn't read it properly. I thought he'd gotten us in as a one-off. I suppose it makes sense that he'd want us there weekly, though."

"I could make some calls tomorrow," I offered. "Maybe some of our clients will agree to us shuffling their schedules around a little bit just for the next few weeks so you don't have to work alone?"

"We can try, but either way, being able to add the Styles Manor to our client list is going to look super impressive, so even if they don't agree, we'll make do. It'll be okay. Speaking of which though, I heard Dallas was spotted in town again yesterday being his usual, douchey self."

"I know." I grimaced. "He catcalled me again. I don't know what's wrong with that guy or how a woman like Lucille Styles could've been related to that."

"She didn't raise him," Brittany said, shrugging. "I'm sure her own kids were a lot better than that entitled prick."

Scott carried the plate with the burgers over to us and huffed out an irritated breath as he sat down. As he slammed his toppings onto his bun, he scowled. "One day that dick is going to get what's coming to him."

Once his burger was made, he took a massive bite and scowled some more, speaking around his food as he kept ranting. "I heard he tore through town like a bat out of hell again and then insisted that Verna move other customers at the cafe to a different table because he preferred the one they were at."

Shooting out of his chair, he grumbled some more as he and his burgers marched back to the grill. "Forgot my beer."

Brittany and I exchanged a look and chuckled, and I pumped my eyebrows at her. "How do you have the hots for him? He's a barbarian."

She shrugged, her eyes sparkling. She leaned in to make sure he wouldn't overhear her. "Who doesn't love a good barbarian? I'm willing to bet all that passion makes him an excellent lover."

I groaned and stood up, shaking my head. I called to her over my shoulder while making my way inside with my empty glass in my hand. "Just for that, you can refill your own damn drink."

She laughed, clearly not too worried about having to get her own drink now that my brother was sitting back down next to her. I gave them a couple minutes, looking at them out the kitchen window as I fixed another soda water.

They were a darn cute couple and we always had so much fun together that it would be a blast if they started dating. As long as they made it work forever.

For some reason, the word *forever* made me think of Landon and my cheeks flushed beet red even if I would never admit what I'd just thought to anyone. If I was being totally honest, I associated that word with him because I would be happy if that was how long he and Colten would be staying.

I felt something with him I'd never felt with anyone else. A connection, perhaps. An ease I couldn't describe. It was nice. More than nice, but it already killed me to know it would only last for the summer.

Just a little less than two short months and they'd be gone, and even though I'd only known them for about a week, I was already dreading the day they were going to have to leave.

21

LANDON

It was a beautiful day in June Lake, but then again, they didn't seem to have any other kind around here this time of year. As it had been since we'd arrived, the sky was a beautiful blue and there were big fluffy clouds floating by lazily.

A slight breeze blew off the lake, just enough to relieve the worst of the heat and not nearly enough to be unpleasant. Colten and I sat side by side on a bike path just up from the beach, shaded by a leafy tree overhead as we waited for Jewel to show up with Brody.

Colt suddenly stood up, literally kicking rocks as he sent me yet another glare. "I can't believe you arranged a play date for me. I'm ten, not four."

I tried not to laugh at his expense, but it was hard to keep a straight face at how deeply miffed he was about this. "It's for your own good, bud. You can't spend all summer at the house."

"Why not?" he asked. "I have everything I need right there."

Truthfully, I didn't really have an answer for that. At least not one that didn't sound mean. The bottom line was that he wasn't socializing well for his age and making friends was a life skill that he would need if he ever wanted to be successful—no matter what kind of success he coveted. He might not become a hot shot lawyer—which was fine by me—or even be career motivated at all, but whatever he did in his life, he had to learn how to deal with people his age.

Whoever he was now and whoever he would become, I would support and embrace him fully, but it was my job to help him build a strong foundation. Friends were key to that. I didn't need him to make friends with every kid he ever met or to become the most popular child in his whole school. That wasn't what this was about.

It was simply a small step in developing a skill he didn't have. Now I just had to hope that this Brody kid hadn't changed his mind.

A few minutes later though, I heard a car pull up on the road behind us and I twisted just in time to see Jewel emerge from it. She was talking to someone—presumably the kid—and laughing at something he'd said as she shut her door.

The next minute, they appeared at the top of the path, still chatting and laughing as they made their way toward us. I took the time to take a quick look at the kid, trying to gauge what kind of person he was.

Blond-haired and tanned, he had a crooked smile and a sporty style. He moved with confidence and Colten seemed immediately intimidated, even shrinking back a little as Jewel walked up to him. She smiled.

"Hey, Colten," she said, her voice friendly and bright. "This is Brody. Brody, meet Colten. He's from LA and he's spending the summer here with his dad."

"That's cool," Brody said with an easy shrug as he extended his hand toward my son. "I'm spending the summer here with my mom. And every other season too."

He offered Colt that crooked smile and Colten took his hand, giving it a quick shake, but his shoulders had collapsed and he was shifting on his feet, apparently uncertain about how to respond. Thankfully, Jewel decided to play mediator, seamlessly stepping into the role as she chuckled at Brody's joke.

"That's a good one. Poor you, stuck here with us year round," she said jokingly.

Brody chuckled. "Hey, I'll take it. At least you guys are cool for grownups. Do you know if Scott is going fishing sometime this week?"

"I'll have to ask him," she replied as she reached out to ruffle Brody's hair. "You want to go up against him again, though? Are you sure?"

Laughter rumbled out of him as he ducked and dodged away from her, but he didn't seem put out by her ruffling his hair. "Do you fish, Colten?"

Once again, my son didn't seem to know what to say, but Jewel was still in that mediator role and she used the opening to segue into something sure to get his attention. "I don't know about fishing, but he kicked my butt in chess on Monday. I'm itching for a rematch."

Colten lit up and I made a mental note to thank her for that. Then I could've kissed her when she used that to point out something they had in common. "Brody is a champion game player too, but his skills are at the arcade in town. Last time I was there, he had the top score in tons of games, so I'm going to have to look into taking him down too."

"Really?" Colt asked, quietly but at least finally sounding curious. "What games?"

Brody shrugged but not dismissively. "I don't really know which ones I still hold the top score in. I've been on the lake and stuff since school ended, so I haven't been to the arcade much. What games do you like, besides chess?"

Just like that, the boys started talking on their own and Jewel sent me a discreet smile as she sat down on the bench beside me. "He's cool, right?"

"Very," I murmured. "I wonder how his mother got him to be so comfortable in his own skin. Any ideas?"

She chuckled. "Well, uh, I think it's just his personality, but Samantha has always kind of just let him be, you know? She's been taking him out on the lake since he was a baby, and as soon as he was old enough to play games, she'd take him to the arcade, but she's never coddled him or spoiled him. She just lets him do his thing."

"So do I, but it seems Colten's thing is chess and not making friends."

"Chess is fine too," she said. "At least his thing is one that will keep his mind sharp as a tack. Besides, it looks like Brody is drawing him out of his shell."

She inclined her head at the boys just as Colten started nodding enthusiastically. He came bounding over to us with a hopeful gleam in his eyes. "Can I have some money? Brody and I want to go to the arcade."

I'd never been so willing to fork over cash as I was when I pulled my wallet out of my pocket. Peeling off a few bills, I handed them over. "Have fun. I'll either be here at the beach or up at the cafe when you're done."

The boys took off, jogging up the path and then disappearing, but I heard Brody's laughter and even some chuckles from Colten filling the air behind them. Once they were gone, I arched an eyebrow at Jewel.

"You're a freaking genius. How did you know that would happen?"

"I didn't, but Brody is easy to get along with. He's not conceited about it, but almost all the kids in town love him."

She had no idea how much her encouragement had helped Colten just then, and I shook my head at her. "Give yourself some credit, woman. You've known him for about five minutes and you might just have helped my son make his first real friend. That's amazing. It's not just because Brody is easy to get along with."

She flushed. "I thought you said he used to have friends?"

"Yeah, sure, but back in the day when friends were the kids he played with at school without even knowing their names. I don't think he's had any since it became a little more complicated than that."

"Well, I'm glad it helped. I was shy growing up too. I know what it's like to need someone to throw you a bone." She nudged me in the ribs. "While they're busy, are you hungry?"

"Are you cooking?" I asked, trying not to sound too wary, but there was every possibility that her food would kill me on the spot.

She shook her head, nodding up at the cafe. "If we go now, we should beat the lunch rush. Let's go grab some sandwiches. I'm buying."

"Uh, okay," I agreed, a bit grudgingly over her buying but following her to the cafe anyway.

We walked in to find quite a few of the tables already taken, but Verna showed us to a table on the patio outside and took our orders for drinks and sandwiches. "I'll be back in a few, kids. You're lucky you got here now. We're filling up fast."

"I thought you might be," Jewel said, smiling at the woman as she took a look around. "It's always good to see the place so full, though."

"Hard work is what summers are for," Verna joked, or at least, I thought she was joking. Then she took off.

Across the street, I could hear the boisterous laughter of the kids in the arcade and I hoped Colten was having fun with Brody. It sounded like there were a bunch of other children in there too, which made me wonder if maybe Brody was introducing Colt to some of the other local kids as well.

"This was a good idea," I said as I turned back to Jewel, staring right into those honey-gold eyes and trying my best to ignore the urge I had to kiss her. Again. "The kids and the sandwiches. And the boating the other day, actually."

She giggled, running the pendant on the chain around her neck from one side to the other. The movement drew my gaze down and I groaned internally when I noticed the swell of her breasts under the fitted tank she was wearing.

I'd been trying so hard not to ogle her, but now that we were alone—relatively speaking, anyway—and her hand was fidgeting right in front of her chest, I let myself look. For just a second.

The tank was a pastel pink and it clung to her every curve. Her blonde hair framed her beautiful face and her lips curved into a semi-permanent smile. She wore no makeup and her hair was loose, the waves in it appearing natural.

"I have a surprise for you when you come back to the house on

Monday," I said, suddenly looking forward to seeing that gorgeous face once she realized what I'd bought from Dallas.

Her chin lowered a bit and her eyebrows rose, but then her long lashes batted as she blinked rapidly and grinned at me. "You're serious? You have a surprise for me? I love surprises."

I do too, I thought. *Especially when they come wrapped up in a body like yours with a smile like that.*

Just then, loud tires screeched on the asphalt and my stomach leaped into my throat as I watched Dallas Styles swing into a parking spot outside the arcade. His red Ferrari lurched over the curb and nearly crashed into the window.

My heart hammered and my muscles tightened. I didn't know just who the hell that guy thought he was, but my kid was in that arcade and so were many others. I didn't give a shit that I was staying in his house or that he came from a family that was revered in these parts.

With that idiotic move, he'd endangered my son and there was absolutely no way I was letting it go.

22

JEWEL

One second, it had been a peaceful Friday afternoon at the café, and the next, Dallas's latest display of recklessness had sucked the peacefulness and relaxation right out of the air. I sat there, blinking hard and gaping as his car landed right next to the arcade window.

My heart hammered in my chest, my mind reeling over how stupid that had been. I'd barely had time to process it, but Landon was already on his feet, marching across the road with deliberate purpose.

To say he looked tense was an understatement. His muscles bulged and his jaw was hard as stone. He didn't look back at me, but I hurried after him anyway, knowing Verna wouldn't think we'd abandoned her without paying for our order.

Cursing Dallas under my breath, I raced up to Landon, gently touching his arm to get his attention. He started, then spun his head to look at me. As soon as he realized who had touched him, the edge in his eyes disappeared.

"Dallas is a handful when he's like this," I warned him softly. "It's best to just leave it alone."

"No," he said succinctly.

At that moment, Dallas spilled out of the car, swearing like a sailor as he looked down at his suit. A bright red stain covered him from neck to waistband, like some drink had sloshed all over him when his car had jumped the curb.

"It's fucking ruined," he complained loudly, yanking his sunglasses off his eyes and glaring at the suit like he could beat it into submission somehow. "That's gonna stain. Fucking food coloring in the fucking—"

Landon stormed right up to him, getting hold of the front of said ruined suit and slamming him against the side of the Ferrari. I stopped in my tracks, not wanting to get any closer if this was about to turn into a brawl.

All around me, other people had stopped too, staring unashamedly at the scene unfolding in front of their very eyes. The truth was that most of the locals were sick of Dallas's bull shit. On so many occasions, almost all of us had tried to beg, plead, or reason with him to no avail.

It certainly hadn't helped us that he knew we wouldn't do anything to him. The donations he made to the fire and police departments ensured that he had them in his pocket and that meant they'd sooner act against the people than the habitual instigator.

Landon didn't know any of this and he'd stormed away before I'd been able to finish my warning, but as I looked at him, I realized he probably wouldn't have listened anyway. He gripped Dallas's shirt hard, the muscles in his arm rippling as he held the man against his fancy sports car.

Although he wasn't looking at me, I could practically see the fireballs spitting from his eyes as he glowered at Dallas and I could definitely still see the tension radiating from him. "What the hell are you doing? There are kids in that arcade and all it would have taken was for you to find the brake a second later and this could've been a very fucking tragic day in June Lake."

Dallas tried to shake him off, peeling his fingers away from his shirt, but Landon held fast, clearly furious and looking for some sort of an apology. I knew he wasn't going to get one, but again, Landon didn't know, and again, I didn't know if it would've made any difference if he had.

As soon as Dallas realized he wasn't going to get away, he sneered at Landon, all bravado and machismo. "That's just how I drive. I knew what I was doing. I was never going to lose control. Now get your hands off me, asshole."

Landon held him for another long moment before his tongue swept across his lips and he dropped Dallas's shirt. He released him and stepped back, but I could feel the rage pouring off him. Somehow, I sensed that this wasn't over just yet, even if he had let go of the man's shirt.

Just then, Colten and Brody came out of the arcade and Landon bit his tongue as he turned to face the boys. Brody spotted the Ferrari, his eyes turning into orbs as he admired it. Dallas, forever searching for a loophole or some way to escape accountability, seemed eager to take the heat off himself.

"You can sit in it if you'd like," he said with that smug drawl in his voice that I hated more than paying taxes. "Heck, you can even touch the steering wheel."

The kid went around to get in the driver's door, looking like he was about to start drooling. Colten followed, but Landon intervened, grabbing Colten's hand and holding him back. "We weren't done yet, Styles. Someone could've been seriously injured with what you just did. You need to be more careful."

"Or what?" Dallas laughed, clearly not taking any of it seriously. "Ease up, my man. Nothing happened. You're just making yourself look like a fool."

He glanced at the crowd that had gathered like he expected a round of applause or perhaps even laughter, but no one was at all amused by what we'd just witnessed. Blowing out a heavy breath, he played it off as if it had been nothing at all.

"Just walk away, Lando. You're a visitor here. A tourist. No one hired you to be the town's safety officer for the summer." Again, he looked around as if he was trying to garner support, but most people simply shook their heads or turned and walked away.

That was the thing about Dallas. He thought he was all that and he'd been getting away with his unlawful and obnoxious behavior all his life, but he wasn't menacing or anything like that. None of us were scared of him. It was more like we knew there was nothing we could do to get rid of him.

Well, that and the fact that anyone who tried to make some kind of move against him would find themselves behind bars while he would, as always, face zero consequences for whatever the problem had been. It was lose-lose for everyone who lived here, and as a result, we'd collectively given up.

Landon hadn't. "Or you'll have to answer to me. You just recklessly endangered children in the presence of at least a dozen people. That's not the kind of thing judges or juries take kindly to, but especially not when there are so many witnesses."

Dallas scoffed. "Oh, you want to charge me? Why don't you go ahead and try?"

Landon kept his head held high, his gaze laser-focused on the other man's. "Your day will come. It always does."

"You'll be gone by the end of August." Dallas scoffed. "Stay out of things that don't concern you."

"Stay away from my son and the places he visits with his friends," Landon retorted, giving Dallas one last warning look.

Brody glanced at me, his gaze flicking to the Ferrari and back again, but I shook my head at him and waved him over. He sighed heavily but didn't argue, probably because he knew his mother would agree with me.

All of the kids had been warned to watch out for Dallas Styles, but even more so when he was in his car. He never obeyed any traffic rules and he didn't seem to understand that a car didn't have to travel at full speed at all times.

As I slung my arm around Brody's shoulders, I flashed him an apologetic look. "Sorry, bud, but I can't let you get into that car."

He sighed again, nodding even as he cast another wistful glance at the flashy vehicle. "I know, but it would've been fun. It's the nicest car in town."

"If by nicest, you mean the most dangerous, then sure." From the corner of my eye, I saw Landon leading Colten back to the cafe as well and I paused for a beat, waiting for them to catch up.

As he took the boys to choose some ice cream inside the cafe, I sat back down at our table and stared at his back through the window, his muscles all bunched up and tense. From our first encounters, I'd known that he had something of a temper, but now I was wondering if I should be as interested in the man as I was.

In my admittedly limited experience, men who were so quick to anger and who didn't hesitate to put their hands on others weren't the most stable. As sweet, kind, and caring as he could be, he definitely had a short fuse, and while I understood why he'd gotten so worked up about what Dallas had done, I couldn't help thinking that perhaps I needed to take a step back.

At the very least, I had to observe carefully how he recovered from this and whether he let it go, or whether he spent the rest of the day obsessing about it. We still had quite a few hours left before I had to take Brody home and I wasn't about to cut the boys' time hanging out together short because of this, which gave me some time to make some decisions about the rest of the summer.

I would keep cleaning Styles Manor. I'd try to help Colten as far as I could with making friends and having a good time in June Lake, but I didn't have to keep spending time with Landon. Not unless he somehow managed to convince me that he had a handle on his temper.

If he could calm down, then fine. I understood completely that he'd had a fright. My own heart had nearly stopped and I hadn't even had a kid of my own in that arcade. So sure. I got it.

But if he was about to go after Dallas again, or if he made me feel in any way uncomfortable, then that was it. I was out.

No matter how hot he was or how incredibly natural it felt to be around him.

23

LANDON

After buying the boys some ice cream, I went for a walk down to the lake to cool off. Jewel had volunteered to stay with them while they ate and to get them some food after. I didn't even care that they'd had dessert first. They'd deserved a treat after all that.

My heart was still racing as I reached the beach, kicking off my flip flops to feel the sand under my feet. I was hoping that it would help calm my temper. It was definitely still spiked for now, and breathing deeply didn't seem to be helping.

Especially not while every time I blinked, my mind conjured up torturous images of the carnage that could've resulted from Dallas's reckless actions. It didn't even take much for me to see those images in mind, since I'd seen countless similar ones while defending the men who hadn't been thinking.

I didn't get like this often, but for a second there, I'd thought my kid was in danger and I'd seen red. And then that nonchalant response I'd gotten from Dallas?

Not. Cool.

As I buried my toes in the sand, I inhaled deeply and exhaled slowly, over and over again until I felt my heartrate starting to normalize. I dragged my hands through my hair, dropping to my haunches once I'd turned a corner and burying my face in my palms.

I squeezed my eyes shut, willing the mental pictures of dismembered limbs and bleeding bodies out of my mind. In my entire career, I'd only defended two people who had caused the kind of accident that could've been, but it had been bad enough that I steered clear of it now.

I could handle all kinds of gore, deceit, and malicious intent, but I drew the line at children being injured. At the start of my career, I'd seen too much of it, and with Colten being a baby, I quickly got to a point where I couldn't take it.

I was still haunted by those few cases I had seen. The devastation that had been caused to so many families—including those of the offenders—that could never be reversed. Those demons would never leave me, my soul never feeling quite cleansed of the strategies I'd devised during those cases.

Pushing back to my feet, I battled against the demons, fighting the rage that tore through my veins. Dallas Styles was a menace to this community, a danger to everyone in it, and he was too dumb to realize it.

Doubtless that he'd gotten away with a lot worse before, I wondered if there was any point in reporting his behavior. Ultimately, no one had gotten hurt today, and while it quickly could've turned into a disaster, it hadn't.

I blew out another slow breath, sitting down on the sand and looping my arms around my knees. As I sat there staring at the water and letting the serenity of being out here soothe my soul, a sweet but tentative voice called out from behind me.

"Landon? Are you okay?"

I turned to face Jewel, a sheepish grin spreading on my lips. "I'm fine. How are the boys?"

Something akin to surprise flashed across her features, but she closed the distance between us anyway and took a seat beside me, not at all bothered by sitting with her ass in the sand instead of on a towel.

"They're good. On their second sandwich each and still going strong. Their appetites have brought back so many memories of Scott at that age. I honestly don't know how any teenage boy's parents can keep up."

I chuckled, baffled by how much calmer I felt now that she was here. No one had ever had that effect on me, but her presence was like a soothing balm to the bleeding parts of my soul. "Honestly, I have no idea how my stepfather kept up with me. All I know was that there were a lot of sandwiches and, later on, a lot of ramen."

A smile lit her face, but then she looked at me—really looked at me—and genuine concern clouded her eyes. "Are you sure you're okay? You seemed kind of triggered back there."

I tipped my head back, allowing the shame to run through me before I looked at her again. "I apologize for losing it back there, Jewel. It's not like me, contrary to what you might believe after how rude I was to you before, but when Colten is involved, I can get a bit overprotective."

"Dallas is an ass," she said slowly, her gaze searching mine. "He tends to bring out the worst in people."

"He's going to hurt someone one day," I said.

She sighed before turning back to the lake. "He already has. Multiple times. Maybe not physically like he almost did today, but he's always been reckless. He's also a total narcissist and those things are a dangerous combination."

I had gotten that vibe from him too. "It's not really my place to ask you to do this, but you should stay away from him. Colten and I will be doing the same while we're in town, even if we are staying in his family's home."

"It's not your place, but I will. I already do, actually. If you ask me, the town would be better off without him, but with the Manor here and no possibility of him passing it on to be managed by his own offspring, we're just stuck with him."

She was still looking deep into my eyes, and I had a feeling I knew what she was searching for. "You're wondering if I'm dangerous too."

Blinking hard, she swallowed, but then she hung her head and sighed. "I won't lie to you, Landon. For a few minutes back there, I did wonder that, but then I realized that you were only standing up back there. For your son, and Brody, and all the other kids who were in that arcade. For the whole town, in some ways. The rest of us leave him be, but you called him out today. That's a good thing."

She lifted her chin slightly, turning so she was peering up at me again even if her head was still hanging. "That doesn't mean you weren't rude before, though. Also, it means something to me that you took a walk to calm down instead of lashing out or worse."

"What would've been worse?"

"Going after him," she said. "Besides, tonight is the night market. Tomorrow is the Lake Warrior contest. Next weekend is the fair. There's a lot to look forward to. Don't let a bad seed like Dallas ruin any of that for you or for Colten."

I saw her logic, even managing a real smile as I nodded. "Thanks for the pick-me-up. I guess we should be heading back to the cafe, huh? The boys will eat the entire place if someone doesn't stop them."

Her answering laughter warmed my soul and my smile widened as I got up and extended a hand to help her up too. As we walked back to the cafe together, pride raced through me at the sight of Colten talking animatedly to Brody.

We drew closer and I heard what he was talking about, groaning as I took a seat beside him. "Are you sure Brody wants to hear all this about chess?"

Colten smirked at me. "He's curious. He wants to play."

Brody nodded, eager as he turned to me. "I've been wanting to learn for a while, but Mom and I don't have a board at home and she's at work when the library is open. Cole can't play either, so he can't teach me and there's other stuff to do at school."

"Can Brody come over to the house sometime?" Colt asked. "We've got that big, fancy board at the Manor just standing there."

I happily agreed. "Yeah, that would be great. Anytime, Brody."

"I'll talk to my mom," he said. His gaze zeroed in on something behind my shoulder and he pushed his chair back. "It looks like Cole and the guys are going to go play volleyball down at the beach. Do you want to come, Colten?"

He looked at me as Brody stood up, and I saw the uncertainty in his eyes. He'd made friends with Brody, but clearly, he wasn't sure about befriending Brody's friends as well. I put a hand on his shoulder, squeezing it and keeping my voice low while Brody waved at the other boys and called for them to wait up.

"Be brave, Colt," I murmured. "It might just be worth it."

Chest rising on a deep breath, he glanced at Brody who was standing at the door, waiting for him. "Yeah. Okay. I'll try it."

"Have fun," I said, giving him an encouraging smile. "Remember that if Brody is nice, the guys he hangs out with probably are too."

Colt nodded, then joined Brody. The two of them strode down the street to meet up with the others. I leaned back in my chair when they were out of sight, glancing at Jewel, who it seemed had been watching me intently.

"What?" I asked when she still didn't look away.

She shrugged. "I'd have felt like the luckiest girl in the world to have a dad who cared as much as you do."

Oh, wow. There's a story there. Not wanting to pry too much, I tried to keep my voice nonchalant as I turned my attention fully on her. "Yeah? What's your dad like?"

A sad smile played on her lips. "He was great. I don't miss him so much anymore unless I'm around other great dads. All of you remind me of what we lost when we lost him."

I grimaced. "I'm sorry. I didn't know."

"It's okay." She stared into the middle distance for a moment before she closed her eyes, smiled again, and then refocused on me. "I know that you didn't know, and I wouldn't have said anything at all if I didn't want to talk about him. What about your dad? You mentioned a stepfather before?"

"Walter," I said, reminding myself to give him another call later. "I never knew my biological father. He passed when I was very young. Too young to remember him at all, but my mom married Walter when I was a kid and he raised me as his own. He's amazing."

She inched forward, her gaze locked on mine. I swore I saw sincere, innocent curiosity in it. Usually, people were only interested in finding out more about me for one of two reasons: my money or my clients.

In Jewel's case, she didn't know about the money or the clients. She hadn't even asked what I did for a living. She was simply interested in knowing me, which did something weird to my insides.

"Amazing, huh? That's high praise. Why isn't he here with you?"

"Because I didn't think that bringing him would be a great idea. He's older and he's in a care facility. Bringing him would've meant bringing a carer along as well, which would've been fine for me, but you know how it goes. Taking people out of a familiar environment just so you won't feel guilty about leaving them there isn't always in their best interest."

She nodded. "I'm sure he would've loved it, though. Maybe next time?"

"Definitely next time. I'm already kicking my own ass for not just bringing him. It was his idea for us to come here, and I figured he wanted Colten and me to have the time together, so between that and the inconvenience, I never even seriously considered it."

"That makes sense," she said suddenly, a playful smile breaking out across her lips. "What you're doing in a place like this, I mean. I couldn't understand it until you said it was somebody else's idea."

I pretended to pout. "Really? It didn't make sense until you found out it wasn't *my* idea? Why is that? Where do you think I would've gone instead?"

She shrugged, eyes sparkling with mirth as she held my gaze. "I'm not sure. Somewhere exotic. Fiji, maybe? Or Bali? Oooo, the Great Lakes?"

Unable to hold it back anymore, I laughed and shook my head at her. "You're right. Left to my own devices, I probably would've dragged him halfway across the world, but I'm really glad I didn't. I'm glad we came here instead."

"I've said this before, but I really mean it, so I'll say it again. I'm glad you came here, too, Landon." My insides did that strange thing again.

It was something between a flop and a tightening, and it felt oddly like a buzzing sensation I'd never felt before. I had no clue what it was, but while it made me a touch uncomfortable, I kind of liked it. It was something new, and definitely not in a bad way.

24

JEWEL

I spent the entire afternoon with Landon and it went by as fast as blinking. After lunch, we had taken a walk through town while the boys played volleyball. It turned out that Colten had enjoyed it and, with a little help from his new friends, had picked up the game pretty fast.

By the time Landon and I had gotten back to the beach, the boys had been big balls of sweat and had needed to cool off, so they'd all gone for a swim in the lake. Meanwhile, I'd found a spot for us to lounge in the shade while they swam and we'd talked for another hour before we'd gone our separate ways.

At the night market now, I waited for them to show up, feeling so much different than I had last Friday. Anticipation filled me, and my head was on a swivel as I searched all the entrances at once trying to find them.

Brittany sat next to me on a bench in the park, sipping a not-so-sweet lemonade and watching the people that passed by. "I'm glad Lacey's mom stepped in with the recipe. This is actually pretty good."

I took a small sip of my drink and nodded my agreement but with my eyes still peeled. "I didn't mind it so much when it was sweeter, but I think she's going to do better selling this batch than the previous one."

A man with dark hair climbed out of a blue truck and I started smiling until I realized it wasn't Landon. Disappointment shot through me and I slumped back again, my shoulders falling as I flicked my gaze to the other entrance.

"He'll be here," Brittany said confidently. "Before he arrives though, it's time for you to admit it."

"Admit what?" I asked, finally managing to yank my eyes away from the entrances for long enough to look at my friend.

Her light eyes were sparkling, a knowing gleam in them as she arched an eyebrow at me. "You have a crush on Mr. Big City. A big, fat crush."

"I know," I groaned, not even trying to deny it. "He leaves at the end of the summer. What am I supposed to do with that? Even if something does happen between us, it's not like it can go anywhere, which means there's no point in even trying."

"That's not true," she said, her head shaking so emphatically that her curls bounced. "Not all crushes have to become relationships. What if you treat this as a summer fling? It could be fun while it lasts, and when it's over, you get to move on with your life without any of the heartbreak or drama that comes with a breakup."

I winced. "Flings aren't really my thing."

She winked at me. "I know, but some men are worth changing *your thing* for, and Landon? He fits that bill."

I fidgeted with my fingers as I thought it over. "What if I get attached?"

"Don't," she said like it was the simplest thing in the world. Shifting to face me fully, she put her hands on my shoulders and looked right into my eyes. "You deserve this, Jewel. You deserve to let go and open yourself up to someone for a change. Have a good time with a gorgeous man for a couple months. You don't have to keep waiting for the man you're going to marry to sweep you off your feet before you get involved with anyone at all."

To me, it seemed like a recipe for disaster, but I nodded slowly as I looked back her. "All of that does sound really good. I just don't want to get hurt, you know?"

"Of course, you don't, but you're going into this with your eyes open. You know exactly how long he's going to be here and you know that when he leaves, it will be over. The key is to enjoy the time between then and now. Let your hair down for a little while, and once he's gone, you can get on with your life."

"I'll think about it," I said. An awareness washed over me that made me turn to look at the entrance again.

Colten and Landon had finally arrived, and they were walking straight toward us. Landon had a sexy, easy grin on his face and his arm was around Colt's shoulders. Colten was looking around wildly, his eyes wide with excitement as he searched for something.

Probably his new friends.

"Hey, Jewel," he said when they reached us. "Have you seen Brody? He said they'd be waiting for me here."

"They're kicking a ball around behind the bandstand," I said. "We ran into him earlier and he said to tell you they'd be there."

"Thanks." He grinned at me before turning to his dad. "Can I go?"

"Of course," Landon replied, the words barely out of his mouth before Colten waved goodbye and bolted to go meet up with Brody and the others.

Pleased that the day had gone so well for them, I smiled as I watched him go, and Landon looked even happier about it than I was. Grinning from ear to ear, he took a seat beside me on the bench, spreading his long legs out ahead of him as he turned to us. "The whole drive over here, he couldn't shut up about how excited he was for tonight. I've never heard him like that. It's like he's a whole new kid."

"Oh, the power of friendship." I giggled.

Brittany smiled and got up. "Unfortunately, the power of friendship doesn't eradicate hunger. I'm going to grab something to eat. Do you guys want to come?"

"Yes," I said immediately, afraid that my stomach was going to start rumbling if I didn't get something into it soon.

Landon chuckled and strode to the food trucks with us. He grabbed a pulled pork sandwich with us and then glanced in the general direction of the bandstand. "I gave him some money. The kids will get something themselves when they're hungry, right?"

"They should," Brittany said easily. "Brody's mom has a stall here, so she can't be running after him with food."

"Cole's mom works here too," I said. "Since they haven't starved yet, I'm pretty sure they'll help themselves when they're ready, but if not, we'll be around."

Scott showed up and nodded hello to Landon before focusing on Brittany. "How do you feel about challenging them to a ring-toss contest? Brad just set it up near Gaston's."

She glanced at Landon and me. "What do you guys think? I'm game if you are."

"I'm always up for some friendly competition," I joked to Scott before I turned to Landon. "By that, I mean it won't be a friendly competition. My brother can't stand losing."

"That must be why I never do it," he boasted with a goofy smirk appearing on his lips. "Let's go before it gets too busy."

Landon glanced between the three of us before he shrugged. "Sure. That could be fun. I have to warn you, though. I haven't tossed a ring in at least two decades."

"That's okay," I said as Brittany and Scott took off and we fell into step behind them. "I can teach you how to do it. Brad sets up the ring toss almost every weekend, so I've had plenty of practice."

Since we were walking behind Brittany and Scott, I couldn't help but notice how close together they were, not quite touching but their hands brushed every so often. Landon must've noticed it too because he suddenly brought his mouth closer to my ear.

"What's up with those two? They seem to be into each other, but I can't quite figure out if they've done something about it yet."

His lips moved my hair as he spoke. A pleasant shiver ran down my spine and I couldn't resist leaning just a little bit closer to him when I responded. "They're still in that will they, won't they stage, but I think it's going to happen soon."

A sophisticated, masculine scent wafted from him, just faint enough that I could smell it but not nearly strong enough to be overwhelming. I couldn't even tell if it was some kind of soap or if it was cologne, but whatever it was, it was enticing as hell. Fresh and clean but with hints of spice and something richer, like leather or maybe smoke from a fire. Either way, it was the kind of scent I could breathe in all day and not grow tired of, too intrigued by discovering the different undertones to get bored of it.

I glanced up at him, seeing mostly his profile from this angle and noticing again how strong it was. The slant of his jaw. The flat of his chin.

His facial hair was neatly trimmed and short enough that it didn't obscure much of his features, and I liked being able to see what he looked like, even with the beard that made him a touch more rugged.

When we reached the ring toss, Scott and Brittany handed over our rings. Scott went first, performing dismally. Every last one of his rings missed and I did a little happy dance before I winked at Landon.

"We've got this in the bag." I glanced at my brother as he smirked at Britt. "What are the stakes and why do you look so happy? You're going to lose."

"Nah. I just wanted to give you a false sense of security. It was part of my game plan."

Brittany laughed. "Was telling her your strategy part of the game plan too?"

"Yep." He cocked his head, his gaze drifting over to Gaston's before he looked back at me. "The stakes are that the losing team has to buy the winning team a spiked lemonade."

"Deal." I stepped up to take my turn and tuned out the live music playing at the bandstand as I focused on impressing the man behind me.

I managed to score some points, throwing my arms up in the air and grinning as I spun back to him. "We've *so* got this."

He returned my grin, but I also saw his gaze wandering, slowly meandering from my face down to my torso until I lowered my arms once more. My skin buzzed with electricity in the wake of his heated gaze and I blushed, quickly going to his side while Brittany took her turn.

As she did, I tried to distract myself from the lust coursing through me by dancing to the beat of the music, but I caught Landon watching me and my good intentions evaporated. Instead of dancing as a distraction, I was dancing for him now, loving the way his eyes seemed to be undressing me with every move of my hips.

Eventually, we won the match despite the lust flowing freely between us, and Scott groaned as he grabbed Brittany's hand. "Let's go get their lemonade so we don't have to be here for the gloating."

She laughed and let him drag her away. Alone and drunk on the good company of the day, I was feeling bold, so I offered him my hand once they were gone. "Dance with me?"

"Here?" He took a pointed look around at all the people waiting in line for the ring toss and I giggled as I shook my head.

"No. Over there." I inclined my head at the tree line behind the game and slightly off to the left. We wouldn't have complete privacy there, but it would be out of the fray.

To my surprise, he nodded, taking my hand and twirling me away before he brought me back in. With a firm grip on my hand, he slid an arm around my hips and drew me closer. His head bent so his eyes were on mine as we went to the trees.

He twirled me again, bringing me back again, but this time, pressing me right up against his chest.

"Smooth moves," I murmured.

"Oh, this?" He exaggerated the sway of his hips against my own. "Thanks. I learned from the best back there."

I threw my head back and laughed, inhaling the scent of his cologne as he held me close. Intoxicated by the twinkle lights above, the joy of the day we'd had together, and that incredible scent, I found myself leaning in, my head still tipped back.

Landon looked deep into my eyes before his gaze lowered to my lips. They parted and my tongue darted out to wet them without my brain having given it the command to do so. Sliding one of his hands up my back, he brushed my hair back and then his head slowly started descending.

Our lips met, tentatively at first, and he kissed me gently, like I was made of flower petals. The world around me faded away to a dull buzz. Light exploded behind my eyes as I pushed my fingers into his hair and kissed him back.

I still wasn't sure I was going to be able to have a lighthearted fling without getting attached to him, but as his tongue pleaded for entry at my lips and the sensation of his strong body pressed to mine stole all sense of reason, I held him closer anyway. I would figure it out.

Just like Brittany had said. I was going into this with my eyes wide open. Landon wasn't the love of my life or the man I would end up marrying, but he was fun to be around and a damn good kisser, and that was definitely good enough.

Surely I could keep my feelings out of it.

25

LANDON

W*ell, this is amazing.*

I wanted this girl something fierce. Everything in me demanded that I push her up against the tree and make her mine, but since there were lots of people and kids around, I was going to have to settle for just a kiss.

It was quite possibly the best kiss of my life, though. My tongue parted her lips and she moaned into my mouth. I crushed it to hers, tightening my grip on her and feeding the addiction I'd just discovered. Jewel was soft in all the right places, her taste sweet and citrusy and her head at the perfect height for me to take her lips without having to break my neck to do it.

I knew we'd have to break apart soon and it killed me. Kissing her was the best fucking feeling I'd had in years. I didn't want it to end, even if I was going to have blue balls forever for having to stop this at just a kiss.

As it was, my dick was straining against the fly of my shorts, my cheeks were hot, and my heart was hammering. I ran a hand down her side, cupping her ribs and dying to cop a feel, but again, *kids around.*

She wrapped her palm around the nape of my neck, the smooth

heat of her sending a bolt of desire through me to feel it in other places. My hips rocked into hers just once, but as that first shiver of pleasure shot through me, I knew it was time.

Hating myself for doing it, I pulled away and reluctantly ended the kiss before I twirled her again. Jewel didn't fight me on it, nor did she seem surprised. Her lips were slightly swollen, her eyes a little glazed over when they met mine again, but she was smiling, which was a good thing.

At least she wasn't pissed at me for kissing her.

Just as I spun her back to me, Brittany and Scott found us. I doubted Scott would've wanted to see me laying one on his sister and especially not since it had gotten so close to getting out of control. Brittany glanced between us, a smug half-smile creeping onto her lips as she handed over Jewel's lemonade.

"Having fun?" she asked lightly, her eyebrows sweeping up just a tiny bit as she looked at her friend.

It was one of those looks that told me they were communicating with a lot more than just words, and Jewel gave her a shy smile in return. I watched them closely until Scott handed over my lemonade.

"A toast to the winners," he said as he raised his glass. "And to the rematch we'll have next weekend."

Jewel laughed and we all clinked our glasses against his. We sipped them as we ambled back to the market and drifted around for a while. Soon enough, Brittany and Scott meandered off on their own again and Jewel turned to face me.

"So, uh, what is this?"

I frowned, staring into those warm, honey eyes and wondering what on earth she was talking about. "Lemonade?"

Lifting her free hand, she pointed back and forth between us. "This."

I wasn't sure what she was getting at and she sighed, a little bit exasperated but still smiling. "Was it just a kiss? You know, a fun, heat of the moment, doesn't mean anything kiss or..." She trailed off, her eyes twinkling before she widened them at me. "Was it like, a *kiss* kiss?"

"A *kiss* kiss?" *God, since when are there so many different kisses? Isn't every kiss a* kiss *kiss?*

She rolled her eyes as she bumped her hip into mine. "You know what I mean. Don't play dumb."

I chuckled. "It was a kiss, Jewel. A *real* kiss. That's the only kind I'm familiar with and that was one I've been thinking about for days."

"It was?" She stopped walking and came to stand in front of me, staring up into my eyes and appearing to be debating something in her head before she came out and just asked me. "What does it mean, then? Do you just go around kissing people like that all the time, or does it mean there's something here?"

"There's something here," I replied without hesitation, my gaze unwavering on hers. "Look, I'll level with you, Jewel. I've never been a big fan of labels. I don't think everything needs to fit into some tidy little box for it to make sense."

"What are you a fan of?" she asked cautiously. "I get not wanting to label everything. I'm totally onboard with that, but I just need to know where we stand right now."

"I'm a fan of chasing good feelings, and of you. I know I want to kiss you again, but that's about as clear as I can be right now."

"That's fine. It's a satisfying enough answer for now, but I need to warn you that I don't play games. I'm a woman, not a girl, and I don't do drama."

"Well, that makes me like you even more," I admitted honestly, reaching up to wind a lock of her soft hair around my index finger. "Other than ring toss, I don't play games either, Jewel. I'm too old and I've got a kid to think about. I've also had enough drama in my past relationships to cover my bases for a lifetime, so you don't have to worry about that with me."

As far as I was concerned, this was shaping up to be a pretty amazing summer. *Thank you, Walt. You wise old man.*

Jewel leaned into my touch for a moment, then nodded and stepped away, inclining her head toward the bandstand. "Good. I'm glad we had that talk. Do you want to go check on Colten?"

"Please," I said, falling into step beside her as we tracked down the boys.

Colt was surrounded by a gaggle of kids, all wearing glowsticks around their wrists, ankles, and necks. When he saw us approaching, he ran up to me with the widest, easiest smile I'd seen on his face since kindergarten.

"Can I go play down at the lake shore with the other kids?" he asked excitedly. "I was just going to come find you to ask."

I eyed the group behind him, all of them laughing as they waited for something. Probably for those who needed to get permission to get it.

I glanced at Jewel and she gave me a reassuring smile. "It's safe down there. There are lights on the main stretch of beach at night and there are always families who choose to take their food from here and go have a picnic on the sand."

Exhaling softly, I nodded at Colten. "Sure. Go. Just make sure you stay on the main stretch of the beach then, okay? I want to be able to keep an eye on you the whole time. Have you had something to eat?"

"You got it, and yes, I have. I had a burger with Brody earlier. Did you eat?"

I nodded. "I did, bud. Go have fun with your friends."

Colten dashed back to his friends, handing out high-fives when he told them he could go. They waited a few more minutes for one other boy to join them before they all took off.

At a run.

God knew where they got all that energy from. I, for one, would not have had it in me after the day we'd had to run right then, but I also wasn't ten. Jewel smiled as if she'd had the same thought as we watched them disappear.

"You've got to wonder how their batteries are always fully charged," she said, shaking her head and wrapping her arms around herself. "I wish I could always run-run-run like that, but I don't think I ever could. Not even at their age."

I chuckled. "I don't remember being quite as bad as they are either, but I guess we had to have been, right? Are you cold? I've got a jacket in the truck."

"Nah, I'll be fine once we get back to the market. Have you tried the salted caramel doughnuts? I love them. They're my favorite dessert here."

I would have preferred to have *her* for dessert, but I also wasn't about to proposition her for a quickie in the woods or in my truck, so doughnuts would have to do. "I love caramel, so we have that in common. You're sure Colten and the boys are safe down there?"

"They should be," she said before she flashed a sneaky smile. "As it happens though, I know about a bench that overlooks the main beach. It's usually empty at night and they won't be able to see us there unless they know to look."

"You're a genius." I grinned. "Doughnuts are on me. Do you want to get another lemonade as well?"

She nodded. "I like the way you think as well."

We got back to the market and I noticed that the mood had shifted. The music was still playing, but it was like there was a sudden tension in the air. Stall owners weren't grinning and chatting to people, mostly because people didn't seem to be lingering at any of the stalls. Eyes were downturned and everyone seemed subdued. I couldn't quite put my finger on it at first, but soon enough, I located the black cloud casting its shadow over the festivities.

Dallas Styles had arrived, looking smug as ever as he strode through the market like he owned the place. His attention almost immediately landed on Jewel. She groaned and glanced up at me. "Well, this was fun while it lasted. Cut straight through from here to the beach and you'll see the bench on your right. I'll see you at the lake tomorrow."

Before I'd even begun to figure out what was going on, she slipped away through the crowd, vanishing.

Dallas came up to me. "Where did Jewel go?"

I shrugged. "I'm not sure. She said something about grabbing some food."

Which was in the opposite direction that she'd gone. Dallas took the bait, spinning around and taking off to look for her in the wrong part of the market. I didn't know why she had literally run from him, but it was obvious she hadn't wanted to speak to the man. I didn't blame her.

Disappointed that we hadn't gotten to eat doughnuts together in a place no one would've seen us if they hadn't known to look, I sighed and strolled through the market, apparently destined to eat my dessert alone.

26

JEWEL

The Lake Warrior contest was one of my favorite days of the summer. I arrived on the sandy shore, prepared with a clipboard and a sign-up sheet, as well as extra sunblock, towels, and a first-aid kit. Just in case.

I always volunteered to help out with the contest. It was a good time. I joined some other locals who were setting up a registration tent in the shade. Sliding my sunglasses to the top of my head, I set down the supplies I'd brought and smiled at the others. "What can I do to help?"

Verna grinned at me as she motioned to a cooler packed with cold waters. "Have one of those and make sure to stay hydrated today. It's a scorcher and it's not even ten a.m. yet. We need to take care of ourselves before we can take care of anyone else."

I chuckled and grabbed a water. Keeping it with me, I went to help her organize the sign-up sheets we'd already received. Working with people I'd known most of my life as well as a few other newcomers, I helped set up for the event. Excitement thrummed through me as the starting time grew nearer.

I loved this event and I volunteered to help out every summer so that we could keep it going. It was a lot of work, but the fun we had every year made it more than worth it. With many hands pitching in, we were completely done with the preparations by the time people started trickling in.

I took my place behind the registration table, giving the contestants their wristbands with their number on it. Already having a blast, I was laughing and talking smack with some of the other competitors about Scott's records when Landon and Colten arrived.

Both seemed apprehensive in their boardshorts and T-shirts. I waved them over. "Come get your wristbands, boys."

Colten raced over to me, proudly presenting his wrist with a huge grin on his face. "I'm going to dominate today. The guys have told me all about it and I'm ready."

I chuckled as I fastened his wristband. "All that matters is that you have fun. Don't worry too much about winning. Enjoying the day is a good victory by itself."

He shrugged, glancing at where Brody, Cole, and a few of the other kids had gathered by the paddle boards. "Maybe that's true, but I'm still going to try."

Turning to his dad, he pointed out his friends and waited for permission before he jogged over to them.

Landon smiled at me. "I cannot explain to you how good it feels to see him having so much fun with those kids. Can you believe that I never even realized how alone he was?"

"Life is busy," I said. "Give yourself a break. At least he's got them now and it's helping him build confidence before you guys go home." I picked up his wristband. "Here you go. I need to put it on for you to make sure you don't swap it out with someone else."

"Why would I do that?" he asked, those vivid green eyes hooking on mine. "It's all just for fun, isn't it? Why would anybody try and cheat?"

I chuckled. "Because saying that the Lake Warrior contest is just for fun is like saying the Super Bowl is just another football game. People around here take it seriously."

Shifting on his feet to take a good look around, he arched his eyebrows and nodded slowly, clearly having noticed the team huddles and all the lone wolves like Scott warming up on the beach. "Why did you just tell Colten not to worry about winning, then?"

"He's good," I said, shrugging. "For the kids, it should just be about having fun. If you ask me, that's what it should be about for everyone, but like I said, our local contestants take it super seriously. Will you just give your arm, please?"

Chuckling, he waved me off and shook his head. "Nah, I'm fine, thanks. I'm just going to watch. I didn't sign up, but I can always help you out here if there's anything you need me to do?"

I laughed and circled his wrist with my fingers, gently strapping the wristband onto him. "Oh, no you're not. We've got things covered here and you're new in town. Everyone and their mother has been talking about whooping your butt out there on the water and showing you how we do things here in June Lake."

He winced. "Now I'm even less inclined."

Colten had run back over to us, catching the last part of our conversation. "Come on, Dad. Be brave and make friends. It's your turn now."

"Well, I guess I can't argue with that," he said, rubbing his finger over his wristband as he glanced at his son. "I thought you were with the kids?"

"I was, but they said I had to come find out from Jewel whose team I'm on for the Beach Ball Relay."

I grabbed my clipboard and scanned the page for the teams of the first event before I smiled at him. "You're in luck. It looks like Brody asked for you to be on his team with his mom, Scott, and a few of the other kids."

"Great." He beamed at me. "What happens after that? Do I need to get any other team assignments?"

"Nope. The teams remain the same for all the events they signed up for." I checked the clipboard again. "Landon, your first event is Paddle Board Jousting. The challengers will be posted for it while they're busy with the Beach Balls Relay. "

"Excellent," he said dryly, glancing at the mountain of paddle boards waiting near the water. "What else will we be doing?"

"Colten's team got signed up for Catch the Flags as well and that will happen after Paddle Board Jousting, though I think Brad will be taking Scott's place on the team for that one." At the confused look that crossed Colten's features, I gave him a reassuring smile. "It's a great game, I promise. It's just like an outdoor version of musical chairs."

"Okay," he said."

"After that, we have the Best Belly Flop, which is from the diving board on the floating dock, and then we have the race, so basically just seeing who's the fastest swimming to the dock and back. You have to run up the shore to touch the lake sign and whoever is there first wins."

"Right," Landon said slowly.

Colten clapped him on the back. "Don't worry, Dad. It's just for fun. I'm going back to my team now, but I'll see you around. Good luck!"

Landon glanced at me and groaned. "This is going to hurt, isn't it?"

"Just a little bit," I teased, then turned to help some other people with their wristbands. Landon joined Scott with his warm-ups.

Loud cheers rang out when Verna's son, the emcee for the day, called the contestants closer for the first event, the Beach Ball Relay. Scott joined Samantha, Brody, Colten, and the others while Landon came to stand with me to watch them.

With the summery scent of sunblock in the air and Verna's son whipping the crowd into an excited frenzy, the contest got underway. Landon watched from beside me, sending me a questioning look as Scott and Samantha laughed with the kids.

"Isn't she his ex?" he asked quietly. "I remember you saying Brody's mom used to date Scott and that's how you knew he was a cool kid to introduce Colten to?"

"Yeah, but they're on friendly terms. They formed this team with the kids back when they were together, and they've kept it going every year even though they broke up ages ago."

"How does Brittany feel about that?"

I smiled. "It's sweet of you to care, but she doesn't mind. Everyone around here knows that there's nothing going on between Scott and Sam anymore. They just both love the contest and their team got pretty notorious back in the day, so they've kept it going for the kids' sake."

"In that case, Brittany is a better person than me," he said. "I wouldn't have liked it if you participated in this with an ex."

A warm tingle ran through me. "Jealous?"

"I would've been, yeah," he admitted, but before I could tell him the same thing, I got called away to post the challengers for the Paddle Board Jousting.

A grin spread on my face when I discovered that Landon would be going up against Scott. He'd walked with me to check the postings and he sighed. "Let me guess, your brother is crazy good at this?"

I reached out to clap on his ridiculously hard shoulder, enjoying being able to touch him even if it was just casual and quick. "Let's just say that I'm going to wish you luck and that you're going to need it. Scott has won this the last four summers in a row."

Landon groaned again. "That's just great. I apologize in advance for the fool I'm about to make of myself."

I chuckled, and Scott came over once his team was done with the first event. "Oh, cool. We're going up against each other, huh? Good luck, man."

"Thanks," he muttered. "Have you got any tips for me on how to knock you down?"

Scott picked up a paddle board and offered it to Landon before he got another for himself. "That depends. Have you ever been on a paddle board before?"

"No," Landon said as they headed down to the lake with their boards and paddles in hand. I accompanied them, listening as Scott chuckled but tried to help Landon anyway.

"Have you ever been on *any* board before?" he asked.

Landon gave him a one-shouldered shrug. "I'm decent at snowboarding and wakeboarding, but this is new territory for me."

"Ever surfed?" Scott asked.

Landon shook his head. "I tried once when I was kid. Wiped out real bad and decided to try something else instead."

My brother laughed. "I'll take it easy on your then, Mr. Big City. Good luck, okay? I'll see you out there."

"Why do I feel like I'm about to suffer a serious head injury?" he joked to me as he watched Scott high-fiving a bunch of people while he ran into the water.

"You'll be fine," I said, but when he stripped off his shirt, I realized that while it might be true for him, it certainly wasn't true for me.

My heart couldn't handle seeing him slowly peel off the fabric that had been hiding his delicious abs from view, and all the moisture disappeared from my mouth to go south as I ran my gaze over the ropes of toned muscle in his back.

"Want me to hold that for you?" I offered, clearing my throat when I heard how breathy my voice was.

Thankfully, he didn't seem to have noticed, giving me a grateful smile as he handed over his shirt and then picked up the paddle board again. Without any further conversation, he strode toward the water and I admired his sun-bronzed skin and those abs, certain that every woman on the beach behind me was doing the very same thing.

27

LANDON

Paddle boarding was not snowboarding. Or wakeboarding. Water wasn't nearly as firm as ice, and with no boat helping me to maintain my balance, it was all on me—and I was not good at it.

As I ducked Scott's assault, a wave swelled beneath me and rocked me right off my feet. I hit the water with a splash and grunted when I broke the surface. The announcer was saying that had been round one.

Which meant I had to get back on the damn board and try again. Since getting back on was no easy feat, I tried to do it gracefully, but the thing kept flipping over as I put my weight on it. Scott laughed, giving me some pointers so I wouldn't look like a fish out of water, flopping around.

"That's it, Landon," he encouraged.

I wobbled but managed to slide my butt onto the board. From there, I rose slowly, ignoring the crowd chanting Scott's name from the shore. Sunlight glinted off the water behind him, nearly blinding me as he lifted his paddle again. I wobbled a bit more as I tried to reach for my own.

Cursing under my breath, I'd barely risen to my full height when

Scott's paddle crashed into mine. I tried my best to put up a fight, but it didn't last long.

Once again, I landed with an enormous splash, this time in no rush to surface once I went under. Instead, I swam down a little deeper, giving myself a minute to hide from the crowd.

I was getting my butt handed to me up there and that wasn't something I was particularly used to. While I was okay with losing at Paddle Board Jousting, it still sucked to do it in front of so many people.

In front of Jewel.

But I knew I had to keep going—be a good sport about it—so I got back up and let him knock me down. Again.

"That's three times in a row for Scott Pendleton, folks," the announcer roared over the microphone. "Victory is Scott's once again! What a show put on by Mr. Landon Payne, but our champ remains undefeated."

I chuckled as I sliced through the water back to my board, exhausted and beyond relieved that it was over. Scott paddled over to me and offered his hand to help pull me up. "That was a good effort, man. For your first time on a paddle board, I'm impressed."

I nodded and smiled. "Make sure to tell everyone else how impressive I was. I doubt they share your opinion."

He laughed. "A few more years of practice and you might just have me."

"Just a few more years, huh?" I scoffed down laughter, shaking my head at him. "I think that was it for my Paddle Board Jousting career. Thanks, but you can have it."

I accepted his help and let him get me back on the damn board for the last time.

"Hey, I've been practicing all my life. Jewel and I grew up doing this," he said happily as we headed back to shore. "She's pretty good herself, actually. Took herself out of the running when she volunteered to help, but she won a few times back in her day."

"Really?" I couldn't quite imagine her trying to knock someone down instead of helping them up, but the woman was full of surprises. Plus, I was really starting to believe there wasn't much she couldn't do—except for cooking, of course. I shivered at the memory.

When we got close enough to the beach, Scott found his feet and walked out of the water with me. "Yeah, she was good as a teen. We still do it for fun when I'm practicing, but it's been a long time since she's been out here for the contest. She thinks it's better to be helping than to be competing."

"Well, someone's got to do it." When kids with camera phones came running up to us, I shook his hand for pictures. Then he started up the beach. "Is that it for us for the day?"

His blond eyebrows jumped and he laughed, his head shaking as he checked his watch. "You've got about forty minutes before the next event starts. Rest up. I'll see you soon."

Sliding his paddle board under his arm, he strode over to the kids, even good-naturedly signing a few autographs and taking some more selfies with them before he went to return the board. I couldn't believe what I was seeing, but I supposed Jewel had told me the Lake Warrior contest was this town's summer Super Bowl.

I guess that makes Scott a rock star around here.

Chuckling as I made my way around them, I searched for Jewel. She was busy with some of the other locals. Colten was with Brody and Cole, playing in the water behind the dock while they waited for their event.

With nothing else to do, I returned my paddle board to the pile and spread out my towel near the water, deciding that I'd watch the other jousting competitors. It turned out that watching the contest was a lot more fun than participating in it, and I genuinely enjoyed seeing Scott progress from round to round.

In the end, the victors competed and then it was down to the two winners, Scott and another sturdy local. I was on my feet with the rest of the crowd, watching gleefully as Scott kicked that guy's ass too. *At least it means it's not just me.*

Clouds drifted overhead as the morning wore on, but they disappeared by the time noon rolled around. Baking in the sun, I stretched out on my towel, completely forgetting that I had another event lined up until the announcer called that it was time for the Belly Flop contest.

I groaned. *I'm really not looking forward to this.*

I got up anyway though, determined to see this thing through now that I'd started. When I'd arrived here this morning, I'd had no idea what to expect, but I'd been convinced I wouldn't be competing.

Mostly, I'd come because Jewel had seemed excited about it, and Colten had been pretty stoked too after his day with the other kids. Sighing, I dusted sand off my ass and waded into the water with the other adults who were competing. Taking a deep breath, I swam out to the dock.

Since no one seemed to be racing to get there first, I took it slowly, appreciating the cool water on my hot skin after all that time in the sun.

"Are you Landon?"

I blinked hard at the sound of my name spoken by a voice I didn't recognize. Twisting in the water, I tried to figure out who had spoken.

An older woman behind me smiled kindly. Probably around mid-sixties, she had wrinkles around her eyes but something about the look in the clear blue orbs told me she still had plenty of mischief in her.

"I am. How did you know my name?"

She let out a burst of laughter and grabbed the side of the dock when we reached it to keep herself from going under. "Everyone knows your name, honey. You're staying in the Styles Manor. It's not often we have guests in town who stay there for as long as you are. Half of us were sure it was haunted. You've gotten all the old tongues wagging."

"Well, I promise it isn't haunted," I said, chuckling as I pulled myself up on the dock. "Are you competing in the Belly Flop competition?"

I didn't want to sound rude, but I had no idea what a woman her age was doing out here with the rest of us who were insane enough to compete in this thing. Her eyes sparkled with mirth, and she had a smirk on her lips as she extended her hand for me to help her.

I took it and gently helped her up. We joined the rest of the contestants in a haphazard line forming. "Of course, I'm competing. I do it every year. My grandkids get a real kick out of it."

My eyebrows swept up. "Here I was thinking I was brave for honoring my commitment to do it."

She chuckled, slicking her graying hair back as she winked at me. "Watch and learn, honey. Watch and learn."

"Got any tips for me?" I asked hopefully.

She grinned. "This event is more about the crowd and putting on a show than it is about best belly flop. Trust me."

With that, she turned away from me and strode directly to the front of the line. She tapped a few people on the shoulder and they made way for her, everyone motioning for her to go ahead. As I watched, she marched confidently to the diving board, climbed up, and threw her arms out to her sides before she dipped into a deep bow.

Cheers erupted from the shore. With a smile, she straightened up, turned toward the water, and extended her arms to her sides once more. Then she plummeted in without any hesitation whatsoever. She landed with a massive smack and I winced, my breath catching as I waited for her to come up.

Jeez, that has to sting.

She broke the surface with her arms raised above her head triumphantly, a grimace on her lips that quickly became a smile. More cheers broke out. People whistled and screamed for her as she swam back to the dock, holding it for a minute to catch her breath.

"Are you okay?" I asked, genuinely concerned for this woman I'd only met a few minutes ago. "Are your organs still in the right place?"

"It's not so bad," she said as she glanced up at me. "You'll be fine. Good luck."

The next few people ahead of me took their turns. Each of them had glaring red bellies when they emerged from the lake. After slowly making my way to the diving board, I reached the front and climbed up with a pounding heart.

"How did I get talked into this?" I muttered under my breath, looking out at the shore where at least two hundred people were watching.

Colten was cheering me on from a spot right at the water's edge with Jewel beside him. She clapped her hands and waved when she saw me look their way. I waved back and reluctantly turned toward the water. *How the hell am I supposed to make this showy?*

The remaining contestants behind me were already getting impatient, grumbling for me to "get flopping already" as they shifted on their feet, preparing to move forward once I'd taken the plunge. Knowing I was out of time, I turned and leaped backward off the board, landing with my arms crossed over my chest.

The slap of my back against the water echoed in my ears. My skin stung and my lungs froze for a moment. It hurt like a bitch, but when I surfaced, the crowd was roaring with applause and that made the burn worth it.

I grinned as I raised my fists above my head, mimicking my new, older friend. I cast a smug look at the others before swimming back to shore. Colten raced into the water to meet me. He dove in once he was at hip height, shaking with laughter.

"That was awesome!" he yelled above the din of applause for the next contestant. "So cool, Dad. I'm sure you're going to win."

Snaking my arms out ahead of me under the water, I reached for him and tossed him over my shoulder. He laughed as I tickled his ribs. "Really? Do you think so?"

"I do!" he squealed, fighting to free himself until I finally let go, rolling him off me to let him land in the water once more.

He was still raving about my back flop when we reached the shore, and Jewel and Scott were there to congratulate me. He smirked as he extended his hand toward me. "That was pretty good for a city boy."

Jewel nodded her agreement, her brown eyes bright and happy as she smiled up at me. "The final contest starts soon. You may want to drink some water and take a break before it does. Your back must really be hurting you right now, but that's not getting you out of the competition."

My back really was hurting me, but the sting was slowly subsiding, leaving more of a singing heat in its wake. Instead of admitting that to her though, I nodded and slung an arm around Colten's shoulders. "We'll be ready. Paynes don't give up. See you soon."

Guiding Colten away from them, I felt her eyes on us as we strode toward the coolers lining the top end of the beach. I smiled. There was no way I was going to win the title of Lake Warrior, but I'd shown her today that I could be a good sport.

Plus, Colten was having a blast, which was even more important. He was opening up and embracing new experiences way outside of his comfort zone. So was I.

Overall, I'd suffered for it, but it was shaping up to be another great day in paradise.

28

JEWEL

Proud of Landon for giving it his all, I hung the cheesy third place medal around his neck. We'd borrowed a tiered platform from the elementary school, and even though he was on the lowest step, it'd elevated him enough that I was face-to-chest with his naked torso, and oh man, it was giving me naughty thoughts as I straightened the medal and took a step back.

The crowd behind me was going wild, hollering and wolf-whistling as the emcee congratulated the winners of the day, but I was barely aware of any of it. It felt like my entire world had narrowed on the broad chest and defined, golden abs of the man in front of me. They were rippling as he laughed at something someone had said, his head tipped back to expose and elongate his strong neck.

It was good to see him laughing with everyone. He was warming up to the town and they were warming up right back. But even that thought didn't break me out of the haze of lust I'd fallen into. I wasn't usually so prone to being consumed by my baser desires, but my attraction to Landon was off the charts. It was next-level stuff and I couldn't help it—nor did I want to.

"That's it for your annual Lake Warrior contest, folks. Thanks for coming out and remember not to go anywhere just yet. The grills are going to be fired up soon and we've got live music coming your way in just a minute, so relax, have fun, and we'll see you all next year!"

As the emcee left the makeshift stage and the band took his place, the winners stepped off the platform and Scott clapped Landon on the back. "Congratulations, man. I don't think we've ever had a newbie on the winner's stand before."

Landon chuckled. "I should be the one congratulating you. First place, huh? I can't say it was unexpected, but well done."

Scott laughed, but he gave Landon a nonchalant shrug as they moved closer to me. "It helps that I do a lot of this stuff on a regular basis. Maybe if you come a bit earlier next year, we can get in some practice and you might stand a chance."

Landon made a noncommittal sound in the back of his throat as he glanced at my brother. "I wouldn't want to dethrone Mr. Lake Warrior himself."

Scott shot him a cocky grin. "I'm always open to some healthy competition. It motivates me. Hey, what's that on your hand?"

Landon turned his hand as Scott asked the question, inspecting the flesh under his little finger before he shrugged. "Oh, it's nothing. I cut myself on the dock earlier."

My heart fluttered in my chest. "I'll get the first-aid kit. That dock isn't the cleanest thing to nick yourself on."

He tried to stop me, but I shot him a look over my shoulder. "I brought a first-aid kit for a reason. Now shut up and let me use it."

Scott laughed, but Landon rolled his eyes before he smiled at me. "Sure thing, Nurse Jewel."

As I walked away, I heard Colten ask Landon if he could go back to his friends, and not a second later, the boy raced past me in the direction of where Brody and some of the others were getting ready for a game of flag football.

The familiar strains of "Brown-Eyed Girl" filled the air as I headed to the registration tent. More and more people settled down around it for the cookout. Knowing my town as well as I did, I knew the festivities would last well into the evening. The contest was only the beginning of the day for most.

Verna was at the registration tent when I got there, packing up the paperwork with a lemonade in her hand as she swayed to the beat of the music. I smiled, glancing around for the first-aid kit and not seeing it anywhere.

"That was a good one, huh?" I asked as I approached her. "I think we can chalk it up as a success."

"A definite success." She returned my smile and waved me away. "And I've got this. Ben and the others will be breaking down the tent in the morning and I'm just taking care of the stuff that can't sleep here. Go ahead and have fun. You worked hard today."

"Thanks, I will, but I was looking for the first-aid kit? Do you happen to know where it went?"

She nodded toward a group of kids sitting on the rocks with adults clamoring around them. "Lacey and her friends were using the paddles for some rock jousting and there was an incident. They're fine. Just some skinned knees apparently, but I'm afraid the kit is in use at the moment."

I glanced at the kids again, my heart aching for them, but I knew they were in good hands. "Skinned knees are the worst. Especially the next day. Thanks, Verna. I'll see you later."

"See you later, honey." She smiled and I left, making my way back to the others as a loose idea started forming in my head.

When I reached my brother, Brittany, and Landon, I shot them a tight smile. "Someone else has already got the first-aid kit. Do you guys mind watching Colten while I take Landon to my place to clean him up? We really need to—"

"It's not a big deal," he started saying, but I leaned in and gave my head a firm shake.

"Hush," I said softly before looking back at Scott and Brittany. "That cut really needs to be cleaned. Do you mind?"

Brittany flashed me a knowing smile but shook her head. "We'll keep an eye on him. Take your time and clean him up properly. We wouldn't want it getting infected."

Scott winced, glancing at a healed scar on the back of his own hand. "She's right. Just listen to them, bro. I didn't and it wasn't fun."

He was totally exaggerating the extent of his injury. I remembered when he'd gotten it and it'd been mildly infected for a few days, but it really hadn't been bad at all. Since he was playing into my plan though, I didn't call him out on it. I simply nodded as I took Landon's arm.

"Colten will be fine here with them. Trust me when I tell you that no one is going anywhere for a long time and we'll be back soon. My place is right across the road."

"Okay," he agreed eventually, glancing at Brittany. "There's sunscreen in his backpack."

"I got it," she said, giving him a reassuring smile as I started dragging him away. "We've got this. Don't worry. Just go let Jewel check you out and don't rush back."

As Landon turned, she winked at me and I blushed a little, grateful that they were going to look after Colten but a little embarrassed that she knew what I was planning. Either way, I took him back to my place and quickly got him all fixed up, but that wasn't what I'd brought him there for.

Standing in front of him, I stuck on a band-aid, not letting go of his hand as my eyes moved up to his. "You know, I thought it was really sexy that you were willing to make an ass of yourself out there in front of a bunch of strangers."

He chuckled. "And here I thought I looked cool."

"Third place isn't half bad," I murmured, gaze still fixed on his as I took a tiny step into him. "Maybe you deserve more than just some tacky medal."

A slight crease appeared between his brows, but he caught on quick, arching a playful eyebrow at me. He put his hands on my hips and moved me with him as he took a step back and sat down on the sofa behind him.

I planted my knees on either side of his hips and straddled him as I took his face in my hands. Wrapping his arms around my waist, he dipped his head back. His eyes drifted to my lips just a moment before I lowered my head and sealed them over his.

Landon groaned, holding me to him. He wound a hand into my hair and tightened his fist around the strands. A tingle of pleasure raced through me, my nipples hardening and goosebumps raising all the little hairs on my body.

I kissed him harder, trying to make it clear that I wanted more than just a kiss this time. He responded with another groan, and his tongue slid out to lick at the seam of my lips. I parted them for him, my arms around his neck.

The scent of sunscreen filled the air around us and his skin was hot from a day in the sun. I knew even in that moment that I was never going to be able to smell that scent again and not think of this day and how I'd been more turned on than ever before.

The space between my legs was slick and aching and my body yearned for more. He flipped us over and laid me down on the sofa. Then he covered my body with his own, holding some of his weight but pressing me into the cushions nonetheless.

Making out furiously, I arched my hips and rolled them against the length of him, so pronounced in his swim trunks that there might as well have been nothing between us. The slip-slide of the fabric was messing with the friction though, not allowing nearly enough of it, and a frustrated moan escaped from me.

Landon shuddered in response. Speaking between furious kisses, he ran a palm along my side, cupping my ribs and flexing his fingers on my skin. "Where's your bedroom?"

"Not far," I replied breathlessly, loathing that I had to break the kiss to do it but sitting up anyway. Instead of saying anything else, I took his hand and led him around the privacy screen that separated the living room and my bedroom in the small studio.

His eyes were on mine, and he used his grip on my hand to twirl me again, bringing me back with a smack into his chest. Then he kissed me again. I wrapped my arms around his neck, stumbled to my bed, and toppled him down on it with me.

I knew we didn't have that much time. Scott, Brittany, and Colten would be waiting for us to get back, but I also knew that they wouldn't be counting the minutes that we were gone. The party was bound to be picking up by now. They would have plenty to distract them.

I was too caught in the moment to care that we were missing it.

For weeks now, Landon and I had been all but ignoring the intense attraction between us, and I wasn't a fool. I knew we probably wouldn't get another opportunity to be together. At least not anytime soon.

So while I had this chance, I let myself be consumed by it, making the most of every last second we had together before I had to let him go.

29

LANDON

Despite knowing we didn't have all day, I took my time with Jewel, savoring every inch of her and committing her to memory. She was incredible, and while I hadn't expected this to happen when we'd come back to her place, I was more than ready to go when she pulled me down on the bed with her.

Harder than I'd been in a long time, I reached for my fly and yanked open the velcro, needing some space before I came in my pants simply because of the friction they were creating. Jewel moaned when she realized what I was doing. Her hands ran down the length of my back before she helped me push the pants off.

I kicked them away, glad I hadn't put a shirt back on, but then I slowed things all the way down, catching her wrist and pressing a quick kiss to it when she tried to reach for me. She frowned, but when I moved my head to her neck and started placing open-mouthed kisses on her throat, she relaxed again.

"Not yet," I murmured against her coconut-scented skin. "If you touch me right now..."

"I know what you mean," she replied in a breathy whisper. A soft moan slid out of her as I ran my hand to the waistband of her bikini bottoms.

It turned out that hooking up fresh out of a lake was a pretty fucking awesome idea. Neither of us had been wearing very much, having rushed just across the street to her apartment to "get my hand cleaned up" without bothering to stop to put on the rest of our clothes.

Dipping my fingers into the fabric, I ran them along the space between her hips, relishing every moan and tremble as she started rocking slightly. I slid off her just enough to give myself the access I needed. Then I brought my mouth back to hers, taking it in a searing kiss that quickly turned us into a writhing mess.

Pleasure rocketed through me with every rub against her leg, but I flexed my thigh muscles and focused on her instead. I slipped my hands all the way into her bikini bottoms and tugged them off. I tried to brace myself for the moment I would finally get to touch her, but when it came, I realized that nothing I could've done would've prepared me for it.

As soon as my fingertips slid between her folds, I kissed her harder, losing whatever part of me had been holding back. Hot and silky smooth, she was perfect and so wet that I nearly tossed all my plans aside.

But no, if I did that and I thrust into her right then, this would all be over in a minute and I didn't want that. I clawed back my self-control and dipped my fingers into her. She mewled. Her legs parted further as my hand moved in and out of her. My thumb found her hard clit and drew circles around it.

All the while, I kissed her deeply, using one hand to anchor her hips to the bed when they threatened to fly off. Her muscles started to contract around my fingers and I groaned, squeezing my eyes shut even tighter to stave off my own orgasm when hers hit.

She screamed into my mouth, spasming under me while her nails dug into my back. I kept going until she was spent. Then I slowed the kiss and waited for her to come back down to earth, but I never let go of her.

Jewel was still panting when she opened her eyes, flicking her gaze to her nightstand. "There are condoms in the drawer."

Thank. Fuck.

Nodding tightly, I rolled over and grabbed one. I'd never been this desperate to get inside someone. My entire tip was shiny with my own wetness as I pinched the latex and deftly covered myself in it.

When I was done, Jewel's eyes found mine. Her arms and her legs opened for me as I moved back to her. Her fingers pushed into my hair. She kissed me gently when she settled underneath me, angling her hips and lifting them to encourage me to sink into her.

Way beyond the point of needing encouragement, I propped my weight on my elbows and broke the kiss to look at her. Then I pushed inside. Since I didn't want to hurt her, I didn't thrust. I managed to slide into her slowly, even if it almost fucking killed me.

The condom did nothing to dull the heat of her. Her tight channel squeezed around me as I sank inside. I groaned and bit my lip as I watched her eyelids grow heavy and a shiver run through her. Once I was fully seated, she squirmed underneath me, pressing her lips to mine once more and whispering between tender kisses.

"I'm okay, Landon. Move. Now, please."

I claimed her lips with my own, kissing her passionately as I finally allowed my hips to do what they wanted to. Withdrawing from her, I thrust in harder the next time, finding a rhythm and losing myself to it, but I never stopped kissing her.

With every deep thrust, I got so much closer. My spine tingled and my orgasm raced toward me. Thankfully, Jewel seemed to be right there with me, moaning into my mouth and shaking. Her muscles contracted around me once more.

"Oh, Landon! I'm—" She never finished her sentence.

I didn't need her to. "Come for me, Jewel. Come all over my cock."

As if she'd waited for me to say it, she went off like a shot. I slammed into her one last time before I surrendered and my climax exploded out of me. Groaning, I came so hard that my vision went black and my brain lost communication with my legs. I was spent.

We collapsed together on her bed, breathing hard as we clung to each other like we would somehow float away if we stopped. Immediately, I wished that we could just stay right there for the rest of the summer. I never wanted to leave her bed.

Despite the fact that I'd just had arguably the best sex of my life, we were probably going to have to leave here sooner rather than later. Just not this second. Her head was on my chest and my arm was draped around her. It felt right. She was something my life had been missing, and leaving the bed would be like walking away from heaven.

I indulged until the worried voice in the back of my head started shouting at me to move. I shut my eyes and groaned, then turned my head to face hers and planted a soft kiss on her hair.

"We should probably get going soon," I murmured. "Not that I want to."

She nodded against me but didn't move at all outside of that. "In a minute."

I chuckled. "Maybe two."

Burrowing into me, she nodded again, sighing softly. I opened my eyes and found myself staring at a bunch of suncatchers against her ceiling. *How did I miss that before?*

Presumably because I'd been completely focused on her. It shouldn't have come as such a surprise that I was only seeing her room for the first time now. The space was small but cozy, with her double bed against the wall and a wardrobe on the other.

Thin curtains hung in her window, and the suncatchers refracted light all over the place in rainbows and prisms. While her furniture was basic, antique-looking wood, and her bedding was a clean, crisp white, the suncatchers made the space seem almost magical, like I'd stepped into a secret, mystical world, and I fucking loved it.

I'd never imagined these little masterpieces when she'd called making them a simple hobby. Captivated by the detail, I found myself wanting to take a closer look, so I stood up to inspect them, buck-ass naked and not giving a damn.

Jewel chuckled and turned onto her stomach, propping her chin up on her elbows as her gaze tracked me around the room. "You just go ahead and take a look around. I'll be here, admiring the view."

I glanced at her over my shoulder and gave my ass a playful smack. "Ogle me all you want. I'll even put on a little show for you. As long as you promise you're still making Colten one of these."

"I am." She smiled and nodded at the dresser. "The one on the left is for him."

Several unfinished suncatchers were on the dresser. I moved toward it, picking up the one she'd mentioned. As I looked at it, I realized that a bunch of the dangling bits were chess pieces and my eyes widened.

"Oh wow." My voice was a little rougher than usual when I realized how much thought she'd put into it. "This is amazing. He's going to love it."

"I hope so," she said.

"I know so." I turned back to her, my gaze locking on hers, and I tried to speak past the depth of emotion within me at the thought of what she'd done for a boy she hardly even knew. "I know so because it will make him think of you every time the sun catches it."

She giggled. "You're a bit of a romantic, aren't you, Mr. Big City?"

I shook my head, snorting as I tried to hold back laughter. After gently putting the suncatcher down on the dresser once more, I returned to her bed and sighed. "I used to be a romantic, but I lost that part of myself a long time ago."

Those beautiful eyes searched mine for a moment. "Can I ask you something?"

I nodded. "Sure. Anything you want to know."

After the sex we'd just had, I couldn't deny that I felt more connected to her than ever before, and I knew it would probably wear off as the endorphins did, but for now, I was happy to answer any questions she might have.

"Did Colten's mother have anything to do with that?"

Again, I nodded. I never liked talking about my ex, but with Jewel, no subject felt too heavy or too difficult. Especially not right then.

Looking right into her eyes, I didn't blame her for being curious but I needed her to know that Kaitlin wasn't in the picture at all. "I, uh, I'm not proud of this, but his mother was actually a one-night stand. Six weeks later, she called to tell me she was pregnant."

Jewel's teeth sank into her lower lip as sympathy softened her eyes. "That must've been one heck of a surprise."

"It was," I admitted. "I gave her my number the next morning in case she wanted to hook up again, not for, well, you know." I blew out a breath through my nostrils and gripped the nape of my neck. "I dropped everything to be there for her and supported her through the pregnancy. We decided to give things a try for the baby's sake, so I moved her in with me. I knew we didn't have the most conventional start, but I figured we'd work it out."

"I'm guessing you didn't?" she asked, eyes moving from one of mine to the other.

"No, we definitely didn't," I said, the memory of that day rising like a dark beast from the compartment I kept it locked in inside my brain. It still made me sick to think about it. "Within a few weeks of Colten being born, she panicked and bailed. I came home from work one day to find him alone in his crib, bawling his eyes out and screaming."

Jewel frowned deeply. "She left him there?"

"Yep." I dragged in a deep breath, fortifying myself before I let slip how much anger I still felt over that fucking day. "With a note that said she was sorry but she just couldn't do it anymore."

Jewel looked like she might cry, but I forced a smile, taking her chin in my hand and shaking my head. "Don't feel sorry for me. Colten is the best thing that has ever happened in my life and I wouldn't change a thing. I'm even glad she left when she did."

"Still, it must've hurt at the time."

"Hell, yes." I let out a husky chuckle. "It was awful, but what hurt me most was that she didn't want her own son. It's a conversation I'm still going to have to navigate one day. I'm just hoping that me wanting him more than anything in the world will make up for it."

"Does he ask about her?" she asked.

I shrugged, despite the rage that simmered in my veins every time I thought about what she'd done, leaving a defenseless baby all alone for God only knew how long. "He used to ask about her, but he knows the truth now. He's a strong kid."

"Because he has a strong father," she agreed, sitting up and wrapping her arms around my neck. She scooted closer, slanted her lips over mine, and kissed me deeply. Sighing, she pulled away. "We should go back to the beach before anyone starts to worry, but thank you for sharing that with me. It means a lot, and for what it's worth, I'm sorry that happened but I think you're an amazing father. He's lucky to have you."

I wasn't so sure about that, but I nodded anyway and then took her hand, helping her off the bed before we started hunting down our clothes. While I never enjoyed talking about Kaitlin, the rage didn't hang around today like it usually did.

Jewel reverted to her friendly, playful self and smiled at me as she smacked my ass just before I covered it with my trunks. I couldn't stay angry. This girl had brought out a light side of me I hadn't even known existed anymore and it felt really fucking good to be getting back in touch with that guy.

30

JEWEL

Back on the beach, I was still buzzing inside. Even my favorite bikini bottoms were uncomfortable after the amazing sex I'd just had. I was also still so sensitive that I was aware of my lady bits with every step I took. It only made me want another round with Landon so much more.

I sighed as I watched him jogging down to the water. He joined a game Colten, Scott, and a few others kids were playing. As he splashed into the lake, I once again found myself checking him out, dragging my gaze over the ropes of muscle in his back and the tiny, almost invisible red half-moons my nails had left behind.

Fresh desire trickled through me at the sight and I almost moaned. My teeth sank into my lip as I tried to hold back the sound. Moaning on the beach while surrounded by so many people would definitely raise a few eyebrows, but I wanted him again. Badly. Fiercely, even.

God, what is wrong with me?

Generally, I functioned on one orgasm every month or two. My trusty vibrator's batteries never ran out. More often, they died from disuse. Yet, I'd already come twice today and I felt like I was far from finished.

Shaking my head at myself, I grabbed my towel and spread it out next to Brittany's where she was lounging in the sun, tanning and keeping an eye on the game going on in the lake. She shot me a look when I joined her. "So, you two were gone a while."

"Were we?" I asked innocently. "I didn't notice."

Brittany laughed and shoved my shoulder. "I'm not dumb, my friend. I know what you were up to. I knew as soon as you insisted on taking him back to your place to clean up a cut that wasn't even bleeding anymore."

"The dock is dirty," I said, shrugging.

"So are you, apparently." She smirked at me, lying back down but keeping her eyes on mine. "How was it? Don't you dare hold back the details when I was babysitting for you."

I blushed a deep red, ducking my head and pretending to rummage through my bag for my sunscreen as I tried to hide it from her. She chuckled, and I realized I didn't want to deny any of it with her.

While I didn't want the whole town to see me blushing, I kept my head down to fake search even as I admitted the truth to her. "It was, uh, unlike any sex I've ever had."

"Really?" Brittany asked, clearly amused but also interested. "How so?"

"Well, for starters, he was tender and rough all at the same time. He handled me with care while also taking charge."

"Well, that does sound different," she said, rolling onto her side to face me.

I took a deep breath, pulled the sunscreen out of my bag, and reapplied it since I'd gone through all that effort pretending to look for it. When I was done, I tossed it back in and braced my palms on the towel behind me. Watching the guys in the water, I let out a dreamy sigh.

"It was flipping amazing, but the problem now is that I want more and I'm not sure I'm going to get it."

She laughed. "You will, but I'm not done with the details yet. Tell me more. Curious minds want to know what else he did to make it so amazing."

I dropped my head back and closed my eyes as I thought back to what had made it feel so special. "Landon is wild. He kissed me like he loved me and fucked like he didn't, but that's all I'm saying. I can't keep talking about this, or I'm going to drag him out of the water and back to my apartment."

Laughing again, she kicked sand on my towel. "You lucky bitch."

I giggled and shrugged as I kicked sand on her towel in return. "Sure, unless you count the fact that he may well have ruined me for other men. And he has a child here, so it's going to be difficult to chain him to my bed so he'll never leave it again. I mean, I'm not cruel enough to force Colten to fend for himself while I spend my days climbing Landon like a jungle gym."

She sighed dreamily. "For that kind of sex, I'd pay someone to watch Colten if I was you."

"Can't," I said, wrinkling my nose. "They came out here to spend time together, so I'm not getting in the way of that, no matter how much he rocked my world."

She grimaced and patted my shoulder, sending me a coy grin. "At least you've got the memories to keep you company, right? That's better than nothing, which is what I've got right now."

Scott wrestled with Brody in the water, both of them shrieking with laughter. I wondered when my brother was finally going to pull his head out his ass. "You should talk to him."

She paused, but then she started giggling. "I can't. God, it would be so uncomfortable. It'll happen when it happens if it's meant to happen."

I shot her a questioning look, but then the guys started wading out of the water, leaving the kids by themselves as they made their way to us. Scott only had eyes for Brittany, and Landon, in turn, made no secret of raking his gaze over me like he was taking a hundred mental pictures.

Once again, I almost moaned but my brother yanked me out from under Landon's spell. "They're serving up burgers at the grill. I'm going to go grab us some. You guys want some?"

"Of course," Brittany said, practically rolling her tongue back into her mouth. I hadn't missed the way she'd looked at him, all wet as he came out of the water.

Gosh, the hormones on the beach today are out of control and it's not even coming from the freaking teenagers.

Scott glanced at me. "Jewel? Burger?"

Oh, right. I nodded, smiling as I reached for my bag. "Here. Let me just give you some cash."

"Nah, it's fine." Scott bent over and swiped up his wallet from his towel. "I got it, and cold drinks are on Landon. So just place your orders and we'll get to it."

"Service with a smile," I joked as I finally looked back at Landon. "I'll just have a Coke. Please?"

"You got it," he said easily, blinking himself out of what appeared to be his own haze of lust. Then he glanced at Brit. She asked for the same.

When the guys came back, we sat and ate together. Colten joined us for just long enough to inhale his own food before he rushed back to meet up with his new friends. I watched him go, taking in the wide grin on his face and seeing the high fives he handed out when he rejoined them.

"He really is like a whole new kid," I said to Landon. "Do you think it'll help him when you get back home?"

"You mean, do I think he'll bring his new social skills with him and maybe be able to connect with the kids in his class?" Landon exhaled heavily. His head shook as he shrugged, his eyes glued to his son. "I don't know, but I hope so."

"Now that Colt has seen how good it can be to have friends, maybe he'll be keen to try a little bit harder," Scott mused out loud, then grinned at Landon. "If push comes to shove, you guys could always move to June Lake. He seems to be fitting in pretty well with the kids around here."

Landon chuckled. "Imagine that. I think I might actually consider it if I had a job I could do remotely, but unfortunately, I don't. Plus, my stepfather is in LA. I'd never be able to leave him to live out his golden years by himself."

"I hear that," Scott said and easily guided the conversation to a different subject while I mulled over what Landon had said.

By the time the sun started setting and Colten and Landon headed home, I still wasn't quite sure how I felt about it, but I smiled at them anyway. "I'll see you guys on Monday."

Colten grinned. "We can't wait. Bye, everybody!"

"Bye, kid," Scott called while Brittany waved.

Once they were gone, I watched them walk up the slope and down the road to their truck. Then I sighed and turned to my brother. "Do you still think Landon is a one-trick pony?"

He laughed, frowning at me as he shook his head. "What do you mean?"

"Do you still think he's just a city boy with a chip on his shoulder?"

My brother's eyebrows jumped up as he chuckled. "Nah. I was impressed with how the guy let his hair down today and became one of us for the afternoon. Maybe he's not so terrible."

Well, at least that's something.

My brother's approval had always been important to me when I was seeing someone. Scott's judgment was scarily accurate most of the time. Lucky for me, while he definitely was protective of me, he didn't think of me as an eternal virgin like some other big brothers might've.

Like he'd read my mind, he reached out to squeeze my shoulder and his tone lowered into a warning. "He's still leaving at the end of the summer. You heard what he said, so don't get too invested."

So that's why he suggested they move to June Lake. I had wondered if it was just something he'd said, but obviously, he'd been trying to get a feel for the guy. Which meant he knew that I was starting to develop feelings for him and he was trying to protect me from getting my heart shattered.

"Yeah, I know," I said, because I did know.

I had *always* known, but that didn't stop me from feeling a bit glum at the reminder. Pushing myself to my feet, I picked up my towel and slid my bag over my shoulder. "I think I'm going to turn in. It's been a long day."

Brittany gave me a sympathetic smile as she nodded. Scott just waved, but I knew he was worried about me. I was worried too.

When I walked back into my apartment, I glanced at my sex-messed bed and the open band-aid and alcohol I had used to clean Landon's cut. *Just more reminders.*

In six more weeks, they'd be gone.

Not even six whole weeks, I was sure.

If it continued like this, I knew that time would fly, and then, when it came to an end, everything would go back to the way it had been. It was a prospect I wasn't too excited about.

I'd always been content with my life here in June Lake, but now that I'd had a taste of having Landon around, I wasn't sure how easily I would be able to go back to my old routines.

In a few short weeks, it felt like he'd turned my life upside down, and I already knew with utmost certainty that turning it right way up again wasn't going to happen nearly as fast. If it ever did.

It was just my luck that the perfect man came with an expiration date.

31

LANDON

On Sunday, Colten and I lazed around the Manor. We'd slept late, gone for a swim, and tossed the ball around a little, and now, we were playing chess.

I wasn't proud to admit it, but I was cornered. Colten had me on the ropes and he had me there after just three moves. It was insane.

Studying the board, I made a move I didn't see as a threat, but Colten grinned like he'd won the lottery and checkmated me. Throwing his hands up in the air, he did a little jig and smiled at me. "Good match, Dad. Well played."

I sighed and offered him my hand to shake as always. "You're getting better by the day. At this rate, I have no idea if I'm ever going to beat you again."

"Not if I can help it," he said playfully. Then he launched into a lengthy and super nerdy tangent about the moves he'd been studying in the chess book Mr. Lafferty had let him borrow before the break. "It's full of tricks and strategy and game plays. I can't wait to get back to the club and experiment with them against some real players."

I arched an eyebrow at him. "I'm not a real player?"

Colten flushed, but he was still smiling as he shrugged. "Be serious, Daddy."

I laughed. "I see how it is. Now that you're getting good, you're leaving old Dad behind, huh?"

He gave me a narrow-eyed look, the humor still shimmering behind it. "Maybe I am, but if you would play me more often, you would get better too. I can let you borrow my book."

"I think I'll leave the chess to you," I said as I picked my phone up off the table. "I'll play you whenever you want, but I don't need to be as good as you are. I just need to be a semi-worthy opponent for you to practice against. As long as it's fun, right?"

"Right," he said, but I could hear his heart wasn't in it. He glanced at my phone. "Do you need to work?"

"Nope, but you and I need to call Walt," I said. "He must be missing our visits."

Colt nodded, getting up and walking around the table to join me on my side. I pulled up a chair for him as I placed the call to the seniors' living facility back home, hitting speaker once the nurse told me she'd go get Walter.

A few long minutes later, my stepfather's voice finally came over the line, and to my relief, he sounded as happy as ever. "My boys! You're both there, right?"

"Yes, we are," Colten said excitedly, leaning forward as he focused on my phone. "We miss you, Grandpa."

"I miss you too." Walter chuckled. "I hope you're managing to have some fun without me, though. You must be since you haven't decided to cut the summer short and come home early. How is the lake?"

"It's awesome!" Colt said loudly, nearly falling off his chair for as much as he was bouncing on it. Walt had always been the only person who could bring out this extremely childlike side of my son, like he felt safe letting his grandpa in all the way, and I truly appreciated Walter's role in his life—for everything, but more so for always making him feel so safe and loved.

God knew, I tried to provide him with the same thing, but it was different. Walt and I were the only stability in Colten's life and I was rarely home, whereas Walter was always available for a chat when

Colt called. A few times, he'd even asked our driver to take him to see the old man without me.

The fact of the matter was that Walter didn't have to do this. Not for either of us. But even if he'd felt some kind of obligation toward me because of my mother, he was truly invested in my son even though he wasn't biologically related to him.

Thank fuck, blood isn't everything.

As I thanked my lucky stars, Colten told Walter all about Brody, Cole, and the other friends he'd made. He told him about learning how to toss a football and have fun in the lake. He also told him about the volleyball, the town itself, the night market, and how all the people here were really nice.

I didn't interrupt him, letting them have their time to catch up while I patiently waited my turn. "You'd love it out here, Grandpa," he said. "You should come with us next time."

"Next time?" I asked and Walter echoed the question.

Colten frowned at me. "Yeah, next time. Brody says the Manor is empty most summers because it's crazy expensive, so I was thinking we could come back next summer."

"Right," I said slowly. "Sure. Yeah. We can think about it."

Walter saved my ass by asking more questions about the place and Colten's friends, and when their conversation started tapering off, I leaned forward. "Why don't you tell Grandpa about the Lake Warrior contest and how you participated as part of a team?"

I knew he'd want to hear about that. Walter had been concerned about Colten's social skills for much longer than I had, a step ahead as usual. Over the phone, he laughed. "What on earth is a Lake Warrior contest?"

"It's this super cool event that they have every year," Colten explained, excited all over again. "Basically, it's like a bunch of little competitions in and around the lake. We spent the entire day yesterday at the beach and Dad even won third place. He did this totally wicked belly flop. Well, back flop, actually, and he got a medal for it. Obviously, Scott came first, but—"

"Whoa." Walter chuckled. "Who's Scott and why is it obvious that he came first?"

Colten brow furrowed. "Oh, right. I haven't told you about him yet. He's Jewel's brother and he's so cool, Grandpa. He even took us out on his boat one day and—"

"Who's Jewel?" Walt asked, interrupting him again. "Is she another new friend?"

"Sure," he said, still speaking so fast that it was like he'd forgotten that he even needed to breathe. "Well, she's more Dad's friend than she is mine, but she's really cool too, so she's also my friend. She's been inviting us to stuff around town and she showed us around after we first got here. Of course, she hated Dad at first, but she was right. He was really mean to her. He almost ran her over."

"I'm sure," Walter mused, obviously having realized that he wasn't going to fully understand who anyone was until he spoke to me. "I'm glad my boys are having such a good time. I've heard it's really beautiful out there."

"It really is," Colten agreed and launched into a detailed description of the landscape before he eventually ran out of steam. "Anyway, goodbye, Grandpa. We'll talk to you soon."

"Bye, Colt," Walter said. "I'll be looking forward to it."

Colten grinned at the phone, then glanced at me. "I'm going upstairs to read my book."

I nodded and took the device from him. When he was gone, I cleared my throat and chuckled. "So that had to be a bit of an information overload."

"I haven't heard him like that in a long time," Walt said, his voice warm with joy and approval. "The break sure seems to be doing wonders for him."

"It is. You were definitely right to suggest this, but how about you? How are you doing?"

Walter laughed. "Well, all the women have been flocking around me like crazy. Something about the summer air has made them frisky. It's making Chester jealous, so if I don't have eyebrows when you get home, you'll know it's because he shaved them off in my sleep."

Cracking up because I truly found the visual of all that hilarious, I laughed and pursed my lips at the phone. "You'd better be using protection, old man. I'm not explaining chlamydia to my ten-year-old."

Walter scoffed. "You're one to talk. Who's this friend of yours Colten told me about? Jewel, was it? That's a pretty name."

"Yep, but it's no big deal." Even as I said it, I knew it was a bit of a lie but I also knew there was no sense in getting his hopes up. Jewel and I were having fun for the summer, but it was hardly like we were going to settle down together. "Life is simple here and Colt was right when he said the people have been really friendly. Jewel has taken us under her wing, including us in the town's activities to make sure we have a good time as tourists."

"Uh huh," he said. "Sounds perfectly innocent. I'm sure that's all it is, but it's alright if you don't want to talk about it. How's it been there for you? It sounds like Colten has been plenty busy."

"He has been, but in the best way. Besides, I've been busy too."

"Not working, I hope," he said sharply.

I chuckled. "Nope, not working. I've barely thought about work at all since we've been here actually. I've hardly even checked my emails and I'm fully embracing the summer off."

"Good," he said, sounding relieved. "That's good, son. What about your inheritance? Have you given any more thought to what you're going to do about it?"

"No," I admitted. "Like I said, I'm fully embracing the summer off, which means I'm not thinking about anything serious. Besides, the money is safe where it is and it's still untouched. There's no rush to do anything."

"Of course," Walt said. "Just make sure that you thoroughly investigate any opportunities that might come up for it, okay?" He paused. "I'm proud of you, my boy. I didn't really think you were going to give yourself the whole summer off from everything, but it's good to know that you are. Colt isn't the only one who sounds happy."

I inhaled deeply through my nostrils. "To be honest, I wasn't sure I was going to manage it either, but so far, so good. It's actually been pretty easy now that I've shut off, you know? It's like that part of my brain is on sleep mode."

Walt laughed. "It'll be there when you need it, but you better use whatever is left of your brain to remember to come home with tons of pictures. I want to see my grandson in action on the lake."

"Yeah, I will. I promise."

We chatted for a while longer before we said goodbye. Then Colten and I went for another swim, ate cereal for supper, and watched cartoons. As we were winding down, he suddenly looked at me. "Hey, uh, Jewel is coming here again tomorrow, right?"

"Right," I said, cocking my head at him. "Why?"

"I like her," he said slowly. "Do you think she'd stay for dinner again?"

"I'm sure she will," I replied. "Are you sure you want her to, though?"

"Yeah, of course," he said before adding worriedly, "We just can't let her cook."

"Not under any circumstances," I agreed, thinking back to that casserole and feeling my stomach lurch. "Pizza, it is."

Colt grinned, turning back to the TV with a satisfied expression on his face. I was glad he liked her. I did too. Perhaps a little too much, but he didn't need to know that.

By the time Colt and I said goodnight and headed to sleep, I was still thinking about her. These days, it seemed she was always on my mind.

Even more so now.

The sex truly had been mind-blowing, and if I was being honest with myself, once hadn't been enough. It had been a long time since I'd had that thought, but it was true.

I wanted Jewel. The only problem was that I didn't know if I'd stop wanting her once we had to leave here. The way I felt right then, I doubted it, but I'd cross that bridge when we got there.

For now, I switched off the lamp on the nightstand and laid my head down on my pillow, consumed by memories of the woman and looking forward to seeing her again in less than twelve hours' time.

32

JEWEL

Things had settled into a good rhythm. My usual Monday clients had let me change some things around so Brittany didn't have to clean on her own and now had long weekends during the summer. We'd arranged to make up for it during the week to catch up on the cleans we missed on Mondays.

She'd offered to come to the Manor with me, but I'd turned her down. I kind of enjoyed having the Paynes to myself when I came out here and Brittany hadn't argued, still wanting to see the inside of the house but not so badly that she'd insist on coming here to clean it.

When I arrived at Styles Manor on Monday morning, my car sputtered to a stop and a suspicious plume of smoke drifted from under the hood like a departing soul. I scrunched up my nose as a vaguely acrid scent filtered into the car itself, bringing with it a sense of dread.

As it was, I'd barely made it down the winding, forest-lined road from town to here, where the Manor sat at the opposite end of the lake. The hood was smoking in earnest now that I'd come to a complete stop. I climbed out and hoped that Scott would be able to come pick me up later.

I doubted I was going to get home with my car in this state. Not until Scott patched her up again. I couldn't worry about that now. I was already late thanks to having to take it slow just so I could get here with it in one piece.

Hurrying around to the trunk, I collected my cleaning supplies and looked up just as Landon came out. He smiled at me, but then he seemed to notice the smoke, and his face fell.

Breaking into a run, he flew down the stairs and looked me over as soon as he was close enough, evidently assessing me for any trace of injury. "What the hell happened? Are you okay? Did you get in an accident or something?"

"Or something," I said, smiling so he'd know I was okay. "It's just old Sasha protesting again. It'll be fine."

He arched both eyebrows at me but nodded, raking his hands through his hair and dragging in a deep breath. "Thank God. I think my heart just almost gave out. If you'd gotten hurt while coming here to clean for us, I'm not sure I'd ever forgive myself."

I chuckled through the dread pooling in my stomach. Smoke was still pouring from the under the hood. I'd thought it would stop now that the engine was off, but that hadn't happened. At all.

"Let's take a look, shall we?" Landon suggested, moving around to the front of the car.

"You don't have to," I started saying when he reached for the metal. Then he yanked his hand back as soon as his fingertips brushed it.

"That's hot." He reached for his shirt and pulled it off by grabbing it at the collar behind his neck.

I swallowed hard, knowing that I shouldn't have noticed how hot that move was when he did it, but shit. I'd rather be thinking about a sexy client than the possibility of Sasha finally having kicked the bucket for good.

Wrapping the shirt around his hand like a glove, he reached for the hood and opened it, releasing yet another cloud of smoke. Carefully leaning over to peek around it, he grimaced and cursed under his breath.

"I hate to tell you this, but I think Sasha has said goodbye. For good."

I groaned out loud. "Well, that's just great. Scott has a way with her, though. Maybe he'll be able to breathe new life into her. Like Frankenstein."

He shot me a dubious look, glancing back at the engine. "How about this? I'll tinker with it while you work. Maybe I'll be able to work some magic on her."

"You really don't have to do that," I said, a little flustered at the offer. "You've already fixed her up once."

"Let me take a look," he said as if it was nothing. "Colten's reading his chess book anyway and I don't just want to laze around."

"That's kind of what you're supposed to do on vacation," I replied, giving him a playful smile. "You do know what a vacation is, right?"

He laughed. "I do, but it's not like this is work. Believe it or not, I quite enjoy working on engines."

"In that case, you're welcome, I suppose." I gave him another smile, still feeling somewhat flustered as I headed inside.

Thankfully, the routine I'd fallen into while cleaning the Manor distracted me enough that I stopped feeling guilty about Landon working on my car on such a beautiful day. Colten was in his bedroom with the book that seemed to be glued to his face whenever he was in here, but he smiled at me when I walked in and immediately set it down.

"I'll help you pick up," he offered, hopping off the bed and getting started before I could tell him to relax.

It seemed the Paynes both had issues grasping the concept of vacation, but I was glad for the company as I continued my normal housework. Once I left Colten's room, I put on music on my headphones, allowing that to drown out the worries about my car.

All weekend, I'd been looking forward to today. To seeing them again while they were still here and now this might just be the last day I'd be able to come to the Manor. If Scott couldn't get my car fixed, a bruised heart was going to be the least of my problems, but I chose not to focus on that, letting the music carry me away completely as I swept and cleaned.

Later in the day, Landon came back inside covered in grease and smelling like oil. As soon as I saw the look in his eyes, my stomach plummeted. "It didn't work, did it?"

"It didn't," he said, that intense green gaze cloudy and dark with remorse. "I'm sorry, Jewel. I tried everything, but I didn't have any luck, so I called a tow truck in town. I'll drive you home later myself."

"Or," he added casually when I didn't respond. "You could stay the night and I can drive you into town tomorrow. There's a lot of house to go around."

My mouth fell open. "Spend a night in the Styles Manor? Yes, please! Imagine that 'yes' in all caps, but only if you're sure it's okay with you."

"It's okay with me," he said, his dirty face breaking out in a smile that made his teeth seem even whiter than ever before.

Colten walked in and he must've overheard what we'd been saying because he was suddenly extremely excited, grinning as he spoke a mile a minute. "You're staying here tonight? That's great. Will you play some chess with me? I've learned a few new strategies today and I'd like to try them out."

"Of course." I laughed, not even my broken car getting me down right then.

Hopefully, they'd tow it into town and Scott would still be able to fix it. If not, well, I'd worry about it then. I wasn't going to let anything mar the memory of my first—and probably only—night here.

After I finished with the floor in the kitchen, I glanced at the fridge and smiled. "How about I whip us up something for dinner? I can get it started before I grab a quick shower. What do you feel like?"

I stowed my mop in its bucket and strode over to the sink to wash my hands. "Maybe I could even try something more sophisticated this time," I said over my shoulder. "But before we get ahead ourselves, I should probably check what you have. You know, since I can't pop to the store to get anything else."

Overwhelmed by the prospect of sleeping in the Manor, I rushed over to the fridge when my hands were dry, cracking it open and inspecting the contents. Once again, it was fully stocked, but I suddenly realized that the boys had fallen quiet.

"Guys?" I asked as I closed the fridge and turned to them. "What do you think? Will it be okay if I cook for you? Do you have any requests?"

"Don't cook," Colten blurted out, the tips of his ears turning red.

Landon pushed Colten behind himself, stepping forward and smiling at me. "What he means to say is that we already had plans to order pizza tonight. There's no need to cook, especially since you've already spent the entire day cleaning. How about we just relax and keep it simple tonight?"

"That actually sounds really good to me," I said, and although I'd never admit it out loud, I was glad they'd already had plans.

While I certainly wouldn't have minded cooking for them, it would be much better to kick back and relax after the day I'd had. Landon nodded and headed for the stairs, grinning at me over his shoulder.

"I desperately need a shower and I'm sure you do too. If you'll follow me, I'll show you the spare bedrooms and you can choose whichever one you like. Almost all of them have adjoining bathrooms and there are towels in them, so you should have everything you need."

"Yes, I cleaned all the empty rooms the first time I cleaned," I said, excitement sending my pulse into overdrive as I followed him up the stairs. Not only was I getting to spend the night in the Manor, but I was going to be doing it while he was here too.

If it hadn't been for my broken car outside, today would've gone down in my personal history as the day some of my most wonderful daydreams had come true.

33

LANDON

Jewel looked beautiful in the orangey, red light of the sun setting across the lake. Her hair was still damp from her shower and her face was all lit up. We were sitting on the large, back patio at the pool eating our pizza, and for some reason, it felt right to have her here with us.

I'd taken a risk earlier, inviting her to stay. I'd definitely been prepared to drive her home, but she'd jumped at the chance to sleep here. I was sure it had more to do with the Manor than it did with me, but it was still pretty fucking amazing to have her here with us even after her workday was done.

Colten cleared the table when we were done eating, even giving us a little bow as he piled the plates on top of one another. "We hope you enjoyed dinner at Styles Manor, Jewel."

She giggled, giving him an exceptionally fond smile as she nodded. "I did enjoy it, young sir. Very much so. Thank you for clearing the table. I really could've done it."

He shook his head. "No, thank *you*. We aim to please."

"You might just make a great restaurant manager one day," she teased. "Assuming you choose to go into hospitality, of course."

"I'll think about it." He picked up the plates and carried them inside.

Once he was gone, I turned to face her and reached for her hand. Surprise flickered across her features, but she let me take it, smiling as I cradled it in both of mine.

"You look fucking gorgeous out here in the sunset," I murmured softly enough that Colten wouldn't overhear us. "Seriously, Jewel. You suit this house so damn well."

"Thank you," she replied, keeping her own voice lower than usual as well. Rosy red bloomed across her cheeks as she glanced down at the spare clothes she'd grabbed from her trunk. "It's kind of you to say so even if I know I look a mess. This outfit has been lying in my car for at least a month and I know how wrinkled it is. Plus, I didn't take my brush when I went to fetch the clothes, so..."

She trailed off and I held her gaze, my head shaking. "Nope. You're perfect."

"I don't think you've lost your sense of romance, Mr. Big City. Maybe it's just been in hiding a while, huh?"

Colten came bounding back outside, and I cleared my throat and let go of her hand. "Can we play chess now?" he asked.

"How about we play some cards?" I suggested. "Chess is only a two-player game and there are three of us."

His eyes bounced from mine to Jewel's. Then he seemed to realize I was right and he nodded. "I'll grab the cards."

When he got back, I dealt us a hand of Go Fish! Colten groaned when he recognized the game, giving me a pointed look as he picked up his cards. "I'm not six anymore, you know? I can handle more than this."

"Oh, I know, but Jewel and I can't. It's been a really long day for both of us, so do me a favor and take it easy on us, okay?"

"Okay," he agreed, but I saw the devilish glimmer in his eyes just before he proceeded to kick both our asses up and down at the game. Jewel didn't seem to mind any more than I did though, apparently more interested in speaking to him than she was in paying attention to collecting cards.

"You're having fun here in June Lake, aren't you?" she asked, her voice gentle and honest. "It's okay if you're not. I'm just wondering so I can see if I should come up with more things for you guys to do. There are a bunch of stunning hikes around here as well as a zipline through the trees, which I don't think I've told you about before."

"You haven't, but I don't need a zipline," he said, glancing at her with a wide grin on his lips. "I love it here so far just doing what we've been doing. Brody and the guys are awesome and we have plans for more beach volleyball this week."

"That's great news," she said, and to my surprise, it seemed like she really meant it.

I'd thought it before, but it looked like she genuinely cared about Colten and his happiness. And then there was that suncatcher she'd made for him. I still didn't have words to adequately express to her how grateful I was for all the things she'd done for my son.

"Thank you for introducing me to Brody," Colten said when I zoned back into the conversation. "I wouldn't have met him or given any of the kids a chance without him, and I'm so glad I did."

She smiled. "I'm just glad you guys hit it off, kiddo. The lake is always more fun with a couple friends by your side."

I watched and listened contently, proud of my son but also realizing that Brody wasn't the only close friend he'd made here. It seemed he'd also connected deeply with Jewel, but even that didn't surprise me much.

She was a role model in every capacity. In the short time she'd known him, she'd shown him what hospitality, empathy, and kindness looked like much more than I ever had. She'd also done it while working damn hard, being involved with her community, and being a great friend and sister.

I honestly didn't know how she did it all, but it hit me like a kick in the gut that I had to leave her in just five and a half weeks. With anyone else, that would've felt like a lifetime, but with her, I knew it would go by much too fast.

It already was.

Pensive while we finished the game, I caught her sending me a few questioning glances, but I shrugged and shook my head. Now wasn't the time to talk about it, but especially not in front of him.

After the game, I gave him a look he knew all too well. "It's time for bed, buddy."

He pouted and glanced at Jewel, but she shrugged and gave him an apologetic smile. "I'm sorry, but there's nothing I can do about it. If your dad says it's time for bed, then it's time for bed."

He sighed deeply. "Fine, but you'll still be here when I wake up, right? We can play chess then?"

"Sure thing, bud," she replied happily, giving him a little wave when he started retreating. "Good night, Colten. Sleep well."

"You too," he sang back to her.

Then I got up and went to put him to bed. I knew I didn't have to do it anymore, but I was enjoying getting to tuck him in at night this summer. It was probably going to be the last opportunity I had to do it.

Once we got back home, I'd have to go back to working the long hours my job required. Even though I'd already resolved to cut down, I knew I wasn't going to be home for bedtime every night. After saying goodnight once he'd brushed his teeth, I left his bedroom door ajar and made my way back to Jewel.

She was still sitting on the patio, sipping a glass of water as she watched the moonlight shimmering off the surface of the lake. I hadn't said anything yet, but she must've heard me anyway because she suddenly spoke up.

"It's even more beautiful out here at night than I'd imagined," she said dreamily. "I don't know what's so different about it from here, but the lake, the reflections, everything just seems better."

I chuckled. "I know what you mean. I may not even have known about this place before I rented it for the break, but it's really grown on me. There's definitely something special about it. How do you feel about a walk around the grounds? You can look around some more."

"Uh, okay," she said, turning to me with a small frown on her features. "It's, uh, it's dark, though. We won't see much. Are you sure it's the best time for a stroll?"

"Just trust me," I said, offering her my arm and waiting for her to take it. "The thing about this place is that it'll take your breath away no matter the time of day."

"What do you mean?" She wrapped her fingers gently around the crook of my elbow and followed me off the patio.

"You'll see for yourself soon," I murmured, leading her around the corner and waiting for the moment she realized what I was talking about.

The sun had set, but the garden was beautifully lit and landscaped, every part of the grounds illuminated along cobbled garden paths that led to the lesser used parts of the property. As I watched, Jewel noticed it. Her eyes widened and they darted around like I'd taken her to Disney World.

"This is amazing," she said quietly, as if she was afraid that raising her voice would break the spell. "I've seen the lights on from the other side of the lake, but this?"

"It's gorgeous, right? I'd love to know which landscaper they used for all this. God knows, my garden back home could use this kind of help."

"Well, they have a caretaker, but I honestly don't know if he's responsible for all this or if they brought in outside help. I suppose you could always ask Dallas?"

I groaned. "I'd rather not. Thanks, though."

She chuckled, holding my arm as we walked through the garden and eventually headed back inside. When we got back from our walk, I suddenly remembered that I still had that surprise for her. Leading her directly to what used to be Mr. Styles' study, I gave her a secretive grin.

"So I've got a little something for you that I thought you might be interested in," I said.

A slight smirk started to spread on her face as her gaze dropped to my crotch. "Let me tell you, it's not little."

"No." I laughed, but I couldn't deny that my dick had been stirring since we took that stroll. "Look here."

I sat her down at the desk and then pushed the jewelry box and journals across to her. A frown puckered her brow. Then she gasped loudly when she lifted the top of the jewelry box and got her first glimpse of the items inside.

"Where did you get this?" she asked in an awed whisper. "This is —why did you say you had something for me?"

"Dallas was selling them and I bought them. For you. I figured they'd mean a lot more to you and to the town than to some collector." As I said it, she picked up one of the journals and ran her fingers over the worn leather exterior. "Do you like them?"

"Yes, of course. I..." She trailed off again, still seeming stunned.

What stunned me in turn was that the journals were holding her attention much more than the jewelry. She cracked open the one she'd picked up, reading aloud from the first page.

Lucille Styles' first entry in it had been about Robert's proposal, and I listened in rapture as she read. Her eyes glittered with tears by the time she finished the entry and closed the journal, bringing it to her chest and holding it close.

"This is the most precious gift I've ever received. I'll cherish it forever." She swallowed hard, her misty gaze on mine. "I can't believe Dallas would sell a family heirloom like this. If I had something like this left of my mother, I'd never let it go."

I gathered her up in my arms, holding her close as she breathed through the wave of emotion that seemed to have overcome her. "I don't know why he'd sell a part of his family history, but I, for one, would like to know more about *you*. Everything you're willing to share. I'm more interested in Jewel Pendleton's heart than I am in Lucille Styles'."

34

JEWEL

I'm more interested in Jewel Pendleton's heart than I am in Lucille Styles. The words echoed through my mind, warming me up from the inside out.

I knew he'd said he wasn't romantic anymore, but for a self-professed non-romantic, he sure knew how to charm a lady. I'd never met someone who said the kinds of things he did. Never known a man to bare his heart that way.

It was late on Monday night, but him saying that he wanted to know more about me had prompted us to come back outside instead of going upstairs to our respective bedrooms. Sitting on a garden patio, we were sipping red wine and talking.

"I never stay up this late on a school night," I said as I cradled my glass in my hands. I had no idea where he'd gotten this wine, but it was the same one we'd had the other night and it was no less delicious now.

Landon chuckled, shrugging as he held my gaze. "I wish I could say the same, but I've always been a night owl. When I was younger, I used to do my best studying after Walter had gone to bed. And these days, I find it's the only time I can really focus in my office. Once the others are gone and the phones stop ringing, that's when my work really gets done."

"You know, I don't even know what line of work you're in." I cast a glance at the Manor, the lights on in some of the rooms inside causing an orange glow to emanate from the house. "It must be something impressive if you can afford to stay in a place like that."

"I'm a lawyer," he replied but left it there instead of exaggerating.

While I wondered why he would stop short, I figured he might open up a little more if I did the same in return. I smiled at him. "A lawyer, huh? I would've thought property magnate. Or maybe something to do with investments."

Those green eyes lit with amusement as he shook his head at me. "Sorry to disappoint you."

"You could never disappoint me," I said before I could stop myself, but while I wasn't usually quite so vocal about my thoughts, I felt safe enough to be open with him. "My father was the town drunk."

Landon blinked hard at the sudden change of topic, the amusement evaporating from his eyes. "I'm sorry."

I gave him a one-shouldered shrug. "It was a long time ago, but you wanted to know more about me and this is it. I was born to a man who loved booze more than his family and a woman who enabled him."

He didn't say anything in response, but I got it. There was nothing to say. It was what it was, and no amount of "I'm sorry's" was going to change it. Besides, I wanted him to know about this. It was only fair. If I wanted to know everything there was to know about him—including why he'd stopped short earlier—then I had to give something of myself in return.

"Everyone knew about his drinking problem." I took another sip of my wine and paused to savor it before I swallowed.

As much as this was my story, it was still hard to tell it to someone who hadn't heard it before and had no idea about any of it. I wasn't ashamed of it anymore, but that didn't mean it was easy to talk about. It simply didn't embarrass me or break my heart like it used to.

"He was a complete embarrassment," I admitted, needing to say those words out loud before I carried on. I found it made it easier for me to explain the rest if I could just admit how I'd felt about it. "I hate to say that about my own father, but it's true. He used to get fall-down drunk every afternoon, and by night time, he was usually passed out somewhere."

"That must've been a tough upbringing," he commented, his voice low and gravelly. "I've known a few people like that in my time and I've never understood how they could do that to their families."

"I don't think they mean to, if that helps. They're ill. I know that now. Alcoholism is a disease, and like any other disease, you can't just snap your fingers and be better, but you're right. It was a tough way to grow up."

I dragged in a deep breath. "The locals around here really rallied around us as a family to make sure our needs were met. I wore hand-me-downs from other kids all my life and so did Scott, until he was finally old enough to put our father out on his ass and tell him not to come back."

Pain flickered in Landon's eyes, but he didn't interrupt me.

"He was only eighteen. It still hurts to think about how fast he had to grow up because of our dad."

Landon reached for my hand and gave it a squeeze. "You don't have to keep telling me about this if it hurts you. I just wanted to know you better, but that doesn't entitle me to your entire life story if it's too painful to tell."

I shook my head. "It's not too painful. Not anymore. I made my peace with it, you know? At first, I kind of defined myself by it. The daughter of the town drunk. But then I realized that I didn't have to be just that for the rest of my life. I'm an adult now and that means that my life is my own. I get to make my own choices and I've chosen to take responsibility for my own story going forward."

"I admire you for that," he said, his tone thick with honesty. "Really. You're so much stronger than I think you realize sometimes."

I chuckled. "I'm not strong. I'm just an eternal optimist who has made the choice not to blame a sad life on the mistakes of my father."

"What about your mother?" he asked. "What was she like?"

"She was amazing." I smiled. "So loving and caring, but I thought she hated my dad. Scott and I both thought that once he was gone, she would finally be happy, but she wasn't. She became completely unraveled after he left and she just couldn't cope."

"What do you mean?"

I sighed. "She started dating online, meeting up with men from other towns, and eventually, she left June Lake and started a new life somewhere else, rarely coming back to visit."

"She left you?"

I nodded. "Scott and I visited her as often as money would allow, but she became less and less reachable over time. We don't even know where she is now."

He frowned, searching my eyes as he cocked his head at me. "I thought you said the other night that both your parents had passed away?"

"Neither of them have been seen or heard from for years," I replied quietly. "All the phone numbers we've ever had for them are out of service. A while back, I realized that if they were still alive, we'd have known about it. Dad would've shown up at some point to ask for money or alcohol and Mom would've brought a new boyfriend home to show off her hometown."

"This almost sounds harder than losing a parent," he said. "At least I have closure but you never got that."

"Thank you for understanding. It means a lot to me." I tipped my head back and slowly filled my lungs with air before releasing it again. "Thanks for listening, but it's not all as sad as it sounds. Scott is my family and so are Brittany and Tiff, and all the people here in June Lake. They've always had my back when I needed someone to lean on and I'll always be here for them too. All things considered, we have a pretty darn good life here."

"Agreed," he said easily. "When we first got here, I didn't understand it but now I think I'm starting to. Life is different here, but it really is pretty darn good."

"What is your family like?" I asked. "Walter is your stepfather, right?"

"Yeah, he is." The corners of his lips turned up in a fond, soft smile. "After my mother died when I was little, Walt stepped up in a huge way and became the parent I so desperately needed. If it hadn't been for him, I would've ended up in the system. I'll never stop being grateful to him for taking me in when he really didn't have to."

"He sounds like a good father," I said.

Landon chuckled. "I'd be lucky to be half the father to Colten that he was to me."

The more he spoke, the more I felt like I knew him and the deeper I wanted to connect. I felt so drawn to him, and with every word he said, his vulnerability became more and more like a gravitational force.

"What about your work?" I asked then, circling back to where we'd started. "What kind of law do you practice?"

"Criminal defense." He waited for a beat, his eyes on mine like he was waiting for a reaction from me.

I frowned. "Okay. What's wrong with that?"

"Nothing, but most people seem to think there's something very wrong with it."

"Why?" My brow furrowed as I thought it over. "Everyone is entitled to a defense, right? Unless I'm missing something somewhere."

Relief washed over his features as he nodded. "You're not missing anything. That's exactly it. Everyone is entitled to a defense, but a lot of people don't see it that way until they're the one in need of said defense. In general, people seem to think that only the worst of the worst, the bottom-feeding scum of a lawyer would defend a criminal."

Disbelieving laughter bubbled out of me. "That doesn't seem right. I mean, you do the crime, you do the time. I get that. I believe in it, but the justice system definitely isn't perfect and committing a crime doesn't always mean we should lock you up and throw away the key."

"Exactly," he said, becoming more animated as he spoke. His face lit up, his hands joining in the conversation. "It's not only about keeping innocent people out of jail. It's also about making sure that the punishment fits the crime."

I smiled. "You clearly love what you do."

He sighed, leaning back in his chair and shaking his head slowly from one side to the other. "I used to. I'm still very passionate about it, but I'm starting to see the cost I've had to pay. Time lost with Walt and my son is time I'll never get back. And for what? To defend criminals all because I believe in the system and I feel responsible for making sure it functions the way it's supposed to? Because I believe in a fair trial and due process?"

My eyes narrowed as my gaze swept across his face, taking in the doubt that suddenly lived in the purse of his lips and the pucker of his brow. "You don't love it anymore?"

"No, I do." He blew out a heavy breath. "I'm just not sure it's worth it anymore. This summer is changing a lot for me. I was already wondering if the juice was worth the squeeze before we got here, but now? I guess I'm just really not sure I should keep doing it."

"It's changing a lot for me too," I whispered, not even really knowing why my voice didn't seem to want to work right then. "The summer, I mean. It's changing a lot of things for me too. I just don't really know what to do about it."

35

LANDON

It struck me as odd that sharing my deepest thoughts with someone would make me physically needy, but as I looked into Jewel's eyes across the table, I was suddenly so turned on that I could hardly breathe. I'd heard that real emotional connection was often behind the best sex and the strongest relationships, but I hadn't believed it until right then.

My jaw tightened and my teeth ground as I wondered if she felt it too. Neither of us were speaking anymore, both just staring at each other completely openly after everything we'd just shared. I didn't know about her, but that was the first time I'd ever spoken so honestly about my life.

About what would have happened to me if Walt hadn't taken me in.

About my belief systems and the emotional upheaval of suddenly doubting that my life's work had been worth doing.

Jewel's honey-gold eyes roamed all around my face, never leaving it as she zeroed in on my lips. Her own parted just slightly. So slightly that I wouldn't have noticed it if I hadn't been staring at her as intensely as I was.

I also saw the tiny flare of her nostrils and I grunted, leaning forward and capturing her face in my hands. She didn't seem surprised, nor did she seem opposed. Instead, she threw her arms around my neck and our lips clashed in a kiss so fiery that it might've burned the world to the ground if that had been possible.

Jewel moaned into my mouth, scooting forward on her chair and not breaking the kiss as she climbed into my lap. I spread my legs to support her better, and my arms snaked around her waist as we deepened the kiss.

I angled my hips up, rocking into her from below. One of my hands wrapped around the nape of her neck, gripping it tight to hold her against me. Her tongue stroked my own with hungry licks that made me desperate to feel it on my shaft. Her own hips quickly moved to match my pace.

Panting and not willing to wait, I slid my hands under her thighs and picked her up, carrying her to the small pool room off the side of the patio. I was taking what I wanted, but I couldn't do it out in the open with Colt sleeping right upstairs.

All I needed was cover in case he should come to the window and a lockable door so he wouldn't accidentally stumble in on us if he was to come looking. Colten and I hadn't used the pool room for anything other than storage of the inflatables since we'd been here, but I knew the sliding door was unlocked.

I stopped in front of the door, balancing her weight as I let go with one hand to slide it open.

"Where are we going?" she asked into my mouth.

"I need you," I murmured hoarsely. "Now."

Another soft moan escaped her, and instead of asking any more questions, she sealed her mouth over my throat, sucking and nipping at the flesh there in a way that told me she needed me just as much. As soon as the opening was wide enough for us to fit through, I carried her past the door and lowered her onto a pile of outdoor cushions, immediately going back to lock the door once I let go of her.

No lights were on in here, but there was enough ambient light filtering in from the house and garden that I didn't crash into anything as I strode back to her. Lying on her back on the cushions meant for the lounge chairs outside, she'd propped herself up on her elbows while waiting for me and her gaze tracked my every move as I crossed to her.

All that blonde hair was up in a messy bun on top of her head, her tank top riding up to expose a sliver of her midriff. I bit my lip as I ran my gaze across that inch of skin. Then I lowered it to the loose pair of short shorts she had on.

"Take them off." I reached for my fly and popped open the button before unzipping. I pulled my shirt off too but left the pants in place for now.

Her lips parted on my harshly spoken command. Eyes hooked on mine, she complied, her hands lowering to the waistband of the shorts before she pushed them off. She left her panties on, shooting me a mischievous smile as she cocked her head and kicked the shorts away.

In the pool of moonlight on the cushion, I could see that her cheeks were flushed, her eyelids heavy as she peered up at me through long lashes. I dropped to my knees between her ankles, wrapped my fingers around each one, and pushed them apart.

Pressing down on them for a moment, I looked back up into her eyes. "Keep them there."

She dropped her chin in a curt nod, watching. I crawled up to her, gathering the hem of the tank in my hands and lifting it over her head. Her back came up to help the material pass behind it, her arms following until the fabric came free.

My heart started pounding in my chest at the sight of her like this, left in just a pair of basic, white cotton panties and a simple, sheer bra that allowed me to see her puckered nipples. With her face bare of makeup and her hair in that carefree style, right now, she was just about the sexiest sight I'd ever seen with my own two eyes.

I groaned, dragging my gaze slowly up and down the length of her curvy body before I slid back down between her legs. With my cock begging to be freed and my breathing coming in rough pants, I placed wet kisses on her collarbones. Ignoring her nipples, I kissed a path down her stomach until my lips grazed against the waistband of her panties.

The scent of her arousal made my dick twitch. My mouth watered to get on her, but I ignored all that too, continuing in my mission to lick and kiss every inch of her even as my fingers dug into her legs to keep them still. They kept twitching like she was trying to close them, but I refused to let her, not wanting to give her that relief of squeezing her thighs together just yet.

Her pleasure was mine tonight. As her vulnerability had been. I had this animalistic urge to claim her as my own. To take her heart, her body, and her story and make them mine. To keep her safe from embarrassment, hurt, and worry from here on out.

But that wasn't really an option.

All I had to give was this. Tonight.

So I was damn well going to make it count.

As I made my way up from kissing her ankles, I ran my hands up her sides and held her hips before placing an open-mouthed kiss right on the front panel of her panties. Her hips bucked, low moans falling from her lips when I licked her through the fabric, blood rushing to my ears at the sweet taste of her.

Hooking my thumbs into her waistband, I finally ripped the panties off and discarded them into the dark, not really caring about having to track them down later. That was later and this was now. Right now, all that mattered was what I was about to do.

Burying my head between her legs, I prayed to the gods of self-control and licked through her wet folds before sucking her clit into my mouth. She let out a keening cry. Her hands landed in my hair and tugged it just hard enough to send little ripples of pain through me as she rode my face.

As worked up as we both were, I knew I was being a little rough and a lot unrelenting, but I didn't stop licking and sucking her until she came for me, screaming my name as she did it. Before her breathing had even returned to normal, she reached for me, pulling me up and laying a hard, meaningful kiss on my lips.

I groaned. My cock throbbed being way too close to its target like this. I tried to pull away, but she kept me where I was, letting go with one hand to push my shorts over my ass. With her slick heat on my pelvis, I lost the fight, reaching for my pants and more than relieved that I'd prepared for this.

I hadn't exactly known it was going to happen, but I'd been hopeful. After taking that shower to wash the grease off, I'd stuck a condom in my pocket just in case. My fingers brushed against the foil packet and I yanked it out, breaking the kiss to bite it open before sitting up on my knees between her legs.

She watched me with rapt attention as I rolled the condom on. Then I lay down on my back and she climbed astride me, eyes on mine. She positioned herself right over the tip of my aching cock. Without further ado, she took my hands for balance and sank down on me, immediately making my body beg to thrust.

I gave in without question, trusting her to tell me if she needed a minute. It turned out she didn't. She was so wet and so ready for me that she started moving with me as soon as I started, keeping the punishing pace I was setting.

As I slammed into her from below, I stared into her eyes and felt my brow furrowing in concentration. The woman felt so fucking good that I didn't stand a chance, especially not after she took her breasts in her own hands and held them as she fucked me.

"Jewel." I barely got her name out before her lips were back on mine, her kisses hot, hard, and hungry once more.

"Come for me," she insisted, repeated the same words I'd said to her before. "Now."

I squeezed my eyes shut, but I didn't hold back. Pleasure raced through me, my muscles tight as the orgasm sucked me dry. Jewel moaned loudly, her own features contorted when I opened my eyes just in time to see her come with me.

Thrusting into her a few final times, I wrapped my arms around her waist and held her when she collapsed on top of me. As we lay there together catching our breath after what had been an unexpected, intense encounter, I wondered if she knew just how connected I felt to her in that moment.

And I also wondered if that was a good thing, or if I ever should've let it happen at all.

36

JEWEL

Waking up in a beautifully appointed, sun-washed bedroom at the Manor, I smiled and let out a soft little moan as I burrowed into the luxurious bed. Seriously, it felt like I'd slept on a cloud surrounded by rainbows and fairies.

With my head still on my soft and amazing pillow that I was definitely going to have to steal at some point, I looked around the room, but somehow, even waking up in Styles Manor paled in comparison to what Landon and I had shared last night.

My body hurt like crazy from the sex—in a good way. I even had some bumps and bruises from him taking me bent over a little table for round two, and I felt him inside me from how deep he'd been for round one, but I didn't mind any of it.

Things had gotten a little crazy between us last night. I didn't blame him for being rough with me. I hadn't exactly held back either.

It turned out that scratching at old wounds and revealing your truest, inner self to someone else was not only a major turn-on when it was with the right person, but it also made you need to get out of your head. What better way to do that than to pour all the emotion into the other person, turning the pain of the talk into pleasure?

If there was a better way, I didn't know it. More accurately, I didn't *want* to know it. I was perfectly happy with the way we'd handled things last night.

Sighing dreamily, I glanced at the clear blue skies outside and sat up in bed, ready to start the day. After grabbing another quick shower and putting on the clothes I'd worn yesterday, having washed them last night, I made my bed and took one last look around the room.

It was spacious and magnificent, with high ceilings, antique furniture, and gorgeous, rich hardwood floors. A bay window off to one side had a little reading nook tucked into it and it was easy to imagine myself there, reading with a view of the lake.

I knew it would never happen, but it really was too bad. On the other hand, even that couldn't get me down. I felt refreshed somehow. Like I'd picked at scabs only to find that the wounds underneath had truly healed over and that the scabs that were now gone had been nothing but an ugly reminder.

It felt freeing. New. I grinned into the sunlight pouring into the room, humming under my breath as I made sure I left the place in the same condition I'd found it. Then I skipped downstairs to track down my host.

Landon and Colten were in the kitchen, cooking up a storm for breakfast. I had to fight the urge to go to them, to give Colten a hug and Landon a kiss. They weren't my family, but they sure felt like more than just a couple of strangers at this point.

Instead, I tried not to notice how good Landon looked in blue shorts and no shirt but an apron that read, *What's cookin', good lookin'?* covering his chest. "Good morning, gentlemen. Can I jump in and help you finish the food?"

"No!" they both practically yelled at me as they spun away from the stove.

I flinched. "Okay, okay. Sheesh. Talk about intense chivalry."

Landon grinned, shrugging a shoulder at me as he gestured toward the coffee machine. "Would you like a cup?"

"Definitely," I said enthusiastically.

When he started moving toward it, I stepped in his way. My skin tingled at our sudden close proximity. "That's okay, I'll get it."

"Nah, I'll get it," he countered, his voice soft and gentle as his eyes ran across my face. "You can just have a seat and let us do all the work this morning."

"Okay," I said slowly. "I was joking about the intense chivalry thing before."

"We're serving *you* this morning," Colten said, bending over to check on the tray of bacon in the oven and frowning. "Is it supposed to be sizzling like that?"

"Only if you like it crispy," I teased. "If you're one of those sociopaths who like it floppy, then you might have a problem."

Landon chuckled, poured my coffee, and handed it over. "We like it crispy. Just relax, okay? Have a break. Colt is right. We're serving you this morning, and once we're done eating, I'll take you home. Does that give you enough time to get to work?"

Glancing at my watch, I was surprised by how late it already was, but I nodded. "Sure. That's perfect. Brittany had the day off yesterday, so I'm sure she wouldn't mind doing our weekly inventory by herself this morning. Let me just text her."

As I pulled my phone out of my pocket, Landon went back to the stove and pushed some scrambled eggs around a pan. Then they announced that breakfast was ready. I looked around the spread, pretty impressed even if all they'd cooked were the bacon and eggs.

They'd also made some toast, cut up some fruit, and taken a container of yogurt out of the fridge. "Well done, boys. This looks incredible. Do you eat like this every day?"

They exchanged a glance, both of their heads shaking before Colten blurted out, "We usually just have cereal or eggs on toast."

I laughed. "That sounds exactly like my usual breakfast. Thank you for this. It really does look incredible. You're spoiling me."

Colten flushed but looked pretty pleased with himself as he dished up. Landon passed a plate to me and made one for himself, and we settled down to eat together at the breakfast table in the corner.

Looking across at me while we ate, Landon smiled, those green eyes sparkling like emeralds in the sunshine on a hot summer day. "I just need to grab a shirt once we're done. Then I can take you home. I've already showered, so we won't hold you up too much longer."

"Yeah, uh." I shot a pointed look at his apron-covered chest. "Do you make a habit of cooking half naked?"

He laughed. "I don't make a habit of cooking at all, but I didn't want fat or oil spattering all over my shirt. This seemed like the safest option."

I chuckled. "Well, you might not be wrong. How's the hunt for the chef coming?"

He shrugged. "Nothing yet. I can't really believe there's no one in this town who seems to want the job for the summer, but hey. Maybe the right person just hasn't seen the advert yet."

"Most of the people in town who are cooks work at the resorts in the area during the summer months," I said. "I could try to ask around for you."

"That's okay. We've been managing alright so far. As long as Colten keeps enjoying burgers and pizza, we should survive."

I laughed. "If you say so. Just let me know if you change your mind. I know some people I could talk to."

"Thanks, but right now, you're the one I'm worried about," he said conversationally. "Do you need a vehicle to drive to your other jobs?"

"Scott said I could use his truck this week. He's off work and next week? Well, I'll figure it out next week."

Landon nodded, but Colten glanced at him like he had something to say. He looked back at me though, sighing as he finished the rest of his breakfast instead of letting us know what had been on his mind.

When we were done eating, I helped them clean up and load the dishwasher. Then we piled into the truck and Landon drove me home. In the backseat, Colten talked our ears off about chess, excited to show Brody some maneuver he'd learned from his book last night.

"You may want to park around the back," I said as we neared my place. "At this time of day, parking on Main Street is usually impossible."

"Got it." Landon took a right and navigated around the building to the street behind it. As he parked, he twisted in his seat to look at Colten. "Wait here, okay? I'll be right back. I'm going to walk Jewel to her door."

Colten nodded at his father and waved at me with the sweetest smile on his lips. "Bye, Jewel. See you soon."

"See you soon, bud," I replied, giving him a wave in return as I climbed out of the car.

Landon got out too, taking my hand as soon as we were around the corner from where he'd parked. A happy shiver ran through me as I wound my fingers around his. Then I dragged him up the stairs with me and looped my arms around his neck. He stepped into me without hesitation, his mouth coming down to meet mine in a steamy kiss that made me tempted to lock him inside with me.

The only thing that stopped me was knowing Colten was waiting in the car. Groaning as I slowed the kiss to a grudging end, I smiled against Landon's lips. "We should both get going, but before we do, I just wanted to tell you that last night was the best night I've had in a long time. Thank you again for listening to me and for understanding, and then, uh, for taking my mind off it, I guess."

A low chuckle rumbled in his chest as he arched a dark eyebrow at me. "Is that what we're calling it now? Taking our minds off things?"

I shrugged. "If the shoe fits."

Sliding his hands into the back pockets of my shorts, he cupped my ass and held me close to him. "You know, uh, if it was such a good night, why don't you come stay over with us again tonight? I'll make it worth your while and I can always come pick you up again when your workday is done?"

I pinched my bottom lip between my teeth. The thought of spending another night with him was almost too much. I needed another shower. A cold one.

"I'd love to," I replied softly, my fingers trailing into his hair. "Wouldn't it be weird for Colten, though? I mean, I don't really have a reason to stay there tonight." I paused. "Oh. I know! I could say I'm going to be your live-in cook."

He blinked. Hard. "Huh?"

"Think about it." I tapped his temple playfully. "Colten won't think anything of me staying over if I'm going to be your cook. It'll allow us to avoid the awkwardness of it all and I'd get to try out some new recipes I've been eyeing that are too big for one person."

Without waiting for him to respond, I took a big step back when excitement surged through me. "I'll go to the grocery store after my last clean. It's the least I can do. I'll see you later."

Landon was still blinking strangely hard and fast, and he rubbed the back of his neck as he nodded. "Okay. Goodbye, Jewel. I'll see you later."

"See you later." I blew him a kiss before heading inside, closing the door behind me, and sighing dreamily.

How is this my real life? When is someone going to pinch me and pull me out of this dream? I made a mental note to take down Landon's ad for a cook when I was at the grocery store later. He definitely didn't need the help anymore.

He had me now, and I was going to do everything in my power to keep living this dream and squeezing as much joy out of it as possible, for as long as I possibly could.

37

LANDON

I got back in the truck, still a little dazed about Jewel's suggestion. While I wanted her staying at the Manor with us for as long as she wanted to be there, I didn't want her cooking and I didn't know yet how I was going to get around it.

First things first, however, I had to clear the extra guest with my son. I liked Jewel. A lot. I loved having her around and I definitely enjoyed having her in bed—or anywhere else, for that matter. But ultimately, Colten was my first priority this summer.

If he wasn't okay with her coming to stay, then that was that.

"So, uh, how would you feel about Jewel coming to stay with us?" I asked as I turned over the engine, glancing at him in the rearview mirror. "Would that be okay?"

His eyes widened, but I also saw the excitement suddenly shining from them. "I'm all for that idea. I love having her around. She's so happy all the time, and she talks a lot. Which is nice. She's also an extra person to play chess with and she's way more patient than you, Daddy. And way better."

I laughed. "Wow. Thanks for that, but there's something else."

"What?" He frowned. "She's not cooking for us, is she?"

I sighed. "I'm afraid she is. Dinners."

His face fell. "What? *Why?*"

I explained the deal to him and he clutched his stomach, his head shaking as he shot me a pleading look in the mirror. "I can't eat another casserole like that. What are we going to do? She can't cook, Dad. I'm better than her in the kitchen and I can't even do anything."

"Yeah, I know, but we can't tell her she's an awful cook. She's too kind. I don't want to hurt her feelings. Do you?"

"No, of course not." He scoffed, his face entirely glum as he sank back in his seat. "We also can't eat her food, though. We'll die."

I grimaced. "Don't be dramatic. We won't die. We might just, uh, starve. A little bit. Only at night, so that's not too bad."

Colt groaned, his head shaking once more. "No, Dad. I can't."

"Yes, you can," I insisted. "All we need to do is take really small portions of her food and put the weight back on when we get home."

I was joking, but something about what I'd said seemed to have made Colten clam back up. Sort of like the way he'd been when we'd first arrived. Turning to face the window, he sighed, staring out as I drove us away from the main street.

"Hey, bud. What's up? What just happened? You don't have to take small portions. I was kidding. Look, I'll talk to her. I'll—"

"It's not that," he said suddenly. "I mean, it *is* that. I don't want to eat her food, but I will. It's just..."

I gave him a moment to collect his thoughts after he trailed off, not prompting him to speak until he was ready. A block or two later, he finally came out with it. "I don't want to put the weight back on when we get home, Dad. I don't want to go home at all."

Stunned into silence, I swiped my tongue across my lips and rolled them into my mouth. First, he hadn't wanted to be here at all and now he didn't want to leave? As soon as the thought hit though, I realized that I couldn't blame the kid.

Life was obviously much better for him here than back in Los Angeles. He had friends in June Lake. He played outside and he didn't have dread hanging over his head about having to go to school every day with kids who weren't nice to him.

I exhaled slowly, but I didn't say anything. What could I say? It wasn't like I could pack up our lives and move here just because he'd made some friends. The best I could hope for was that the social skills he'd learned here translated once we got back to the city.

We stopped at a red light, and just as I was about to suggest to him that he might make friends at home if he treated them the same way he did Brody, something slammed into our back end. Colten and I both jolted forward and he let out a startled shout.

My features snapped into a scowl as I checked my mirrors, not at all surprised to see a bright red Ferrari behind us. *Dallas fucking Styles.*

"You have got to be kidding me," I growled, unclipping my seatbelt before shooting Colten a meaningful look. "Stay here, kiddo. Let me deal with this, okay?"

I got out of the truck to find Dallas stumbling out of his crumpled car, clutching his phone. Rage simmered in my veins when I realized he'd obviously been texting and driving, but of course, he glowered and laid into me for it.

"Why the hell are you stopped in the middle of the road? What is wrong with you, man? That's not a parking spot."

Grinding my teeth, I pointed at the red traffic light. "I'm not parked there. In case you missed it in driver's ed, red means stop, but I suppose you have to be looking at the road to see a red light."

I pulled my phone out of my pocket and called the cops. Once I was told that the police were on their way, I started taking some pictures of the scene just in case I needed them. Meanwhile, Dallas was getting more and more worked up and a crowd was starting to gather.

"Bullshit! That light wasn't red. Are you suggesting that I wasn't looking at the road? The light was green, idiot. You stopped for no reason."

I sighed but didn't respond. The light had been red. Colten had been with me and he'd seen it too, but moreover, I was sure there would be a way to check these things. Besides, the truck he'd just rammed into was his own.

Or his family's, at least.

A few people in the crowd were holding up their cellphones, but I was actually pretty glad they were here. Dallas noticed it too, smirking at the damn cameras like he was some kind of celebrity as he kept shouting at me.

"You seriously need to get out of town, man," he ranted. "You're doing nothing but causing trouble here. I mean, who parks in the middle of a damn road? The light was green."

"You can keep saying that as much as you want," I finally ground out. "Saying it doesn't make it true. Let's just wait for the police, okay? Calm down."

"Calm down?" He scoffed, his face turning the same color as his car.

In his temper tantrum, his slicked-back hair had fallen over his face. The graying strands over the tomato red of his skin created a sort of sickly contrast. I had no idea how the people around here put up with this guy, but I'd just about had it myself.

"*You* calm down, asshole!" he yelled at me. "This is all your fault. You stopped right in front of me for no reason. Don't you dare tell *me* to calm down. Look at my car! It's wrecked."

I shrugged. "To be fair, the truck is yours too, so that's two wrecked vehicles."

"You're going to pay for this," he demanded, borderline hysterical as he clenched his fists at his sides.

It seemed my remaining calm was really getting under his skin, but there was nothing I could do about it. The cops would be here soon and then hopefully we'd be on our way soon after. Dallas started pacing up and down, his shoulders hunched. He stopped to smirk at a camera every once in a while, but I didn't think anyone was buying the act anymore.

"You are going to pay for this," he snarled, stopping the pacing to shoot me another glare. "You fucking asshole! You just slammed on the brakes without any warning. You're an irresponsible, pathetic, fuck—"

As he got more heated, using foul language now and jabbing his finger in my direction, Colten suddenly rolled down his window and called nervously for me. "Dad? Daddy!"

I strode around to his side of the truck, forcing what I hoped was a reassuring smile to my lips, but my heart jerked when I saw how pale Colten was. "Daddy? Are you okay?"

"I'm fine, bud. Are you okay?"

He stared at me for a long beat, his eyes much too bright. "I think so. Why can't we just leave? That man is really angry."

"I know, but we can't leave the scene of an accident, so we need to wait for the police to get here. Everything is okay though, kiddo. As soon as the police come, I'm just going to have a quick talk with them and then we'll be done."

Dallas was still fuming, snarling at a few of the bystanders who were trying to calm him down. I glanced at him before looking back at Colten. "Just stay in the truck for now. The police will be here real soon."

While I was trying to set him at ease, Dallas suddenly stormed toward me, his middle finger raised and the look in his eyes slightly unhinged. "You're going to be sorry you ever did this. I'll make sure of it. I—"

"I didn't do anything except stop at a red light. Now take it down a notch and wait for the police to get here."

He got right in my face, spittle flying out of his mouth as he kept yelling at me. "Don't tell me what to do. You did this! This is your fault!"

"Take. It. Down. A. Notch," I repeated slowly, enunciating every syllable and every word. "You're scaring my son, Mr. Styles. Just calm down and wait for the police to get here. They'll take our statements and we'll all be on our merry way, but simmer down and back away from this truck and my child. Now."

38

JEWEL

Brittany and I made our way into one of our clients' houses together, quickly falling into our usual steady routine. We worked vigorously side by side to clean from top to bottom, starting in Mrs. Harris's primary bedroom and working our way out.

"Make sure you hit every surface," I reminded Brittany and myself as we strode into her bathroom. "Remember that time she said she saw a speck of dust on the window after we left?"

Brittany giggled and rolled her eyes. "Good old Mrs. Harris. I love her, but heaven knows, she goes over this place with a fine-tooth comb after we've been here."

"Yeah, except that there was no speck of dust when we left," I said, smiling as I thought back to how hard she'd tried to get a discount from us after. "Either way, let's just make sure that we're extra thorough. Otherwise, we'll have to give her twenty bucks off again."

"You got it," Brit called from the shower cubicle as she climbed into it. "Open the windows for now, would you? She desperately needs some fresh air in here, and even if she doesn't, I do."

I chuckled, inhaling the musty air and wondering why the old lady never seemed to open any windows or doors. Then again, she lived here by herself, and even though she was just down the road from Scott's house and knew she could call him any time if she needed help, I supposed I couldn't blame her for being cautious.

It made me wonder about my own future. Would I be a lonely old woman one day who hated fresh air? I couldn't imagine it, but that didn't mean it wouldn't happen.

I sighed as I gathered my supplies and went down on my knees to scrub the porcelain throne. Pulling on my gloves, I reflected on my morning with Landon and decided that I would not, in fact, become a lonely old woman.

Obviously, I wasn't going to be growing old with *him*, but there had to be at least one more where he'd come from, right? Sooner or later, I would meet the other-Landon. The one who wanted a simple, small-town life and perhaps already had one in a neighboring town or something.

The difference between Mrs. Harris and me was that she said she'd already had the love of her life. Her late husband, Harold, had married her at twenty-one and he'd spent every day of the rest of his life with her. I wanted that kind of love too. The kind where you committed to someone and stuck by them for as long as you were on this earth. Through thick and thin, for richer or poorer, and all that stuff. I wanted it so bad and I honestly thought Mrs. Harris could have another shot at it, but she wasn't interested.

She said a person only got one love like that and she was content enough on her own, knowing she'd been one of the lucky ones to have had it at all. Memories of my night with Landon flickered through my mind again, but not the sex this time. The talking.

Opening up to him and feeling safe enough to bare my soul. To tell him about all the bad that had happened in my life and to trust that he wasn't going to take off running because of it. That had been huge for me, but I couldn't afford to start thinking about him as my *one*.

While it still hurt to think about Landon leaving someday soon, I had realized this morning that he was as intent on making the best of our time together as I was. Six weeks was better than nothing and I was determined to make this the best summer ever, and then after, I would move on.

I'd been thinking about what Brittany had said about going into this with my eyes wide open, and since there was no avoiding my attraction to him or our connection any longer, I figured I'd go with Brit's advice. Have some fun, let my hair down, and don't worry too much about the after.

The after that I knew would suck but hopefully only for a little while. Whatever happened in the after though, I couldn't let it steal this opportunity to be with him. In whichever capacity was possible.

With my thoughts to distract me, the morning flew by in a blur of hard work and cleaning products. Lemon scented and with freshly scrubbed hands, Brittany and I left Mrs. Harris's when we were done and I turned to her when she climbed into Scott's truck.

"We've got a few minutes before we need to be at the next client's place. Do you just want to eat in the truck?"

We were both a sweaty mess and I knew what she was going to say before she'd even said it. "Sure. Lunch break in Scott's truck. Why not? Or we could go swimming."

"We can't go swimming. We're not done for the day yet."

"Maybe we can stop on our way to Ms. Pam's?" she suggested. "Just a quick dip—"

She was cut off when my phone rang and I smiled when I saw my brother's name. "We're not done yet, if that's why you're calling, but yes. We'd love to go out on the boat with you later."

"I wish that was why I'm calling, but it's not." My heart stuttered at the serious tone of his voice. Scott was almost never serious, but when he was, it was never good news. "Did you hear about the fender bender on Main Street today?"

I frowned deeply. "No. What happened?"

Scott sighed. "Dallas rear-ended Landon."

My stomach flipped over. "Are they okay? Was Colten in the truck too?"

"Yeah, he was, but it sounds like they're all okay. A little bit shaken up, I'd assume, but no injuries." He paused for a beat. "Well, actually,

Dallas might not be okay. From the sounds of things, he got his panties twisted up in a pretty tight knot and the cops even cuffed him before they took him away."

"They cuffed him?" Disbelief made my brain feel disconnected from my body for a minute. "The police department here, in June Lake, arrested Dallas Styles?"

"Yep," Scott said, some of the seriousness finally easing out of his tone now that he'd broken the news to me. "It looks like it might've been a DUI."

"A DUI?" My blood ran cold. "You're absolutely sure that Landon and Colten are both okay?"

"That's what I heard, but maybe you should give him a call later? I'm sure he'd appreciate it. I spoke to Don, who was at the scene this morning, and he told me Dallas really tore into Landon."

"And Landon?" I asked curiously. "Did he lose his cool?"

"Not according to Don. He said Landon just kept telling Dallas to calm down and wait for the cops, but you should really talk to him about it. I wasn't there."

"I will. Thanks for letting me know. And Dallas? What's going to happen to him?"

I could practically hear the shrug in his voice. "Don't know, don't really care. Except that it's about time they slapped a pair of cuffs on that man. I just hope he doesn't pay his way out of it. It'll be real nice if they toss him in jail for a bit too, keep him off the streets and out of our hair for as long as they legally can."

I hummed my agreement, but my heart and limbs felt heavy with worry. I needed to know that Landon and Colten were okay before I'd be able to think about anything else.

Scott hung up the phone and I navigated to Landon's number. I also filled Brittany in quickly, seeing the concern for them clouding her eyes as well. "Check in with them, but Jewel? Physical injury isn't the only thing you have to worry about. I'm willing to bet Dallas is going to try to blame the accident on Landon."

"I'm sure he already has, but it was still Dallas who got arrested. Let's hope that means they didn't believe him."

The call connected and my heart stammered in my chest. "Landon? Are you there? Are you okay? I just heard about the accident."

"I'm here," he said.

The relief that ran through me at the sound of his voice, as even and reassuring as ever, nearly brought me to tears. On the other end of the line, he let out a soft chuckle. "It really wasn't that serious at all. Just a fender bender. We're fine. I'm kind of surprised it even made it to the town's gossip line."

"*Everything* makes it to the town's gossip line." I chewed my cheek for a moment before I lowered my voice, needing him to know how much I wanted him to be honest with me. "You're sure you're both okay?"

"Yeah, we're fine. Dallas just got a bit aggressive and he spooked Colten. We actually just sat down to talk it all over. Can I fill you in on everything later?"

"Of course. I just wanted to make sure you were alright. Say hi to Colten for me and tell him I said Dallas is more bark than bite. He doesn't need to be afraid of him."

"I will, but it might help him to hear it directly from you later. I'll call you, okay?"

"Okay. Also call if either of you need anything at all. I'm here for you." I said goodbye then, relieved to have heard that they hadn't been injured, but it was still difficult for me to finish the workday.

I was distracted with thoughts of how bad it could've been and worried about poor Colten. I'd seen Dallas mad a few times before and it wasn't pretty. He probably scared the kid witless and made a huge scene, even if it sounded like the accident had been his fault.

Drifting around Ms. Pam's house, cleaning but not really focusing on what I was doing, I nearly knocked over a lamp and Brittany arched an eyebrow at me. "Okay, so I know the answer to this should be obvious since you weren't actually in the accident, but are *you* okay? You don't look like you are."

"Yeah. No. I mean, I'm fine." I exhaled heavily, licking my lips as I tried to put my thoughts into some kind of order. "I guess I'm just hoping that Dallas gets more than a slap on the wrist this time around."

"What are the chances of *that* happening?" she asked, resignation in her eyes as she shrugged. "That's just how the world works, Jewel. Rich people have connections and those people they're connected to help keep them out of trouble."

"Yeah, but it's not right. He's really going to hurt someone one of these days. He's been getting worse and worse, and I can't stand the thought of us all just watching and waiting to see how bad it has to get before the police department realize that their buddy poses a genuine threat."

"I know. Let's just hope they charge him today, okay? Usually, they just let him go, so if they keep him locked up this time, it means they've finally come to their senses."

I wasn't hanging onto much hope that it would happen, or so I thought until I saw Dallas leaving the police station. On my way home, I drove past it and it was only as all that hope crashed and burned that I realized I'd really put my faith in the department to do the right thing this time.

Frustration bubbled through me. As always, they were just letting him go because of who he was, his wealth, and his connections. Being a Styles in this town had always bought him a certain amount of leeway, but after he'd taken over the family estate and everything from his parents, who had been Robert and Lucille's children, he'd really been getting out of control.

I knew he donated a lot of money to the police, to town hall, and to local charities, which redeemed him in the eyes of some, but not as far as I was concerned. It wasn't like he had decided to make those donations. He was simply keeping them up now that his parents weren't around anymore.

As I drove past him, he saw me, whistling and even blowing me a disgusting kiss. *That's it. I've had enough.*

Flipping him the bird out the window, I wished there had been a puddle on the side of the road I could've driven through to splash him with some dirty water, but for now, giving him the middle finger would have to do. He laughed it off though, probably telling himself that I was still just playing hard to get, but at this point, I didn't know how I could make it any clearer.

He was the most revolting, vile creature I'd ever had the misfortune of coming across and I'd rather move across the country than go on so much as one date with him. Eventually, I hoped he'd realize it.

Leaving him behind me, I drove home and packed an overnight bag. Then I headed to Scott's house to drop off his truck. Landon and Colten would be picking me up from there later and I couldn't wait to see them.

Just the thought of what might've happened if it was true that Dallas had been driving under the influence made my heart cave in on itself. They could've been seriously injured. Or worse—and the way that made my chest feel like it'd been turned inside out was the first clue I got that it might not just be a casual relationship to me.

Despite what I kept telling myself, I was developing real feelings for this man and I truly cared about his son. But that didn't scare me. It just meant I was going to have to really work at making the time I had with them worth it.

And then move in with Mrs. Harris once they were gone. Just two lonely women, one of whom had had the love of her life already and the other having only known hers for a summer.

39

LANDON

Colten and I sat down in the kitchen with a soda each and a plate of chips between us. I looked at my son from across the table, noticing the hazy gleam in his eyes and the slight furrow of his brow, and worry ratcheted my insides.

The accident itself had been minor, the damage to the truck barely noticeable. Dallas's car was a different story altogether, but even that wouldn't be totaled. As far as accidents went, we'd gotten lucky.

Colten dragged a chip slowly through the dip, turning it over before bringing it to his mouth and biting into it as if he was in a daze. I knew this had been his first experience with a car accident and that, fender bender or no, he had to be at least a little bit traumatized, but I had a feeling that wasn't what was bugging him.

"Okay, kiddo," I said, trying to keep my voice calm and reassuring as I fixed my gaze on his. "Let me have it. What's going on up there?"

I tapped my temple, then leaned back, waiting for him to open up. Colt popped the rest of the chip into his mouth, but even his chewing was different. Too slow and like he was savoring the taste of the ordinary, salty snack.

Frowning, I inhaled deeply and mentally cursed Dallas for acting like such a nutjob earlier. Colt swallowed the chip before he suddenly flicked his eyes to mine. "It was an accident."

He said it slowly, almost like he wasn't sure if he was right. I nodded and gave him a small, encouraging smile. "Yes, it was. How are you feeling about it?"

He shrugged, those green eyes far away and thoughtful as he spoke. "I'm okay. I just don't understand why Dallas was so angry. It's just an accident. He didn't hit us on purpose and we didn't do anything wrong."

"You're absolutely right. He didn't hit us on purpose and we didn't do anything wrong, but some people get worked up a lot faster than others. Especially when they know that something was their fault."

"But that's just it. It was *his* fault. He wasn't looking where he was going, so why was he so angry at you?"

Because you can't fix stupid and entitled.

Instead of saying that though, I tried to explain it in a more constructive way. "He has a quick temper and I don't think he's used to taking responsibility for stuff. That's why it's so important to learn to say sorry when you've been in the wrong. All people usually want from you is an acknowledgment of fault and an apology that you mean. If we're not taught about accountability as kids, then sometimes, as a grownup, it is hard to apologize. For some grownups, it's much easier to just get angry and point fingers."

"Like Dallas?"

I nodded. "Exactly like him. I don't know if he was ever taught about taking responsibility and saying sorry, but even if he was, it doesn't look like he truly knows how to do it. He might not even believe that he was in the wrong today, but we know that he was, and thankfully, there were enough people around us who saw what happened. That means that no one else blames me. It's just him and that's okay because what he believes is none of my business."

Colten's head tipped as he stared deep into my eyes. "You're not scared of what's going to happen next?"

"Nope." I gave him a smile I hoped would convince him that I was being honest. "There's evidence that we didn't do anything wrong and enough witnesses that will say that we didn't just stop randomly. The police will also be able to access any cameras in the vicinity of the accident and they can even look at the data from the traffic light. That's evidence and what it means is that whatever happens next, it's not our problem."

"So you're not scared he's going to come after you?" A shudder traveled through him and I reached out, gently laying a hand over his forearm and giving it a soft squeeze.

"I doubt he's going to come here to yell at me some more or to start a fight, if that's what you're worried about. By now, he would've calmed down and he's not stupid. He's not going to cause any more trouble for himself."

"But this is his house," he said slowly, fear shimmering in those eyes when they locked on mine. "Doesn't that mean he can come inside whenever he wants?"

"Well, I don't know if he has spare keys, but we do know that he can open the gates, so how about this? We'll make sure that we put the deadbolts on the exterior doors tonight. Will that make you feel safer?"

He dropped his chin in a nod and I smiled. "Great. That's what we'll do then, but you don't have to be afraid of him, buddy. He just lost his temper, is all. It's normal for people with egos as big as his to go off on others when something happens that they don't like, but that's all it is. His ego was bruised. He won't want to draw any more negative attention to himself by having another tantrum. Worst case scenario is that he tells his buddies in a bar about some guy who stopped for nothing right in front of him."

"We don't care about that?" he asked carefully.

I chuckled. "We don't care about that. We have the law, the evidence, and the witnesses on our side. That's all we care about. Besides, I don't think he has too many buddies around here anyway who will give him the time of day. He doesn't strike me as the kind of person who attracts too many friends. That's the problem with people like him. His ego is so big, it doesn't leave much room for anyone else in his life."

Finally, Colten managed a tiny smile. "We're going to be alright?"

"Absolutely," I said confidently. "It's really not anything to worry about."

The front doors opened then and I stiffened, immediately jumping up while arching an eyebrow at Colten and telling him to stay put. To my immense relief, it was Jewel who walked through the door, smiling and carrying armfuls of grocery bags.

A wide smile spread on her lips when she saw me. "Scott dropped me off. We didn't want you to have to come all the way back into town to pick me up after what happened earlier. You're sure you're okay?"

"We're fine," I said easily, striding over and taking some of the bags off her hands. "What's all this? You really didn't have to go shopping."

"I know, but I wanted to," she said brightly. "If I'm going to be your cook for the summer, I needed to pick up some things that I'm going to need. Plus, I didn't want you to have to worry about what we'll have for dinner tonight, so I've got it covered."

"That was very thoughtful," I said.

"How's Colten?" she asked as she preceded me to the kitchen. She smiled when she saw him frozen in place at the table. "Hey, kiddo. I was just asking about you. Are you okay?"

His gaze dropped to the grocery bags in her hands and he grimaced but smoothed his features quickly to give her a smile instead. "I am now. Dallas just freaked me out a little bit, but Dad says it's nothing to worry about."

She chuckled and dropped the groceries on the counter before she went over to give him a hug. "Your dad is absolutely right. Dallas is our local idiot in June Lake. I'm sorry he hit you and I'm so relieved that neither of you are hurt, but don't mind him. If I had a dollar for every time he's yelled at people who haven't done anything wrong, I'd be richer than him."

Colten got up after she released him, hovering as she walked back to the counter and started unpacking the groceries. "What are you cooking tonight?"

"Lasagna," she said excitedly, glancing at him and pumping her eyebrows. "It's comfort food for me and I figured you could use a little comfort. It's also not the easiest dish to make in really small portions for just one person, so it always feels like a waste to make it just for myself."

As she separated the groceries into things she'd need tonight and other stuff to be packed away, Colten and I jumped in and helped take things to the pantry or the fridge. Those golden eyes of hers met mine as I walked back to the counter, softening as she raked them over me as if searching for injury.

"I'm so sorry he crashed into you," she said quietly. "That man has always been an accident waiting to happen behind a steering wheel. If you ask me, his license should be revoked, but obviously, that's not going to happen."

"Don't feel too bad for us," I said. "The kicker is that he rear-ended his own truck, seeing as how it comes with the Manor for renters to use. It really is no skin off my back."

She chuckled. "Is it bad that I'm really getting a kick out of that? Out of everyone around here whose property he could've damaged with his recklessness, it was his own. That's brilliant. Karma really does have our backs."

Colten came out of the pantry and pulled up at a stool at the island. He watched carefully when she started with the lasagna and peppered her with questions as the process continued. "Are you sure the recipe calls for that much salt? Shouldn't the layers be a little deeper? Is it, uh, supposed to smell like that?"

She answered them all good-naturedly, but when she turned away to check the oven, I nudged him. "Let her cook. There's nothing we can do about it now."

Thankfully, she didn't hear me and his worry about the dish seemed to have gone over her head. When he went off to set the table and she began with a salad, my phone rang and my heart leaped when I saw Walt's name on the screen.

"I need to take this," I muttered, sliding my thumb across the green bar as I strode out of the kitchen. "Walter? Are you okay?"

"I'm fine. I'm fine."

A pit of worry formed in my stomach. "Are you sure? You sound kind of off."

"Worrywart," he teased, but even that lacked its usual luster. "You worry too much. I really am fine. Better than fine, actually."

I frowned, walking to the sliding doors leading out to the balcony and peering at the lake beyond. "How do you know that?"

Walter chuckled. "Well, for starters, they keep a close eye on us here, as you know. I just got my bloodwork done today and the doctor said that I'm fit as a fiddle. For an old man anyway."

"What's going on then?" I asked, that worry still nagging at my gut. "I know there's something, so spit it out."

"There is something, but it's not about me," he said carefully. "I'm calling because someone showed up here today looking for you. Someone I really wasn't expecting."

"Who?" I asked, half distracted when I turned back to the kitchen to see Jewel pouring something into a pot on the stove while Colten scrunched up his nose.

"Kaitlin," Walter said and I spun back to the windows instantly, my stomach going ice cold at the mention of my ex's name.

"What the hell was she doing there?" I asked. "Why would she be trying to track me down after all this time? Unless, of course, her guilty conscience has finally caught up with her. It only took her ten years to reach out to check on her own damn son."

"Uh, no." He sighed heavily. "She didn't even ask about him, son. It sounds like she knows about your inheritance. She seemed to remember that you were supposed to get it all when you turned thirty, and obviously, she knows how old you are. I think she's sniffing around to see if she can cash in on some of it for herself. I just wanted to warn you."

"Fuck." I cursed under my breath, exhaling through my nostrils before I nodded. "Thanks for letting me know. I'm pretty sure you're right about her intentions. I should've seen something like this coming."

"Kaitlin always has been the gift that keeps on giving," he said lightly. "I should be turning in soon. You have a good night, my boy. Send my love to Colt."

"I will," I promised before ending the call. Then I took a minute to collect myself before heading over to the table where Jewel and Colten were sitting down to eat.

Once again, the meal was atrocious but the salad was crisp and fresh. I managed a few bites of the lasagna, happy to have the salad to wash it down with. Meanwhile, Jewel's tastebuds didn't seem to pick up on the salt overload masquerading as pasta and she smiled at me.

"Is everything okay? You've been a little quiet since you took that call."

"Yeah." I glanced at Colten, but I knew I had to be truthful here. If Kaitlin was after some of that money, she wouldn't stop at the senior living facility. There was every possibility she'd be waiting naked in my bed when we got back home or something equally ridiculous. "Walter warned me that Colt's mom showed up. Apparently, she's been looking for us."

The color drained from his cheeks and he pushed his plate away, ashen faced as he shook his head. "I just lost my appetite."

Clever, I mused, knowing he was using this to get out of finishing the horribly salty meal, but he couldn't fake how pale he'd gone. He truly was worried about his mother coming out of the woodwork, and if I had to be completely honest with myself, so was I.

Kaitlin Crew was selfish, greedy, and didn't even know the meaning of the word *empathy*. Jewel gave me a curious, confused look, but I glanced at Colten once more, not wanting to get into the nitty-gritty in front of him.

All he had to know was that she'd shown up and that it might happen again. He definitely didn't need to know that I was far more worried about what she was up to than about what Dallas was going to do next. Compared to her, the local idiot—as Jewel had correctly termed him—was as tame as a newborn puppy.

Kaitlin, on the other hand, was trouble. And apparently, that trouble was headed directly for me.

40

JEWEL

Twenty-four hours after Walter had called to warn them about Colten's mother, I was taking a long soak in the en suite bath in my luxurious room at the Manor, giving Colt and Landon some time to speak privately. All day long, the boy had been quiet and withdrawn while Landon had tried to keep things cheerful and upbeat, but even I had been able to see the worry in his eyes.

I couldn't imagine how it felt for Colt to have a mother who hadn't wanted to raise him. I also didn't envy Landon the task of having to navigate it all. While I didn't know much about Kaitlin, it seemed to me that she'd once again put Landon in an impossible position and that, by itself, was enough to tell me that she had to be an incredibly selfish person.

First leaving him with their son without any notice or consideration for either of them, and now by showing up at his stepfather's living facility out of the blue. Surely, she had to have known that Walter would reach out and tell them, and that in doing so, all sorts of old wounds would be torn open.

Lying there in the warm, citrus-scented water, I dragged my hands across the surface, wondering how any mother could be so thoughtless. My own had abandoned me too, but only once I had been much older than Colten was even now. Plus, she'd kept in touch for a while after she'd left. At least she hadn't simply disappeared overnight without a trace.

Still, having had my own mother walk out on me, I related to Colten and the uncertainty he had to be feeling right now. Neither of them seemed to know exactly why she'd shown up at Walter's care facility, though I had a feeling Landon suspected something he wasn't saying out loud.

For both their sakes, I was hoping she'd simply been checking in. Perhaps even seeking them out to apologize. But while I was naturally optimistic, wanting to give people the benefit of the doubt, I wasn't naive.

I knew that her surfacing like this likely wasn't good news. Sighing as I lathered some soap into a sponge and washed myself, I pondered what this meant for Landon and Colten. Would they cut their summer short and head home to deal with her?

The mere thought made my chest ache. I only had a few more weeks left with them, but I desperately wanted those few weeks. I would hate to have to say goodbye to them even earlier than I'd known I'd have to.

Eventually, clean and wrinkled, I got out of the bath and changed into comfortable sweats with a light, long-sleeved T-shirt that hung slightly off one shoulder. It had started raining earlier, and while it wasn't cold, it was definitely nippier than it had been earlier.

Heading out of my room, I saw that Colten's light was off, but there was still a glow emanating from downstairs which told me that some of the lights down there were still on. Following the glow, I found Landon sitting by a window in the parlor, watching the rain fall with a glass of whiskey in his hand.

"Hey," I said softly, not wanting to startle him. "Mind if I join you?"

"No. Of course not. Come on over here." He glanced at me, those greens soft but still a little cloudy with worry. "I didn't realize that it rained at night around here during the summer."

I chuckled. "Rainy nights are rare this time of year, but I love them. They always smell so incredible. Especially out here at the Manor."

We were surrounded by so many trees and so much grass. The windows in the room were open and I sighed dreamily as I sat down beside him on the sofa. Curling into his side, I put my hand on his knee and breathed in the earthy scent floating in on a refreshing breeze.

"How did the talk go?" I asked quietly. "Is he okay? He seemed a bit down today."

Landon shrugged, snaking a warm arm around my shoulders and drawing patterns on my bicep as he returned his gaze to the rain. "He deserves better than the likes of Kaitlin. The kid has a good head on his shoulders, you know?"

"He really does," I agreed thoughtfully. "No doubt he's questioning a lot of things right now."

"That's what bugs me," he murmured, lowering his head to rest it on top of mine. "I've never kept any secrets from him. As soon as I knew he was old enough to understand, I told him that his mother left because she chose to. That it had nothing to do with him."

He released a shaky breath. "I told him that she's always wanted to put herself first, and that's what she did when she left. It's who she is and who she will always be."

I glanced up at him. "And now? I hope he still believes that it wasn't his fault."

"I think he does, but he's a kid. What kid doesn't want to know their mother? It's only natural, but I had to make sure that he knows she's probably going to put herself first again this time around. Whatever she wants from us, I needed him to know that he has to manage his expectations."

"Shit, that's tough," I said, burrowing deeper into his side and holding him a little closer. "What did he say?"

"That he's already come to the same conclusion basically. It sounds like his main concern is that she's going to hurt me again, which she won't. She doesn't have that kind of power over me anymore, but Colten? He's too young to remember how much she hurt him."

He went quiet for a long time after that and my heart went out to him, bleeding for the pain they both must've experienced at her hands. "It must've been really hard having such a young baby and becoming a single father."

"It was the hardest thing I've ever had to go through," he admitted. "I'd, uh, I'd go to him when he was crying. Pick him up out of his crib and cuddle him. Change his diaper. Give him a bottle. Whatever I could think of to make him stop crying, but I knew I couldn't give him what he really wanted, which was his mother. He couldn't ask for her yet, but I mean, it doesn't take a rocket scientist to figure it out. There were nights when he was inconsolable, but he and I got through it eventually."

"I admire you for that," I said, completely honest. "I cannot even imagine how difficult it must have been for you, holding a crying baby all night long and not knowing what to do about his longing for the one person who should always have been there for him."

"It wasn't fun. I can tell you that much. But the thing is that I really wouldn't change it because, in the end, he stopped crying for her. Colten is mine in every single way and we've always been so much better off without her. The thought of her coming back now and trying to sink her claws into him? It makes me so fucking furious and protective. I feel like an animal in a trap ready to gnaw my own limbs off to defend what's mine."

I felt a rush of attraction toward him that spiked my blood pressure so much that it damn near made me dizzy. This man was just so incredible. So strong and so real. I rolled my head on his shoulder to look up at him, bringing my hand to his face and stroking his cheekbone with my thumb.

"You are an amazing father and a provider unlike any other I've ever met. Colten is lucky to have you and I'm quite sure he knows that. No matter what she does now, she can't change the past. He *is* yours and he will always know who was there for him."

"Sure, but she's still his mom," he murmured.

"Whatever happens, I have your back and his." I turned a little more into him so my torso was facing his as I held those beautiful eyes. "Do you have any idea what she wants?"

"Money," he said as if it was a lot more than just an educated guess. Like he knew it for a fact. "When I turned thirty, I received my inheritance from my parents and she knows about it."

"Do you think that's why she's suddenly circling? Are you worried she wants your inheritance?"

He nodded, his next words chilling me to the bone. "What I'm most worried about isn't the money itself. It's that she's going to file for custody so that she has some form of a claim to it."

I shook my head, my eyes widening at the thought of anyone doing something so truly vile. "I'm no expert at this, obviously, but it doesn't sound like she has a leg to stand on. Maybe you should call a lawyer, though. Just in case."

"I am a lawyer." He laughed, brushing a few damp locks of hair out of my face.

"A family law lawyer," I said, smiling up at him. "From what I've heard, it's never a good idea to take your own case to court."

"It's not, but I also don't know anyone I trust more than myself with this." He moved his thumb to my mouth, dragging the pad of it across my lips as he drank me in like he was marveling at my very existence. "Thank God, you're here. I'm not entirely sure what would've happened if you hadn't been, but I think there would've been a lot more spinning out."

"I doubt it," I said confidently. "You seem to have all this under control, even if it's not easy."

"Sure, but knowing you're here has been keeping me calm. We're in this beautiful place, we've got you with us, and even if she's out there somewhere, trying to find us, she can't take this from any of us, you know?"

"I do know." I climbed into his lap and smiled as I wound my arms around his neck.

Mild surprise flickered across his features, but his hands fell to my hips and he gripped them tight as I whispered in his ear. "Now let me distract you from your troubles, Mr. Payne. Right here and now, it's only us here and I think we should take advantage of that. Don't you?"

41

LANDON

Jewel had been an absolute blessing this week. Not only did she help get us through the initial shock of Kaitlin showing up at Walt's, but she'd been doing everything in her power to make sure we were still enjoying the time we had here in June Lake.

She played chess with Colten during the day and took us out on Scott's boat, and she'd spent most nights in my bed and listened whenever I'd wanted to talk. For the most part, now that the initial shock had subsided, things had all but gone back to normal.

Kaitlin had never reached out to me and I was hopeful that she couldn't track me down here. Even if she could, she was hardly the sort of woman to be interested in traveling to a tiny town like this one. Walter hadn't heard from her again either, so while the worry in my gut was still there, I was trying not to let it get to me too much.

If she dropped by once we got home, I'd find out what she wanted then, and if she didn't, then she'd obviously realized she had no legal claim to any money from me. I suspected she wouldn't just let it go, but for now, she was either considering her options, didn't know where I was, or was working on some kind of strategy, which bought me time to keep enjoying the summer.

Meanwhile, Dallas hadn't been seen around town all week and everything was settled with the insurance company about the fender bender. Colten didn't seem concerned about any of that anymore and whatever mild trauma he had suffered as a result of the accident seemed to have worked itself out.

All of which meant we were having a carefree Saturday at the town fair. Colten barely had any time for me, running around with kids his age and some a bit younger or older, playing carnival games and going on rides I couldn't imagine him having been brave enough to go on back home.

In such a short amount of time, I'd seen tremendous growth in him and I was immensely proud of him for it.

Jewel giggled as she bumped her hip into mine, drawing my attention away from my thoughts. "Should I even ask what you were thinking about to make you smile like that?"

I winked at her, my lips tugging into a slow smirk. "Well, since you've already asked, you might as well know that I was thinking about you, actually. I'm not quite sure how to thank you for everything you've done for us, but especially for introducing Colten to Brody. I can't believe he's the same kid I brought here with me. He's really coming into his own with those kids."

Her eyes tracked to where they were being taught how to walk on stilts. "I think you should give credit where credit is due. All I did was introduce them. Colten is the one who grabbed hold of the opportunity and made it count."

"True, but still, thank you," I said. My hand slid to the small of her back as I guided her to the line for the Ferris Wheel. "I haven't been on one of these things since I was a kid. You're sure this one is well maintained, right?"

She shrugged, her eyes sparkling with laughter as they met mine. "Not really. All I know is that we haven't had any incidents with it before."

"Well, that's comforting," I joked, honestly just happy to be getting back to having fun without anything to really worry about.

Breathing in the fresh air, I felt the warm rays of late afternoon sun on my skin and grinned. Colten wasn't the only one who was coming into himself here. I felt like I was getting reconnected with myself as well, remembering all the things that were truly important in life.

Like Colten. And like taking a step back, slowing down, and literally focusing on enjoying all the little things that brought me joy.

Finally feeling completely relaxed and at ease, I joked around with Jewel as we inched closer to the front of the line. Just as we were about to get on, Scott and Brittany climbed off, both of them giggling like kids and blushing.

My eyebrows swept up. They spotted Jewel and immediately stopped in their tracks, turning even more red than they had been before. She rolled her eyes at them both. "You're terrible at hiding your crushes on each other. If it matters, you have my blessing for whatever this is." She gave Scott a stern look. "Just don't break her heart, or I'll have to kill you." Turning to Brittany next, she propped a hand on her hip and nodded at her friend. "Be good to him. He's my big brother, so if you hurt him—"

"You'll have to kill me too?" Brittany grinned.

"Yep. As long as we're all clear about that, I don't really care what you do with each other." Her nose wrinkled. "Just, uh, spare me any graphic details."

Scott smirked at her and mimed zipping his lips, but Brittany did her best to look innocent, batting her eyelashes as she shook her head. "There are no graphic details to share. We just kis—"

He suddenly slid an arm all the way around her shoulders, pulling her into his side and laughing as he clamped his palm over her mouth. "She said to spare her the details. Let's just go. Have fun on the ride, you guys."

Brittany shook with laughter against him. Her eyes flicked up with a look of adoration in them as she stared at him and said something too muffled to make out. He dragged her away but turned to call to us over his shoulder.

"Remember to keep it PG up there," he warned. "It's not as easy as it might sound."

Jewel pretended to gag. I nodded at him, took her hand, and pulled her onto the ride. We sat down on the hard seat, waiting for the attendant to lock the bar in place over our laps before lurching when the bench started moving again.

"Can you believe him?" She grimaced and leaned into her seat beside me. Her hand was on my thigh but her eyes were on the horizon as we rose slowly higher into the air. "Keep it PG. I mean, it's not like we're going to forget how many kids are around."

I laughed. "You might not, but I can't make any promises."

We stopped for more people to climb on below, and I turned to her, taking in the slight rosy flush on her cheeks and the bright light in her eyes. "I tend to lose track of things whenever I kiss you. So you might have to put on the brakes if I forget about the kids. Deal?"

Her lips parted, and her tongue came out to wet them. She shook her head, her voice a little more breathy than usual when she spoke again. "Uh uh. You can't say stuff like that to me and then expect me to put on the brakes. It's not right."

"How so?" I asked, amused by her reaction to what, to me, had been a relatively simple truth. "You already know that you do things to me. Why can't I say it?"

She groaned. "Because it's hot, that's why."

"Is it?" My head jerked a little to one side. "I thought everyone around here was honest, so I thought you'd be used to hearing stuff like that."

"Honest doesn't mean that we engage casually in dirty talk," she said.

I laughed, bent my head closer to hers, and spoke against her hair. "That's not dirty talk, baby. If you want dirty talk, how about—"

"No," she squeaked, her cheeks even more flushed now, and she pulled back to look into my eyes. "We can't do that up here."

I stopped staring at her for long enough to take a quick look around, noticing that we were nearly to the very top. I couldn't see any people from where we were currently stopped and it seemed a good bet that they didn't have a good view of us either.

"Why not?" I asked, my cock rousing as I slid a hand up the inside seam of her jeans. "Think of it as foreplay."

"Foreplay?" Her eyebrows quirked up. "We just got here a little while ago. If we start getting all hot and bothered now, it's going to feel like forever before we get home."

"Yeah, but the anticipation will just make it that much sweeter." Capturing her chin in my free hand, I brought my mouth to hers, kissed her hard, and stroked my tongue into her mouth.

She melted into me and wound an arm around my neck, forgetting all about her inhibitions for a moment. A moment I savored as I tasted the tangy lemonade on her lips and breathed in the clean, sweet scent of her.

"You and I are going to take a shower together later." I relished her sharp intake of breath when I ran a thumb across her pussy over the denim. "When we do, I want to see your lips wrapped around my cock again. I'm not going to last, but don't worry. I fully intend on spending the rest of the night making it up to you."

She moaned her assent, leaning into what quickly became a steamy make-out session that I put a stop to before I came in my pants like some boy. Chuckling against my lips, she rested her forehead against mine, just holding it there for a few beats as we caught our breath.

"Looks like you were the one who remembered after all," she murmured. "Note to self, don't let Landon speak to me alone while we're in public."

I groaned and turned to the view before I started showering the attendant with cash from above just to keep us up there a while longer. "Yeah, I might've gotten a little carried away with that. Think they'll miss us if we slid away to your place for an hour once we get back down?"

Humor shone through the lust in her eyes when I glanced at her. "No sirree. You wanted the anticipation to make it sweeter, so have at it."

I laughed, swiping my palms over my face and regretting my

choices as I tried to claw back my self-control. "I need you to not touch me for a minute."

She giggled and poked me in the ribs. "Oh, really? Does this count as touching?"

Scooting as far away from her as I could get, I chuckled and shook my head. Then I focused on the view so that I didn't have to look at her right then. The lights from the fair, the rides, and the tents reflected on the surface of the lake as the sun set, and it might just have been the most beautiful sight I'd ever seen.

Second to the woman sitting beside me, of course.

As the thought occurred to me, I took her hands and felt the sudden urge to level with her. "You've made this the best summer of my life, Jewel."

She blinked a few times in surprise, but then she nodded and squeezed my fingers. "I feel the same way."

A strange but profound sadness crept into her eyes and I closed the distance between us, scooting closer to her again. I slid a finger under her chin and gently lifted it. "Hey, what's this? What's happening right now?"

"I just, uh, I know it's silly, but I don't want you and Colt to go back to LA. I mean, I know you have to and everything. This isn't me begging you to stay. I just can't really stand to think about you leaving."

I pulled her close, folded my arms around her, and closed my eyes. "Let's not think about that right now. Let's just enjoy tonight, okay?"

Now that she'd said it, though, I had to admit that I didn't want to go back to LA any more than she wanted us to, and I already knew Colten didn't want to go home. We had to do it, though. We had to leave here eventually, but I didn't want to overthink it.

We still had four more weeks here and I wasn't going to ruin them by dreading the moment we had to leave. For the first time in forever, I was truly living for the moment and it felt damn good.

Just like Jewel did when she was in my arms like this. It really was just too damn good to let a little something like reality come in and steal it all away from me.

42

JEWEL

Landon Payne was too darn irresistible for my own good. In one fell swoop, he could melt my heart and set my body on fire. It was ridiculous. It should've been illegal for one person to have it all the way he did—the silver tongue, the heart of gold, and the physical features of a god.

It made my knees weak and my chest feel like it had a hummingbird trapped in the middle of it. After a Ferris Wheel ride that I would never forget for a variety of reasons, we went on the some of the other rides and then played a few carnival games with Colten and a handful of the friends he'd made.

I couldn't deny that I still wanted to drag Landon straight to my bed if I'd been given half a chance, but I also just loved seeing him engage with the kids. He was so playful and such a worthy role model for all of them that I had a hard time not swooning and falling over.

Seriously.

With that dark hair deliciously mussed from my fingers and the light breeze and his blue T-shirt clinging to all of his toned muscles, he laughed with the kids, showing off his pearly white teeth as well as his easy sense of humor. *What woman in her right mind would leave all that?*

I certainly never would've. Kaitlin must have had her reasons, but honestly? If he had ever been mine, I never would have let him go.

As we threw darts at balloons, tossed rings on glass bottles, and played every other game we could, I couldn't help the melancholy that lingered deep within. He and I had promised to just enjoy the night together, but I'd finally come out and said it.

I'd told him that I didn't want them to leave. It'd been selfish and probably far too clingy for a girl who'd only known him about a month, but I hadn't been able to stop the words from coming out. Only now that they were out there, I wondered if there was any possible way in which they could stay.

I doubted it, but still, saying it out loud had made me realize just how true it was. I would give anything for them to stay here with me forever instead of just having a few more weeks with them, but I was determined not to let him know that.

I'd already told him how I felt. I wasn't about to let him in on the exact depth of those feelings, so I was doing my best to keep my promise and enjoy the fair.

As we were leaving the fishing game, Samantha came over, chatting to her son for a moment before smiling at us. "Brody and I are going to join the musical chairs competition. Would you guys like to come too?"

Colten immediately shook his head. "No, thank you. Everyone has been talking about it. There are going to be too many people watching."

I glanced at him, sensing that he needed some encouragement, and I jumped at the chance. "Can I join you? I used to freaking love that competition. I never won, but it was still fun."

Samantha chuckled. "Maybe you'll win this year, huh? I should warn you though, I've been practicing in my free time."

She winked at me and I laughed, arching an eyebrow while hoping my enthusiasm would rub off on Colten. "I have a natural talent. I don't need to practice."

"Oh, is that why you kept losing?" she teased lightheartedly. "Because of your natural talent?"

"Nah, that was just me giving all the rest of you guys the chance to shine. This is my year for sure. Don't expect me to go easy on you again."

As she and I started heading in the direction of the circle of chairs that had been set up, Colten eventually fell into step behind us. To my surprise, Landon joined us too. Soon after, we were all embroiled in a goofy round of musical chairs from which Sam emerged as the victor.

She tossed her hands into the air as she did a happy dance that made her son blush and cringe. "You're not going to go easy on me? Too bad you didn't ask me to go easy on you instead."

"You really need to learn how to talk smack," I said playfully. "You're not doing it right, Sam."

She laughed, ignoring her son's embarrassment. She and I bantered back and forth a bit. From the corner of my eye, I saw Colten patting his friend on the back, saying something that made him laugh before he joined Landon and me to get some refreshments.

The three of us grabbed some deep fried potato tornadoes and waters, then found a spot to sit on the grass while we watched Brody and Sam compete in the three-legged race. As we sat down, Colten was downright giddy, having so much fun that he couldn't seem to stop smiling.

Landon was also totally in the moment, laughing with his son like he didn't have a care in the world. As I sipped my drink, I watched the two of them together, laughing and goofing off, and I realized that I could easily listen to them like this for the rest of my life without growing bored of it.

Resting my chin on my hand, I let out a soft sigh. *Why do they have to live so far away? Why couldn't it have been easier?*

Los Angeles was nearly four hundred and fifty miles away from June Lake. It wasn't a terrible amount of distance, but it was enough that it would be hard to continue a functioning relationship if neither of us moved.

Chances were that even if Landon and I were to decide to attempt a long-distance relationship, we'd see each other on weekends at most. A lot of that time between leaving work on a Friday and before we'd have to be back on Monday morning would be eaten up by traveling, which made me wonder if it was even worth it to do it every weekend.

Probably not, if I was being honest. Plus, I knew how hard Landon worked when he wasn't here. I also knew that he spent a lot of time in the office after hours, and with him already having decided to try to spend more time with Colten, I didn't know if he'd have any of it left for me.

I also had no idea if he'd even want to try it. *Why would the universe tease me like this?*

It had given me the man of my dreams and a kid I could easily grow to love, but only for a couple months. It wasn't really fair and I really didn't know if I should let it continue going in the direction it was. I already knew I was going to suffer when they left.

That much, I'd been certain of for a while now. *Maybe I should spare myself a bit of hurt by pulling back now instead of spending the next several weeks getting in even deeper with them.*

Even as I thought it though, I doubted I could even if I tried.

The fact of the matter was that I was already in too deep, and at this point, I couldn't imagine that it would make it any easier on me to get out now. Knowing I was going to lose them had bothered me from the very beginning, but I'd gone for it anyway and now I was already in.

"What are you thinking about?" Landon asked suddenly, yanking me out of my thoughts.

I blinked a few times in rapid succession, then smiled and gave my head a light shake. "I was just enjoying the show. The two of you bantering like that is pretty entertaining."

He chuckled. "Did you hear me ask if you were about ready to go for a walk through the fair? I feel like we haven't even seen half of it yet."

"That's because you haven't." I stood up, folded my empty food and drink containers together, and tossed them in the trash before dusting grass off my butt.

Colten chucked away his empty containers too, but Landon kept his water with him, chatting to us as we wandered through the rest of the fair. We bumped into Brittany and Scott again when we turned a corner, and I lifted my eyebrows at the massive fluffy purple teddy bear my brother was carrying.

"What is that?"

Brittany was absolutely glowing as she grinned at me. "It's the prize he won for me. She's cute, right? I'm calling her Tiny."

Scott was drowning under the size of the bear and I snorted as I tried to hold in my laughter. "Tiny seems appropriate. Jeez, Scotty. Could you not have won her a proper prize?"

My brother grumbled. "I'm going to put this damn thing in my truck before it crushes me."

Brittany giggled and winked at me before she hurried after him. We turned to watch them leave. Colten laughed at my side as Scott nearly ran a woman over with the giant bear obstructing his vision. The next moment though, his laughter cut off abruptly when the woman came into view and I heard Landon suck in a sharp breath.

Glancing up at him, I saw his carefree expression shift right back into the mask of nothingness I remembered from the first time we'd met. I followed his line of sight, realizing that he was staring directly at the beautiful woman my brother had nearly bowled over.

In a bright yellow sundress with a denim jacket over it, she was stunning. Her high heels accentuated her slim figure and long legs. Her glamorous makeup showcased every one of her dramatic features. Her brow was high and smooth and her blue eyes were wide and gorgeously olive shaped.

Long black hair in a fresh blowout hung to her waist, drawing my attention to how trim it was in comparison to her full bust. She was a definite looker, the kind who was making heads turn even as she just stood there.

As my gaze darted back to Landon's face, however, I didn't even need to ask who she was. I already knew that this must be Kaitlin, the woman who had walked out on them and broke their hearts to pieces. Seeing her now in a dress that reminded me of sunshine and eyes like a summer sky, I wasn't sure it would matter what she'd done in the past.

After all, she was Colten's mother and Landon's ex. She was one of the most beautiful women I'd ever seen, but she might be here to cause them further heartache. Either that, or to win back her man now that he'd inherited however much money he'd inherited.

My first thought was to jump in front of them, protect them both from her for as long as I could, but my second was for myself. Because if a woman like that had come after her man, then I'd already lost him.

In fact, he might never have been mine to lose.

43

LANDON

You have got to be fucking kidding me.

I gritted my teeth, wondering why Kaitlin had to pick tonight of all nights to show up in June Lake. The best night I'd had so far.

But her timing had always been terrible. The decade we'd spent apart didn't seem to have changed that. Kaitlin Crew knew exactly when to pick a time for whatever she was doing to have the most negative effect it could have on my life. It was just the way it was.

As soon as she spotted me, her eyes darted to my side and she zeroed in on Colten, confidently striding over to us and speaking only to him. She put on her best baby voice, treating him like he was five years old.

"Colten? Oh, look how big you are, my boy. Mommy's little man. Come here and give your mama a hug."

Instead of complying, he gave me a panicked look and immediately retreated, side-stepping until he was half hidden behind me. I glanced down to check on him. He slipped his hand into Jewel's and my heart gave a weird squeeze.

Without even realizing it, she'd become a safe space for him. Just like June Lake had. The instinct to protect them both reared up in me and I shifted to stand even more in front of them, stopping Kaitlin from getting to Colten or being able to look into his eyes at all.

She'd lost that right when she'd walked away.

Colten's deadbeat mother planted her hands on her slim hips, a scowl on her features as her gaze came up to meet mine. Somehow, her expression was flirty and pouty at the same time.

Those cornflower blue eyes that had ensnared me one lonely night under the strobe lights of a club in LA focused on me now. They brought back so many memories I'd have been happy to forget, but unfortunately, they were burned into my brain like a brand.

Kaitlin was beautiful. More so than I remembered. In my mind's eye, I'd been picturing her with devil's horns and flames in her eyes for so long that it was weird to see her without them, but I still knew that her beauty was a trap.

As I looked at her, she did the same to me, slowly raking her gaze up and down before she brought it back to my eyes. "You look good, Landon."

I didn't return the compliment, giving her a stony stare instead. I had nothing to say to her and I certainly wasn't in the mood to exchange pleasantries. Whatever she'd come here to say, I'd rather she just got it over with.

Giving Jewel a dismissive look, she turned back to me, her Snow White looks as deceiving as ever. This wasn't the woman who bit a poison apple—she *was* the poison—but when she smiled, even I might've been fooled if I hadn't had a taste of it before.

If I hadn't been reminded of that taste every damn time I looked at our son. The boy she'd abandoned just a few months after giving birth to him.

"You've really grown into yourself," she purred, cocking the hip with her hand on it. "I expected a bit more than blue jeans and a T-shirt, though. What with your family's wealth behind you now, I'm sure you can do better, but that's nothing that can't be fixed."

My jaw clenched tighter. "What are you doing here, Kaitlin?"

Those long, jet-black lashes fluttered for a moment, like she was confused or taken aback by the question. Then she gave me a surprised smile. "I'm here to reconnect, Landon. Talk. Meet and get to know my son and get some fresh air. What else would I be doing here?"

I scoffed, but before I could tell her what I thought, she took a tiny step forward. It was more of an adjustment of her position than an actual step, but it put her in wafting distance of me. On my next inhale, I caught a whiff of her sophisticated, slightly peppery scent.

It made me want to hurl, but I managed not to. Although when the look in her eyes became more flirty, it became more difficult to hold it back.

She breathed in deeply and gestured down at the lake. "Will you take a walk with me? We have a lot to discuss."

I begged to differ, but when I glanced at Jewel, she nodded for me to go ahead. "I'll hang back with Colten. We'll go find Brody and the others."

"Yeah," I said. "Okay. I'll come find you in a few."

Kaitlin remained silent during the exchange, but she did finally spare Jewel more than a quick, dismissive look. Her nose turned up a little though, letting me know what she thought of the small-town girl she was looking at.

Focusing on me again, she started walking and didn't wait to check that I would follow. She already knew that I would. As much as I hated leaving Jewel and Colten, I'd been waiting for the other shoe to drop where Kaitlin was concerned.

To be fair, I hadn't expected it to drop tonight—or while we were in June Lake at all—but I'd suspected it was coming. The lawyer in me knew it was best to just get this over with. I considered this talk as my opportunity to find out what her true motives were and to try to figure out how to make her go away before it got ugly.

We walked in silence to the beach, which somehow felt less magnificent with Kaitlin than it had looking out at it from the Ferris Wheel with Jewel. Especially when she started talking nonsense at first.

"Thanks for asking how I've been," she said lightly. "I suppose I can't blame you after the way we ended things, but you should know that I'm doing well."

I snorted. *The way we ended things?*

Oblivious, she kept rambling. "I finally started my own business working as an aesthetician and masseuse."

Who gives a fuck? I slid my hands into my pockets, pausing when she did and walking with her when she started forward again. I still didn't have anything to say, but Kaitlin never had cared much about the sound of anyone's voice but her own.

"I've done well for myself," she said, looking up at me as if searching for my approval, but she was going to be waiting a long time because she wasn't going to get it. Sighing softly, she nodded and stared straight ahead again. "I run the business out of my home and I have an established and loyal client base. It was slow going at first, but I can't complain too much. I've made quite a name for myself."

An exasperated huff came out of her when I still didn't respond, but then she shook her head and tried a different tactic. Glancing up at me as she walked, she smiled softly. "How's work going for you?"

I shrugged. "It's fine."

"That's good. I'm not surprised. You were always going to be an excellent lawyer. Although part of me thought you'd have moved on by now. Imagine my surprise when I found out that you were still working in criminal defense."

I grunted and a slight smile spread on her face. "Walter looked well when I saw him. Healthy as a horse. You must be pleased that he's doing so well."

I nodded and her smile widened slightly. Midstride, she glanced up at me again without stopping, her features now relaxed. As if she thought she was getting somewhere with me.

"Is Walt still obsessed with sports cars and things that go fast?" She suddenly giggled. "Are you still obsessed with that too? Living fast and hard with all the pretty things in life by your side?"

I shook my head, but my lack of verbal responses didn't slow her down.

"I'm glad you're doing well, Landon. I've missed you. When did you put Walt in a home? I never thought you would, but I suppose it's been a long time. A long time during which you definitely haven't achieved your fullest potential as a lawyer, but just like your look, that's nothing we can't work on together."

It didn't escape my notice that in all of this, not once had she asked about Colten. Finally, tired of waiting for her to land the damn plane, I stopped walking and turned to face her. "Why are you really here, Kaitlin?"

She blinked at me innocently. "For a chance to put my family back together."

"That ship has sailed," I said in no uncertain terms, my jaw hard as I stared down into her eyes. "You walked out. Never checked in. Never cared enough to call, even just to find out if your son was okay."

"I—"

"No, Kaitlin," I said firmly. "There is no excuse. Even tonight, Colten's well-being seems like it's the furthest thing from your mind. We're not your fucking family and we never were."

For once in her miserable life, she didn't leap to her own defense.

Picking up speed, I shook my head at her, my eyes narrowing. "You made the right decision when you left. You weren't fit to be a mother and that's okay. I made my peace with it and so did Colten. Things have worked out just fine, so if you're here to clear your conscience, you don't need to. Our slate is clean in my books. I'm even grateful you left, but if you're here for something else, I'll see you in court."

She folded her arms. "Something else?"

"My money, Kaitlin," I said flatly. "If that's what you're after, then you're shit out of luck, so save your breath for your lawyer. I'm not giving you a cent, and I'm not buying into this crap that you're selling about reconnecting or putting our family back together. Just level with me. What are you really doing here?"

44

JEWEL

Landon parked the truck in the garage and Colten and I both dragged our exhausted bodies out of it. The poor child had fallen asleep on our way back from town, but regardless, now that his eyes were open again, he shot his father an imploring look.

"What happened with Kaitlin, Dad?" he asked. "Where is she? Where is my mother?"

"I'll fill you in tomorrow, bud," he replied as we walked into the house.

They paused in the kitchen to get some water and I heard Landon sending him off to bed, but I didn't stop to ask the questions rattling around in my own head.

Heading directly for my bedroom instead, I didn't stop walking until I'd reached the closet, opened it, and pushed up on my toes to retrieve my bag. I opened it and hurriedly grabbed as many things as I could at one time to pack them into my waiting bag.

I was almost done when Landon popped in, first just sticking his head inside, but when he saw what I was doing, he frowned and came in, carefully shutting the door behind him. "Why are you packing? Where are you going, baby?"

I shook my head as I crammed my things into the bag, wishing I could be anywhere else. "I don't think I should be here anymore, Landon. I'm probably only confusing things, and confusing Colten. You need space to sort this out with Kaitlin. I'll call Scott to come pick me up."

Green eyes on mine, he stopped in the center of the room and slid his hands into his pockets as he regarded me. "Why do you think you're confusing him?"

"Because I'm *here*," I said, glancing up and seeing him watching me closely. I sighed and straightened up. "She came all this way to talk to you. The least I can do is to get out of the way and let you guys figure it out."

"There's nothing to figure out." Suddenly in motion again, he crossed the distance between us in two long strides and caught my face in his hands, peering at me from between thick eyelashes. "The last thing I want from you is space, Jewel. I didn't invite Kaitlin here, nor do I want to speak to her again. I will, for Colten's sake, if I have to, but she and I are over. We have been for a long time."

As he looked into my eyes, his mouth descended to my own and he took my lips in a searing, somewhat desperate kiss. I melted instantly and looped my arms around his neck as relief coursed through me. I'd given him an out and he hadn't taken it.

In fact, he'd completely convinced me he didn't want it. I wasn't about to hold her unexpected, unwelcome appearance in June Lake against him if he still didn't want anything to do with her.

Landon gripped my hips. His tongue parted my lips as he pushed me back on the bed. I went willingly, kicking the bag off as I lay down. If he didn't want me to leave, I wasn't going anywhere. His legs slid between mine, spreading them at the ankles, and he settled on top of me.

I held on to him like a clingy koala bear, half afraid that he was going to change his mind and yet somehow knowing deep down that he wouldn't. While I had no intention of coming between a family, that wasn't what they were.

From what I'd heard, I knew Colten better than Kaitlin did, and when she'd tried to talk to him, it was my hand he'd taken. Finding a measure of comfort from that knowledge, I kissed Landon back with abandon, remembering my promise to have their backs no matter what.

As he kissed me, low groans rumbled in his chest and his hips rolled, sparking pleasure deep within. His hard, warm body pushed me into the mattress. All that desire from earlier on the Ferris Wheel came back with a vengeance. My nipples peaked and my panties got damp fast.

Landon's hands traveled up and down my sides, the flat of his palms hot and his fingertips gentle as they danced under the hem of my shirt. I arched my back, silently begging him to peel off the fabric and he complied, gripping it hard before breaking the kiss to pull it smoothly over my head.

His lips crashed back into mine as soon as it was clear, his hands now hot against my bare skin. A pleasurable shiver rushed through me and I moaned into his mouth, nipping his lower lip before reaching for his shirt in turn.

He helped me take it off, bunching the fabric at the nape of his neck into his fist before he pulled it clear and tossed it away to join mine somewhere on the floor. In every kiss and every touch, I felt his desperation to convince me to stay and I fed on it like an emotional vampire.

I'd had so many doubts about whether it was the right thing to do, getting involved with him, and yet, when we were together like this, it felt inevitable. Like I'd never really had a choice at all.

Something in him spoke to something in me, our very souls calling to one another until we gave in and let them be together. Logically, I knew it wasn't possible and all my worries about them leaving were still there, but I couldn't deny that it felt like we fit together in a way I'd never felt with anyone else.

Sliding his fingers under my knee, he hooked it up and held my thigh as he rocked into me. His hips were now perfectly positioned for me to grind against his hard length. With my entire body taut with tension, I took the relief he was offering and kissed him hard.

He groaned again and I suddenly remembered what he'd said about us in the shower together. Wrenching my lips away from his abruptly, I smiled and arched a teasing eyebrow at him. "I thought we were starting with you in the shower tonight."

Eyes burning into mine like twin green flames, he shook his head. "That was before. This is after. Maybe later, though."

"Maybe." I slanted my lips over his once more, reached for the waistband of his pants, and slid my fingers in between us.

When I finally reached his button, it took some maneuvering to get it open, but I managed and nearly preened with pride when I unzipped him and tugged his pants off along with his underwear. Now completely naked, he rolled us over so I was on top. For a moment, I just looked at him.

Tucking my hair behind my ears, I let my gaze linger on the sharp lines of his face, the dark slashes of his eyebrows, and his arrow-straight nose. The longer bits of hair on top of his head were tousled and I smiled, loving that *I'd* been responsible for making him look so disheveled.

My gaze caught on his before it lowered to his strong jaw and the elegant column of his throat, then to his broad smooth chest and the chiseled blocks of his abdomen below. He groaned as I toyed softly with the happy trail of dark hair that ran from his belly button to his pelvis. His hips arched when I lifted my own to sit on my knees between his thighs.

I could feel his eyes burning into me as I finally reached for his long, curved shaft. I wrapped my fingers around his girth and gave him two slow, leisurely strokes. When he didn't stop me, I ran my thumb across the glistening wetness at his tip and leaned down to taste it, intent on giving him what he'd wanted on the Ferris Wheel.

This man—all of him—was mine for tonight. Maybe it would just be for tonight, or maybe it would be for the next few weeks. Perhaps it would even be for a few more months after that. I didn't know, but in this moment, the only thing that mattered was showing him how I felt about him *now*.

A low growl tore out of him when my lips met his hot flesh and I brought my hands to his hips, holding them firmly. I sank my mouth over him. Glancing up to look into his eyes, I ran my tongue along the underside of his shaft, loving that I could see how his pupils dilated and his brow furrowed in concentration.

His lips parted. His fingers wound into my hair, gripping it tight. I withdrew before starting the whole process over again. I took it slow, wanting to drag it out for as long as I could. This wasn't a race. There was no rush, and I cared about him too much to make it a quick blowjob just to get things done.

The muscles in his stomach rippled as I kept going. His thighs tensed and his hips rolled gently into my mouth. Murmured curses fell from his lips as he held my hair in his grasp, still in control even though I'd thought for a moment I was.

I let him have it, though. Willing to take his guidance, I ran a hand down from his hip to his thigh, cupping between his legs just before I felt him swell in my mouth. A deep groan rumbled out of him a moment before he tried to wrench free, but I wouldn't let him, wanting everything he had to give and feeling the floodgates open between my own legs when he came.

Afterward, I kissed a hot path back to his lips and then sealed mine over them, wondering if he was going to recoil from his own taste on my tongue, but he didn't. It was weirdly erotic, the first time I'd done anything like it, but Landon pushed himself up on his elbow, his breathing still uneven, and he rolled me onto my back and gave me the same treatment I'd just given him.

Undoing my jeans, he pushed them off and unhooked my bra, taking his time with the garments and never letting his mouth stray too far from my skin. As my nipples were bared to him, he sucked them in each in turn, his tongue swirling around them, and he pushed a finger into me.

A loud, keening noise escaped me. My hips came off the bed, but he wasn't deterred, his lips on my chest and his fingers making magic down below. Neither of us had said a word in ages, but right now, it felt like we were communicating in a whole different way.

This didn't just feel like sex or fucking. It was so much more than that, even if I wasn't at all ready to think the actual words. When his thumb came up to circle my clit, pleasure raced through me like lightning and I let go, hanging onto him as the climax made my toes curl and my ears ring.

By the time I came back down to earth, he was already kissing a trail down my stomach, settling between my legs before tenderly cleaning me up—with his mouth. The mere thought of it should've made me cringe, but it didn't. Instead, more pleasure sparked through me, and eventually, the next orgasm sneaked up on me like a wildly sexy ninja I didn't stand a chance against.

Our entire night was like that, slow and gentle with neither of us holding back or doing anything we felt we had to. When Landon finally sank into me, he held my hands and looked into my eyes. After, as we fell asleep, he held me close, his breathing evening out at the same time as my own.

I might not have wanted to think the words, but they were right there at the forefront of my mind when I finally drifted off. Landon and I had made love tonight, and now, more than ever, I had absolutely no idea how I was supposed to let him go.

45

LANDON

Colten and I had sat down yesterday and talked about my conversation with Kaitlin. Surprisingly, the kid had handled it pretty well. He was confused and frustrated by her sudden appearance, sure, but he hadn't spun out because of it.

Ultimately, he'd simply made it clear that he didn't want anything to do with her and that he was afraid she was going to come between the two of us. As soon as I'd assured him I wouldn't let that happen, he'd seemed much happier.

Now, however, it was Monday afternoon and the workday would be coming to an end soon. I'd put in a call earlier to a colleague of mine who specialized in marital law, and while I'd been worried the guy wouldn't get back to me today, I grabbed my phone as soon as it rang.

"Hey, Brandon. Thanks for calling me back."

"Yeah, of course, man. What's up?"

"Can you hang on a sec?" I glanced at Colten lounging on the sofa and showed him that I'd be a minute. Then I got up and strode to the study. Once I was there, I shut the door behind me just in case. "So, uh, I need your advice about something. I'm pretty sure I know what my legal position is, but it was recently pointed out to me that I don't work in your field."

He chuckled. "It's always best to get an outside opinion on personal matters anyway. I guess I just didn't realize that you were married."

"I'm not," I said. "You don't have to worry about a messy divorce. This is actually about my son and his mother, who has shown up after a decade of not having any contact with us."

Brandon scoffed. "Seriously? She wants custody after not seeing the kid for that long?"

"I don't know," I mused out loud. "Frankly, I'm not actually sure what she's after. I asked her point blank, but she was squirrely about it. Didn't give me a straight answer. It might have something to do with an inheritance I just received, though."

"Ah," he said knowingly. "Yeah, the past tends to come back to haunt people once there's a nice chunk of change on the table. You said you hadn't had any contact with her for a decade before she showed up?"

"Yep. She walked out on our son when he was just a baby. Left him in his crib while I was at work with a note saying that she couldn't do it. He's ten now and Saturday night was the first time she's seen him since."

"Shit." He let out a low whistle. "Has she tried to contact either him or you in that time? Sent birthday cards or Christmas presents?"

"No, no, and no," I said. "To the best of my knowledge, she's never tried to reach out. I still have the same number and Colten goes to the school we've been wanting to send him to since he was born. They haven't said anything about anyone trying to see him there or to get any information about him and she sure as hell hasn't called me."

"Let me get this straight," he said after a brief pause. "She abandoned your son with you as a baby and disappeared until Saturday?"

"That's about it."

He chuckled. "You don't have to worry about losing a custody battle, Payne. She doesn't have a case and I'm so confident about it that I'll put my money where my mouth is. If it comes down to it and we lose, you won't have to pay my fees."

Relief slammed into me, so powerful that I had to sit down until it passed. "That's what I thought."

"Look, I'm not saying she's not going to try, but we can't stop her if that's what she's going to do. She has every right to approach the court, but she'd have to hire the best lawyers to even have a shot at unsupervised visitation at this point. Let alone custody."

"As far as I know, she simply won't be able to afford an army of lawyers." She'd said she was doing well for herself, but I knew what these guys charged per hour, and I also knew there was no way she'd be able to pay for as much of their time as it would take to try and build a case for her.

"If she does take you to court, give me a call," he said easily. "It would be pretty cut and dry to prove that her intention is not to reunite her family or whatever, but to try to stake some kind of claim on your inheritance. Why else would she show up now?"

"My thoughts exactly," I murmured. "Thanks, Brandon. I owe you one."

"No worries, man," he said. "I might have to take you up on owing me one soon, though. I've got a client who's in a bit of trouble with the law. I'm trying to sort it out for him, but if the deal I'm negotiating as part of the divorce falls through, I'll let you know."

"Any time," I said. "Thanks again."

We hung up and I stayed where I was for a long moment, just sitting behind Lucille's old desk staring at the grandfather clock in the corner. It was good news that Brandon didn't think she had a case either. At least it meant that my understanding of marital law wasn't that rusty.

On the other hand, if she started by asking for visitation and agreed for it to be supervised at first, then she still had a shot at getting back into his life. My life. I'd fight it tooth and nail, but it wasn't impossible she'd be granted the right to see him.

At the same time, that would raise questions of her having to pay child support, though. It wouldn't take much for a judge to see that I didn't need the money, but it was an argument I could make that might deter her.

Sighing heavily, I braced myself for the next conversation I'd have to have with Colten and got up, checking the time before I left. Since she'd been staying here, Jewel hadn't cleaned the Manor despite it being Monday. She'd been keeping it sparkling since she'd moved in —even though I'd told her it wasn't necessary—and as a result, she and Brittany had gone to do some of their other Monday clients' homes.

After I left the study, I found Colten outside in the sun reading his chess book. I strode out to join him, taking a seat on the lounger beside his.

He kept his finger in the book but shut it, bringing his cautious gaze to mine. "What is it? What happened?"

"That was my friend on the phone," I explained. "He's a lawyer too, but he works with divorces and custody issues. That kind of thing."

Colten's eyes widened, his jaw tightening as he stared at me. "Custody issues?"

I reached out and squeezed his knee, giving him a reassuring smile. "I spoke to him just in case Kaitlin decides to take me to court."

He got panicky then, his legs starting to bounce as he looked around like a caged hyena. "A court case? About me? Do you think she's going to take you to court to get custody? Can she do that? Can she take me from you?"

Before I could even respond, he kept rambling, his hands trembling as he lifted them to his hair. "All the kids I know who have divorced parents stay with their mothers. I don't know about many who live with their dads, but my mom is a stranger to me. I don't want to live with her, Daddy. I don't want to go to court either. I just want her gone again."

So do I, bud. Getting up, I moved onto his lounger and wrapped my arms around him, holding him tight so he would know I wasn't going anywhere. "I'm not going to let her get custody, kiddo. My friend doesn't think she has a case and neither do I. I wanted to let you know what was going on, but I don't want you to worry about it."

Just then, Jewel walked out after her long workday. She was wearing bleach-stained clothes and her hair was up in a messy bun with damp tendrils of hair that had fallen out of it framing her face. I still hated knowing she'd been scrubbing other people's toilets and floors all day, but I'd never been as happy to see someone as I was to see her right then.

It was clear she'd come straight back here after work, and as soon as Colten pulled away from me and saw her, he broke down. Like instantly.

Tears welled in his eyes and suddenly spilled over. His shoulders shook as he covered his face in his hands. She glanced at me with questions in her eyes, but I shook my head as she rushed over to him, sat down on his other side, and gathered him up in her arms.

Hugging him fiercely, she kissed his cheek and leaned back just a little, brushing his hair off his forehead. "What is it, Colt? What happened? What's wrong?"

I felt her compassion coming off her in waves. Felt her worry about a child she hadn't even known all that long, yet she was there for him, holding him like he was her own and waiting until he was ready to talk after asking him what was the matter.

In all the time I'd been a father, I'd never seen or felt anything like this. Usually, the only people who were there for him were Walter and me, but this was a woman, and judging by how he'd broken down as soon as he'd seen her, it was different.

Shit, I thought as I watched her holding him, hugging him tight and stroking his hair. She rested her head on top of his, her eyes closed. She inhaled and exhaled deeply, murmuring for him to breathe with her. *I just fell in love right here on the spot.*

It was massively inconvenient and it would be very much impossible to carry on an actual relationship with her, but things had been inching that way for a while now. This moment, however, her genuine compassion for my son and the fact that her heart was so big that she'd come to him without question had pushed me over the edge.

I was in love with Jewel Pendleton. She was the woman I'd been waiting for all my life without even knowing it. She was our missing piece. The one we needed to make our family complete.

But she lived and worked over four hundred miles away from us. She loved her town and all the people in it. Her life was here. Ours wasn't.

Fuck. How the hell did I let it get this far?

46

JEWEL

For the last two weeks, things had been blissful. There were now only three weeks or so left before the Paynes were leaving, but neither of them had brought it up and neither had I. For now, I was choosing to live in a bubble of denial.

Kaitlin hadn't shown back up to try to steal her son from his father. Dallas hadn't shown his face in town again. Work was going well and I'd been spending all my free time exploring every nook and cranny of the Manor to my heart's content.

I was convinced that I knew it better now than even the Styles family ever had and it had definitely been a dream come true to get to do it. As I sat in the sunroom now, reading more of Lucille's journals, I sipped a cup of tea, completely enthralled by her writing style and how it somehow made her story come to life.

It was like I could hear her voice in my ear and see her walking these halls, sitting perhaps exactly where I was right then as she'd written the entry I was reading. It was excerpt from a few days after Dallas Senior, the current Dallas's father, had been born, and I practically felt her pain in my own chest as I read about it.

From a distance, this house and their incredible love story had always seemed so perfect to me that I'd never imagined there had been such agony here, but Lucille's journals were proof that I'd been wrong. Tears burned the backs of my eyes as I read about her struggles as a new mother, how alone and abandoned she'd felt, not at all prepared for motherhood.

Although this had been written over sixty years ago, it was so raw on the page that I felt it slicing through my heart as I read about it. I was stunned that a woman who'd had it all had been having such hardships behind the scenes, but her life definitely hadn't been all sunshine and rainbows.

As I continued reading, I discovered that Robert had avoided his wife and the baby after he'd been born, keeping to himself in his study instead. He'd been here, in this very manor with them, and yet, it didn't seem like he'd been involved at all.

Disappointment raced through me and I closed the journal, dismayed that the love story I'd coveted all my life hadn't been nearly as romantic as I'd thought it was. Everything I'd thought I knew about them? Untrue.

Sighing as I got up, I carried the journal and my empty mug to the kitchen to make some more tea. While I waited for the kettle to boil, I cracked the journal open again, disappointed but also needing to know more. I couldn't stop now that I'd started, itching to get more of a peek behind the curtain.

As I read, I stumbled upon another entry. Lucille was pregnant again, but she knew the baby wasn't Robert's. My mouth fell open.

No. Way. No fucking way. Lucille Styles had an affair?

I flipped through the pages, eager to find out who was the father of Lucille's second oldest child and unable to believe the plot twist that had just come my way. I knew they'd been real people, but I hadn't expected anything like this from them at all.

Before I could find an entry giving any detail about the baby daddy, I was interrupted by a knock at the front door. My eyebrows mashed together.

Colten and Landon were out getting groceries for the week. Something they'd insisted on doing without me as apparently it was father and son bonding time. Personally, I didn't get the appeal of bonding over a choice between rice or potatoes as a side for dinner, but it seemed to work for them.

Pushing away from the counter, I reluctantly shut the journal once more and wondered who on earth was at the door. In the time I'd been staying here and even before that, when I'd only come in to clean, there had never been any visitors.

Brittany and Scott were the only people in town who might've decided to pop in unannounced, but I was pretty sure they would have texted me if they had been planning a visit. Curious but also filled with an odd sense of trepidation, I went to the door, swinging it open to find Kaitlin waiting on the steps.

She had her back to me at first, admiring the grounds from behind a pair of huge sunglasses. Although I knew she had to have heard the door opening, she didn't turn immediately, taking her time to drink in the view before she slowly spun to face me, pulling her sunglasses off at the same time.

My heart stammered in my chest. The woman was even more gorgeous in the sunlight than she had been at the fair a couple weeks ago. Her black hair glistened in the sun, loose and so sleek and shiny that it looked like a wig.

Her eyes were as blue as the lake beyond and she had full, pink lips that shimmered with some kind of gloss. With her body encased in a striking, bright red sheath dress and another pair of sky-high heels on her feet, she looked like a freaking supermodel.

My mouth dried up and I had the strangest urge to cower. Or flee. Or something else that lesser creatures did when faced with one that was clearly superior. I stood my ground, though. The woman might've been radiantly beautiful, but I had the upper hand when it came to what was inside.

"Can I help you?" I asked crisply, staying in the doorway and making no move to invite her inside.

Her eyes narrowed on mine. "I'm here to see Landon."

"He's out," I said. "I'm not sure how long he'll be gone. It's probably best not to wait. It could be a while."

Kaitlin huffed, but even that sounded graceful coming from her.

"That's fine. Let me in. I'll wait inside while you do whatever it is you do around here?"

Her gaze dragged up and down the length of my body. Disapproval practically radiated off her once she brought her eyes back to mine. Arching a steep eyebrow, she cocked her head and took a step forward. "A maid, I presume? Nanny perhaps as well? It figures. He never could take care of everything himself."

My face burned with shame. Kaitlin had seen me with them at the fair. She knew I wasn't here only as Landon's housekeeper and yet, in a sense, I kind of was. Cleaner and cook. That was my reason for staying here with them.

I hadn't been invited to live at the Manor as a guest or a girlfriend. I'd offered my services and he'd taken me up on said offer.

A rush of anger, jealousy, and, to my surprise, even hatred sped through me. She was the kind of woman who belonged in a place like this. With a guy like Landon.

She looked every inch the part of a lady of leisure, summering at the lake with her gorgeous family and rich, attractive, successful husband. While I was the kind of woman who worked for them.

It had never bothered me before. Never brought me shame. But as I stood there, faced by this haughty beauty who was clearly still expecting me to let her in, I sure felt ashamed.

She and I both knew I didn't belong here, yet Landon had pleaded with me to stay when I'd tried to leave. Her son had cried on my shoulder more than once over the possibility of having to see her again. I was the one who cooked for them at night and who waved them goodbye in the morning.

Just a few hours ago, I'd been playing chess with Colten while drinking coffee with Landon reading the paper on his tablet beside us. She had chosen to give all that up and I wasn't going to just hand it back to her.

Not after what she'd done to them.

How can someone be so vile as to abandon their own child? How could she never have checked in? Never cared? Not until now.

Now that she knew there was money on the table.

As all these sour thoughts raced through my head, Kaitlin stepped closer, her eyebrow still arched. She waited for me to move, but I wasn't going to. As she'd correctly pointed out, I was the maid. It was my responsibility to keep any unwanted visitors from coming in while the lords of the manor were out.

It wasn't my house. I couldn't just let people in and offer them tea, now could I?

"Where are you staying?" I asked. "The inn, the motel, or a vacation rental?"

"The inn," she responded sharply.

I nodded. "Very well. I'll pass along the message that you were here and I'm sure he'll call you. Now go."

I slammed the door in her face, my heart pounding and my cheeks still hot. I'd never been so rude to someone in my life, but I'd also never met anyone who deserved it as much as her. Except maybe Dallas, but he wasn't the one who'd shown up on their doorstep today.

I locked the front door behind me just in case she decided to come in anyway, and I drew in a deep breath, hoping I'd done the right thing. While I knew the Paynes didn't want to see her, I supposed she would always be Colten's mother.

In my opinion, that didn't entitle her to entry, but I wasn't always right. Doubt gnawed at my insides for a moment before I let it go.

I knew where she was staying and the inn's telephone number was freely available. When Landon got back, I really would tell him she'd been here. It would be his choice whether he wanted to call her to talk or if he wanted to invite her over.

All I knew was that if she was coming back here, I was leaving. Even if only for the time of the visit. I wouldn't subject myself to feeling the way she'd made me feel.

She was a despicable person underneath that beautiful veneer. Looks had never mattered much to me beyond a first impression. I could appreciate the genetic gifts a person had been given without letting my opinion of them be formed by how blessed they had been by the gene fairy.

Kaitlin had made my skin crawl, but she'd also made me feel inferior. Even when I knew I wasn't. She was intimidating as hell, and clearly, she thought she was entitled to Landon's time. Even though she wasn't.

Confused and feeling like I'd been hit by a truck, I returned to the kitchen and made my tea, wondering what Landon had ever seen in her. Aside from the obvious.

It also made me wonder what he saw in me. I let out a deep sigh as I stirred my tea, trying to shove the insecurities aside. One look from that woman had me question and doubt myself more than I ever had in my life.

Thank heavens I had some time alone to sort through it all before they got home. Landon had enough on his plate to worry about without me having to add to his burden. Besides, as I stood there, reminding myself of who I was and what I'd survived, I decided in no uncertain terms that if I ever saw her again, I wouldn't let her intimidate me.

Now I just had to figure out how to follow through.

47

LANDON

After bringing Colten back home and unloading the groceries, I found Jewel in the sunroom, engrossed in one of Lucille's journals but with her whole body sort of caved in on itself. She sat with her knees drawn up to her chest, squeezed into one corner of the sofa with her arms hooked around her shins.

"Hey, you." I walked in and took a seat beside her, leaning over to press a kiss to the exposed skin of her shoulder. "Are you okay?"

"Uh, no," she admitted. Her eyes lifted slowly from the page and flicked from one of mine to the other. For a moment, I thought she was going to leave it at that, but then she sighed. "Kaitlin came by while you were out."

"Fuck."

Jewel grimaced as she nodded, her lips downturned and everything about her somehow smaller than usual. "She's uh, she's staying at the inn and she wants to talk to you."

Dread pooled in my stomach. "Was she horrible to you?"

One of Jewel's shoulders rose on a shrug, her gaze not quite meeting mine. "Not outright, but she makes me feel things that aren't so nice."

"Same," I agreed, taking her chin in between my thumb and my index finger and gently tipping her face up to mine. "I was hoping she'd left town, but if she's still here, I need to go see her."

"I know," she said softly, finally letting go of her legs and scooching a little closer, taking both of my hands in hers. "I know you said you didn't want space to figure things out with her, but if you change your mind, you just need to tell me, okay?"

I held her gaze intently. "Kaitlin isn't here for me, Jewel. She's here for my money, and even if she's not, it doesn't matter because I'm not interested in her."

"You guys share a child," she said. "A past."

"Yeah, but just because I have a past doesn't I mean I want to live in it. What Kaitlin and I had, even before, wasn't some great love, Jewel. It was a hookup that resulted in a child she wasn't prepared to raise. It's not romantic. There are no unresolved feelings for a first love or anything like that."

"She did break your heart, though."

"Sure, but only because I was invested in making it work for Colten's sake. My heart also didn't break for her as much as it did for him." I took her face in my hands and looked deep into her eyes. "I'm going to go speak to her to find out what she wants and then I'm going to come home. To you. Unless you want to come with me?"

"No," she said quickly, her head shaking as she glanced over my shoulder. "I'd much rather stay here with Colt. Or is he going with you?"

"Definitely not," I replied confidently. "Alright, then. I'll see you soon. The inn is that building just off Main, right?"

She dipped her chin in a nod, then followed me out of the sunroom and disappeared to find Colten. A pang shot through me at the thought of leaving them here alone in favor of going after Kaitlin, but I needed her to leave and the only way to do that was to see her.

It wasn't like I was choosing to spend time with her rather than them. I just needed to get this out of the way.

With a heavy heart, I drove back into town, all the while wondering what Colt and Jewel were getting up to and wishing I was with them instead. I found the inn easily enough, then tracked down Kaitlin suntanning at the pool.

Decked out in jewelry, makeup, designer sunglasses, heels, and a tiny scrap of a bikini, she was scolding children for splashing in the water and getting her wet. As I approached, she cursed loudly, got up, and dragged her chair away from the edge of the pool.

She hadn't seen me yet, but when she did, she slapped on a charming smile and pulled her sunglasses down to the tip of her nose to peer at me over the solid black rims. "Took you long enough. I've been waiting for you all day."

I sat down across from her, not in the mood to play games. My entire heart was back at the Manor, and while I would have loved to toss Kaitlin into the pool, I refrained, wanting nothing more than to put this behind me.

"Why did you come to the Manor?" I asked directly. "Give it to me straight this time."

"Fine." She sniffed softly, like she was offended, but then pushed the sunglasses back to the bridge of her nose and lifted her chin. "I've spoken to my lawyers and I'm going to do whatever it takes to be part of yours and Colten's lives."

My jaw unhinged itself. "You want to be part of *my* life?"

She nodded. "Of course, I do, baby. I know I've made some mistakes, but I can't take them back. All I can do now is to make it right. That's all I'm asking you for. A chance to make it right."

"There is no making it right, Kaitlin," I said, quietly seething. "You left him. Alone. In his crib. As a tiny, defenseless baby who couldn't do anything for himself. The least you could've done was to give me a fucking heads-up so that he didn't have to wait for God knows how many hours before I got home."

"The housekeeper was there," she said emphatically. "I'm sure Colten was just fine."

"Are you?" Both of my eyebrows shot up. "How are you so sure he was fine? I checked with her, you know. The housekeeper. I asked her if you told her you were going out. She said no."

Kaitlin reclined on her chair, blowing out a frustrated breath. She gathered the hair on top of her head in her hand. "I've already said that I know I've made mistakes, Landon. There's no need to rub them in."

"Oh, yes there is. And I'm telling you that there's no way for you to make it right. Not after what you did. Not after all these years. If you'd come back the next day or even the next month, *maybe* we could've tried again, but now? You've got to be shitting me."

"I hate that expression," she said, her features pinching for a moment before she sighed. "All of that is water under the bridge anyway. I don't care about our history. I only care about our future."

"We don't have a future," I said firmly. "Have you ever stopped for a minute to think about what Colt wants? What I want? Because it's not you."

She pushed her sunglasses into her hair and rolled her eyes at me. "You might not want me, but he's only ten. He doesn't know what he wants. What he deserves is to know his mother."

"He doesn't want to," I explained impatiently. "I realize that there's no way you could know this, but he's a smart kid. He does know what he wants and he doesn't want anything to do with a deadbeat like you."

"How do you know that?" she asked with a flip of her hair over her shoulder. She turned so she was facing me, stretched out on the lounger like she was posing for a painting or trying to entice me. "How do you know that he won't want the chance to know me if we offered it to him? Maybe you're the one who needs to think about what Colten might want."

I gritted my teeth but kept my cool. "Your absence hasn't been missed, Kaitlin."

"Of course, it has. I'm his mother." She pursed her lips at me. "That's the point of this, isn't it? He knows I haven't been there, but he doesn't know why not. I'm sure he'll want those answers."

"I've never lied to our son," I said, stating it as frankly as she had. "He knows who you are and what you did, and he doesn't want or need you. He knows that you chose to leave him with me and that you didn't want to raise him. He also knows that he can't trust you."

She dismissed everything I'd said with a slight wave of her manicured hand. "I don't believe you. I think you're just saying what you think you need to say to get rid of me."

"I'm not going to pretend that I don't want to be rid of you. I do, but that doesn't make anything I said less true. Colten knows all about you, Kaitlin. He also knows it's not his fault that you left and that he's better off without a mother who couldn't take care of him."

She sniffed again. "My lawyers warned me this might happen. That you might lie and say hurtful things. You can say whatever you want to say, though. I know what I want and I know what my son will want."

Leaning over, she fished a business card out of her pool bag and handed it to me with a smug smirk appearing on her lips. Like she thought giving me a lawyer's card was the silver bullet she needed to tear a hole through my heart. "If you don't want to be civil about this, you can call them to discuss how we're going to be moving forward."

I threw the card in the pool without even glancing at it, my gaze on hers instead. "Do what you need to do. I'm not calling anyone or having any discussions with them about moving forward with a future I don't want."

"I always get what I want though, Landon. You of all people should know that."

I leaned forward, my elbows on my knees as I finally got real with her. "Just level with me already, would you? I'm really not in the mood to play these games. If you wanted me back, you'd have come crawling long before now, so what is it that you really want?"

"I already told y—"

"No, not all this bullshit you've been spinning," I said, cutting over her. "At the end of the day, I need to know why you would suddenly come all the way out here ten years after the last time we heard from you. Be honest with me about the bottom line, and if I can, I'll make it happen. What's it going to take, Kaitlin?"

She eyed me suspiciously and I sighed, exasperation snaking through my veins. "Fine. Give me your phone."

Her eyebrows inched up, but after holding my gaze for another moment, she picked up the device and smacked it into my waiting palm. I blew out a frustrated breath and turned the screen to her. "You need to unlock it. Otherwise it's worth about as much as a brick."

Reaching forward, she did what I'd asked without commenting about it or questioning me, simply pressing her finger to the screen until it emitted a bubbling noise that told me it was unlocked. After that, she watched closely as I searched for her recording app and opened it.

Hitting the red circle with my thumb to record what I was about to say, I brought my eyes back to hers, holding them while I spoke into the receiver.

"This is Landon Payne. I'm with Kaitlin Crew in June Lake, California," I said clearly, making sure to pronounce each word properly. "If Kaitlin and I ever end up going to court over custody of our son, Colten Payne, I will strike this from the record, but I want an honest answer from her as to what she wants from me and I hereby pledge that if I can accommodate it, she can have it."

Her eyes glittered with mischief—and victory—and she pulled the sunglasses from her head, finally sitting up straight and letting her feet drop to the ground. She was about to strike a deal and I knew it. I had her right where I wanted her, finally ready to tell me just how much money it was she'd come out here for.

Because as much as I wished for Colten's sake that he had a mother who actually cared about him and who wanted to know him, this wasn't that. Kaitlin had come after us for one thing and one thing only—and that one thing wasn't her son.

48

JEWEL

Nervously waiting for Landon to come home, I sat opposite the chess board from Colten, but neither of us were paying much attention to the game. For the first time since I'd known him, the little boy seemed far more interested in something else—me.

The frozen pizza I'd cooked sat on the plates beside us, but where mine was almost untouched, he'd practically inhaled his. I couldn't recall ever having seen him eat as much at dinner time, but now that his stomach was full, it looked like he was on a mission, and this time, it wasn't to defeat me.

It was to question me.

He folded his hands on the table in front of him, his eyes focused on mine as he stared at me. "If I ask you a question, will you answer it honestly?"

"Yes."

My heart pitter-pattered in my chest, but I had nothing to hide from him. Nothing except of course the truth that he ended up asking me for.

"How do you feel about my father?" His chest rose on a deep breath, but his eyes never left mine. Landon had said Colten was considering becoming a lawyer one day and right then, I had to admit that I thought he'd make a pretty darn good one. "Please don't tell me you're just his friend. I already know it's not that and you already promised you'd be honest with me."

Because I wasn't expecting you to come right out and ask me the one thing I don't know if I can tell you without discussing it with your dad first. In the end though, he hadn't asked what was going on between us. He'd asked how I felt about Landon, and that was my truth to share or to decide not to.

As I stared back into those glittering green eyes, I couldn't find it in my heart to lie to him. Colten cared deeply about his dad and he was already terrified about why his mother had shown up. He trusted me and he wasn't wrong. I had promised to be honest.

Drawing in a deep breath, I fidgeted with the chess piece I'd been holding, and then finally, I just dropped both hands into my lap to hold them still. "The truth?"

He nodded silently.

"Okay, then," I said. "Before I tell you that, I want you to promise me something in return."

His head cocked. "What?"

"Whatever I tell you, you can't tell your dad," I said. "I'm going to tell him myself one of these days. I just don't think the timing is quite right at the moment. What with your—With Kaitlin showing up. I know it's been a lot for both of you to come to terms with."

"I won't say anything," he promised after a moment of consideration. "You have my word."

I managed a small smile, nerves making my stomach feel like it had a whole swarm of butterflies in it. "In that case, the truth is that I'm falling for your dad. I really, really like him, and even though I know it's not the easiest time for you guys, I'm hoping that I'll be able to get to know him a little better."

Colten smiled. "I think he likes you a lot too. You shouldn't be scared to tell him. It's your turn to be brave. Just like I had to be when we first got here."

"I see what you did there." I grinned at him, relieved that he didn't seem angry about me having feelings for his dad but also still nervous. Not only for Landon's return now, but also that Colten might say something about what I'd confessed. "Thanks for the tip, though. I will be brave. Soon. I promise. I just think it's important to let him work out whatever needs to be worked out with Kaitlin first."

Colt paused for a moment, swiping his tongue across his lips. His eyes hit the board instead of remaining on mine. "I hope she doesn't take us to court."

"I know, sweetheart. Let's not worry about that until your dad gets home, okay? I'm sure he'll have some answers for you now that he's spoken to her."

He sighed but nodded. "I have a secret too."

My eyebrows swept up. "You do?"

"I don't want to go back to LA," he rushed out, still not bringing his gaze back to mine. "I want to stay here. Forever. I've told my dad that I don't want to leave."

Blinking rapidly, I tried to hide how stunned I was by his revelation, but I doubted I'd succeeded. Either way, he was deliberately not looking at me now, moving his eyes to the window and staring out of it at the lake with a longing expression on his face.

"Why do you feel that way?" I asked quietly. Since he'd already told Landon, I didn't think there could be any harm and having a conversation with Colten about it. I might even be able to help. "Lots of kids don't want to go home after a vacation, though. I think it's normal."

"No, it's not that," he said, sounding much older than his ten years all of a sudden. "I think that's what my dad thinks too, that I'm just a kid who wants to be on vacation forever."

"Okay," I said slowly. "If it's not that, then what is it? Why would you rather stay here than go home? From what I've heard about it, LA is a pretty cool place."

He shrugged. "It's not bad. I like my teacher back home and the chess club, but other than that? I just feel like I'm lonely there compared to how it is here."

"Well, it's easier when your dad isn't working, I'm sure. It allows him to be around a little bit more."

"It's not a little bit," he said, still staring at the lake like it held all the answers. "At home, I spend more time with our house staff than I do with my dad. It's always been that way. I never see him when we're home, but here, we spend time together every day. We're closer now than ever. We've never laughed like this together and I've never felt like he understands me, but then we got to June Lake, and suddenly, it's like he sees me and he knows who I am."

My heart cracked. "Thank you for sharing that with me, Colt. I think this is something you need to talk to your dad about, though. One thing that I know for sure and that I can promise you from the bottom of my heart is that your dad loves you very much."

"I know." He sighed and dragged a hand through his hair before he finally glanced at me again. "I just don't want things to go back to the way they were. You don't know how much he works, Jewel. He works like, all the time, and even if I do get to see him, it's only for an hour or so while he's still distracted by the case he's working on."

I wished I could say something to make him feel better, but I had nothing. "For what it's worth, I know he misses you while he's working and I know he'd much rather spend that time with you."

"I feel so bad for feeling this way," he admitted after another brief pause. "I know my dad helps people. I also know some of them deserve all the help they can get and others don't, but I need him too, and when we're at home, I never have him."

Slowly moving his eyes back to mine, he was on the brink of tears and so was I, but it didn't look like he was done yet. "And I think..." He trailed off, sighed, and then looked away again. "I think I need you too."

I held back my tears, feeling the pressure of them behind my eyes and in my chest, but I couldn't let them fall. The kid was going through enough as it was and I didn't want him to think he'd upset me if I started crying now.

Besides, he wanted to stay and I wanted them to stay too, but that didn't mean it was going to happen. It wasn't a decision Colten and I could make. I didn't even know if it was a decision Landon could make. I had no idea how big his practice was or even if he had his own firm. I didn't know much about his work situation at all, other than what he'd told Scott about not being able to work remotely.

As someone who couldn't work remotely at all either, I completely got it. Plus, they had Walter in LA and all that. It was a lot more complicated than just a kid and girl wanting them to be on vacation forever.

The only thing I could do now was try and comfort Colten and to cheer him up before Landon walked in on us both sobbing on the floor. Reaching across the table, I cupped his cheek in my hand and gave him the best, brightest smile I could muster.

"You big softy, you," I murmured.

He laughed and swatted my hand away. "I'm not a softy. I'm just honest."

"I like people who are honest," I said, pushing back my chair and standing up. "Alright, I need to do the dishes before your dad gets home. We don't want him walking into a dirty kitchen after everything he's had to deal with today."

Colten got up immediately and came to help me. We chatted about less serious things as we washed the dishes together and waited for Landon to get home. As I listened to him telling me about some of the antics the kids in his chess club had gotten up to, it occurred to me that I'd fallen for more than just Landon.

If I was being completely honest with myself, I'd fallen for his son too. For their little family and my small role in it.

On a high from connecting so deeply with Colten, I got playful, taking the hose attached to the side of the sink and blasting him with it. He yelped in surprise. Those twinkling green eyes shot to mine and told me I had just started something he was going to end.

Sliding his hand into the full sink that he'd been rinsing the washed plates in, he suddenly sent a spray of water my way. I laughed as warm water dripped down my face and hair, and I blasted him with the nozzle again.

Before long, we were engaged in an all-out water fight in the kitchen that ended with a slippery floor and both of us on our butts, laughing hysterically. It was going to be a nightmare cleaning all this up, but as I watched Colten laughing from his belly, cracking up every time he slipped trying to get up on the wet floor while he was still laughing, I decided that the cleanup would be worth it.

Every little moment and every memory I got to make with them was.

49

LANDON

What a fucking day.

Bleary eyed, I got home late, emotionally spent after my negotiations with Kaitlin. I dragged my ass out of the truck and into the house, feeling the tension bleeding out of me now that I was here. It was quiet and cool inside, all the lights off except for the kitchen and a few others that would help me find my way.

The scent of melted cheese and pepperoni hung faintly in the air and I inhaled deeply, bummed to have missed pizza night but happy that it had been worth it. A sense of peace settled over me like a cloak as I strode further into the house, heading to the kitchen first in the hopes that they'd saved me a slice.

As I walked in, the first thing I saw was Jewel, her hair damp and up in a messy ponytail, her head buried in one of Lucille's journals. She was in her pajamas with a light summer robe over them and her fingers wrapped around a cup of tea.

She looked up, smiling when she saw me. "Welcome home. How did it go?"

"It wasn't easy, but I think we reached a resolution." I didn't stop walking until I reached her. Then I pulled her into my arms and kissed the top of her head. "How did it go here?"

"It was fine. Fun. Colten's asleep."

"I figured. I'm sorry to have missed him." Breathing her in, I held her for another moment before I let go, reached behind me for a stool, and sat down. "Thanks for staying with him."

"It wasn't a problem at all." Those warm brown eyes rested on mine. "Can I make you some tea?"

"I'd love some." As I went to get up and tell her that I would make it, I noticed that the kitchen behind her was a disaster. There was water everywhere, with towels on the floor that had been soaked through. I frowned. "Whoa. What happened here? Did a pipe burst or something?"

She giggled as she shook her head, standing up and leaning across the island from me. "Colten and I had a water fight. I started it."

I chuckled but only a little. I was too exhausted to offer much more than that. "Who ended it?"

"We both did. It seemed better to call a truce before the kitchen became a swimming pool." Pushing away from the island, she turned and walked over to the kettle, filled it with water, and cocked a hip against the counter while she waited for it to boil. "Do you want to talk about it? The resolution you reached with Kaitlin."

"I paid her off," I said simply.

Her expression fell. "She took money from you?"

I nodded. "It took some doing, but eventually, she admitted it was all she wanted. Apparently, she felt like I owed it to her."

"Owed it to her?" she echoed incredulously. "Why? She walked out and left you to raise your son all by yourself. If anyone owes anyone, she owes you for taking care of Colten for all these years."

"You'd think, but nope." I watched as she fixed my tea and made herself some more. Gratefully accepting the cup when she handed it over, I took a sip, winced, and set it down to cool a bit before turning back to her. "According to Kaitlin, she sacrificed her body to give me the greatest gift of my life. My son. It seems she's always felt that she deserved some kind of compensation for that."

Jewel's features had gone completely blank. When she sat down again, she sagged onto the stool like her legs had been about to give out. "I can't believe it. What kind of person does that?"

I shrugged. "At least she gave me a number eventually. Two and a half million dollars and a promise that we'd never see her again. Obviously, I agreed."

Her eyes filled with tears and she brought a hand to her mouth, averting her gaze like she was trying to fight a sob. It didn't work, though. Her shoulders started shaking, and when she blinked, the tears spilled down her cheeks in hot streams that didn't look like they would ever end.

Surprised and confused, I leaned forward and squeezed her leg. "Hey, are you okay? What's going on? You don't have to worry about the money, Jewel. It was small change if you consider what I got in return. It—"

Her eyes snapped back up to mine and she gave her head a soft shake. "I'm not crying about the money, Landon. These tears aren't for you. They're for Colten. To have a mother care so little about her son..." She trailed off, sobbing in earnest as she covered her face in her hands. "I just can't wrap my head around it. Our moms are supposed to love us no matter what. They should turn down all the money in the world for a chance to know us."

I blinked hard a few times, and then it occurred to me. "This is triggering for you, isn't it? With your own mom taking off the way she did?"

Jewel jerked her chin in a nod. I got up and wrapped my arms around her, holding her while she sobbed. For my son. For herself. Probably for every other kid out there who'd had the misfortune of drawing a mother who didn't give a shit in the lottery of life.

The more I thought about it, the more my own heart ached. All I'd felt before had been relief for the fact that Kaitlin's sudden reappearance in our lives had been so temporary. I'd never thought about how it might make Colten—or even Jewel—feel to know that she'd only been here for money.

It fucking sucked.

I didn't remember much about my mom. I had some snippets, flashes of memory I wasn't sure had been real or whether I'd conjured up those mental images based on stories Walter had told me. But even though I'd been so young when she'd passed, I'd always known that she'd loved me more than anything.

Walter had made sure to keep her alive in my head and my heart, talking about her endlessly and constantly telling me how proud she had been of me. How proud she would've been. He'd told me about the promises she'd made him give her about caring for me as his own and how she'd only agreed to marry him after he'd sworn that he'd love me unconditionally.

Drawing in a shaky breath, I stroked my hand up and down Jewel's back, trying to take care of her even if my own cup was darn near empty. When the sobs finally started subsiding, she wrapped her arms around my hips and stayed in the circle of mine as she lifted her head to look up at me.

"I adore your son. I'd do anything for him and I've only known him for, like, a month and a half. I guess I just don't understand how Kaitlin could accept money and promise to stay away from him. Surely, he should mean more to her than that."

"He should," I agreed wholeheartedly. "Kaitlin isn't like me and you, though. She wasn't ready to be a mom when she got pregnant with Colt and I'm not sure if she ever will be ready, but she doesn't value the same things we do. I'm jealous that you got to have a water fight with him tonight and I wasn't here to join the fun, but she would've had kittens if she'd come home to this."

I waved a hand at the mess. "To her, living isn't spending time with a kid and that's also fine. It's not for everyone. Do I hate that my son has a mother like that? Sure. Do I wish that she would've turned down the money? Yeah, I kind of do. If I'd trusted her intentions, I would've allowed her into his life in a heartbeat, but I didn't trust them and it turned out I was right to be suspicious."

"I know. It just makes me so angry that she came and let him see her, and now she's gone again and you're going to be left to pick up the pieces. If she wanted money that badly, why not just call? Why show up and tell him that she wants to reconnect? That's just cruel."

"I agree, but I wouldn't have given her money if she'd just called. Perhaps if she'd threatened to show up, I might've been willing to negotiate, but she did what she thought she had to do. You don't have to worry about Colten. He'll be okay. I'll make sure of it."

"I know you will," she murmured, dropping her head against my chest once more and inhaling deeply. "I'm sorry. You've had a rough day and I'm making it even worse. I think I'm just going to go to bed."

"Nah, you'll never get any sleep like this." I ran a hand down her arm and twined our fingers together. Then I pulled her up and led her to the second primary bedroom—my bedroom, since Colten had claimed the first.

Guiding her into the bathroom, I let go of her hand to open the faucet for the tub, running her a bath in the hopes that the warm water would ease her worries. This wasn't her burden to bear, and if I was being honest, I could use it myself.

Various bottles and jars of scented bath products lined the windowsill on the opposite side of the tub and I grabbed a bottle of bubble bath and poured a generous amount of liquid into the stream. With that done, I headed over to the vanity, pulled a lighter out of the drawer, and went around the room to light the candles that had been left in here.

Dotted around the surfaces, I noticed them before but I hadn't used them yet. This seemed like the time, though. Once the little flames were dancing around the wicks, I switched off the lights and went back to Jewel, this woman who already cared for me and my son in a way his mother never had.

A woman I'd fallen for without even trying. It all came so easily with her. So naturally that I hadn't even fought it because why would I? It felt pretty damn good after being on my own for so long. I'd had all my walls up when we'd arrived, but Jewel, with her fiery soul and huge heart, had broken them down without me even realizing and now I was already in it.

I wasn't the type to run or hide. I'd always faced whatever had come my way head on, and that was exactly what I was doing now.

As the water cascaded into the tub, I pulled off my shirt and kicked off my shoes, finally getting rid of my pants before I turned to her. Her face was bare of any makeup, her cheeks red and her eyes swollen from all the crying, yet she was still the most beautiful woman I'd ever seen.

Vulnerability shone like a beacon from her eyes and a protective monster roared within me, demanding that we claim this woman as our own and keep anything from ever hurting again. While I wasn't in a position to touch that particular instinct with a ten-foot pole right then, just for tonight, I could ease her pain.

I could protect her from further hurt and help her sleep well instead of tossing and turning all night, marinating in the pain of her own abandonment. Stepping into her, I kept my gaze on hers as I reached for the sides of the robe, pushed it off her shoulders, and let it fall to the floor.

My eyes itched to drop to her chest when I pulled off her shirt. I loved her boobs. A deep, true love that I would never get enough of, but since tonight wasn't about sex, I just looked deeply into her eyes instead.

Once the shirt was gone, I pushed off her pants and panties, then stepped into the bath and offered her a hand to help her in. Everything in me begged to touch her, to bury myself deep inside her body and lose myself in it for the night, but I didn't give in to the urge.

Tonight, I wanted to take care of her. With the warm glow of the candles and the sweet scent of the bubbles in the air, I sank down into the water and rested my back against the edge. Then I pulled her down to sit between my legs.

She rested her head against my shoulder, her eyes closed as she leaned into me. Sliding an arm around her shoulders, I felt the even beat of her heart against my forearm and I found my own eyes closing as I laid my head on top of hers.

Today had been long and grueling, but getting to end it like this was fucking bliss. It was something I could definitely get used to. If only I could figure out a way to make it last for longer than the three weeks we had left here.

50

JEWEL

I felt like crap for bursting into tears when Landon had told me about the deal he'd struck with Kaitlin. Colten wasn't my child, and no matter how I felt about him, it wasn't my place to cry over it.

It also hadn't been my intention to make it all about me and my mom, but the truth was that when Landon had told me that Kaitlin had taken the money, my heart had shattered into millions of tiny, sharp little shards that had sliced through the rest of me.

It had hurt so much that I hadn't been able to hold back. I'd tried, but I just hadn't been able to claw back my composure. Even now, those cuts on my insides were still smarting, though the hot water and Landon's arms were working miracles for the emotional pain.

"Are you sure you're okay?" I murmured quietly to Landon, gently wrapping my fingers around his forearm as I shifted my head back a little to look up at him. "It's got to be pretty terrible to have to pay off your ex just so she won't fight you for custody of a child she doesn't even care about."

I knew I'd stated it harshly, but I was so torn up about this that I couldn't find it in myself to be much kinder when it came to that woman. At least my own mom had only left us after she'd fallen apart because my dad had left.

Before that, growing up, she'd been a wonderful mother. We hadn't had the easiest of childhoods, and we definitely hadn't been well off, but she'd taken us swimming in the lake in the afternoons after school and she'd cooked us pancakes every Sunday morning.

I couldn't imagine what it was going to feel like for Colten one day when he was my age, knowing that his mother had chosen a payday over him. It was unconscionable to me.

Landon opened his eyes and looked into mine, the green of them so soft and warm in the romantic candlelight that I just wanted to crawl into them. He managed a tired smile, his lips curving up at the corners, but it was clear that he was exhausted.

"I'm okay," he replied, his voice low and slightly hoarse, as if the emotion of it all was tightening his throat. "I'm just sorry I didn't realize how triggering it was going to be for you. And how hard it's going to be for Colt to accept even if he doesn't realize it now."

I hummed, tipping my head back a little further and giving him a small smile. "He's got you, though. I know I've said it before, but he really is lucky to have you. He's going to be just fine, and when he is, it's going to be because he has a father who loves him more than anything."

"Well, I mean, I love bacon a lot too, so—" I smacked his arm and he laughed, eyes coming back to mine. "Okay, fine. You're right. I do love him more than anything. He's pretty lucky to have met you too, though. He likes you."

"I like him," I said, drinking in his strong profile and wondering just how much to tell him. "We had a good talk today while you were gone. He really misses you when you're working."

Landon's chest rose against my back and he blew out a deep breath. "I'm going to do better from now on. I don't quite know how yet, but I am."

"I believe you." I lifted one of my wet hands out of the water and brought it to his cheeks, running my fingertips along his cheekbone. "You'll figure it out. I'm pretty sure you're the kind of guy who can do anything he puts his mind to. Hell, you even almost had Scott beat at the Lake Warrior contest."

A soft snort came out of him as he bit back a laugh. "Your definition obviously differs from mine of almost having him beat, but this is something I can figure out. I will. I just need time to think about how I can shuffle things around."

I nodded. "You'll get there. Actually wanting to do it is half the battle won."

Smiling as he held me tighter, he lowered his head and pressed his lips to mine. It was a gentle kiss, tender and meaningful, and I savored it. Moaning softly, I wrapped my arm around his neck. At the sound that escaped me, he groaned in turn and I felt his cock stirring against my lower back.

"I didn't get you naked expecting anything," he murmured into the kiss. "Quite the opposite, in fact. We're supposed to be relaxing."

"We are relaxing." I smiled against his lips as I snaked my hand along the flat planes of his abdomen. "Isn't part of relaxing also just doing whatever we want to do, though?"

"Yes," he hissed through clenched teeth as I wrapped my fingers around his rapidly hardening shaft. "As long as you know you don't have to do this."

"I want to," I assured him, watching him closely as I started stroking up and down.

Landon's head fell back, the tops of his cheeks flushed and his lips parting. He leaned back a little further, allowing his hips some space to move as they began rocking into my touch.

A thrill shot down my spine. I loved that I had this effect on him, but I also loved that I could be this close to him. That he'd let me in even after the kind of day he'd had. Besides, I really wasn't doing this because I felt any sort of obligation to. I just wanted to be with him. I wanted to make him feel good and remind him that life didn't have to be hard.

It could be fun. Pleasurable. Passionate. A person didn't have to overthink everything or overcomplicate it. I knew he hadn't brought me to the bathroom to have sex, but it was really pretty simple. I wanted him and I knew he wanted me too, so I didn't see any reason to deprive ourselves.

His jaw tightened and the muscles in his throat started working. I leaned my head closer and pressed an open-mouthed kiss to his neck. A soft growl vibrated through his chest and my nipples hardened in response.

Being with Landon like this was the best feeling in the world. Just a little while ago, my heart had cracked open in front of him and I'd bled my emotions all over the poor man, vulnerable and sensitive as hell, and then he'd taken care of me.

He helped me put myself back together, and now, even though I might've been embarrassed about falling apart in front of anyone else, he was making me feel wanted and loved. My emotions were raw and I knew his were as well, but that was the beauty of it, letting each other see everything there was to see and still wanting to be together.

As my hand moved, he drew me to him, kissing me deep and hard, his wet fingers winding into my hair as his tongue parted my lips. This was raw too, the kiss. We were both laying it all out there and I'd never felt so safe doing it.

I pumped my fist a little faster, an ache starting between my legs. One of his hands released my hair, running sensually with the flat of his palm against my face, throat, and neck before he cupped my ribs. I arched my back, silently begging him to touch me in any one of the many places that wanted to be touched right then, and he indulged me without question, circling his thumb and index finger around my nipples and pinching them.

Sparks of pleasure flew through me and I moaned into his mouth, rubbing my thighs together before I did something really embarrassing—like touch myself just because I couldn't wait any longer. It was the weirdest thing, being so turned on physically while feeling so connected to him on every other freaking level.

I'd never been as emotionally invested in a man as I was with him, and while that deep current of intense feelings should've turned me off, it really didn't. Instead, it made every brush of his fingertips against my skin feel that much better. It should've scared me because I knew it meant that I really was in love with him, but I just wasn't afraid.

I wasn't afraid of my feelings, intense as they were. I wasn't even afraid of the heartbreak I knew was headed my way. In the moment, all that mattered was nurturing the connection between us. Feeling what I felt and what he made me feel.

As another long, loud groan came out of him, his thighs tensed but then he took my wrist in an iron grip, instantly stopping my movement. Breathing hard, he pulled away, his eyelids heavy as he rested his forehead against mine.

"Let's go to bed."

I nodded. He climbed out of the tub, and I took his hand when he offered it. My legs were shaky, but he wrapped me up in a towel before quickly drying himself. Then he led me into the bedroom and dried me off as we reached his bed.

The friction of the towel and his hot hands over it drove me crazy, but he didn't make me wait, bringing his mouth to my core just as soon as he'd tossed the towel away. Moans spilled out of me as he sucked my clit into his mouth. His hands were on the insides of my thighs, spreading them to give himself better access as I stood there, hanging onto his hair so I wouldn't fall over.

I was almost at the edge when he pushed me down on the bed, grabbed a condom, quickly rolled it on, and sank into me. While the lights in his bedroom were off, there was ambient light from the candles in the bathroom. I could see the wildfire in his eyes as he withdrew and the immense relief when he sank back in.

I pushed my fingers into his hair, my gaze locked on his as our bodies moved together and pleasure streaked through me. It curled my toes and exploded in bubbles of elation through my veins, but even in the midst of the most powerful orgasm I'd ever had, those words were right on the tip of my tongue.

I loved Landon Payne, and unless I was very much mistaken, he loved me too.

51

LANDON

Why is the world shaking?

My eyes flew open at the thought and I sat up in bed, the glowing green dials on the clock on the nightstand telling me that it was three a.m. I frowned, still groggy and disoriented, but then I realized that the world hadn't been shaking.

Colten was shaking my arm, his face just inches away from my own. "Wake up, Dad. Wake up!"

I squeezed my eyes shut and opened them again, but he was still here. And so was Jewel. My stomach sank when I realized we'd just been caught in bed together. I opened my mouth to explain, grasping for words I couldn't find in my foggy brain, but as soon as my eyes adjusted in the low light and I saw Colten's face, I realized that he seemed frightened.

He didn't seem to care at all about Jewel being in bed with me. Instead, his eyes were wide and round, his lips mashed into a thin white line. "Daddy, wake up. Are you awake?"

I jerked my head in a nod, reaching out and putting my hand on his shoulder. "Yeah, bud. I'm awake. What's going on? What's wrong?"

"There are three cars parked outside," he muttered in a rough, half-whisper. "One of them is that red car that crashed into us the other day."

At those words, I was hit with a rush of adrenaline. Immediately, I knew something was wrong. I didn't doubt for a moment that he was right. He hadn't dreamed it. Dallas was here, and apparently, he'd brought backup.

Jewel was slowly coming to and I glanced at her, my voice low and urgent. "You two need to get dressed. Right now. Colt, run back to your room and grab some clothes. Bring them here. Jewel will help you pack a bag. Jewel, you need to pack too. Stay inside."

Colten nodded, pale in the silver moonlight filtering in through the window, but he took off, giving Jewel and me the minute we needed to cover up before he came back. Jewel glanced at me as she pulled on the pajamas she'd been wearing earlier.

"What do you think he wants?" she asked, obviously having come to the same conclusion I had about who was out there.

It seemed she didn't think someone else had the same car as Dallas either. It was definitely him. I shrugged as I shoved a T-shirt over my head. "I don't know, baby. Just go get dressed and pack a bag. Keep Colten with you please. I need both of you to be ready to leave if we have to."

"Yeah, okay," she said nervously. "Are you really going to go down there?"

I nodded. "I have to. If I don't, they'll come in and that's the last thing we want. Just stay out of sight, okay? I'll meet you guys back here as soon as I can."

I could see the nerves etched into her features, the anxiety shining from her eyes. When Colten came running back into the room with a stack of clothing and his bag, I saw the same thing from him. Annoyance raced through me, setting my blood to simmer as I marched downstairs.

I didn't care what had happened between Dallas and me. I'd paid him to stay here for the whole summer and it was absolutely unacceptable that he'd show up like this in the middle of the damn night.

As I got to the foyer, aggressive knocking started against the front door. The banging thundered through the silent house. Aggravation tightened my muscles and I ground my teeth as I yanked open the front door, throwing up a hand to shield my eyes against the flashlights that were suddenly blinding me.

"Get the hell out of my house," Dallas slurred the command, swaying slightly as he jutted his hand toward the front gates. "You're not welcome here anymore. Not after humiliating me in front of everyone and getting me that DUI. So get the fuck out."

While I knew it hadn't been my fault, it was easy to see that Dallas was drunk again. A quick glance at the men who were with him told me they weren't just regular townsfolk. They looked like goons, hired guns for our eviction.

Both of them wore tight black T-shirts, and they were huge. Built like houses with dangerously vacant gleams in their eyes. With Jewel and Colten inside, I decided not to pick a fight. I needed to focus on getting them out and away from here safely.

Tomorrow, I could take up the matter of this rude intrusion and demand a refund of the money I'd already paid. But for tonight, all I needed was to keep Colten and Jewel safe. There was no telling what he'd do in this state and Colt had been traumatized enough, by Dallas and by Kaitlin.

I wasn't risking any more drama or trauma.

"Fine," I spat at him. "I'll leave, but I need to get my son."

Dallas smirked, the scent of bourbon radiating from him as he shot a pointed look at his goons. "The kid is scrawny. He won't be able to take us, so let Daddy go get his baby, boys. We don't want a nerdy boy like him hanging around anyway."

He made a few more rude comments about "the kid" that made my blood boil, but I retreated anyway, focused on my mission to get them out before these men came in. As I reached the staircase, however, I heard the front door smacking open against the wall and their footsteps rang out as they strode into the house.

Fuck.

My pulse spiked, my level of concern suddenly sky high. I didn't want Dallas to know that Jewel was here. There was no telling how he'd react. I knew he had a thing for her. She'd told me that he always made a point of stopping by her place when he was in town and that he'd asked her out numerous times.

Spinning around with my hand already on the banister to ascend the stairs, I gave them a hard look that stopped all three men in their tracks. "Stay right here until we're out. I'm willing to leave, but I won't have you anywhere near my son. We'll need a minute to pack things for the night."

Dallas sneered, but one of the men grabbed his arm and held him back, exchanging a glance with the other guy before he nodded at me. His voice was cold and stony as he inclined his chin toward the stairs. "We'll give you five minutes, but then you need to be gone."

"Yeah, yeah," I muttered, not at all afraid for my own safety.

If it hadn't been for Jewel and Colten, I wouldn't have hesitated to dig in my heels. I knew this type. Dallas had probably picked them up at a biker bar somewhere, promising payment of some sort if they provided him with some scowling faces to help scare me away.

I didn't doubt he'd hatched this plan while drinking tonight, but I would make sure he'd regret it in the morning. For now, though, I turned and headed upstairs, breaking into a jog as soon as I was out of sight.

Throwing the lock on the bedroom door once I was inside, I turned to face Colten and Jewel. Three packed bags sat on the edge of the bed, and she had her arm around his shoulders where they'd been waiting right next to the bags.

Apprehension stared back at me from both of their expressions, their eyes glossy with concern and fear. Keeping my voice down and even, I strode to pick up the bags, slinging all three over my shoulders.

"Dallas is here," I said to confirm their suspicions. "He brought backup and he wants us out. He's drunk again, so it's safer to comply for now, okay?"

I glanced at Colten and flashed him what I hoped was a reassuring smile. "They're not going to do anything to us, bud. Remember what I told you about big egos? This is just part of Dallas's. He's still embarrassed about what happened the other day and the only thing he can do is to chuck us out of his house."

Colt sighed but nodded. "They didn't hurt you?"

I chuckled dryly and shook my head. "They didn't even try. If they had, the police would already be on their way here."

Once he looked mildly less panicked, I turned to Jewel. "I need you to go out the back, baby. Don't let them see you. I don't want Dallas knowing you're here in the state he's in. There's no telling what he'd do."

Her face was ashen as she stood up and touched her fingers to my cheek. Her eyes were full of worry but it didn't seem to be for herself. "Are you going out the front?"

"We're going to have to. He needs to see us leaving, but we'll meet you on the south side of the house, okay? I have a feeling we're going to be walking. He won't let us take the truck, but I'll call the driver that brought us here just as soon as we're clear."

She nodded. "We'll be okay. Let's just focus on getting out of here first."

"Be careful," I warned her quietly, not wanting to alarm Colten more than he already was, but I really didn't want Dallas to know she was here.

She might've told me that he was more bark than bite, but in my profession, I'd seen what alcohol could make men do. When they'd had enough to drink, some people just couldn't help themselves. They committed heinous acts that they didn't have the courage for when they were sober.

Jewel's eyes latched on mine. "Don't worry about me. I'll be careful, but I've gotten to know this house pretty well. They won't see me. Are they in the foyer?"

"Yep, I told them to stay put while we packed a few things for the night."

She inclined her chin in a nod at me to let me know she'd heard, but then she bent at the knees and looked at Colten, even managing to give him a reassuring smile of her own. "We need to go our separate ways for now, but I promise you that I'm going to be okay and I'll meet you right outside."

Colt suddenly threw his arms around her, giving her a tight hug as he nodded. "Just be safe. That guy is scary."

She chuckled, but the sound was more high-pitched than usual. As much as she tried to appear calm, she was afraid. "He's not so bad. I'll see you soon."

The thought of both her and Colten being so scared of one drunk asshole made me want to rip his head off his shoulders with my bare hands, but I didn't let either of them see the fury eating me up inside.

I need to keep them safe. I need to get them out of here.

With that mantra in my mind, I crossed back to the bedroom door and unlocked it, checking that the long, wide hallway outside was clear before I nodded at them. "Okay, let's go."

"I think it's best if I take my bag," she said as they approached the door. "It'll save you having to answer questions about why there are three."

I sighed but handed it over. "Stay safe, Jewel. South side. Remember."

Voices filtered up to us from downstairs, but it was mostly Dallas's, boasting to his goons about how much money he had. *Not a great idea, buddy.*

They were almost certainly going to insist on being paid more now that he'd let them see this house and he was telling them all about it, but that wasn't my problem. Watching as Jewel stole off to the side to take one of the smaller staircases, I waited until she'd disappeared from sight before I took Colten's hand.

"I'm sorry about this, kiddo. We're going to be okay, though. Just keep your head down and follow me. Let's do this. Let's just get out of here."

52

JEWEL

I gripped the bag I'd packed while Landon had been downstairs. Inside were the journals from Lucille, the most precious things in the house to me except for the guys who were also heading out right now.

Clothes were replaceable and so were the few other things I'd brought here. If Dallas got his hands on these journals again though, I wasn't sure he'd honor his agreement with Landon. He'd probably take them and try to sell them again, even if he'd already been paid.

Either way, I hadn't wanted to take any chances with them. They were heavier than a change of clothes would've been, but thanks to the adrenaline coursing through my veins, I barely even noticed the weight.

My heart pounded every step of the way as I sneaked out of the house, grateful for the winding and broken-up layout of the manor. It kept me hidden from view even if I could hear their voices not so far away.

Sending up a little prayer that Landon and Colten were already out, I darted out the back door, sticking close to the wall until I could take to the shadows in the yard. I kept moving, all but holding my breath until I saw Landon and Colten turn the corner.

Releasing all the air in my lungs, I breathed a sigh of relief and waited for them to join me, my heart still pounding. Now that I knew they were safe though, I knew it would start returning to normal. Landon's features were hard as they approached, tension vibrating from him, but he held it in check, tipping his head in the direction of the pedestrian gate in the wall.

"Stay in the shadows," he said quietly, his hand gripping Colten's as he took mine in the other. "Dallas may not be able to make out three shapes moving away from the house instead of one, but I think his goons might."

I wound my fingers tight around his and ran across the grounds with them toward the main road. Once we were off the property, we disappeared into the shadows of the forest lining the street before we stopped to catch our breath.

Far enough away to speak normally now, I fished my phone out of my pocket. "I'm going to call Scott to pick us up. You can stay with him until all of this is sorted out. I'm sure he won't mind."

I would've offered to have them stay at my place, but it was a tiny one bedroom. Nearly a studio suite. They'd be much too cramped there and I didn't know if it was appropriate for Landon and me to share a bed habitually while Colten slept just a few feet away on a sofa.

While he had found us in bed together earlier, that was different to it becoming a norm. My thoughts raced until my brother picked up, his voice thick with sleep. "Yep?"

"Scott, it's me," I said quickly. "I'm in the forest about half a mile away from the Manor. Dallas showed up. It's a long story, but can you come pick us up?"

A string of curses escaped him, but at least they made it clear that he was awake and alert now. "I'm on my way. Stay where you are. I'll call when I get close to you."

He hung up and I nodded at Landon. "Scott will be here soon. We should sit down. Are you guys okay?"

Colten collapsed onto a big rock, his little face so pale in the moonlight that it made me want to kick Dallas for doing this to him, but he nodded. "We're safe. Are you okay?"

I smiled at him, dropping my bag in the dirt and going over to sit on the rock next to his. "I'm all good. That was exhilarating. Quite an adventure for the middle of the night, don't you think?"

He frowned, but then he started chuckling and the sound was like music to my ears. "I don't think I've ever had an adventure."

"Come on, bud," I said, trying to keep my voice light and breezy instead of cluing him in on the fact that the adrenaline was fast draining from my system, leaving me feeling shocked and scared. "Every day is an adventure if you let it be one. This was simply an adventure I wouldn't like to repeat."

He rolled his head onto my bicep as he nodded back at me. "Me either."

We settled in for the wait with Landon pacing on the forest floor, his muscles wound up and bulging as he marched back and forth. He didn't say anything other than to check on us periodically, but he also didn't lose his cool.

When my phone pierced the deafening silence of the night, he shouldered all three bags once more and led us back to the road. A moment later, Scott's headlights turned the bend and relief raced through me once more.

We piled into the truck with no hesitation, and I motioned for Landon to take the passenger seat while I got into the back with Colten. He curled up against me immediately, passing out almost as soon as a seething Scott turned the truck around and put his foot down on the way back into town.

"What an idiot," he spat quietly, glancing up to check on Colten in the rearview mirror and keeping his voice down, but seething nonetheless. "What the hell was he thinking? This is the last stunt he's going to pull, I swear. I'm done putting up with Dallas's bullshit."

"Same," Landon agreed, white-knuckling the grab bar on the ceiling of the truck. "Thank God he let us go without incident, though. He just snarled some crap at me on our way out."

"Yeah, but someone could've gotten hurt if you hadn't kept your head tonight," Scott said. "This was the last straw. Good on you for not going off on him, but if it'd been me, I'm just not sure I'd have been able to do the same thing."

"You would've if you'd had your sister and a kid to think about," Landon reasoned, but I heard the venom slicing through his tone. "I didn't have much of a choice, man. Trust me, if it hadn't been for them, I definitely wouldn't have gone so quietly."

"You guys are sure you're alright?" Scott asked, glancing at me before turning his attention back to the dark and winding road. "If he so much as laid a hand on you, I—"

"He didn't," I said quietly so as not to rouse Colten. "Landon told me to stay out of sight and I did. Some of my stuff is still there, but other than him digging through the closets in the bedrooms, he won't even know I was ever there."

"I wouldn't put it past him," Scott said. "We'll have to go pick up your stuff in the morning. Where are we going, by the way? Jewel's place?"

"Actually, I was hoping we could just stay with you tonight," I said, silently begging him to agree. "I don't really have enough space and I think we all just need to get some sleep."

"Sure," he said without even taking a second to think about it. "That's a good idea. I'll feel better knowing you're with me anyway. If he does go through your stuff and realizes who it belongs to, he might show up at your apartment next."

"I doubt it," I said, but I hadn't thought he'd show up at the Manor like that either, so it was possible that I was wrong.

"Thanks, man," Landon said when Scott and I both fell silent. "It'll only be for tonight. We'll figure the rest out in the morning."

"Yeah, of course," my brother said graciously, surprising me by how readily he was agreeing to all this. "All that matters now is that we get the little man to a bed where he'll be safe for the night."

My heart swelled with appreciation for my brother. Like me, he had a real heart for kids and I'd never loved him more for it than I did right then. Especially because I knew he was uneasy about whatever was going on between me and Landon.

He hadn't brought it up in a few weeks, but I'd seen him and Brittany shooting me worried glances whenever they saw me with Landon. They didn't want me to get hurt and yet, we all knew which way this ship was sailing.

As the two of them started talking about Dallas and how much of an ass he was again, I agreed, but I didn't say so. Instead, I rested my head on top of Colten's and held him tight, promising him in a quiet whisper that everything was okay now.

After the talk he and I had had just yesterday, I knew how sad being tossed out of the Manor was going to make him. It had become a safe, happy space for him. A place where he'd bonded with his dad for the first time in a long time and which had held only memories of laughter and fun until tonight.

Anger at Dallas for ruining all that bubbled in my veins. One drunken night and he'd stolen this little boy's happy place right out from underneath him. Without a second thought, he'd yanked the rug from under this child's feet and I hated him for it.

Fiercely and vehemently.

Although I didn't know what Scott had in mind when he'd said he wasn't going to put up with Dallas's bullshit anymore, I knew in that moment that I was with my brother. Whatever steps he decided to take against Dallas after this, I was in.

I was sure most of the people in town would be too.

Colten let out a soft sigh in his sleep and I pressed a kiss to his hair, hoping that he could feel how safe and loved he was right then. His mother might've had no idea what she was missing by taking two and a half million dollars instead of loving this boy, but I did.

I knew and I wouldn't accept a hundred times that in exchange for even just a day spent with him. This little boy had crawled so deep into my heart and knowing that he'd potentially been in danger tonight had just made it that much more obvious to me how much I cared about him.

I would have tackled Dallas myself if he'd tried to hurt Colten. I definitely would've lost if I'd tried to take him on, but I would've put my body on the line without a second thought to protect this child.

Heaven only knew, after everything he'd been through, it was the least I could've done.

Colten didn't deserve all the hurt, the loneliness, and the abandonment. He deserved only all the good things in the world. All the best things, and if it were up to me, I would've devoted my life to making sure he got it.

53

LANDON

Only a few hours after our rude wake-up call, I was in the kitchen with Scott, drinking coffee instead of sleeping in with Jewel and Colten. I'd tried to go back to sleep after Scott had shown Colt and me to his guest bedroom, but I hadn't really gotten much more than a few winks after that.

It was seven a.m., but Scott was up again as well, his eyes red-rimmed from lack of sleep as he regarded me from the other side of the kitchen island. "You manage to get any more shut-eye after we got in?"

I shook my head. "Not really, you?"

"Nah. Too busy plotting against Dallas," he said, but I wasn't quite sure if he was joking.

I chuckled. "Whatever you decide to do, let me know. I've got your back. Someone needs to do something about that guy. He's a menace." I paused. "Thanks for coming to our rescue last night, Scott. I really appreciate it."

"Thanks for keeping your head and protecting my sister," he replied seriously.

"It was a close call," I admitted. "I almost lost my mind. The only reason I kept my shit together was because I was worried about Jewel and Colt being in the house."

"So what's your plan?" he asked, cocking his head at me as he held my gaze. "What happens now?"

I shrugged. "I don't know. It's his house. I don't have any legal grounds to force him to let us—"

"No," he said, cutting me off and shaking his head. "I don't care about that. Dallas is an ass, but I'm sure he'll give you your money back if you lean on him a little bit. You'll be better off staying someplace else anyway, now that you've pissed him off. What I meant is what happens now with you and my sister? What's your plan? You're still leaving in a few weeks, right?"

I went quiet. I'd been pretending that little fact wasn't real, thinking about it every now and then and dismissing it again. But it was real. Our time here was coming to an end fast and I couldn't ignore it anymore.

"I don't know what to tell you," I said honestly. "My life is in LA. My job. Colt's school. Walter." When he gave me a questioning look, I added. "My stepfather. He raised me and he's the only family we've got. I can't just leave him in some facility hundreds of miles away."

Scott grimaced, but I saw the understanding in his eyes. "I respect whatever decision you make, but don't string Jewel along if the decision is already made. Don't dangle it like a carrot in front of her face that things might work out between you."

"I'm not," I protested, but he let out a humorless chuckle.

"I know my sister and she's in love, Landon. The ship has sailed. It's too late to do anything about it now, but don't hurt her any more than you have to. Don't make her think this is something it isn't."

The weight of his words settled on my shoulders.

I've let this go too far. Now I'm going to hurt her, myself, and worst of all, Colten.

Scott didn't rub it in or make any threats about breaking my kneecaps if I didn't do something. He just gave me a tight nod and then strode over to the fridge to pull out a tray of eggs. Meanwhile, I felt like I'd had the wind knocked out of me.

I needed to talk to Jewel about this. Today. We couldn't ignore it any longer, skirt around it, or decide to live only in the moment. The time had come to actually deal with it.

Sighing as I rubbed the back of my neck, I turned as Colten and Jewel walked into the kitchen together for breakfast. She smiled at me and came to my side, slinging her arm over my shoulders and casually touching her temple to mine. "Colt and I have an idea to pick up everyone's spirits."

"Yeah, what's that?" Scott asked.

She shared a conspiring look with my son. "A good, old-fashioned day on the boat. We can go tubing and swimming, and maybe pack a picnic to eat on the beach?"

"I'm always down for that," Scott said, breaking some eggs into a pan. "Let me just scramble this. We'll have a quick breakfast and then Colten can come with me to buy the fuel?"

Colt nodded enthusiastically. When the food was ready, he vacuumed it up and waited impatiently for a laughing Scott to finish. As soon as he was done, Colten bolted to the door, yelling goodbye to Jewel and me before running out to Scott's truck.

The guy gave me a look that said he was buying us this time alone to talk, and I was grateful for it. As grateful as I was surprised that he was handling it all this well.

When they were gone, Jewel carried our bowls to the sink and came back to me with a mischievous smile on her lips. Instead of going to her seat, she crawled into my lap, locking her arms around my neck as she smiled down at me.

"I know yesterday sucked, but I told Colten we'd have a better adventure today." She planted a kiss on my lips that made me want to do anything but tell her the truth, especially when she pressed her lips to my ear and whispered against it. "Who knows? You and I might even be able to sneak away while they toss the ball around."

I groaned, wishing I could just let it all go again, but I had to talk to her and I knew it. Pulling back, I looked her square in the eye and leveled with her. "I'm in love with you."

She blinked a few times fast. Then a slow smile spread on her lips and her eyes fluttered closed before she focused on me again. "I love you, too. I've just been waiting for the right time to tell you."

My heart soared and broke at the same time. Excruciating agony mingled with the purest joy, and together, the two conflicting emotions nearly tore me in half.

Jewel kissed me like she meant it, but I pulled away before I got caught up in the moment. It would be too easy to revel in this. In her. In knowing that the most amazing woman in the world loved me back.

"I still have to go home," I murmured against her lips. "We can't keep doing this, Jewel. It's just going to make things harder at the end of the summer."

She lifted her head away from mine. "What?"

"I think we should stop before we go too far." I hated saying it, but it had to be done. "I'm sorry, baby. I just don't think this is a good idea anymore."

Her head jerked back as if she'd been slapped. Scooting backward off my lap, she stumbled to the kitchen counter and gripped it for support. "We've already gone too far, Landon. We love each other. Are you really trying to break up with me less than a minute after you told me that you're in love with me?"

"I am, Jewel. I am in love with you, which is why I have to put a stop to this."

Her honey-gold eyes widened and she scoffed. "Is all of this really only occurring to you now? Because I've been thinking about it for a while and I don't know what we're going to do, but I think it's at least worth trying to make it work."

"How?" I asked flatly, my chest aching but my features stoic as I remembered what Scott had said about dangling carrots. "It's common knowledge that long distance relationships don't work indefinitely."

"Don't have any capacity to try?" she asked with disbelief cutting into her tone. "What about speaking to Walter about moving here? Or what if—"

I shook my head. "I can't uproot my father, Jewel. He's doing well because of where he is, and Colten has school and responsibilities. The chess club. I can't just yank him around either."

She looked right into my eyes, searching, but I didn't know what for. There was no way we could make this work. I wanted to desperately, but wanting something didn't make it possible.

"I have work, Jewel," I said, needing her to understand that moving here simply wasn't an option for me at this time. "I have a firm to get back to. Open cases with clients who have been waiting for me to get back."

She opened her mouth to say something, but no words came out. Tears started glittering in her eyes, her beautiful face slowly turning slack. "There has to be something we can do, Landon. If we love each other, we have to fight for it, right? Love isn't something you just throw away."

"It shouldn't be, but I don't see any options for us, Jewel. Not unless you want a relationship in which we only see each other for maybe one weekend a month and text back and forth until we run out of things to text about."

"You're giving up," she whispered a moment later, giving her head a hard shake. "I didn't think you were the type."

"I'm not," I said emphatically, fixing my gaze on hers. "If there was any way to make it work, I'd have done it, but realistically, the only way to do it is if one of us moves. You've got your business here. Your responsibilities. All of mine are back in LA."

I shoved a hand into my hair, feeling that ache spread from my chest to the rest of my body like poison spreading through my veins. I fucking hated every moment of this. I couldn't even tell her how much I deplored what I was doing right now, but just because something was easy didn't make it right.

Falling in love with her had been easy, but it wasn't right. It couldn't be when there was no way to make it last. "I have Walt. I have work. I have Colt. I have to sort out my inheritance instead of just letting it sit there because I'm overwhelmed by it. I have to decide what my next steps are in my career."

Fat, heavy tears welled on her eyelids, spilling over on her next blink to track wet streaks down her cheeks. "So this is it, then? Just like that, it's over."

I threw my arms out to my sides, feeling like my blood was turning to sludge. I could hear my heart pounding in my ears, that ache taking over my entire body. "What do you want from me here, Jewel? I love you, but that doesn't mean I can just uproot my entire life and move to June Lake to be with you. People depend on me."

"So do I," she said tearfully, giving me one last look before she shook her head and left in a rush, slamming the door behind her.

I collapsed back in my chair, shoving both of my hands through my hair this time. "Fuck!"

That ache turned to excruciating pain, but it wasn't physical and I knew it. It was just my heart and soul ripping themselves out of my body to follow her. *That's all, no biggie.*

Everything in me pleaded to go after her. To run down the street and throw myself at her feet to beg for her forgiveness, but I didn't move.

As much as it hurt, I knew it was for the best. I also knew Scott had been right earlier. I had been stringing her along. Not intentionally, but that didn't make it any less true. I'd been acting as if the day we would have to leave would never come, or like things would work themselves out before then.

But there had never been any real possibility of this ending any other way than it just had. I'd done what had to be done, even if I already knew I would never be able to forgive myself for it.

And I had a feeling Colten wasn't going to forgive me either.

54

JEWEL

Back at my apartment, I poured my heart out to Brittany. A few blocks away from Scott's house, I'd finally realized that I couldn't walk all the way home and I'd put in a hysterical call to my friend, sobbing so much that she'd barely made out that I was asking her to come pick me up.

That had been about an hour ago and I was only calming down enough to talk now. She sat on the sofa facing me, her legs tucked underneath me and a beer in her hand. As soon as we'd arrived, she'd popped down to the store to buy a six-pack and she'd given me one too, but I hadn't even been able to take a sip yet.

It might be a beautiful day full of rainbow lights from my suncatchers, but it felt ugly and lonesome after what Landon had just done to me. "I just can't believe it. These last few weeks have been pure magic. Damn near perfect. Then he tells me he's in love with me, but we have to end it? What kind of bullshit is that?"

"I'm still a little lost about how you ended up at Scott's to begin with," she said, her brow furrowed and her eyes glossy with sympathy. "What exactly happened with Dallas?"

"He showed up at the manor at three a.m. to tell Landon to get out. Drunk as a skunk and with two thugs in tow. I was so scared, but

Landon made sure that Colten and I were safe. He never let his ego take control. We were in a good place, you know?"

"It has looked that way," Brittany said, her voice soft and gentle. "When you first told me his ex had shown up, I thought trouble might've come to paradise, but then you got through that and I thought that was it. That you'd figured something out."

"I thought it was over then too," I admitted softly. "I figured that if a woman who looked like that, *and* that he has a history with, wanted him, then I didn't stand a chance, but he was so sweet about it. He made me feel so secure in whatever it was we had. We didn't figure out how we were going to keep seeing each other, but it sure felt like more than just a summer fling."

I sighed, my breathing shaky as I felt my face falling all over again. "That's the worst part about all of this. It felt so right. It all just happened so quickly and so easily that even though I knew it was going to have to end, I don't think I really expected it to. Especially after Colten told me that he wanted to stay."

Brittany's eyes flew wide open. "What? Are you serious? When did he tell you that?"

"Yesterday," I admitted unhappily. "He said he'd already told his dad about it, but he also said that he needed me. I didn't make any promises or anything like that, but I kind of thought that was it. That if Colten wanted to stay and Landon knew about it, then..."

"Then he wouldn't leave," she concluded for me. "It's not that easy, though, babe. He has a whole life in LA."

"I know, but he likes it here. Plus, he paid off his ex to leave them alone and he's made it plenty clear that I've been good for Colten, so I think I just, in the back of my mind, thought that when push came to shove, he'd stay."

"Wow, he paid her off?"

"Yep. Two and a half million dollars is the going rate for promising to leave your kid alone forever, it seems."

She flinched. "Ouch. That's a lot of money. I mean, we knew he was rich, but that's like, mega bucks."

"Yeah, I know, but he acted like it was nothing." I sighed. "Either way, with Kaitlin out of the way and after my talk with Colten, Landon and I just felt like we were on solid ground. I let myself be so vulnerable with him, Brit. I don't know how to go back to my normal life now that I've had them in it."

She scooted over to give me a comforting hug. "Would you ever consider moving to LA with him? It's not like it's on the other side of the country."

The mere thought of it made my stomach flip over. I shook my head. "No, I haven't really thought about it. This is my home. I could never just leave."

"What's keeping you here, though?" she asked. "You could always just give it a chance?"

"My family is here," I said slowly. "Everything is here. You. Tiff. Scott. The business."

"Yeah, but June Lake will always be here to come back to," she reasoned. "I'll always be your best friend and Scott will understand. I mean, Tiff might come and go if she's got anything to say about it, but you'd see her again too."

For a crazy, wild minute, I tried to envision moving someplace else. I tried to imagine packing up and leaving with them, not knowing when I was going to be coming back again. As I tried to picture making a life with Landon in LA, memories of the last time I'd seen my mother played through my mind.

Her smiling face as she waved goodbye, her long blonde hair blowing in the slight breeze as she shrank into her boyfriend's side. The way she'd looked up at him just before the cab had turned the corner, like it was more important to check on him than it was to see us one last time.

As it all came back to me, I shook my head and refocused on my friend. "I'm not leaving here to follow a man. That's just not who I am, and let's say I do it. Let's say that I swallow my pride and go with him. He's just going to pour himself into his career as soon as he gets back. The shine of having me with him will wear off, and I'll become a glorified babysitter to his son that'll make him feel better about leaving him for as long as he does."

I exhaled. "My life is here and I love it just the way it is. I've loved this time that I've spent with them too and I won't deny that it hurts, but I'm not chasing after him to some city I've never even been before and where I'll likely never even get to see him. I'm not changing a life I love for anything."

"Good," she said with a sigh of relief. "For a second there, I thought you might think it was a good idea. I had to ask anyway."

That got a smile out of me, but it was short lived. Just because I wouldn't move to LA didn't mean it was easy to let go of them. When they finally left for good, I was going to miss them deeply. Their absence was going to hurt. Bad.

"You warned me," I murmured as I looked into Brit's soft brown eyes. "You told me to keep my heart out of it and just have a bit of fun. I tried to listen, but my heart got sucked into it anyway."

She chuckled, shaking her head before dropping it to rest on top of mine. "I've got your back while you heal, girl. You're going to be okay. I know this sucks so much, but Scott and I are here for you, and in the end, it's going to work out for the best."

I didn't know about that, but I was grateful to have a friend like her even if I was heartbroken that Landon was ready to call it quits. I had been hanging onto these next three weeks we could've had together like a lifeline, hoping that something was going to give before they passed.

Foolish as it might've been, I'd thought that in time, we'd manage to come up with a plan that would allow us to stay together. I'd been willing to give long distance a try. Anything that wouldn't involve breaking up, but obviously, Landon just didn't feel the same way I did.

"One day, you're going to look back on this and understand why it happened the way it did," Brittany said softly. "Maybe it'll be because your one true love is just around the corner or maybe the dinosaurs will come back and take out all of LA. But whatever it is, there will have been a reason for it."

I glanced up at her. "Dinosaurs?"

She shrugged. "It was the first thing that popped into my head."

We lapsed into a comfortable silence as I tried to process how fast that conversation had turned around. When he'd told me he was in love with me, it had been like my entire being had been filled with sprinkles of elation.

Our future together had fallen open like a road map, with so many different paths to choose from, and I would have been happy with any one that allowed us to reach the same destination in the end. In my mind's eye, I'd pictured being there for them from now on.

Giving Colten pep talks over the phone when he went back to school. Reminding Landon to go home at night. Spending the holidays with them here for winter break. Keeping the spark alive with Landon in a variety of interesting, digital ways until we saw each other again.

It wouldn't have been ideal, but it sure would've been better than this. I sighed, pushing my fingers into my tangled hair and pulling them through it.

I hadn't even gotten around to brushing it this morning. I'd simply pulled it into a messy ponytail when Colten had come bounding into Scott's bedroom where I'd been sleeping on a spare mattress, enthusiastic to share his idea about a day on the lake.

"I wonder what he's going to tell Colt," I mused out loud, feeling a fresh wave of tears coming on. "How do you think he's going to take it? Do you think I'll have the chance to say goodbye?"

The thought alone made that fresh wave break free and hot tears started streaming from my eyes again. There was no stopping the tide today, and I wasn't trying to. I knew from experience that bottling up emotions never made them better. It only made me feel them that much more intensely when I finally had no choice but to confront them.

I'd done it with my dad all my life, shoving down all the pain he'd made me feel until after he'd left. Letting go enough to find acceptance had been a slow, excruciating process I had no intention of repeating. It had taken me years to come to terms with it all.

"It's going to be okay, babe," Brittany said as she snaked her arms around me for another hug. "I know it doesn't feel that way now, but it will be."

As she said it, all I wanted was to fast forward to a time when I'd be able to believe those words. A time when I'd feel like myself again, but that time definitely wasn't today.

Out of all the men in the world, I'd gone and fallen for one who not only lived nearly five hundred miles away, but who also refused to even consider staying with me. He was sweet and kind, smart and funny, and perfect for me in every way—and he'd fallen in love with me to boot—but none of that mattered.

I'd thought Landon was a fighter, but it turned out that I'd completely misjudged him on that front. Or maybe it was simply because he didn't love me enough to try.

55

LANDON

I pulled up in front of the Manor in a rental SUV. Sighing as I got out, I shielded my eyes against the sun and saw Dallas in the yard. He was holding a golf club, wearing nothing but a robe, boxers, and sunglasses as he whacked balls into the lake and drank beer.

Glancing at the house, I noticed that the front door was wide open, so I headed in that direction instead, strolling inside as if I had a right to be there. Which I did, considering that the time I'd paid for hadn't run out yet.

After I left here, I'd sort out a refund, but at the moment, the only thing I wanted was our stuff. I would pack Jewel's things too and drop them off at Scott's on our way out of town. It felt like the least I could do.

As I walked into the house, Dallas finally realized I was there, hollering as soon as he saw me. "Stop! Do not go in there, Payne. It's my house and I'm denying you access."

I didn't listen. Crossing over the threshold, I made for the stairs first. Dallas followed me in, snarling threats as I reached the first step. "If you don't stop right now, I'll call the cops."

I rolled my eyes and gripped the banister, ascending fast but staying calm. Dallas scoffed before I heard his bare feet smacking against the hardwood floors behind me. "I mean it, Landon. Leave or I'm calling the cops. You're trespassing."

I spun around and took the few steps between us two at a time, getting right in his face. His eyes were red and watery. The stench of stale beer wafted from him. With his thinning hair sticking up in all directions and a sickly pallor, he wasn't as intimidating today as he obviously thought he was.

"Stop threatening me." I issued the command quietly, but even I heard the low, dangerous warning in my tone. "I've fucking had it with you, Styles. I'm here to collect my things, and once I have it all, I'm leaving. The Manor and June Lake. For good. You'll be hearing from me about the money I've already paid, but unless you're willing to refund me right the fuck now, I'm going to get my shit without you in my ears and then I'm out of here."

He averted his gaze and threw his hands up. "Fine, but make it quick."

"I'll be done when I'm done." I turned again and stalked up the remaining stairs, heading to Colten's room first.

Once I'd packed up his stuff and made sure that I had everything, I went to my bedroom, leaving Jewel's for last. *That one's going to hurt.*

Just being here fucking hurt. It was like the very air in here was infused with her presence, reminders of her everywhere I looked.

Like how she'd made sure the curtains in the windows were draped just right every morning and how she'd moved the potted plant in the corner at least once a day to sweep behind it because, apparently, that was where the dust would gather. Her earrings were on my nightstand and the bottle of bubble bath I'd used that night still stood in the wrong place next to the tub.

Memories of her bled into my brain and there was nothing I could do to stop it as I shoved my stuff into my bags. When I'd discovered that Kaitlin had left us back in the day, it had stung. There I'd been, sacrificing my way of life for her and our baby while apparently she'd been unable to make any sacrifices of her own.

It had bruised me to know that I'd been willing to get married and spend the rest of my life with her when she clearly hadn't wanted me. My heart had broken for Colten, but not so much for myself. For what lay ahead, sure. For a million other little things that being a single dad would entail, but not because I would miss her.

Our relationship just hadn't been like that. It had been one of necessity and we'd both known it. For a while there, we'd tried and I'd even liked her, but it had never developed into more than that.

This, however, right now? This fucking sucked. I was leaving a girl I loved for no reason other than logically, we couldn't be together. *What kind of bullshit is that?*

It was practical and realistic, but my heart didn't care about either of those things. It wanted what it wanted—practicality be damned.

Unfortunately, my heart wasn't calling the shots here. My brain was. Colten and I had a life to get back to. As I strode out of my bedroom and into Jewel's, I tried to remember that.

Every breath I took in there felt like a dagger being buried in my chest, but I got through it despite the pain and her scent lingering in the air. I got through it because I had to. I had a kid to think about. An old man. Clients. A career I'd spent my entire adult life building.

A career I still wasn't sure was worth it anymore.

Even if I decided to get out of criminal defense, I could still be an attorney. There were dozens of things I could do with my knowledge and experience, but every last one of them was in LA.

Once I had everything, I slammed Jewel's door behind me like it would give me some kind of closure and then I grabbed all our stuff, shouldering past Dallas on the way out. He'd been guarding the front door like some kind of tipsy sentinel, as if he'd been afraid more unwanted guests would be arriving.

Without another word to the worst host I'd ever had, I left the Manor and didn't look back. June Lake had been a little slice of heaven until it hadn't been. The way I felt right then, I couldn't get away from there fast enough.

As I climbed into my car, Dallas called after me. "It's about time you get the hell out of Dodge and stay out, Payne. We don't need the likes of you around here."

I snorted. *These poor people sure as hell don't need the likes of you either.*

I wasn't about to argue with him, though. Dallas Styles wasn't my problem anymore. If Scott ever told me he needed help dealing with the guy, then sure, I'd step up and do whatever I could, but he hadn't brought it up again at all.

Gunning it back to his place after I left the Manor, I found Colten sitting with Scott in the backyard. They were spread out on the grass with a couple sandwiches, a football lying next to Scott and a sheen of sweat on both their foreheads.

"Hey, man. You get everything?" Scott asked as I walked out. "We were just tossing the ball around, but then Colten told me you guys haven't been on a hike yet. That's a sin, I swear. We've got some of the best hikes in the state. We're thinking of taking a short one this afternoon."

I glanced at Colten, who nodded his agreement enthusiastically. Knowing I was about to break my son's heart, I looked back at Scott. "Actually, I think it's time for us to head home. Thank you for your hospitality and for letting us stay, but we don't want to impose any longer than we already have."

Scott's features tightened, his gaze darting from one of my eyes to the other in a questioning look. Then his own eyes widened and he pushed into a standing position. "Sure. Yeah. Of course. I'll just give you two some privacy."

Sliding his phone out of his back pocket, he strode into the house and I knew he was going to call Jewel. I hadn't told him yet that I'd ended things with her. Once he found out, I doubted he was going to want us around anymore.

Colten didn't know yet either, and his jaw had all but hit the ground as he glared at me. "*Home* home? Like, LA home? That's where you want to go?"

"Yeah, bud." I walked a little closer to him and sat down on the bench in Scott's garden, my feet planted apart and my elbows resting on my knees. "I know you don't want to, but that's one of the reasons why it's better for us to go now. Before we become even more involved with this place and its community."

His eyebrows shot up and he shook his head hard. "No. I'm not leaving. I'm happy here and we have at least three more weeks. I'm not going anywhere."

"I'm afraid it's not open to negotiation, Colt. We're leaving. Today. All of our stuff is already in the car and I called the pilot on my way back from the Manor. He's fueling up as we speak."

Tears welled in his eyes and he drew his knees up to his chest, wrapping his arms around them as his head kept shaking. "No. I won't go. I don't want to go back to LA and you can't make me."

"Yes, I can. I'm just hoping it won't come down to that."

"What about Jewel?" He narrowed his eyes to slits. "Are you even going to say goodbye to her?"

"I already have."

"Well, I haven't," he spat. "I'm not going back there. I hate it there. I hate everyone who lives there. They're mean and they're always too busy. *You're* always too busy when you're there. I hate you!"

Ouch. While I knew he was just lashing out, my heart cracked in half at hearing those words from my son. I'd been told to expect them at some point, but nothing could've prepared me for it now that it was happening.

"You're allowed to hate me today, buddy," I said, not wanting the argument to get any more heated than it already had. "I understand, but that doesn't change that we're leaving."

I had never had to lay down the law with him like this before, and to be honest, it probably hurt me at least as much as it hurt him—if not more—but ultimately, this was better for both of us. Colten had already started talking about not wanting to go back to LA weeks ago. I suspected that he had thought I would never make him leave after he told me how happy he was here.

It killed me to do it, but we had to go. Standing up, I looked right into his eyes and tipped my head toward the house. "I'll be waiting for you at the car. Say goodbye to Scott. We're going straight to the airport from here."

Twenty-four horrible hours later, my son had still barely said a word to me. He'd met me at the car outside of Scott's house, but he'd given me the silent treatment all the way to the airport and for the whole flight home.

I'd tried to talk to him, tried to explain, but he'd folded his arms and given me his back. As soon as we'd gotten to the estate, he'd stomped up to his bedroom and I hadn't seen him again until this morning.

When I'd told him we were going to come visit Walt today, he'd nodded and gone upstairs to get dressed, but he'd hardly even looked at me. We'd never had a fight like this, and as I sipped my juice sitting across from Walt at Green Acres, it seemed the old man had picked up on it.

"What's wrong with my boy?" he asked, watching Colten where he sat with Chester, looking just as miserable and glum as his opponent in the game of chess they were playing. "I've never seen him so sad."

"He's pretty pissed at me," I admitted, proceeding to tell him all about how things had gone and why we'd left early.

Walter listened intently, and by the time I was done, disapproval was like a living thing in his eyes as he shook his head at me. "I'm disappointed in you, Landon. That's not something I've felt very often in my life, but I've got to say, I sure feel it now. I raised you better than that."

"What? Why?" I frowned at him, searching his dark, frustrated gaze but not finding any answers. "We live here, Walter. In LA. Colten's school is here and my work. You."

He sniffed and looked away from me. "Don't try to blame me for this, kid. It's not my fault you didn't learn anything this summer and that you didn't listen to your heart."

Feeling like I'd let everyone down, I exhaled heavily and dropped my face into my hands. I'd thought Walter, of all people, would understand why I'd come home. He'd suggested a summer at the lake, not a lifetime.

He knew more about responsibilities than anyone else, what with having taken in a kid that wasn't even his and raising him as his own simply because he'd made a promise so many years ago. The man had taught me everything I knew and one of the main lessons he'd hammered into me had been about reliability and responsibility.

Without applying those to every aspect of life, he'd said, you'd never get very far. I'd lived by those words and now I was starting to wonder if I'd missed something somewhere. The old man stood up and ambled over to Chester and Colten, pulling up a chair to join them. He started murmuring to my son, concern in his eyes as he leaned forward to speak to him.

I sighed, squeezing my eyes shut and wishing I'd never taken his advice to begin with. This summer had been both the best and worst of my life, but it seemed like the worst part of it had followed me home.

56

JEWEL

Two weeks after the Paynes had left, I was out on the boat with Scott, Brittany, and Tiff. It had been a rough day of cleaning for Britt and me. One of our clients had been sick and missed a couple weeks of our regularly scheduled cleans. An afternoon on the lake had sounded like the perfect way to wash off all the ick.

Now that we were out here though, I realized what a gigantic mistake it'd been. Ever since they'd left, I'd avoided the Manor as far as I possibly could, not even looking in its direction from the parts of the beach or town from which one could see it.

Scott had driven us out to the center of the lake this afternoon, and from there, there was no avoiding the place. Styles Manor sat as regal and beautiful as ever across the sparkling lake, a constant reminder of the heartache I'd been living with for half a month now.

I knew it wasn't that long, but it felt like it had been years. Like my heart would never stop aching and the pain would simply become part of me one of these days.

As I settled back on the boat, my eyes hidden behind a pair of aviators I'd borrowed from Scott as I lounged in the sun, I looked at the Manor and sighed. This summer had changed everything for me. I'd finally gotten to have my own love story, but it had turned out to have a lonesome ending instead of a happily ever after.

On the other hand, my story was seemingly rather similar to Lucille's. I'd spent most of my free time these last couple weeks reading more of her journal entries and I'd learned that their story had been far from perfect itself.

All my previous beliefs about them had been shattered now that I knew how things had really been between them. Rather than having had this epic romance for the ages, I now knew that Lucille and Robert had lived separate lives for years after their children had been born.

He hadn't been a natural father at all and he'd really only stepped in once the kids had been over the age of five. Lucille had carried the weight of their family alone for years before he'd taken an interest in their children.

During that time, it seemed they'd grown apart so much that they'd practically become strangers to one another. While they had shared that big, beautiful house, she'd spent her time with the babies or chasing after them once they'd become toddlers. She'd cooked their meals and cleaned their bodies and their home. She'd given the kids her all while Robert had been primarily in his study.

It had gotten so bad at times that he hadn't even taken his meals with the family. From what I'd read, it seemed he'd basically become a recluse, snapping and snarling at the kids when they disturbed him while he worked. Which had been all the time.

Once the kids had been old enough to reason with, to listen, and to have conversations, he'd finally stopped his crap. Slowly but surely, their marriage had gotten better again but I still felt in Lucille's entries that she'd never fully forgiven him.

Nor had she ever told him that their second child had been born from an affair she'd had with the local bartender in town. A man she only referred to as "H."

When I'd first discovered the secret, I'd been tempted to go digging. To find the identity of the man who had not only fathered one of her children, but who seemed to have kept her sane and supported her during long years of estrangement from her husband.

In the end though, I'd decided against it. I respected Lucille's right to have kept this a secret that she'd taken to her grave, never wanting the truth to see the light of day. Some things belonged in the past and it just wasn't my place to go disrupting her family history.

Brittany's voice pulled me out of my thoughts. She must've realized I'd been staring at the Manor because she suddenly brought up the one topic she'd been skirting around for weeks. "Have you heard from Landon at all?"

I shook my head. "I don't expect to, either. It's better this way, though."

After the initial shock of his decision had worn off, I'd realized that all Landon had done had been to make the call I hadn't been strong enough to make. It still hurt deeply, but I understood why they'd had to leave.

I just wished I'd had the chance to say goodbye. That was what had really upset me—that they'd just gone.

While it was true that I hadn't heard from Landon, Colten had reached out to me via text a couple days after they'd gotten back to LA. We'd also spoken on the phone.

Well, tried to speak, anyway.

I'd wound up crying like a baby and he'd cried too. My heart had broken for him as he'd told me how sorry he was that they'd just up and left me. How he wished things could be different. How much he hated his father for making him leave.

That last part, I'd managed to talk to him about, though. I'd told him that Landon had done what he thought was right and that he deserved some grace. He was probably hurting too, and ultimately, there really had been no other way.

Colten had agreed about his dad hurting, confiding in me that he knew Landon was having a tough time, but he'd also told me that it was just too hard. That for now, he was still too angry. I understood that. I was angry too.

In spite of the anger, I realized after they left that I had expected Landon to do what I vehemently refused to do myself. Move.

A long-distance relationship might've been one thing if it'd been for a specific period, but ours wouldn't have been. My life was and always would be here, in June Lake, while the same could be said for Landon and Colten's in LA.

Sometimes, I still wondered if we should've at least tried, but deep down, I knew that would only have been delaying the inevitable. What kind of future might we have had together unless one of us ended up moving to the other side of the state?

I didn't know for sure, but the obvious answer was that we never would've been able to live happily ever after. Although I'd given it some more thought, I'd come to realize that moving to LA would never have made me happy.

With them, perhaps I might've found a measure of happiness there, but I knew I would have grown to resent Landon for it. Which wouldn't have been fair. So finding a way to live happily ever after by following them wasn't an option as it would never be completely happy.

Once I'd realized that, I'd also realized how unfair it was of me to have asked him to move here to June Lake. If I couldn't consider moving, how could I ask it of him? Having thought of it like that, I'd been relieved that he'd shot down the idea.

Heartbreak sucked, but living with a man who resented me would've been much, much worse. As a result, that wouldn't have been a happily ever after either.

All of which meant that as much as it had felt like it was meant to be, it simply hadn't been. Landon hadn't been my forever love, and the sooner I could accept that, the better.

"Has Colten contacted you again?" Scott asked, gently pressing down on the throttle to steer us away from Styles Manor. "He keeps sending me funny videos. Sweet kid. I feel sorry for him."

"So do I," Brittany said, sighing as she turned to me. "If you have heard from him again, do you really think it's a good idea to keep talking to him? I know you adore him, but it might end up making it harder on him, which I know you don't want to do."

"I really don't," I agreed. "I haven't heard from him again, though. The last time we spoke, I told him that I would always be here for him and so would everyone in June Lake, but that it was probably for the best if we didn't talk for a while. Just to give us both time to settle back into our own lives. He seemed to understand."

Scott grimaced. "Poor kid. That had to have been rough for both of you, but it was the right thing to do. He knows you're here if he needs you."

"I guess he just hadn't needed me," I said, sitting up to grab a water from the cooler. "Enough of this. Can we please change the subject now?"

"Finally." Tiff laughed and lifted her sunglasses so I'd see her give me a wink. "I've got your back, girl. Actually, I have just the thing to take all your minds off Those Who Shall Not Be Mentioned."

"Yeah, what's that?" Brittany asked eagerly.

Tiff smirked. "There's a new challenge going around social media. It might be fun if we all—"

Scott groaned and shook his head. "Nope. There's no way. All those challenges are pure idiocy and they always get people sent to the hospital. Or worse."

Brittany agreed with Scott, and while they bantered back and forth with her sister about the merits and dangers of social media challenges, I glanced back at Styles Manor over my shoulder. For the rest of the afternoon, I had fun on the lake with them all, but my mind was mostly still lost in the memories I'd made this summer and what might have been.

I'd had some of the best times of my life in that beautiful old house with them, but just like Lucille and Robert's story hadn't been quite as perfect as I'd once thought, mine and Landon's hadn't been destined either. Maybe one day, a young couple would move in there and give the Manor the beautiful, happy family a place like that so richly deserved, but I doubted I'd even be around to see it.

Dallas would have to sell it or have kids of his own for that to happen, and neither of those things were likely to happen in my lifetime. *The asshole.*

Releasing one more sigh, I turned my back on the Manor and didn't look at it again for the rest of the day. As hard it might be, it was time I start putting all those memories and what-ifs behind me.

Colten and Landon were gone, and at this point, I doubted they would ever be coming back, even for a visit.

57

LANDON

At the beginning of September, the new school year was underway and I was hoping this would be a better one for Colten. After dropping him off myself for a change, I watched him get swallowed up by a crowd of excitable children and sent up a quiet prayer that he'd use the skills he'd honed this summer to make some friends now that he was back.

So far definitely hadn't been so good.

I'd tried to talk to him on a few occasions and I'd even encouraged him to invite the chess club over to our place for a pizza night or something to reconnect before school started, but *nada*. He just wasn't interested.

At least he was speaking to me again. Sort of. It wasn't the same as it had been in June Lake, but I took it as a good sign that the silent treatment had worn off.

Blinking myself out of my thoughts, I refocused on the road and backed out of my parking spot. Merging with the traffic, I turned my attention to the day ahead. First up, I had a discovery meeting with a client, the prosecution, and their client.

The man I was defending today had been accused of harassment and stalking. The charges were pretty mild in comparison to some of the other cases I'd tried, but some of the stuff he'd allegedly done was pretty out there.

Apparently, it had started with him brushing up against the complainant at work. The usual stuff. A few accidental touches and brushes here and there, but it had quickly devolved into him supposedly groping the woman and it had culminated in him exposing himself to her in his office one day.

In addition to all that, she was alleging that he had been following her around, showing up at places he had no business being while she was there and sitting in his car outside her house at night. Supposedly, he'd also sent her abusive text messages whenever she'd turned him down, followed by photographs of a sexual nature as he propositioned her again.

As far as I knew, all the texts in question had been deleted shortly after she'd supposedly read them and I'd seen evidence of deleted messages, but there was no way of telling what had been in them. Striding into my office, I headed directly to the conference room and sifted through the paperwork I'd asked my assistant to deliver here for me.

My client, as well as the opposition, would be arriving soon and I had to make sure that I was well versed in every single aspect of this case before they arrived. I'd been working on it for a couple weeks now and I was pretty clued in to the facts, but something was bugging me and I still couldn't put my finger on what it was.

Outside the conference room, beyond the opaque glass walls, the firm was slowly coming to life. Pretty soon, the hallways would be bustling with people rushing around, their heads buried in their own paperwork and their sixth or so espresso of the day in their hands.

The pace of life in LA had never been as tedious to me as it had been since we'd returned. It had also never been as obvious how wrapped up everyone was in their own lives. Back in June Lake, no one constantly stared at their phones. They walked around with their heads up, greeting the people around them with friendly smiles and stopping for a quick chat.

Even when they were in a rush, they weren't practically running around, looking like they'd smash right through any barrier that got in their way. As a partner at Adams Incorporated, I knew full well how busy our practice was.

The firm was old and established, the targets for billable hours sky high. No one ever had any time to waste on something as simple as chitchat—unless of course it was office gossip—but since I was the head of the criminal litigation department, that had always been something I'd been proud of.

Having a team who hustled and busted their asses day and night had been a bright and shiny feather in my cap. Now, however, I kept wondering how many years these people were going to live if they didn't slow down sometimes—and what their quality of life was actually going to be while they were here.

It was downright sad, really, that so many of them didn't seem to have lives outside of this office. Shaking my head at the direction my thoughts had taken, I looked up just in time to see my client walking in.

A tall man with broad shoulders and the bulging muscles of the amateur bodybuilder he was, Jason Gripp maintained that he was innocent. He grinned when he saw me and I stood up to shake his hand. "Remember what I told you, Jason. Let me do the talking, okay?"

"Sure," he said as he gave me a firm shake. Then he took the seat next to mine as I waved him into it. "This is bullshit, though. Daph had a thing for me. Everyone knew it. She's just pissed that I wouldn't fuck her."

I suppressed a sigh. I'd explained to him a dozen times that he couldn't use that as a defense. Just because she might've enjoyed his advances at one point in time didn't mean that he hadn't harassed her once they'd become unwelcome.

Plus, for a guy who said he was innocent, he sure did have a lot of vulgar things to say about the woman. A woman who walked in with the prosecutor not long after Jason had sat down and shut up at the look I gave him.

She was quiet and slight, and to my surprise, I saw a lot of Jewel in

Daphne Sinclair. She had blonde hair with kind brown eyes and smile lines around her eyes and lips, but it didn't look like she'd been smiling lately. As she sat down across the table, she wrung her hands, looking everywhere but at me or my client.

My stomach hardened into a rock. It was at that moment I knew what had been bugging me about this case. Jason kept telling me he hadn't done what she alleged he had, but I suddenly knew that she was telling the truth.

Despite having just been told to shut up and let me do the talking, Jason started mouthing off almost as soon as they sat down. "Why are you being such a bitch, Daph? I don't deserve this. Everything I ever did, you wanted. You—"

"Shut. Up," I seethed quietly to him. "Let me just finish reading this statement, then we'll get started."

Snorting obnoxiously, he shrugged and slammed his back into the chair, but a few seconds later, he spoke up again. "You know I didn't do any of the shit you're accusing me of. I never—"

Finally unable to take it anymore, I got to my feet abruptly and braced myself against the table. Glaring at my client, I shuffled all the paperwork into one neat pile and straightened up. "You're a foul fucking excuse of a man who deserves to be slapped with these harassment charges and, at the very least, a restraining order. I'm done. I quit. You're going to have to find yourself another lawyer."

Jason was pissed, his head rearing back as he leaped to his feet. "You can't do that, asshole. I've already paid your—"

"I don't give a damn," I said as I gathered my things and glanced at the prosecutor. Both he and Daphne were watching me with wide, disbelieving eyes. "I'm afraid we're going to have to postpone this while Jason secures alternative legal representation."

Jim, the prosecutor, jerked his chin in a nod, but he looked dazed, like he couldn't believe what he was seeing. Frankly, I couldn't believe it either, but this meeting had brought with it a huge reality check for me. I also suddenly had a certain clarity for the first time ever.

I didn't want to do this anymore, defending assholes from what they deserved just because I was trying to uphold a system that had been flawed for a very long time. While I knew I was exceptional at my job, that just made this worse.

My exceptionalism had stood between countless victims and the justice they deserved. I couldn't do that anymore and I knew exactly why—Jewel.

I saw her in that young woman across the table who was currently staring at me like I'd sprouted a second head. I knew I couldn't put her in harm's way just because I was "doing my job." Someone else could do it.

"I'm sorry you've had to come all this way and sit across from this asshole for nothing today," I said to her as I snapped my briefcase shut. "You're in good hands with Jim. He's a fantastic lawyer and he's going to get you the justice you deserve."

As she nodded, I gave her a reassuring smile and then turned back to Jason one last time. "I suggest you get your shit together because if I ever run into you on the street, I will not be acting as your attorney. I'll give you justice myself."

I leaned in a little closer, knowing that I was breaking every ethical and professional rule in the book, but I just really didn't give a shit. "And you won't like it if that happens."

Having said my piece, I stormed out of the conference room and strode directly to the receptionist, not bothering to keep my voice down as I made my announcement. "Anne, would you be so kind as to tell Bruce and the others that I quit? They can call me if they have any questions or concerns. I'll make sure that my office is packed up and vacated before the end of the week. Thanks for everything you've done for me. You've been great."

Around me, colleagues, clients, and delivery people alike came to a standstill, but I didn't give a flying fuck. I'd been so uncertain for so long now, feeling like shit sometimes about what I did for a living but clinging to those few souls I'd actually helped who really had been innocent.

Today, for the first time ever, I'd realized that this job—no job—was worth my soul and that was what it was costing me. So I was done. I refused to compromise my humanity and my sense of justice for anyone.

No matter how much they paid me or how many opportunities I might just get to defend one or two more innocent people who came across my path coincidentally along the way, I was done—and I'd never been happier about anything.

58

JEWEL

With only a handful of Friday night markets left before harvest season, I'd decided to take a chance. Once the markets ended, they'd be replaced with pumpkin-carving events, fireworks, and home-brewed cider competitions. I loved summer the most in June Lake, but fall wasn't half bad either.

What it meant, however, was that I only had so many more markets left this season to shoot my shot, which was why I'd decided to do it tonight. For the first time in years, I'd set up a booth at the market and I was displaying the suncatchers I'd made recently.

I'd never had a chance to give Colten his, and I hung it up to sell before I thought better of it. As unlikely as it was that I would make any sales tonight, I couldn't bear to part with this one. Not yet.

Gently placing it back in its box, I finished my display and took a step back to admire it when I was done. I was proud of how good it looked, the prisms and rainbows sparkling in the last of the late afternoon rays.

As always, the air was scented with barbecue and frying sweet stuff. Children's laughter rang out. I took in my stall, feeling my heart swell at how pretty it had come out. Even if I didn't sell anything tonight, I'd taken a big step forward by just doing this and no one could take that away from me.

One day at a time, I was rebuilding my life from the ground up, shaping it into something that more closely resembled what I'd always wanted. Suncatchers were a part of that. I loved my business with Brittany, but it had been chipping away at my soul for years that I'd given up on trying to sell my beautiful little crafts. Setting up this booth tonight was proof of how much I'd grown this summer.

In the last few weeks, I'd spent more time crafting and building these works of art than I had in ages. Heartbreak would do that to a girl, but so would the confidence Landon had instilled in me.

Above all else, I was grateful to him for that. For believing in me so much that even in his absence, I had the courage to display things even the fancy city boy had thought were gorgeous. I was also just grateful that I'd had something to pour myself into.

It had really helped, giving me something I cared about and enjoyed doing to distract myself from how sore I was to know Landon wasn't in town anymore. As people started arriving for the market, I inhaled a deep breath and took that moment to manage my expectations.

The last few times I'd tried this, I hadn't sold anything. I couldn't afford to let it get me down if I didn't sell anything tonight either.

Moving in behind my table, I smiled and readied myself for the crowds of admirers, none of whom would wind up purchasing the piece they'd admired, but I was determined not to let it get to me. To my utmost surprise, I made several sales right off the bat, with the first few admirers immediately choosing items they wanted to buy.

On a whim, I snapped some pictures of my display and grinned. Tiff had helped me set up an Instagram account recently and she'd encouraged me to post photos of my work on it. I'd followed her advice and my DMs had already started to fill up with special order requests that were going to keep me busy for at least the next couple of weekends. But I'd been skeptical about it all.

Now, however, with a few instant sales under my belt, I posted a few more pictures to the account, hoping it would attract a little more attention. My inspiration to use the vibe and aesthetic of Styles Manor in my creations seemed to have helped me find an audience, and it was looking like, if I could just keep the ball rolling, I might actually be able to get somewhere with this.

It would be a damn nice side hustle, and since it was something I was passionate about too, I was suddenly filled with excitement about it. Still grinning as Brittany and Scott wandered over to me, I glanced at their joined hands and felt a sharp pain shoot through my chest.

I was happy that they were finally together and that things were going so well for them, but I couldn't deny that I was also jealous that they'd found love right here in June Lake. Neither of them had to worry about traveling to LA or losing their hearts to people who were never coming back.

I sighed, but smiled when Brittany handed over a coffee they'd ordered for me. "There you go, babe. The stall is looking so good. How's it going?"

"It's actually going really well," I admitted, thankful for the hot drink now that the sun was going down. The evenings were already getting a bit chillier, and with the cool air blowing in a breeze off the lake, I was glad Lacey had swapped out her lemonade stand for a coffee bar. "I've already made a few sales."

Brittany beamed at me, letting her head drop to Scott's bicep as she grinned. "That's awesome. I'm so happy for you."

"Thanks." I held up the coffee. "Thanks for this too. I needed it."

Scott nodded, wrapping his arm around Brit's shoulders. I hated how envious I was of the way they held hands and each other. When he kissed the top of her head, it even felt like I was going to be sick with jealousy.

But I didn't let it show. I just made sure the smile froze on my face, which wasn't that hard considering that I honestly was happy for them. Besides, it wasn't their fault that I broke up inside every time I was reminded of what I'd lost.

"I should get back to it," I said, injecting forced cheer into my voice. "Thanks again. I'll catch up with you guys later?"

They nodded as one, as if they shared the same mind. Then they turned away as one too, meandering down the lane I was in and finally disappearing into the crowd. Happily, a little girl ran up and grabbed my attention when she squealed.

I smiled at her, feeling that ache in my chest subside just a little bit at the joy on her face when she admired one of the suncatchers. It had pink feathers and antique-looking, rose-gold details. "This one, Mommy. *Pleeeease*?"

Her mom chuckled, rushing to catch up to her and glancing at me when she did. "How much are these?"

The woman's cheeks were flushed, but between the cool air and the exertion of having to keep up with the energetic little girl, I couldn't blame her. She reached for her wallet, but I waved it away, reaching for a box and unhooking the delicate suncatcher to lay it inside.

"When is her birthday?" I asked.

The mom frowned. "About four and a half months from now."

I smiled. "Consider it an early birthday present, then. Thank you for appreciating my work, little angel."

The girl grinned up at me and the mom looked flustered, but they took the gift box and hurried away, both appearing just a little bit lighter than they had a minute ago. I watched them leave, glad to have done something to make the little girl happy after her joy had made me feel better.

Sensing a presence approaching the table, I plastered another welcoming grin on my face, then turned and looked up. Right into the face of the very last person I'd expected to see tonight.

Landon.

That gorgeous, thick dark hair of his hung just so over his forehead, not styled as it had been when he'd first arrived here months ago, but in the relaxed, natural way it had settled into while he'd been here. His intense green eyes crinkled with his smile. His long fingers slipped into the pockets of his jeans.

For a moment, I thought I was dreaming, but when his familiar, masculine scent wafted over to me, it hit me right in the heart that this was real. He was here. My mouth dropped open and my stomach nearly fell out of my butt.

"What are you doing here?" I breathed.

"I forgot something when I left," he said.

I cocked my head, my heart beating a mile a minute. "Oh?"

Landon leaned across the table, taking my face in his hands as his gaze swept across it. I melted into him, my entire being longing to throw myself into his arms. He stroked his thumbs across my cheekbones slowly, like he was memorizing the contours of them. Then he kissed me.

It was no more than a soft, gentle press of his lips to mine, but it slammed my heart into overdrive. Racing at an explosive pace, it skipped and jumped as he eased his mouth away and murmured against it. "I forgot my girl."

Before I could even begin to start questioning what that meant, Colten came running around the back of the table, appearing out of thin air and throwing his arms around me. Giving me a huge bear hug, he squeezed me tight.

"I missed you, Jewel."

"I missed you too, buddy," I whispered, bursting into tears as I hugged him back. "What are you doing here? When did you get in?"

He laughed as he took a step back and swept his arms out to his sides. "We came straight to the market from the airport. We wanted to surprise you, or else I'd have warned you that we were coming."

"Well, I'm definitely surprised." I screwed my eyes shut, half expecting Colten to be gone when I opened them again, but he wasn't.

Neither was his father.

While my eyes had been closed, he'd walked around the table too, coming to stand next to his son, but his eyes weren't on me anymore. They were locked on the suncatcher I'd placed so carefully back into its box just a little while ago.

"This is for you," I said to Colten as I turned and picked up the box, nervously presenting it to him for the first time. As far as I knew, he hadn't even known that Landon had asked me to make him one, and honestly, I didn't know if he was going to like it. "I made it while you guys were here. So you'd always have something to remember June Lake by. I just never got around to giving it to you."

Colt reached slowly for the box, taking it from me with an almost reverent expression on his face. His jaw was slack, his brow furrowed as he flicked his gaze back to mine. "It's got chess pieces on it."

"Yes, it does." I smiled, reaching out to ruffle his hair. As my fingers touched the soft strands, it served as a reassurance to me too, telling me that I really wasn't dreaming.

I blinked hard once more, but again, they didn't disappear. Colten was lifting the suncatcher out of the box carefully, turning it over in his fingers and grinning at the chess pieces. Landon's attention seemed to be split between me and his son, but it settled on me as Colt spotted Brody coming toward us.

"I'm going to go say hi," he said excitedly, giving me a playful smirk. "He knew we were coming, but I only told him once we landed. See you guys!"

With a cheeky wave, he took off running toward his friend and Landon held a hand out toward me. "I'll understand completely if you say no, but would you like to take a walk with me? I'd really like to talk to you."

59

LANDON

After asking Verna to watch her stall for her, Jewel and I went for a walk on the beach. In the month since we'd been gone, it'd gotten much cooler here, especially next to the water. The breeze coming off the lake had an icy edge to it, the sand beneath my feet already cool even though it'd been baking in the sun all day.

We were both dressed much more warmly now than we had been before I'd left, but a shiver ran through Jewel as we strode along the shore. Silently, I offered her my hoodie but she shook her head. "I'm fine. Thank you."

It was about as many words as she'd spoken to me since we'd surprised her, but at least there was no venom in her tone. She wasn't being short with me or simply shutting me out. She just didn't want my jacket.

"I owe you an apology," I started. My hands were in my pockets but my forearm brushed against hers every so often as we walked. I glanced at her, seeing that her eyes were staring straight ahead, a thoughtful expression on her features. Since she hadn't said anything or walked away, I kept going, watching her closely as I spoke. "I know that saying I'm sorry will never make up for the way I left, but I really am sorry."

After another long minute of just staring straight ahead, she finally shot me a sidelong look, her chin tucked low against her chest. "If you're so sorry, why did you do it? Why did you come back? I feel like I don't know anything right now. Not what you're here for. Or for how long. Or what it means that you're here. If it even means anything."

I exhaled a long, slow breath and nodded. "I thought I was doing the right thing when we left. It felt like the only thing I could do to spare us all this pain, but I only realized after that all I was doing was being a coward. Thinking only about myself and what I wanted."

"You're allowed to think about yourself, Landon. But none of that tells me what you're doing here now."

"See, that's the thing. At the time, I thought that was what I wanted. I thought I wanted to get away from here. I thought I needed to go back to my life and that it would be better for everyone that way, but I hurt Colten and I hurt you. And I'm sorry. I'm so, so sorry, Jewel. I was so wrong."

She crossed her arms to hug herself, glancing up at me as she stopped walking. In the pale moonlight, I couldn't see the exact golden color of her eyes, but I could see the hurt shining from them. "What do you want, then? If you don't want to be back in your own life, where do you want to be?"

"I want to be here," I said emphatically. "I want to be with you. I want you, me, and Colten to be a family. I want to find something meaningful to do with my life, and I want to do it from here. I want this, Jewel. Us. If you'll still have me, of course."

Her lips slowly parted, her jaw growing slack as she stared at me. "Are you serious? You've moved here?"

"Well, I mean, not yet. I've got a lot of stuff I need to wrap up back in LA, but I quit my job. At least that's a start, right?"

"You quit?" She stared at me like she was expecting me to tell her I'd adopted a rhino next.

I chuckled sheepishly, nodding as I rocked back on my heels.

"Yeah, I kind of went down in a blaze of glory. Or a meltdown. Depends on how you're looking at it, but the end result is the same. I no longer have a job."

"That's..." She trailed off, then suddenly smiled at me. "That's amazing, Landon. I'm so proud of you. You've got balls of steel."

I did a double-take, then started laughing. "Really? We're talking about my balls now?"

She shrugged, a small smile playing on her lips as she turned and started walking again. Chuckling as I fell into step beside her, I nudged my elbow into hers. "So what do you think? Do you still want me now that I'm unemployed?"

"I don't know," she said quietly, glancing at the sand and the footprints we were leaving behind. My heart started sinking until she spoke again. "I don't really care about your employment status, but has anything else changed? What about Walt? And your inheritance? And Colten's school and his responsibilities?"

"Last I checked, they have a school here," I said lightly before I got serious. "Look, in all honesty, I do still have a lot to figure out, but you asked me if I'm willing to fight for us and that's what I'm doing. I'm just sorry it's taken me so long to do it."

"So you're willing to consider moving to June Lake?" She stopped walking abruptly, turning to face me with hope sparkling in her eyes. "Forever?"

"I'm not just willing to consider it," I murmured, facing her in turn and reaching for her hands. "I'm ready to put the wheels in motion to do it. I haven't had time to figure everything out, but where there's a will, there's a way. I can sort out my inheritance from here. Colten's chomping at the bit to start school with Brody and the others. Walt..."

I drew in a sharp breath. "For now, he'll have to stay where he is. I'll have to go back and forth a lot for at least the next few months while I settle things over there, but he's supportive of this move. Green Acres was the first place I went after I quit. We talked. He wants me to do this."

My heart hammered in my chest as I waited for her to respond. At the moment, she was just staring at me again, her jaw unhinged as she blinked like she wasn't sure she understood everything she'd just heard.

"What do you think?" I asked. "Have I blown it, or do we still have a chance?"

"It's been a hard month without you," she started slowly and softly, vulnerability shimmering in her eyes as the corners of her lips turned down. "I felt betrayed and angry, but I finally got to a point where I understood why you'd done it. I even believed that it had been for the best. How do I know this is really going to happen?"

"I've already enrolled Colten in June Lake Elementary," I admitted. "He'll be transferring in next month. I can show you the email if you don't believe me."

"No, I..." She blinked a bunch of times really, really fast. Then she ran her hands up the length of my arms to my shoulders. "You're really moving here for me?"

"Yeah, I guess I am," I said. "To be fair though, it's not only for you. It's for Colten too, and for me. But for us, yes. I'm moving for us."

She pushed her fingers into the hair at the back of my head as a slow smile spread her lips. "In that case, I forgive you. You really hurt me and I'm not just going to get over that, so I might need a bit of constant reassurance from you for a while, but I'm willing to give you another chance."

"You are?" My heart went crazy, galloping as relief flooded my system and a grin broke out across my face. "For real?"

"For real," she murmured, stepping into me and pressing her chest against mine. "I'm serious about that constant reassurance, though."

"I can give you that," I promised her as my hands found her hips and I gripped them hard, afraid that if I eased up even just a little that she'd suddenly disappear from my life again. "As much of it as you need."

She smiled. "Good."

"I wasn't sure what to expect showing up unannounced like this,"

I admitted, holding her closer just to breathe her in. "You're amazing. Do you know that?"

She shrugged. "Nah, I'm just in love. I missed you and Colten every second of every day that you were gone and I've daydreamed about a moment just like this. I never thought it would happen, but you came here. You apologized. You're doing exactly what I've been praying you would decide to do, even when I know I wouldn't have been able to do the same thing."

I lowered my forehead to hers. "Colten and I were meant to find June Lake. We were meant to fall in love with this place and with you. This is where we're supposed to be, Jewel. I know it."

With that, I slid a finger under her chin and lifted it, sealing my lips over hers for a kiss that doubled as a promise. I wouldn't pull any of that shit again. From now on, I was putting her and my kid first, and everything else could be damned.

Jewel grabbed my hand and inclined her head back toward the market with a coy smile playing on her lips. "Sam, Brittany, and Scott are still watching Colt, right?"

"Why?" I asked teasingly, already following as she dragged me across the beach to the street. "Do you need to fix up my hand again?"

She tossed me a wink over her shoulder as we hurried to her apartment. "Something like that. Mostly, I just want to welcome you officially to June Lake."

I groaned. "God, please don't tell me you welcome everyone who moves here like this?"

"Nah, only the guys I love." She flung her arms around my neck as soon as we'd stumbled into her apartment.

I kicked the door shut with my foot, my hands in her hair and my lips against hers as I spoke between searing, hungry kisses. "I love you too, Jewel Pendleton. I don't know what the fuck I was thinking when I left, but I'm never doing it again."

"Good," she murmured into my kisses as I walked her backward to her bed. "I'm holding you to that."

"I'm counting on it." As soon as her knees hit her mattress, I dropped my hands to the hem of the sweater she had on and pulled it unceremoniously over her head.

She laughed, unzipped my hoodie, and pushed it off my shoulders while kicking off her shoes. There was nothing romantic about the way we were ripping each other's clothes off, but once we were naked, we finally slowed down. A little bit anyway.

I laid her down on her bed and crawled over her, kissing her deeply and thankful for the condom I'd hurriedly rolled on. Sliding my fingers between hers, I held her hands above her head, pressing them into the mattress as I sank into her.

She felt like coming home, hot, and wet, and perfect. I groaned into her mouth, deepening the kiss as she writhed underneath, her hips keeping time with mine. This was the very best possible outcome to have gotten from us surprising her, but as we made love that night, I vowed to myself that one day very soon, I would surprise her again.

With a ring next time.

So many things in my life were up in the air right then, but the only thing I knew for certain was that I'd made the right decision coming back here. As soon as I knew exactly how I was going to make it all happen, I would ask her to be mine.

Forever.

In the meantime, I was going to make sure she knew just how much I loved her—starting right here and right now. She was never going to doubt how much she meant to me ever again.

EPILOGUE

JEWEL

Six Weeks Later

Fall had officially arrived. The forest surrounding the lake had turned from green to amber, brown, and red, creating a vibrant tapestry of warm colors to signal that the winter was well on its way. Bundled up in a fleece blanket, I wondered why the hell Landon had insisted so vehemently that we take Scott's boat out on the lake.

Now that the end of October had arrived, trips out on the boat were rare for me. Occasionally, I would come out with Scott when he wanted to go fishing, but those trips were few and far between.

I hadn't been given much of a choice in the matter today, though. Landon had woken up with a bee in his bonnet about it and here we were, gliding across the shimmering surface of the lake while I clung to my blanket, my teeth almost chattering.

It was a chilly but sunny day, and the lake looked like a mirror, not a breath of wind to ripple the water and no other boats to make waves. I glanced at Landon where he stood behind the wheel, his hand gently easing back on the throttle.

"How long are we going to be out here?" I asked as he started slowly. "I love being out on the boat as much as the next girl, but I may just turn into an ice cube before we head back."

He nodded at the Manor, regally guarding the shore on the other side of the lake. "We won't be much longer. I just wanted to get another look at it."

As his gaze moved to the old house, I stood up and rested my head on his shoulder as I stared at the Manor. "I read Lucille's journals while you were gone. I don't think I ever told you."

"Yeah?" The corners of his lips inched into a soft, almost wistful smile. "Learn anything interesting?"

"I did actually." I hadn't told anyone else about it, but it seemed safe to share Lucille's secret with Landon. "It turns out that everything I thought I knew about Lucille and Robert was a sham. After they had their first baby, the romance turned into a whole big mess of drama."

He chuckled. "Kids can put a strain on any relationship."

"Not like this," I said softly, imagining Lucille out there next to the lake chasing after the children all by herself. "Robert disappeared into himself for years. He practically locked himself in his study. Eventually, she had an affair."

"Whoa, I wasn't expecting that," he said.

I sighed. "I guess their love story wasn't nearly as glamorous or spotlessly smooth as I thought it was."

"The best ones never are," he said as he touched his head to mine. "We've had our speedbumps, too. Our challenges may have been different to theirs, but it wasn't just smooth sailing."

Bringing his hand back to the throttle, he slowly pushed down and drove away from the Manor, guiding us to Soulmate Beach. I smiled at him when he docked at the stretch of beach where Robert had proposed to Lucille and I'd bonded with Landon and Colten for the first time.

"I haven't been here since that time we came together," I said as he helped me off the boat. "When Scott started getting Colten into football."

He laughed, leaving me alone for a moment as he went to retrieve a picnic basket from the boat. "Well, I didn't bring a football today, but I do have a thermos of hot chocolate and some treats."

I blinked back my surprise. "I'll take that over a football any day of the week."

After he pulled a blanket out of the basket, he laid it out on the sand and we sat down, cuddling together and admiring the lake, which was shockingly blue on the crystal clear, cold day.

"I knew you were still a romantic deep down inside," I teased as I slipped my hand into the crook of his arm and held on tight, relishing the solid heat of him at my side. "You do know that a picnic on Soulmate Beach is considered almost like a promise around these parts?"

He glanced down at me. "Is it?"

"Yep," I said, grinning. "You better go fetch a football if you don't want me to think this is more than it actually is." I sipped on my sweet hot chocolate as I winked at him. "We're just going to have to toss it around gently. My fingers might snap off if I catch it wrong. They're so damn cold."

He wrapped an arm around my shoulders and pulled me close, taking both of my hands in one of his and rubbing them. "I'd rather not have any of your fingers snap off today, so I suppose it's a good thing I really didn't bring a football."

As I chuckled, he reached over to the basket and started pulling out some of the snacks he'd brought. Little sandwiches and a thermos of soup. Also some cut-up fruit, a variety of cheeses, olives, and some crackers. Spreading them out on the blanket, he brought those electric green eyes to my own and I saw the current running through them. I just couldn't tell if it was nerves or excitement.

"What's going on?" I asked. "All of this looks amazing. You don't have to worry that I won't love it. I do, and I also really appreciate all the effort you went through."

He smiled, but even that was suddenly tighter than normal.

"Could you grab the last surprise from the basket? It's just in the side pocket."

I reached in and my fingers brushed against something smooth and hard. Frowning, I closed my hand around some kind of cube and I pulled it out, curious as to what kind of surprise came in a small, square box.

As the thought hit, my heart started racing at the first possibility that occurred to me. *No. Nooooo. No, he didn't. He couldn't have.*

But as I pulled out the box, I saw that he could have, and he had. When I pulled it out, I found myself holding a deep purple, velvet-encased ring box. I flipped it open and gasped when I saw the gorgeous ring sitting on a perch inside.

The diamond in the center caught the sun, nearly blinding me until I shifted the box in my palm. For a long moment, I just stared at the ornately designed ring with its antique-looking engraved shoulders and the tiny beads of metal used to create scalloped borders.

It was absolutely stunning, so beautiful and perfect that it brought tears to my eyes as I lifted them back to Landon's. I sucked in another sharp breath of air when I found him on one knee, grinning as his gaze settled on mine.

"When I was much younger, I asked Walter once why he'd chosen my mother. She'd come from an old money family who weren't exactly pleased that she was involved with a guy like him, who didn't have money or a family name."

He stared into my eyes intently. "Plus, as an added complication, she also had a little boy from a previous marriage in tow. It didn't make sense to me that he'd willingly take on all that, but when I asked him about it, he told me '*when you know, you know, and trust me, son, one day, you'll know.*'"

"I didn't understand it at the time, but then I met you, and suddenly, it was like all the lights went on inside. I knew. I just didn't realize it at first."

Tears welled on my eyelids as I nodded my agreement. I'd known too and I *had* realized it. I'd just thought we were star-crossed lovers and that we'd never really get to be together.

"You came into our lives so unexpectedly, bringing with you a world of color, and love, and warmth that I never knew existed. Every corner of my life that used to be filled with darkness and doubt is now filled with purpose."

He took my hands and held them tight. "My purpose is to love you, Jewel. To cherish you and to make you laugh. To protect you and Colten too. I want to do that for the rest of my life if you'll let me."

"Yes!" I practically squealed, throwing my arms around him. He laughed as he caught me, holding me tight for a minute. Then he pulled away and took the ring from me to slide it onto my finger.

The tears were leaking out of my eyes. Joy unlike any I'd ever known swelled in my chest. Landon's eyes were misty too, the grin on his face so wide that it looked like it would never leave.

"Well, that's a relief," he said. "Do you see now why we couldn't risk your fingers snapping off?"

I nodded faintly, my eyes torn between his and the gorgeous ring. "Did you really think I was going to say no?"

"I hoped you wouldn't," he said, and the slight vibration in his tone made me glance back up at him. "Because I have another surprise for you."

Butterflies hatched and started racing around in my stomach. I lowered my head slowly to one side. "What else do you have up your sleeve, Payne? Isn't this enough?"

I wiggled my finger at him, marveling at the weight that would live there from now on.

Sliding his hand into mine, he drew in a deep breath and shrugged. "I've bought us a house here in June Lake."

I gasped. Again. I'd known he was planning on starting to look at places soon, but I'd had no idea he'd found one. For the last month and a half, he'd been commuting between June Lake and LA, tying up all the loose ends there while Colten stayed here with me.

At first, they'd gone back to LA after that weekend for Colt to finish out his last month of school there, but once he'd started here, I took care of him whenever Landon had to go. His trips had been less frequent since, though.

"You bought a house?" I asked breathlessly, blinking hard as I tried to wrap my head around what this meant. "This is it, then? You're going to be here from now on?"

"Mostly," he said. "I'll still have to go back and forth until I have Walter settled and if I have to see clients or go to court, but outside of that, yes. I'll be here."

More tears streamed from my eyes. I couldn't believe that this day was finally here. While I'd believed it would happen eventually, I hadn't been at all sure when. I definitely hadn't been expecting that day to be today.

Especially since Landon was getting involved with various nonprofit organizations within the criminal justice system. He was acting as an outside consultant they could utilize as a resource, but I had figured he would need to get all those ducks in a row before there would be any possibility of him being here permanently.

"I'm so happy right now," I said, my voice catching as I shook my head at him. "When?"

He chuckled, pulling me close and holding me against his chest. "Last week. We couldn't keep bouncing between AirBnBs and the motel any longer. Colten needs a home base now that he's at school, and obviously, your apartment is too small, which is why I didn't ask if we could just move in with you."

I smiled, touching my palm to his cheek and drinking him in. "You're amazing. I hope you're going to be so happy at your new house. I'm sure you will be."

"Your new house too," he corrected me lightly. "We all needed somewhere we could settle together. A place with space, where we can make memories of our own. You don't have to move in right away if you don't want to. We'll be ready whenever you are."

"No, I want to," I murmured. "I'm ready, and besides, I'm practically living with you anyway. I love being there to make Colt breakfast in the mornings and to help him with homework in the afternoons. No way am I giving up that time with him."

Landon chuckled. "In that case, when can you move in?"

I arched a playful eyebrow at him. "As soon as you tell me where the house is. I can't exactly move if I don't know where I'm going."

He grinned and pointed across the lake at the Manor. "It's right there. You remember the way, right?"

My mouth fell open. "You didn't!"

He gave me a cocky smirk before he crushed his lips to mine, murmuring against them in between kisses. "Why, yes. Yes I did. I think it's the perfect place to live out our happily ever after, don't you?"

The End

ABOUT THE AUTHOR

Weston Parker
EVERY good girl DESERVES A bad boy

Hey there. I'm Weston.

Have we met? No? Well, it's time to end that tragedy.

I'm a former firefighter/EMS guy who's picked up the proverbial pen and started writing bad boy romance stories. I co-write with my sister, Ali Parker, but live in Texas with my wife, my two little boys, my daughter, two dogs, three cats, and a turtle.

Yep. A turtle. You read that right. Don't be jealous.

You're going to find Billionaires, Bad Boys, Military Guys, and loads of sexiness. Something for everyone hopefully.

OTHER BOOKS BY WESTON PARKER

A Wedding Bells Alpha Novel:

Say You Do

She's Mine Now

Don't You Dare

Promise It All

Give Me Forever

Feels Like Love

Mine to Hold

Love by Accident

Two Become One

Love Me Not

I Choose You

All for Love

A Faux Love Novel:

Fake It Real Good

Fake It For Money

Fake It For Now

Fake it For Real

Fake It For Love

Fake It For Us

Fake It For Wealth

Fake It For Good

Fake It for Fame

Fake it for Fortune

Fake it for Glory

Fake it for Him

Searing Saviors Series:

Light Up The Night

Set the Night On Fire

Turn Up the Heat

Ignite The Spark Between Us

The Worth Series:

Worth the Risk

Worth the Distraction

Worth the Effort

A Wild Night Novel:

Between the Sheets

Under the Covers

Bad Boy Greeks Series:

Fake It For Me

My Favorite Mistake

Pretending to Be Rich

A Military Man Romance Novel:

Air Force Hero

Let Freedom Ring

Maybe It's Fate

All American Bad Boy

All For You

Guard My Heart

A Bad Boy Bachelors Novels

Bad Boy Bachelor Claus

Bad Boy Bachelor Cupid

Bad Boy Bachelor Bunny

Bad Boy Bachelor Summer

Bad Boy Bachelor Thanksgiving

Bad Boy Bachelor Christmas

Bad Boy Bachelor Valentine

A Match Me Up Novel:

You and Me, Baby

Pull Me In

Never Let Go

A Last Time Novel:

My Last Chance

My Last Secret

My Last Song

My Last Shot

A Parkers' Christmas in July Novel:

Such A Hot Christmas

Standalones:

Captain Hotness

Hot Stuff

Deepest Desire

My First Love

My Last First Kiss

My One and Only

Mine Forever

Trying to Be Good

My Holiday Reunion

One Shot at Love

Always Been Mine

Caught Up in Love

All About the Treats

Good Luck Charm

Love Me Last

We Belong Together

Main Squeeze

Brand New Man

Made for Me

Follow You Anywhere

Show Me What You Got

Have Your Way with Me

Heartbreaker

Keeping Secrets

Going After What's Mine

Give Me the Weekend

Take It All Off

Backing You Up

Come Down Under

Need You Now

Desperate for You

Standing Toe to Toe

Take It Down a Notch

Take A Chance On Me

Spring It On Me

Come Work for Me

All Good Things

The Billionaire's Second Chance

Pay Up Hot Stuff

Bad for You

Showing Off the Goods

Our Little Secret

Runaway Groom

Love Your Moves

Rich Fake Witch

Fair Trade for Love

Match Me Up

Not Fake for Long

Dropping the Ball

Last First Date

Hometown Hottie

You Know You Wanna

Some Kinda Romance

Summer Nights

Printed in Great Britain
by Amazon